The Multiplex Man

The Multiplex Man
The Multiplex Man
The Multiplex Man
The Multiplex Man
The Multiplex Man
The Multiplex Man
The Multiplex Man
The Multiplex Man

JAMES P. HOGAN

BANTAM BOOKS
NEW YORK TORONTO LONDON SYDNEY AUCKLAND

THE MULTIPLEX MAN

A Bantam Spectra Book / December 1992

Library of Congress Cataloging-in-Publication Data

Hogan, James P.
    The multiplex man / James P. Hogan.
      p. cm.
    Title is repeated 7 times on t.p.
    ISBN 0-553-08999-4
    I. Title.
PR6058.O348M84   1992
823'.914—dc20   92-21596
                                           CIP

Published simultaneously in the United States and Canada

Bantam Books are published by Bantam Books, a division of
Bantam Doubleday Dell Publishing Group, Inc. Its trademark,
consisting of the words "Bantam Books" and the portrayal of a
rooster, is Registered in U.S. Patent and Trademark Office and
in other countries. Marca Registrada. Bantam Books, 666 Fifth
Avenue, New York, New York 10103.

PRINTED IN THE UNITED STATES OF AMERICA

RRH   0 9 8 7 6 5 4 3 2 1

To Henry Palka
With thanks for being a lot of help
with a lot of things

The Multiplex Man

Jarrow
Jarrow
Jarrow
Jarrow
Jarrow
Jarrow
Jarrow
Jarrow

one

The flashing signs on both sides of I-94 south into Minneapolis read: POLICE CHECK AHEAD. PREPARE TO STOP. Farther on, past a disused overpass, the morning traffic was slowing to a crawl as barriers with winking red lights funneled it into a tailback along the inner two lanes. A line of delinquents stood pulled over on the shoulder. Jarrow was glad that Larry had picked him up earlier than usual. It would all clog up quickly, even though traffic these days wasn't as heavy as the moving nose-to-tail jams of times gone by. He was due to see Valdheim at 8:45, and the thought of being late for doctors' appointments was one of the things that made him anxious.

"They do it on purpose," Larry muttered as they eased into line. "This time of morning everyone's in a hurry and snarly, and they just want you to give them a hard time. You talk back, and then they hit you with the works. Their scores go into their records. The meanest ones get the promotions."

Larry liked to think of himself as a man who believed in saying what he thought, with the result that no topic escaped without receiving the imprint of his opinion. Jarrow saw it more as an inability to refrain from airing views that most people would have considered better left unsaid. That would have been careless at best on anyone's part, and bordering on foolhardy for a halfway-prudent professional—which in itself would have been enough to make Jarrow uncomfortable. But for a teacher at junior high school, charged with a responsibility for the shaping of young minds, it crossed the line into recklessness and invited suspicions of subversive designs. And that made Jarrow positively nervous.

"Get a load of this guy coming up behind," Larry said, nodding at the rearview mirror. Jarrow moved his head to see in the side mirror mounted on the door. The vehicles following them were squeezing over to make way for a limousine impatiently flashing an official blue-and-yellow light. From the silver badge on the front, Jarrow guessed it to be from one of the international regulatory agencies. Larry stayed in the center of the lane, pretending not to see the irate wavings of the state trooper marching forward from among the uniformed figures ahead.

A two-note siren blast came from behind, and then a voice cut in over the pop jazz playing from the vehicle's sound system. *"Pull over, ahead. You're obstructing official business."*

"Now, there's what I call creature comfort," Larry said, contemplating the lines of the limo, now thrusting up close behind them like a motor yacht trying to nudge past a tugboat. It was large and majestic, probably capable of cruising at 150 on smooth-burning hydrocarbon synthetic. By contrast, the electric getabout that he and Jarrow were riding in was stark and utilitarian, and could putter along at fifty with up to four people, at a squeeze, and hundred-mile hops between cell changes.

"For God's sake let it through," Jarrow grated, rubbing his moist palms together. He had an inborn dread of confrontations, and more than suspected that Larry was doing this deliberately to rattle him. Larry had a strange sense of humor that way.

Larry spread his hands briefly. "That's our money they're driving around in, isn't it? Why should we be kicked out of the way like trash on the street?"

The siren sounded again, insistently. Larry stayed put for several more agonizing seconds until Jarrow really thought that he was about to get them a ticket, or worse, and then pulled over at the last moment. The limousine swept by disdainfully and was waved on past the barrier.

Jarrow wiped his hands on his knees. "If you want to complain about the system, there are proper channels," he said tightly.

"Right. And they'll get you the same place as the other tubes too." Larry opened the window and turned on an innocent expression as the trooper hove to, purple-faced, outside.

"Is something the matter with you, mister? You deaf as well as blind? Maybe you shouldn't be out on the street."

"We were talking. I guess I got absorbed."

"Well, that's not good enough. If you're in charge of a vehicle, you're supposed to know what's going on, okay? Let me see your papers."

The traffic check was nominally to catch cars with even-date-only tax stickers being driven on an odd day of the month—the enforced ride-sharing that this imposed was the only reason for Larry and Jarrow to be traveling together—but no cop was going to let a chance go by of grubbing for other morsels too. Larry passed out the wallet containing his operator's license, owner's registration, road-tax receipt, insurance certificates, vehicle-inspection certificate, environmental-compliance certificate, metropolitan area usage permit, medical statement detailing blood type, drug allergies, and current treatments, and whistled silently to himself while the trooper scrutinized them. From Larry's other side, Jarrow watched the blue-chinned mouth framed by the window, bunching in a grim, downturned line and snorting as each document failed to show a fault. Larry glanced across and winked confidently.

The trooper fished a compad from one of his tunic pockets and punched in the registration, but he was already scowling in anticipation of the CLEAR OF VIOLATIONS response that appeared on its screen a moment later. He backed off a couple of paces and stood, fists clenched on hips, surveying the vehicle from end to end.

"That wheel's wearing low. There's vibration at the rear end. Get your bearings looked at."

"Yep, reckon I'll just do that."

"On your way."

"You have a nice day too." They moved on through, speeding up and staying to the right to continue south, skirting the downtown area of Minneapolis. Larry waved to indicate the direction ahead, in which the limousine had disappeared. "You know, there was a time when anyone who had the money could own a machine like that. Now you have to convince some bureaucrat that you've got the need. Why the hell should it be anyone else's business?"

Jarrow sighed. "Oh, come on. You know how it was with those gasoline burners." Everyone knew how it had been. Why did Larry have to ask pointless questions all the time?

"Well, I'm not so sure about that, Dick," Larry said. "I know a guy who used to be an engineer in the business. He says that ten percent dirty cars caused fifty percent of the problem. All they needed was a tune-up. It could have been fixed for peanuts compared to what they spent tearing the industry apart. So maybe it wasn't the way everyone gets told. Maybe a lot of other things back then weren't the way everyone gets told, either."

They were passing Loring Park. An exit sign ahead indicated Groveland. Jarrow leaned forward in his seat and pointed, glad of the chance to drop the subject. "That's it, this one coming up now. Stay over on the inside. We need to go right at the first intersection."

"There at the light?"

"That's it."

The light changed to red as they approached. Larry grunted and eased to a halt. He drummed his fingers on the wheel, humming tunelessly to himself, then glanced across at Jarrow while they waited. Jarrow stared ahead, waiting for him to pick up the theme again, but Larry read his mood and decided for once to leave it at that. For him simply to remain silent, however, was too much to hope for. "What is it that you need to see this doc for—just a checkup or something? If it's not personal."

"No, that's okay. . . . It's a neural thing. Not anything wrong, really. More just something they're curious about—some kind of irregularity in the brainwave pattern, to do with the sleep rhythms." Jarrow shook his head. "I don't really understand it myself."

"Is it anything to worry about?"

"They're not sure. Apparently, it's a new area they're just getting into. There's a theory that it could trigger unconscious stress patterns and affect all kinds of other things. That's why they're interested."

Larry grinned as the light changed, and they moved off again. "You see, Dick. It's what I've been telling you all along: You take life too seriously. Try easing up a little."

"So now it's medical advice, as well, eh? You're an M.D. as well, all of a sudden?" Jarrow hadn't meant to sound that sarcastic. Really, he was reproaching himself for being more forthcoming with detail than was called for, as if he needed to justify himself.

But if Larry noticed, it didn't show. "Just a detached but perspicacious observer of life. . . . Anyhow, it didn't cost you a nickel. Where do we go now?"

"Straight on past the trees. . . . It's one of the houses now, the green one with the laurel. . . . Okay, this'll do fine."

The car pulled up in the service lane, separated from the road by a strip of grass. Its two occupants made a contrasting pair: Larry younger by at least ten years, easygoing and relaxed with his collar-length yellow hair, and dressed casually in a fleece-lined jacket and wool sweater against Minnesota's April cold; Jarrow in black overcoat with collar and tie, trimmed mustache, hair graying at the temples. Jarrow felt that working for the State was to represent the State, with a duty to project an appropriate image. Larry's kind didn't worry about things like that.

"Need a ride into the school later?" Larry asked as Jarrow was getting out. "I have to go into town at lunchtime on an errand. I could detour this way if you like."

"It's okay. I can catch the mono."

"Wouldn't be any trouble."

"No, I'll be fine. Besides, I'm not really sure how long it's likely to take. . . . Er, thanks."

"Okay. See you around later, then. Oh, and I'll catch you later this afternoon sometime for that book."

"Book? Oh, yes, sure." Jarrow had promised to let Larry have a book that he still had out from the staff library.

The car pulled away, and Jarrow turned toward the house. Larry was young and headstrong, but really not so bad inside, he told himself. He had been wondering if a quiet word with Irwin Shafer, the principal of Linden Junior High, about some of Larry's indiscretions wouldn't be out of place. But on reflection, as he came to the end of the path and stopped at the door, he decided against it. It was something that could keep until another day.

He extended a finger and pressed the bell push beside the engraved brass plate reading: DR. M. R. VALDHEIM, M.D., PH.D., M.A.P.A., M.I.P.N. CONSULTANT NEUROPHYSIOLOGIST.

two

Dr. Valdheim, wearing a white coat over shirtsleeves, appeared in the hallway while Jarrow was still completing formalities at the reception desk. He was in his sixties, Jarrow guessed, a tall, gangling man with thick, metal-rimmed spectacles, who managed to combine a broad, straight-shouldered frame with a gaunt, hollow-cheeked face topped by a balding dome, looking as if it had found its way onto the wrong body.

"Mr. Jarrow, good morning. Right on time as always. And how are you feeling today?"

"Not too bad. At least the weather's easing up."

"It has been a tough one, yes. I thought the snow was here forever."

Valdheim's voice had a trace of a foreign accent that Jarrow had never been able to place but hadn't asked about. Despite his senescent features, his manner was always brisk and sturdily robust. Jarrow wondered if that was his way of seeking to impart professional reassurance. If so, it never quite worked, for Jarrow always found himself with a feeling of something sinister in the background, like a shadow lurking just beyond his limit of vision. He wasn't sure why.

Marje, the receptionist, ran Jarrow's verification coder through a slot on her terminal to confirm the details she'd entered, and handed the card back. "That's fine, Mr. Jarrow. How are those kids treating you at the school?"

"Oh . . ." Jarrow fumbled for an answer. He had always suffered from an acute awkwardness with women, which taxed his thinking faculties even over questions as innocuous as this.

"I guess you've been there long enough to know how to look after yourself," Marje said.

"Er, yes. I guess so."

"This way please." Valdheim rescued him with a gesture in the direction of the passageway leading to the treatment room. "You're the first," he said over his shoulder, indicating the empty waiting room with a nod as Jarrow followed. "We can go straight through."

Jarrow had been attending these sessions periodically for almost six months now, although the circumstances leading to them had begun some time before that. In the course of his mandatory annual checkup the previous summer, he had described periodic attacks of lethargic depression and emotional confusion, sometimes bad enough for him to take time off work. Suspecting an incipient cerebral disorder, the local clinician referred him to a specialist for diagnostic tests, who in turn brought in a neurologist from the Regional Health Authority's Ramsey Hospital in St. Paul. The condition turned out to be a mild inflammation that soon yielded to a course of antibiotics and drugs.

But to Jarrow's consternation, he was informed that the tests had revealed certain irregularities in underlying patterns of neural activity, which were thought to have induced the condition. In other words, although the prescribed treatment appeared superficially successful, the suspicion was that it had addressed the symptoms rather than the cause. Nobody could be really sure, however, since that area of psychopathology was on the fringe of contemporary research. However, Minneapolis had been selected as one of several national test sites for a new piece of diagnostic equipment that was being developed for decoding and analyzing deep-seated brain activity, and Jarrow was approached to volunteer as a model case study. Jarrow agreed, and the introduction to Dr. Valdheim had followed soon afterward.

They entered the treatment room, which Valdheim had once described as housing a "glorified video reading head." All the same, it still managed to require the inevitable carts with rubber tubes, glassware, and trays of implements that doctors everywhere seemed incapable of functioning without, and the sight of which always made Jarrow feel slightly sick. The room itself had a bench and a sink along one side, with shelves and a glass-fronted cabinet full of jars and bottles above. A control console with a keyboard and several display screens, along with two cabinets of electronics, took up most of the wall opposite. The centerpiece of it all was an assembly of electrical apparatuses, focusing guides, windings, and cooling coils that dominated the space in between. From its center, a leather-topped couch extended into the room, its head end surrounded by a radial array of metal tubes and crystal plates laced by wires and optical fibers, around which the room's other fittings seemed to stand in respectful reverence like the lesser trappings in a chapel before the main altar.

It was called QUIP, which Jarrow now knew stood for Quantum Interferoencephalogram Processor. Valdheim had told him so. Valdheim had also been more than generous with his time in trying to explain about superconducting current loops, quantized molecular magnetic moments, and resonant phase patterns deep in the brain; but that kind of thing really wasn't Jarrow's field.

Although he tried to nod and shake his head and say the right things at the right times, he still didn't have a clear-enough grasp of how the device worked to have hazarded any attempt at describing it to anyone else. But apparently the detectors could sense changes in electrical current as small as a millionth of a millionth of a millionth of an ampere, which Jarrow gathered was about the same fraction of the current in a small flashlamp as the thickness of a piece of tissue paper was to forty times the sun's distance from the planet Pluto. After that, he hadn't even bothered trying to follow. His first impulse had been to flaunt this newfound knowledge at Larry, but it would only have given Larry, who taught sophomore math and physics, the satisfaction of snowing him with more technicalities. So in the end, Jarrow had decided against it.

Valdheim went over to the console, flipped some switches, and commenced a dialogue with one of the screens via the keyboard. "You're becoming something of a celebrity, you know, Mr. Jarrow," he said over his shoulder.

"Oh, really?" Watching Valdheim checking the responses and then entering another command put Jarrow in mind of a virtuoso organist enraptured with his natural medium. He himself found the ubiquitous thickets of buttons and cryptic symbols, which barred the way to seemingly everything he wanted to do in the modern world, incomprehensible. You had to be under fifteen or Japanese to understand anything these days. Or one of those people whose business it was, like Larry—and which Larry never let slip an opportunity to demonstrate.

"Yes," Valdheim said. "Your case is being talked about in professional circles."

"It is?"

"Well, a certain rather specialized group of professionals, anyway. It has some interesting features."

Jarrow had never thought of himself as important. He felt mildly flattered.

Valdheim touched another button, entered a code, and looked up expectantly as one of the screens that had been blank came to life. "Let me show you a little of what we found last time," he said. Jarrow followed his gaze obediently. The screen showed a mass of what looked like scores of richly branching trees of various colors, all densely intertwined and enmeshed together. Some seemed to flicker in highlights, with branches suddenly disappearing from some places while others added themselves elsewhere, darting their way erratically through the forest like fingers of multiple-forked lightning feeling pathways to the ground. Other patterns came and went spasmodically, while still others propagated smoothly, changing and distorting like smoke rings moving through turbulent air. Valdheim had shown Jarrow similar things before. And still, none of it meant anything. To Jarrow, it could all just as easily have been a computer reconstruction of autogenesis in a petri dish, or a surrealistic vision of colliding galaxies.

Valdheim stepped a pace back and explained, still looking at the screen. "Here's a recurring cycle of activated dendritic arboration paths occurring in a region of your inferior temporal cortex. That's one of the regions where visual primitives resolved in the striate cortex are combined into coherent imagery. It also receives an input of emotively significant associative weightings from the neocortex. But the configuration of synaptic modifications established as a consequence is inhibited by oscillations correlating with the conscious state, which are communicated from the thalamus." He pointed from one entanglement of meaningless, pulsating luminescence to another, then turned to look at Jarrow inquiringly.

"Fascinating," Jarrow said.

"We are looking at what goes on inside your brain, you see," Valdheim went on. "This is where the images that you see begin to come together. Man is a visual animal. Images are very important to us. We weight them with various emotional associations, depending on our experiences." He gestured again. "Normally, of course, the images are driven by signals coming in from the world outside, which is how they keep in step with reality and hopefully reflect what's happening there. But the region can still function when there are no signals coming in to direct it. Then it invents images of its own."

At last, a glimmer of something that made sense. "As in dreaming," Jarrow hazarded.

Valdheim returned a perfunctory nod, as if to a moron who had just grasped the connection between *A* and *Apple*. "What we have here is a repeating pattern of just such a nature, which represents a persistent set of images and connotations that will affect the processes taking place in the further areas that this region maps into. And this, we believe, might be the root of the depressions and disturbances that you described when you came to us."

Jarrow thought he followed that part. "These images . . . am I supposed to know what they are?" he asked uneasily.

"No." Valdheim shook his head. "As I said, the activity is suppressed during the waking condition. Hence you have no conscious awareness of the form in which it manifests itself. And our techniques at present are not sufficiently sophisticated for us to tell you. But later, we would like you to take a series of psychological tests to help us try and establish that." The doctor rubbed his palms together. "In the meantime, back to work, yes?" He showed his teeth in a skull-like parody of a smile. "Or at least, I shall do the work while you relax. To activate the pattern, we will have to put you to sleep again."

Jarrow knew the drill by now and was already removing his jacket. He hung it on the stand by the door, added his necktie, then slipped off his shoes and sat down on the leather couch. Nurse Callins—Valdheim's stern-faced, middle-aged, and terrifyingly efficient assistant—entered through a rear door as Jarrow settled himself back and lowered his head onto the rubber headrest at the center of the radial array.

"Good day, Mr. Jarrow," she said, at the same time handing Valdheim a folder filled with papers, charts, and printouts.

"Hello again."

"A three-seven soporific, please. Same dose as before," Valdheim said. Nurse Callins turned toward the bench and the sounds came of tablets being dropped into a beaker and liquid being stirred. Valdheim moved over to the couch and began positioning supports and fittings around Jarrow's head. Jarrow felt soft pads tightening snugly beneath his ears and cold contact heads probing through his hair to touch his scalp. Although he knew that the procedure was noninvasive and painless, an involuntary nervous reaction asserted itself, and he found himself talking reflexively.

"It must be pretty expensive—all this stuff you've got here."

"You wouldn't want to pay the insurance premium," Valdheim agreed.

"I'm surprised that a private practice would have equipment like that."

"I'm cooperating with a national trial program, don't forget. The government owns it."

"Isn't it kind of unusual for it to be in a place like this? I mean, why wouldn't they set it up in one of the state hospitals somewhere?"

Valdheim watched a readout while he adjusted a control. "Head still now, Mr. Jarrow. No more talking, please."

Nurse Callins moved into view and lowered a shallow drinking cup with a shaped lip. "Here you are. Easy, now."

The liquid tasted mildly tannic. Jarrow drained the last of it, then raised his eyes to find Valdheim's face peering down at him, seemingly from afar and yet filling his field of vision. The drug was taking effect already. Valdheim's voice sounded distorted and hollow. "That's the idea. Nice and comfortable. Watch my fingers as I count. You'll be away before I get to ten. We'll see you later in the recovery room. One . . . two . . . three . . . four . . . five . . ." The fingers blurred into each other, and Valdheim's face receded to become a pink smudge. For some reason his eyes, gleaming through the metal-rimmed spectacles, still remained distinct.

The voice boomed, emanating seemingly from everywhere: *"Six . . . seven . . . eight . . ."*

three

Jarrow regained consciousness slowly, to a feeling of softness and warmth enveloping him. Subdued light penetrated his eyelids, gently tugging him back to wakefulness.

A muted voice, a man's, was babbling in the background. Jarrow stretched his legs and felt smooth sheets sliding against his skin. He turned onto his side, and his face pressed into yielding pillows. His arm came up to rest on another pillow alongside. Cool air found a chink by his shoulder; he pulled the blanket closer around his neck. He hadn't felt so relaxed for years.

The babbling voice resolved itself into the vibrant logorrhea of TV announcers everywhere—which should have been illegal when people were trying to sleep. Jarrow pulled the blanket over his ear and tried to burrow deeper into the pillows, but the voice infused itself through the cracks like water into a leaky shoe.

". . . announcement of a new national enforcement agency to be set up under the Bureau of Environmental Control. Modeled on Europe's 'Green Police,' the organization will employ agents at federal and state levels to secure tighter compliance with regulations and planning requirements. The agents will have arbitrary powers of search and entry to conduct spot checks, and—get a load of this—will operate on a *percentage* basis of the fines imposed by a delinquency tribunal. In Stockholm last night, conservation secretary for the Western Consolidation, Gustav Moller of Germany, applauded the news, but called for stronger moves to pressure the Southern World and FER states into line. We'll have more on that later. Meanwhile, a time check: it's just coming up to seven-thirty on this chilly but clear Tuesday morning. . . ."

What? Jarrow rolled back over and opened his eyes.

"And to lighten things up a little, we've got a story about two penguins who've decided to live in a city fountain. And here to tell you about it is Mavis Young. Mavis, good morning. I must say, you're looking great today."

It wasn't Tuesday, it was Thursday! And how could the time be 7:30 A.M.?

It came to him then, suddenly, that a lot of things were wrong. What was a TV doing here? The bed was too big for a doctor's recovery room. And Jarrow was naked in it. Then he realized to his consternation that the pillows had an odor of perfume.

"Hi, Brad," a woman's voice said from the TV. "Why, thank you, kind sir."

"So, what's this about vagrant penguins?"

"Well, it all started with . . ."

Jarrow sat up. There was another queen-size bed alongside, untouched except for some women's clothes strewn on the quilt. On the bedside unit between the beds was a cigarette pack and lighter, an ashtray with several butts, and two glasses, one with an inch of amber liquid.

He gazed around in bewilderment. There was a vanity-cum-bureau running along the far wall, and on top of it, he could see a black briefcase, a lady's purse, a man's wallet, loose papers, a set of keys, and some change. None of the items looked familiar. Along with them was a part-emptied bottle of Canadian Club and an ice bucket. Near the bed was a chair with a striped shirt and underwear tossed carelessly over the back. A table with a tray holding dishes and what looked like the remains of a meal stood with two more chairs by a window. The drapes of the window were closed. There was an armchair nearby. On the other side of the room, opposite the window, was a folding luggage stand bearing a leather traveling case and a shoulder bag. A double closet completed the room, which appeared to have two doors opening off from it. One of them was half-open, and Jarrow could see from the view in the mirror above the vanity that it led to a bathroom.

The place had every appearance of being a hotel. This whole situation was insane. Jarrow hardly ever touched alcohol; he abhorred tobacco. Even raunchy jokes embarrassed him, never mind sleazy amourettes in hotels. And the men's clothes thrown over the chair weren't his.

He scrambled up hastily, but hesitated when he caught a glimpse of his reflection. There was something odd about his appearance. For the moment he wasn't sure what. Then, feeling insecure in his nudity, he went into the bathroom for a towel. There, he found a man's traveling kit by the sink, with toothbrush, shaver, nail clippers, and hairbrush—and again nothing was familiar. There was also a woman's red zip-up cosmetic purse, pushed to one side and spilling lipstick, compact, nail polishes, and hair grips; nearby was a pack of Band-Aids. Jarrow hitched a bath towel around his waist and went back into the main room to check the window.

Wherever this was, it lay among high-rises in what was clearly a large city center. But whichever way he tried projecting the angles, he couldn't reconcile it remotely with any view of Minneapolis. He let the drape fall back and stood rubbing his brow, eyes closed, as if hoping to massage the illusion away. But nothing had changed when he opened them again.

Baffled, he turned away from the window, and his eye came to rest on the plastic stand on the table beside the tray, containing copies of the hotel directory and various promotional materials. He picked up the directory and opened it. The introductory page carried the face of a smiling black woman in a yellow blouse and blue tunic. "Welcome!" the caption read, ". . . to the Atlanta Hyatt."

Atlanta?

Jarrow hadn't been to Atlanta since a weekend over ten years ago, when he'd attended an educational conference. He could think of nobody that he knew in the area, nor any business that might have brought him there. He swallowed hard as the realization sank in that something very strange had happened to him; his confusion began giving way to fear.

First, he needed to get dressed. He went back across the room to inspect the closet. It contained a couple of suits, one light gray, one dark with a thin pinstripe, several clean shirts, neckties, a pair of casual slacks, a maroon bathrobe, and a blue, hip-length topcoat. As with the other items in the room, he had never seen them before. The other side of the closet revealed a blouse and skirt, a pair of blue jeans, a woman's green coat, and an orange dress. No sign of any of his own clothes.

He tried the leather traveling case: socks, underwear, handker-chiefs, clothes brush, and other personal items—all a man's, but not his. A plastic bag inside at one end contained laundry. He looked briefly in the shoulder bag, but as he had anticipated, it was the woman's. Frantic now, he searched the drawers of the vanity, the cupboard units at either end, the shelf above the closets, and even the space beneath the sink in the bathroom. Nothing. He straight-ened up, filled one of the tumblers from the cold faucet, and took a long drink. Then he came back into the main room and stood, staring at the clothes in the closet again. As was his tendency when he was thinking, his hand came up unconsciously to pinch at his mustache. But his fingertips met a smooth upper lip.

He turned and looked at himself again in the mirror on the closet door. There was a bruise, a day or two old maybe, on his temple. And he had a Band-Aid on one side of his neck a short distance below his right ear. When he explored the spot with his fingertips it felt tender and slightly sore.

But the face was familiar: clear-skinned and clean-shaven, with black wavy hair and dark eyes; and he could detect nothing unusual about the lithe, swarthy-skinned body. Yet the sight seemed to jar with strange stirrings half remembered. He'd had the same kind of feeling, momentarily, when he first caught sight of himself in the larger mirror upon getting up from the bed.

He was sure that he had a habit of pinching his mustache when he was thinking or brooding; indeed, hadn't the reflex just mani-fested itself? But how could that be, when he didn't have a mustache? Maybe he'd had one once, and—along with a lot of other strange things that seemed to have been going on—had forgotten getting rid of it. Or could it be simply the remnant of an uncommonly vivid dream? . . . He needed a shave, he noted. But that could wait.

A door opened and closed somewhere nearby in the corridor outside. Voices sounded loudly for a few seconds, then receded, reminding Jarrow of the impending confrontation that could come at any moment. He looked at the woman's things scattered around the room, the remains of the meal and the drink, the untouched second bed. The vision of casual, abandoned intimacy repelled and un-nerved him. Even without the disorientation of his predicament, facing the aftermath would have been ordeal enough. He had to get away and find somewhere to think alone without this kind of complication. And there was only one way. . . .

He took down the pants of the gray suit and measured them against his leg. They seemed to be about his size, anyway. He draped them on the edge of the bed and held the jacket against himself. It was the right width and length. Fumbling in his haste and anxiety, he took some socks and underwear from the traveling case, pulled on the pants, and buttoned himself into one of the clean shirts hanging in the closet. He found a pair of men's black leather shoes tossed near the wall by the bathroom door, which again fitted perfectly, and selected a plain dark blue tie from the rack. Finally, he slipped on the jacket and moved across the room to survey the items on the bureau-vanity more closely.

His next shock came when he opened the black briefcase and found a pair of guns staring up at him. He knew nothing about weapons, but one was a large automatic pistol and looked powerful, while the other was small and slim, lighter in construction, probably intended for concealment. With them was a plastic case containing an assortment of what looked like tools, drills, and other gadgets that didn't mean anything, along with a number of electronic devices, equally baffling. Jarrow stared in horrified fascination for several seconds, then closed the briefcase decisively and pushed it aside. He didn't have time now to worry about what it meant, and he certainly wasn't about to risk complicating this situation further by taking it with him.

The loose change went into one of the pants pockets, and after a moment's hesitation the keys. There was also a hotel memo pad with the top sheet turned over and several phone numbers scrawled on the one that was exposed. They didn't convey anything. He turned back the top sheet and found scrawled on it the words:

Headman to ship out via J'ville, sometime Nov 19. Check ref "Cop 3."

Jarrow shrugged and dropped the pad into one of the side pockets of his jacket, along with the room's electronically coded passcard. He took a handkerchief from the traveling case and then picked up the wallet. Inside was a personal ID card in a transparent window—and that was when he got his next shock, causing him to gasp aloud. The ID card was made out for a Maurice Gordon, said to be from Philadelphia; but the face looking back out at him—smooth-shaven, olive-skinned, with black wavy hair—was his own. A hasty check of the wallet's other compartments revealed that Maurice Gordon was cleared by the IRS to leave the country at will, belonged to the Eastern Pennsylvania Chamber of Commerce, and had recently visited Washington. Also, he believed in being prepared for emergencies: the wallet contained almost $2,500 in cash. Jarrow stuffed the wallet into an inside pocket, went to the door, and then as an afterthought retrieved the blue topcoat from the closet. He went back to the door again, paused for a deep breath to steady himself, and let himself out.

A sign a short distance away directed him to the elevators. When he was halfway along the corridor, a woman came around the corner, heading the other way. Certain that it was his unknown companion, Jarrow tensed for the encounter, but she passed by with just an uncertain half smile, sensing his apprehension. Getting too jumpy, he told himself as he pressed the call button at the elevator. Calm down. Got to calm down.

The car arrived. Despite his admonition, he felt himself tensing again as the door opened, but the car was empty. "Which floor do you require?" a synthetic voice asked from a grille as he got in.

"Main lobby."

In his present state of mind, a thousand-mile overland trip back to Minneapolis was out of the question. Flying was a far more restricted affair than had once been the case, and a ticket would only be issued on production of a valid internal passport carrying a certificate of compliance issued by the taxation department of one's state of residence. Since the only travel category authorized in Jarrow's internal passport was the low-priority grade that came with his junior high-school teacher's status, he had resigned himself to the prospect of a long wait at the airport.

But the thought occurred to him as the elevator descended that the ID he was carrying meant that he would have to collect the mysterious Maurice Gordon's passport from Reception on checking out, and from the quick assessment he'd made from the contents of the wallet, there seemed a good chance that Gordon might have a higher-category authorization. So one small blessing could be that he'd get home sooner.

When Jarrow came out of the elevator, a man in a white hat was disputing something with the clerk at the desk, gesticulating furiously and then starting all over again whenever the clerk tried to answer. Jarrow watched from behind a pillar. The problem seemed interminable. Another woman came out behind him from the adjacent elevator and again he froze, but she ignored him and went out the front door. Finally, the dialogue at the desk ended, and the man in the white hat stomped away. Jarrow emerged and approached warily.

The clerk greeted him matter-of-factly. "Good morning, sir."

"Hello. Er, room . . ." Jarrow looked at the passcard in his hand, then realized that he didn't know the room number. For security reasons the code printed on the electronic passes wasn't the same as the door numbers. He slid the passcard across the counter without finishing the sentence. The clerk inserted it into a terminal.

"Mr. Gordon, room 1406?"

Jarrow nodded, at the same time swallowing involuntarily. "That's right."

"How can I help you?"

"I need to leave right away."

"Okay. Let's see, there are a few extra charges I have to add in here. It won't take a second." The clerk consulted unseen oracles and tapped at keys.

Jarrow looked around anxiously, expecting at any moment to hear a shout or see somebody coming toward him from the elevators. A call-tone sounded from a phone behind the desk. Another clerk took it. Jarrow watched uneasily. The clerk said something into the handset, listened, and his eyes came to rest on Jarrow. In his mind, Jarrow could picture security staff already rushing to the lobby, police cruisers drawing up outside. He felt perspiration rushing down his back, certain that every line on his face was a beacon broadcasting that something was amiss and screaming for attention. But the clerk's gaze drifted casually away again, then he grinned to himself and started ribbing whoever was at the other end. Jarrow looked away, telling himself again to calm down.

"If you'll just okay that, Mr. Gordon."

"What? . . . Oh, yes." Jarrow inspected the bill that appeared on the customer screen built into the top of the counter. "It says three nights. Is that right? I've been here three nights?"

"Today is Tuesday, sir. According to the record, you arrived late Saturday afternoon without a reservation. Isn't that correct?"

"Sure. I was just checking. That's okay."

"I need your coder, sir."

"Er, pardon?" He hadn't thought to check that he had one.

"Your personal verification coder, Mr. Gordon. I need it to verify the bill."

"Oh, of course." Jarrow reached inside his jacket and drew out Gordon's wallet. Rummaging inside he found a PVC with the name MAURICE J. GORDON embossed in visible print. The clerk took it and pushed it into a slot while Jarrow watched woodenly, waiting for the inevitable rejection, or for some other irregularity to signal itself.

"That's fine, Mr. Gordon. Here you are." The clerk returned the coder, along with a U.S. internal passport. Numb with relief and not a little surprise, Jarrow accepted them and nodded mutely. He looked at the passport and saw that it was made out in the name of Maurice J. Gordon. The picture alongside the thumbprint was his own. It was in order and carried a high-priority flight authorization. "Thanks for using the Hyatt. Come and see us in Atlanta again sometime."

"Thank you. Can I get a cab to the airport?"

"Sure. There should be a couple outside. The doorman will take care of it."

"How far away is it?"

"This time of morning, aw, about twenty, twenty-five minutes. What time's your flight?"

"I haven't booked one yet. Thanks. . . . Thanks again."

"Have a good one."

Jarrow got a cab straightaway at the main entrance, but it was several miles before he felt safe and could settle back in the seat to begin taking stock of his circumstances.

"Driver, what day is it?" he asked, leaning forward, just to double-check.

"Tuesday, all of it, last I heard."

Jarrow sat back again, shaking his head. It was crazy.

four

It had been several years since Jarrow last flew. He didn't enjoy it. The terminal had a worn and shabby look, seeming to exude the weariness of a world that was running down. There was growing concern about the effects of jet exhaust on the stratosphere, and the government had been talking about cutting the annual mileage allocations auctioned to airlines and raising rates to reduce the number of flights further. Jarrow hadn't realized that the measures were so far advanced, however. Half the airport's facilities appeared to be closed, and the departure lounge into which Jarrow eventually found his way was packed with anxious and harassed travelers milling around the check-in desks as they jockeyed for places, or sitting out interminable waits amid piles of baggage and restless children. Taking in the scene, Jarrow resigned himself to the inevitability of a long delay. But to his grateful relief, Gordon's passport got him onto a United flight due to depart, as luck would have it, in less than an hour, with a stop at Chicago. He hadn't realized that the fares had gone up so much, either, but Gordon's cash reserve took care of that.

The man who lowered himself ponderously into the seat next to Jarrow's was fifty pounds overweight, breathed wheezily, and smelled of stale perspiration. He overflowed the armrest with his elbows and invaded the aisle space on one side and Jarrow's legroom on the other with his knees. Jarrow pulled himself in as far as possible and prepared himself for an uncomfortable flight.

The man leaned back, spreading his elbows wider to unfasten his necktie, then sideways, thrusting a shoulder across, to fish a pack of gum from his jacket pocket with the other hand. "These flying sardine cans don't get any better," he drawled.

"Right." Jarrow had the sinking feeling that this was the prelude to something that could go on all through the flight. During the cab ride from the hotel and amid the bustle of the airport, he had been waiting for a few hours of quiet to pull himself together and collect his thoughts.

"You do this route often?"

"Er, no."

The wrapper came off one of the wafers of gum, and the gum went into the mouth, which proceeded to chomp noisily. "I used to do it all the time. I know the scenery from here to the Windy City like my local road into town. Had to cut it back some in the last six months, though—with the new restrictions."

"Oh."

"I'm in tiles and flooring. How about you?"

"Pardon?"

"What line are you in?"

"Oh. Teaching. I teach."

"That's nice." There was a short silence, apart from the gum cracking. The information had evidently provoked no further thought or curiosity. Jarrow was just beginning to hope that perhaps he would be permitted some peace for his own reflections after all, when the man shifted his bulk heavily again and leaned closer. Jarrow caught a whiff of bad breath mixed with the odor of gum. "Of course, you know what it's all about."

"What?"

"All this cutting back and clamping down. Why we can't catch a plane anytime we want anymore, or why you can get fined for running an air conditioner if it's below seventy-five. You know what's really going on?"

Jarrow sighed. Everybody knew why such things were necessary. He didn't want to get into this. "It's a limited world," he recited. "The Profligate Era overstretched everything. We have to get back to a proper balance, conserve resources."

A thick-fingered hand waved itself in front of his face. "Nah, that's not why. It's because they know what's down the line. The Russian heap of cards came apart, right, and now it's all a mess over there. The old firm's supposed to be junked, and now they're all going their own way, okay? . . . But that ain't the way it is. See, the way I figure it is, them Communists are still out there, in the space bubbles and on the Moon. That's who's really running things out there. And one day they're gonna be coming back to settle the old action, and our people know it. So everything's gotta be put into the military, and it's why we have to have all this security. We can't afford luxuries for now."

Jarrow groaned inwardly. Yes, Earth had to remain on its guard against the Offworlder threat, but this half-wit had it all wrong. The danger was simply one posed by economic reality: their reckless expansion of industry and population was bound to outrun the capacity of their resources to sustain, and when that happened they would look to Earth's, which were strained enough as things were. Anyone who couldn't see that, or who needed to conjure up the ghosts of defunct political ideologies to explain the situation, wasn't someone to waste breath arguing with. And just at this moment, Jarrow wasn't interested in arguing with anybody.

"I'm sorry, I've had a couple of tough days," he said. "Nice talking to you, but I need to catch up on my sleep." Without waiting for a response, he slid down in his seat, closed his eyes, and began going over what he could remember.

Three days. . . . The clerk at the Hyatt had told him he had checked in on Saturday. And it seemed that Jarrow had acquired all the trappings and identity of Maurice Gordon by that time. His visit to Dr. Valdheim's had been on Thursday. What had happened during those missing forty-eight hours?

The fat man crashed about in the seat next to him again, derailing his thoughts. The ceaseless noise of gum-chewing sawed at his nerves.

The last thing he could recall before waking up in the hotel was looking up from the QUIP apparatus as he went under. At the thought of the probes and contacts around his head, all his misgivings about anything technological—and medical technology in particular—returned. Was it possible that he hadn't awakened at all, and all of this was taking place in his mind?

Weariness came over him with the effort of trying to make sense of it, and he drifted into a genuine, if fitful, sleep. At Chicago the fat man, thankfully, deplaned. His place was taken by a wan-faced woman who said not a word and was no trouble. After takeoff,

Jarrow dozed again, awakening only when the cabin attendant roused him for the descent into Minneapolis. Through the window on one side as the plane banked, he caught a glimpse of a curve of the Mississippi and the plains to the south of the city, and saw to his surprise that there was plenty of snow about. He thought it had just about cleared. Maybe there had been a freak storm late in the season while he'd been gone, as sometimes happened.

When he got out, he decided that must have been the case: the weather had turned *cold*. He was glad that he'd brought Gordon's topcoat with him.

Since his divorce, Jarrow had lived alone in what was called Brooklyn Center, eight miles north of the metropolis. The apartment, one of sixty in a twin-tower layer cake of gray concrete and aluminum-ribbed glass shamelessly flaunting the name Orchard Lea Court, had seen better days. With the extension of urban rent controls, landlords and builders had been showing typical social irresponsibility by pulling out of the private-residence business, and it was now necessary for dwelling space to be allocated on a number-of-occupants basis. In fact, Jarrow was above par in getting what he had. That was one of the areas where being a teacher could help.

It must have been quite a storm, he concluded, seeing the piles of cleared snow along the sidewalks as he began tottering and slithering the two icy blocks from the nearest autoshuttle point. But when he had gone no more than a few yards, he saw that the snow was dirty and in many places lay on top of compacted slush that looked as if it had been there a lot longer than three days. He puzzled over this oddity as he walked—and then stopped dead as the realization hit him that the assumption he'd been carrying uncritically all the way from Atlanta was completely without foundation.

He had presumed that his visit to Valdheim had been *last* Thursday, two days before he checked into the Hyatt. But there was no reason, of course, why it should be so. In fact, it was now so obvious from the changes that had taken place that whatever had happened must have involved far more time than three days, that he could find no explanation for taking so long to see it. Perhaps it was all affecting him even more than he realized. He began moving again, his pace quickening despite the treacherous surface under-foot, in growing disquiet and agitation.

And then, on reaching Orchard Lea Court, he stopped again to stare at the block across the street. Unless he'd been walking in and out for weeks without noticing, it had suddenly acquired a whole new frontage. Surely, the last time he'd seen it, hadn't it been empty, with a sign advertising a takeover by new owners and plans for converting it into offices? Now it was in business, with a new door and entrance hall, fresh paint, and logos on the windows advertising several brave enterprises now in residence. That hadn't happened over the weekend, either. More puzzled than ever, Jarrow turned and walked up the steps to the entrance of "B" tower.

Inside, he paused and stood looking around. The lobby area looked even more run-down than he remembered, with walls scuffed and scratched and the carpet on the stairs by the elevator worn threadbare at the edges. He walked over to the elevator and pressed the call button. The machinery inside responded with creaks and rumblings. And then as he waited, mentally playing through the picture of entering his apartment and wondering if any new surprises were lying in wait for him there, he realized that he probably didn't have a key to get in. He felt inside his pocket and pulled out the keys that he'd picked up in the hotel room. As he'd feared, none were his own. The car arrived and the door in front of him slid aside. But there was no point in getting in. He stood looking around him in a quandary.

There was a movement in the janitor's room by the main entrance, and a figure rose behind the window facing out over the lobby. Moments later, a gnarled, whispy-haired Hispanic shuffled out, wearing a blue workshirt beneath a tan, kapok-padded vest. Jarrow had never seen him before.

"You lookin' for somebody in here, or sump'n?"

"Ah, just the man." Jarrow tried to force a disarming grin, but it wouldn't quite work. "Look, I've got a small problem here. I've lost my key, and I'm locked out. Can you come up and let me in? It's 703."

The janitor flashed him a suspicious look. "703?"

"Right."

"I can't let nobody in except a resident. Who are you, anyhow?"

Jarrow wasn't in a mood to be given even more of a hard time than he was having already. And he didn't like the man's tone. "Look," he said tiredly, "if you're new to the job, give yourself time to learn all the faces before you try that kind of stuff. I *am* the resident, okay?"

"Get outta here."

All the tension that had been accumulating since early that morning erupted. "Look at your list, for God's sake," Jarrow snapped. "The name is Jarrow. I want to get into my apartment."

"Jarrow, huh?"

"Right." The janitor wasn't budging. Jarrow's voice rose higher. "Look, what the hell is this? I've been out of town, and I haven't had the best of weekends. So will you quit trying to be a hardass, or whatever you're playing at, and just do what I'm asking you to?"

The janitor backed toward the doorway he had emerged from. "What kinda asshole are you? I ain't never seen you before, an' I ain't never heard o' no Jarrow. Now I'm warnin' yuh, if you don't get out I'm callin' the cops."

Jarrow sighed, then changed tactics and spread his hands imploringly. "Look, I'm telling you I'm Richard Jarrow. I live in number 703. Why is that such a hard thing to believe?" Inwardly he was seized by a sudden misgiving as he realized that all he needed now was for the janitor to ask for some ID. Jarrow didn't have a shred that he could produce.

"What are you talkin' about?" the janitor rasped. "People called Ryan live in 703. Have done as long as I've worked here."

"And how the hell long is that?" Jarrow challenged, getting angry again.

"Three months now, just over—if that's any o' your business. So don't you go tellin' me I need to learn any faces."

Jarrow gaped, all the belligerence evaporating out of him. But even that didn't add up. He turned and stared out through the doors at the mounds of snow piled along the sidewalk. Three months would put them into midsummer: June or July. This was getting even crazier.

He turned a baffled face back toward the janitor, who was hovering just outside his cubbyhole with obvious doubts as to Jarrow's motives or sanity.

"What's the date today?" Jarrow whispered.

The janitor retreated into his room and reappeared with a

stained copy of the *Minneapolis Star & Tribune.* "November seventeenth."

"*November?* That's impossible!"

"That's what it says, right here. Think I can't read or sump'n?
Take a look yourself." The janitor thrust the paper out, at the same
time keeping his distance. Jarrow took it and read the line below the
banner disbelievingly. The janitor's voice mumbled on in the background. "Comin' in here tellin' me I don't know my job, sayin' he
lives here. Asshole don't even know what month it is."

Jarrow handed the paper back numbly. His last recollection
before finding himself in Atlanta was his visit to Dr. Valdheim. That
had been on the third of April.

He had lost over seven months of his life.

five

When he was ten years old or so, Richard Jarrow had become a Galactic Ranger. Membership was acquired by filling in an application from the back of a breakfast cereal box and sending it in with ten dollars and five tokens. In return, the prospective interstellar lawman received a visored communicator helmet; space navigator's equipment belt and sidearm; official ID card and badge; a top-secret manual containing various codes and signaling procedures, instructions for dealing with a host of unlikely situations, charts of the organizational command structure, rules and regulations, and the Ranger's Code of Honor. It also included a tear-out registration form to be completed and returned for filing at Galactic Strike Command Headquarters, care of the Krispbix Foods Corporation, which among other things listed height, weight, color of hair and eyes, and any other distinguishing features.

In response to the last question, young Jarrow had described a birthmark on his left forearm, vaguely shaped like South America. For some strange reason he couldn't actually summon to mind any visual recollection of what it had looked like. But he remembered quite definitely filling in the answer. The stranger thing was that there was no trace of such a mark on his arm now.

He was also becoming aware of other, similar peculiarities concerning events he was certain he remembered as having happened, but that he was unable to reconcile with his circumstances now. There had been an occasion in his teenage years, for example, when he went on vacation with some friends to Texas in July and had been badly sunburned. He remembered the doctor who treated him commenting that with his fair skin he should have taken it easier for the first few days. But how could that have been, when Jarrow had olive skin and a Mediterranean complexion?

He sat on the edge of the single bed in a nondescript room with faded wallpaper and cheap drapes, and tapped a number into the keypad of the viewphone. For refuge, he had sought out one of the small hotels in downtown Minneapolis, which, for cash, would waive the regulations requiring ID. Maurice Gordon, he'd decided, would be better buried for the time being, until he found out more about him.

The girl who answered the call was thin and pallid, with dark hair fluffed out around her head like a smoky halo. She wore a bored and indifferent expression. "D.K. Properties."

"Hello. You're the company that handles the rentals at Orchard Lea Court in Brooklyn Center?"

"Yes, we do."

"Ah, I wonder if you can help me. I'm trying to trace a Mr. Richard Jarrow who used to be in number 703. Can you tell me—"

"Hang on one second." The girl turned away, and the sound of computer keys being hammered came over the audio. A phone rang somewhere in the background. "703, you said?"

"Right."

"What was the name again?"

"Jarrow."

"Right. . . . Well, he ain't there no more. It's let in the name of Ryan. Jarrow's contract terminated end of May last year."

"Er, do you have any indication of why?"

"We're not into life histories here. We just rent apartments, okay?"

"I understand. Oh, one more thing. Does it say where he went? Do you have a forwarding address, anything like that?"

"All it's got here is that the contract ran out at the end of May. That's all I can tell you."

"I see. Thanks anyw—" The screen blanked out.

Jarrow touched a key to disconnect, swung his legs up off the floor, and lay back against the pillows stacked at the head of the bed. He had been lying there like this ever since he checked in, groping for a hint of a lead that never came. A whole chunk of his life, from the April 3 that he remembered through to November 17, which he had to accept was the current date, had vanished. On top of that, even his recollections from before—from times that he had no reason to view as having been abnormal—were sprinkled with details that couldn't be true. And as if that wasn't disconcerting enough, he had returned to find himself surrounded by evidence of a life-style that wasn't his, and in possession of the clothes and ID of somebody he'd never heard of.

He stared at the picture of buffalo hanging above the brown-painted chest of drawers on the other side of the room. The buffalo didn't have an answer to offer. Jarrow thought for a few minutes longer, then got up, took the blue topcoat from the hook behind the door, and went back down to the street.

The time was just coming up to four in the afternoon when Jarrow arrived at Linden Junior High. After his experience with the janitor the day before, he was wary of relying on being recognized to get him past the security desk—especially since he had no documentation to verify who he was. Respect for authority and the kinds of safeguards necessary for the orderly functioning of society were essential in the makeup of future citizens, and the educational environment was designed to instill familiarity and acceptance from an early age. Students carried electronically coded IDs, filled in forms, and had to get permits for just about everything, and were organized into progressive levels of seniority that taught due deference to higher ranks. They were reviewed periodically in a "personal profile" that included assessments of such qualities as group conformity and social adaptability, as well as academic performance, and this constituted the beginnings of a cumulative record of appraisals that would accompany them through, and in many cases have much to do with determining, their careers.

However, the buildings also contained a number of staff doors that could be opened by number codes, which Jarrow knew. He went around to the side of the central building, which contained the staff rooms and offices, entered the digits into the touchbox, and a few moments later appeared from a side corridor leading into the main hall. There, he paused to take stock of the general situation.

A new door had been installed at the end of the corridor leading to Ms. Filey's and Chet Orne's classrooms, but by now Jarrow was learning to expect things like that. The posters around the bulletin board were different. One was a chart of the human body populated by caricatures of directors in suits inhabiting the head and sending out orders, and depictions of assorted professionals, public servants, tradespeople, and workers in various places carrying out their assigned tasks. The slogan above read: EACH PART HAS ITS PLACE. SO DO WE. Another extolled the virtues of group conformity by showing a ridiculously portrayed pig with artificial wings strapped to its back about to leap from a tree, while other pigs looked on from below in various attitudes of scorn and derision. BE SMART: PLAY YOUR PART, the caption exhorted. Farther along, some shelves had been put up in the hall area to accommodate overflow from the library.

Jarrow had arrived as classes were changing, and students were free to move in the corridors without passes. The younger faces were unfamiliar to him, which was to be expected if they were from the September intake. As he moved on past the library, heading for the staff living room and general office, a group from one of his own freshman social integration classes came around the corner from the refectory. Sally Bolin was giggling as usual, sharing a joke with Wendy Redcliff; behind them were Jerry Hodge, a few pounds heavier, and Abud Taraki, the large-eyed Iranian, still wearing the same red neckerchief with gold-embroidered eagles' heads. They'd all be sophomores now.

All at once, being in familiar surroundings again, seeing faces that he knew, brought the first feeling of respite from the confusion that had been racking Jarrow ever since his strange awakening that morning. Relief flooded through him, drowning the doubts and bringing a conviction that somehow, everything would work itself out now. Forgetting all misgivings, he changed direction to intercept the group and grinned at them delightedly, yet in a way that couldn't come close to expressing what he felt at that moment.

But the two girls looked through him as if he weren't there and went on their way sniggering and chattering, while Jerry and Abud exchanged glances just long enough to confirm to each other that this guy was acting strangely. Abud stopped to look at Jarrow inquiringly, while Jerry slowed a few paces ahead.

"Are you looking for someone?" Abud asked cautiously.

"Abud. Don't you remember me? I can't have changed that much." Jarrow spread his hands in appeal, at the same time broadening his grin to a point that he realized too late was inane.

Abud backed off a pace. "No, I don't."

Jarrow's smile faded into incomprehension. He turned to Jerry. "*You* must know me. Don't you?"

Jerry shook his head. "Sorry." He looked at Abud. "Come on. We'll be late. Pass-break'll be over in less than a minute."

Abud retreated after Jerry. "The school office is that way," Abud threw back over his shoulder, pointing. "They'll be able to help you in there."

And then a commanding voice spoke from a speaker somewhere behind and above. *"Attention, person wearing the blue coat."* Jarrow spun around and looked up. One of the surveillance cameras was trained on him. He was so used to walking about the place oblivious to them that he had forgotten. *"This is security. You have not been identified as authorized to be on the premises. Remain where you are."*

Panic hit, a desperation to find somebody who would know him. He turned and fled for the staff living room, opened the door, and went through.

The first impressions to filter through his muddled senses were of everything inside being much as he remembered: the same pair of worn armchairs and a couch, the mural TV framed by bookshelves, forming the centerpiece of the far wall, the coffee urn on its table by the door into the cloakroom. But a couple of the faces that looked up in surprise at the hastiness of his entry were new. Louise Kreishner, who taught first- to third-year English, was filling a mug from the urn; Ivor Nimmo, the gym coach, was talking to another man, unknown to Jarrow, in the easy chairs by one of the two low tables in the center of the room; and Jenny Lauer, who taught conservation and deindustrialization, was marking papers at the long desk by the window.

There was an awkward silence as whatever conversation had been going on a moment before ceased. Then Nimmo raised his eyebrows inquiringly, without a flicker of recognition. He was a solid, loose-limbed man with a healthy, ruddy-skinned face and fringes of golden curls hanging on doggedly to a head that was mostly smooth. He had on a maroon track suit and blue-and-white sneakers. Jarrow was not fond of sports and had always found Nimmo intimidating.

"Yes? Can we help you?"

Jarrow shook his head incredulously. "Ivor. It's me."

Nimmo's brow knotted. "Sorry, but it's not obvious. . . . Have we met?"

"Met? We only worked together for three years." Jarrow waited. Nimmo showed his palms and shrugged. "Well, I'm Richard Jarrow, for God's sake!"

At this, Louise Kreishner straightened up from the coffee urn and turned, holding her mug in her hand, and Jenny Lauer stared from her chair at the desk; but neither of them showed any more sign of knowing him than Nimmo had.

Jarrow looked from Nimmo to Louise, to Jenny, briefly at the strangers, who were all attention by now, and then back at Nimmo. "What the hell is this, guys? Look, I know this might be something of a surprise, but people can reappear after long absences, you know. Why are you all looking at me as if I'd walked in with two heads?"

Nimmo frowned, then looked away at the others as if for support or suggestions.

"Go and get Irwin," Jenny muttered from the desk in a low voice, clearly meaning Irwin Shafer, the school principal.

Then the door behind Jarrow opened again and a man in a blue police-style shirt stepped through, the flap of his gun holster unfastened and his hand resting pointedly on the butt of the weapon. Jarrow knew him at once: Chip Rogers, one of the security officers, but Rogers obviously didn't know him. "Who are you?" he demanded curtly. "Didn't you hear the order to stay put out there?" He looked at the others. "Does anyone know this guy? Has he got business here?"

Nimmo shook his head. "Never saw him before."

"You'd better come with me," Rogers said, loosening the gun further.

Jarrow looked from one to another again protestingly. "But this is crazy! I know *you*. You're Ivor Nimmo. You teach phys ed here, right?" He stabbed a finger in the direction of each of the others in turn. "And I know *you*, Louise, and *you*, Jenny. Christ, doesn't anyone's memory go back as far as April? Is there some kind of mass blackout going around that nobody's told me about?"

The new people in the room exchanged uncomfortable glances and shuffled in their seats. Louise put down the coffee mug and crossed over to the door. "He says he's Jarrow," she explained, speaking with the low, overly calm condescension of somebody anxious not to provoke a lunatic. "Will you come with us to Irwin's office, Chip?"

"I'll come too," Nimmo said, bracing his arms on the sides of his chair and rising.

Louise led the way back into the corridor, Jarrow following, and Nimmo bringing up the rear with Rogers. "We're going to Irwin Shafer's office, right?" Jarrow said, turning his head and making an empty-handed gesture. "You see, I know . . ." He saw that the words were making no impression. Suddenly he felt foolish, and his voice trailed away.

Minutes later he was standing by Shafer's desk, watching the same mixture of hostility and suspicion spread over the principal's heavy-jowled moon of a face as Louise related the story. Behind them, Nimmo stood watching with his back to the closed door, Rogers alongside.

"Who are you, and how do you come to know so much about us here?" Shafer asked finally in his quiet but intense, half-whispering voice.

"How else would I know if I wasn't who I say I am?" Jarrow demanded. "Irwin, we've known each other for years. You hired me. Will somebody tell me what the hell's going on here?"

Shafer seemed to consider his options for a few seconds, then looked up. "Do you really believe what you're saying, or is this some kind of sick joke?"

"Why should it be a joke? Look, I'm Richard Jarrow. Check your files and I'll tell you anything from them that you want to know."

Shafer looked somberly at the other two, seemingly ignoring Jarrow entirely. Then he emitted a long sigh and lifted himself from the chair. He moved around to the wall behind Jarrow, where a collection of group photographs was hanging in frames, and took one down. "Do you recognize anyone in that picture?" he asked, handing it to Jarrow.

Jarrow looked. The picture showed three rows of students, the front row sitting on the ground, second on chairs, third standing, with staff members clustered in the center. "Why, sure," Jarrow said. He pointed. "That's Jenny Lauer in the middle, who was back there in the living room just now. Ken Yallows is next to her. I know most of these students: Xedong, here, Matthews, Casey, Wilheim, Rostalli. . . . You want me to go through the whole list?"

"How about him, there?" Shafer indicated with a finger. "The one standing on the other side of Jenny Lauer."

Jarrow peered at the man. He seemed to be more or less medium in build, with graying hair, and a pink, babyish face masked by a mustache. Jarrow shook his head. "I don't think I know him."

Shafer took the picture back. His eyes had the steely look of a hanging judge who had just heard all the evidence he needed. "Well, that's very strange," he said huskily. "You should, because *that* is Richard Jarrow. And now, mister whoever-you-really-are, *I* want *you* to tell *me* what the hell's going on, before I have the police called in. Richard Jarrow died from a stroke in May. All of us that you're talking to in this room attended the funeral."

six

Some of the stores in the mall a couple of blocks from the school were closed, with FOR LEASE signs and whited-out windows, but the Farm Griddle steak-and-pancake restaurant that Jarrow had frequented for over three years didn't seem to have changed. He approached it across the parking lot, walking quickly and glancing back as if he expected to have been followed. He had escaped from the school on the pretext of using the bathroom, and then left via a side entrance.

He wasn't conscious of having walked the two blocks, or of making any decision to come here, but driven by pure habit had stumbled in a fog of confusion, too stunned by what Shafer had said to know what he was doing. But once at the door, he hesitated. Would Shafer have dismissed him as just a crank and told the others to forget about it? Or might he have taken a more serious view and called the police? They could already be scouting the vicinity. Jarrow wavered irresolutely, wondering if he should widen the area farther before he stopped moving. Then the familiar sight of the food counter, the row of booths inside the window, and the large menu board by the door brought home to him that apart from a modest lunch on the plane, he hadn't eaten all day. And in any case, he told himself, if anyone was out looking for him, he'd be less conspicuous inside than on the street. He went in.

The girl taking an order from a table at the far end was Mandy from seven months ago, but the others that he could see were new. Eamon, the assistant manager, was still there and conducted Jarrow to a booth by the window, but with no sign of recognition. Jarrow was past feeling any surprise.

The menu seemed to have lost a few items since he was last in, particularly from the range of pancakes, waffles, and desserts. He noticed that the syrup dispensers had disappeared from the tables. There had been talk of banning excessive-sugar foods from public places, he remembered. Egg, beef, pork, and chili dishes now carried health warnings, as well as regular coffee, alcoholic drinks, and chicken, which had done so before. Jarrow settled for a tuna salad with wheat crackers. As the waitress left with the menu, he caught the eye of Eamon, standing near the cash desk, and raised a hand to summon him over.

"Is everything all right, sir?"

"Oh, sure. I just wanted to ask you something. Tell me, do you happen to know of a Dick Jarrow who used to come in here?"

"Dick?" Eamon's face clouded. "I guess it's been a while since you were in here, eh?"

"Well, yes as a matter of fact. Why?"

"You mean the guy who used to teach at the school just along from here, right?"

"Used to? Did he leave or something?"

Eamon shook his head. "'Fraid it's worse than that. He died . . . gee, it must have been sometime early in summer. A stroke, somebody said it was."

"Oh." Jarrow had been ready for it, and accepted the statement woodenly. "That's too bad."

"He was kinda quiet, but okay. Were you a good friend of his?"

"Not that much, really. You know, bumped into him every now and again. I guess you don't realize how time flies. Scary, isn't it?" On impulse Jarrow added, "What reminded me was, earlier today somebody mistook me for him. Would that seem likely to you?"

Eamon looked down and shook his head disbelievingly. "No way. Did the guy have dark glasses on, and a dog?"

"That's what I thought. I just wondered if he still came in here, that's all."

"Well, sorry I had to be the first to tell you. Is there anything else I can do?"

"I guess not. Thanks."

"Enjoy your meal."

Halfway through his salad, Jarrow's digestion was ruined when he saw a city police department cruiser drawing up outside, and two winter-jacketed officers came into the restaurant; but they sat down at the far end without giving the place a second glance. Jarrow returned to his meal, his chest thumping like a basketball being bounced. He wasn't sure how long he could go on like this; and there was no way of telling how long he might have to, because he had no idea what he was going to do. But Gordon's money would only last for so long, and that set a real limit, whatever other ideas might occur to him. He'd need to sit down tonight, back at his hotel, and do some budgeting.

Nothing made sense. If his appearance had been changed through some elaborate process—by whom? for what purpose?—why, apart from the oddities among his recollections that he was unable to explain, did he seem normal to himself? And it wasn't simply a question of appearances. The woman in the hotel room in Atlanta, the drink, the guns in the briefcase—all pointed to his having been somehow transformed into literally a different person, physically and psychologically, for over half a year. And then somehow, since this morning, the mental part only of that person had apparently reverted to its former self. It sounded impossible, but what other explanation was there?

Yet even that didn't account for all of it. If he was transformed, who was dead? The only trail he had to follow was the memory of an ordinary, everyday routine that ended abruptly in April. What, then, had happened in that last visit to Valdheim?

He checked himself right there. Why did he assume that whatever had happened to him had anything to do with Valdheim? Only because it was the last thing he remembered. But the cause could have been something that happened after that, but with some kind of retroactive effect—as when people knocked out by a blow on the head supposedly lost all recollection of what went before. So, the first thing to find out more about was what had happened immediately after that visit. Had he acted normally? Had something else happened at a later date that might have led to the predicament he was in now? The last person he'd talked to, other than Valdheim, Valdheim's receptionist Marje, and Nurse Callins, had been Larry Banks, when Larry dropped him off outside. And Larry, he now recalled, had promised to catch him in the afternoon to pick up a book that Jarrow had borrowed from the staff library. Larry, then, would have been looking for him later. It would be interesting to know if Larry had found him. That would be as good a place as any to start, he decided.

Jarrow finished his meal and went to one of the phone booths by the door to consult the directory. It showed that Larry Banks still lived at the same address in Champlin. But after pondering the matter, Jarrow decided against calling him right away. He was still too shaky and mixed up to know, really, what he wanted to say. If people thought he was dead, and if the reaction of Shafer and the others at the school was anything to go by, he would have to have a better line prepared than simply blundering in and saying he was Jarrow. Hopefully he'd have things clearer in his mind by tomorrow.

He brought a local Champlin area map onto the screen to check the location, paid a quarter for a hard copy, and put it in his pocket. Then he went back to the desk to pay the check, nodded a good night to Eamon, who was back at his post near the desk, and went back out. It was getting dark, and the evening was already chillier. He went to the K mart a short distance along the mall and bought himself some warmer socks, a scarf, and a couple of thick sweaters. The clerk there told him that a bus would be leaving the mall in twenty minutes that would take him back to Minneapolis center. That left the question of what to do with the rest of the evening. It was one of those rare occasions in his life, Jarrow decided, when he could use a drink.

seven

There had been a time when men plundered the planet to light empty buildings all the night long. But reason and discipline had finally prevailed over vanity, and the towers of Minneapolis now loomed dark and faceless into the wintery night.

Jarrow got off the bus a few blocks short of the Hennepin Avenue bridge, crossing the river at Nicollet Island. He avoided the area west of the avenue, where some of the plusher bars and lounges were to be found. They were places where people went to see and be seen. He just wanted to hide. Instead, he headed into the central city and eventually found one of the smaller downtown bars. It was a bit garish for his taste, but a lot warmer than the sidewalk, and homey in its own rough kind of way.

He ordered a gin, adding less tonic than he normally took, and installed himself on one of the stools. The TV above the bar was showing a police movie, complete with the virtually obligatory cast of ethnic tokens: white protagonist (angry, maverick), two blacks (police chief, mature and tolerant; protagonist cop's partner, street-wise and loyal), one Hispanic (Catholic, dedicated family man), one liberated female (naive, learning fast—but not fast enough to avoid getting laid by maverick cop). Jarrow personally found the formula tiresome, but he accepted that it was necessary to instill correct notions into the masses.

After a while, a bearded, dark-haired man wearing a black woolen cap and navy donkey jacket sat down on the next stool. From his exchange with the bartender when he ordered a beer, his name was Paul. Meanwhile, on the screen, the plot line delivered as trustily as Old Faithful: maverick cop finally pisses off overtolerant chief and gets suspended ("I'll take the badge and the piece"), but tries to hunt down villains independently, wasting family-man partner in the process. Official team arrives in time to save the mess, maverick cop consigned to deserved oblivion, while wiser-now female gets promoted and will manage okay from here on. All a packaged lesson in the ultimate wisdom of appointed authority and the folly of individualists who think they can go it alone.

A barrage of commercials followed, showing cute kids eating breakfast, cartoon knights in gleaming armor chasing mucilaginous germs through a drain, and a moron and wife barbecuing steaks (with requisite health warning) for their ilk on a patio. Jarrow ordered another drink.

Next came the news. The lead item concerned a ground laser station that should have been boosting shuttles up from Florida two years ago (Jarrow remembered it as over a year behind schedule). Apparently it had failed some more tests, and the National Directorate of Technology was now saying that a major section of the project would have to be redesigned and rebuilt. The leader of the European Moderation Party, which opposed any expansion into space, had said the whole thing should be scrapped, and environmental groups were gleefully derisive. Meanwhile, Aerospaceflot of New Muscovy, the capital province of the loosely tied Federation of Eurasian Republics—roughly speaking, what had once been called the USSR, plus a number of former Eastern European and Asiatic Moslem territories—had inaugurated a regular passenger service to connect with the Offworld lunar transporters plying between Earth orbit and bases at Copernicus and Tycho. The new enforcement agency to be set up under the Bureau of Environmental Control had been relegated to third place since morning, but the account was pretty much the same as Jarrow had awoken to in Atlanta. To underline the need for draconian measures, it was followed by a report of how, in a computer model produced by two of the Bureau's scientists, unregulated emissions from FER industries could disrupt atmospheric ozone.

"Bullshit," Paul muttered from the stool next to Jarrow.

"Excuse me?" Jarrow said, turning his head automatically.

Paul gestured toward the screen without looking at him. "That's bullshit. They've been coming up with garbage about ozone ever since CFCs were banned at the turn of the century. What it was really all about was that the patents were running out, and what used to be called the Third World was about to take over a market worth billions."

"Really?" Jarrow said. For his part he considered the official position understated—he would hardly have held a job as a teacher if it were otherwise. But he wasn't going to get into arguments with strangers in bars over it.

Paul downed a swig of beer. "Now they're trying to build up world pressure on the Eurasians to meet Consolidation standards, which would undermine the FER's Offworld connection. What else do you think the Consolidation is for?"

He meant the political and economic union composed primarily of North America and the western states of Europe, which in the last few years had officially designated itself the Western Consolidation as a way of underlining its commitment to collective solidarity against the decadence and disorder threatening to engulf it from the east. "The new Mongol hordes" was how the danger was usually described.

Jarrow stated the obvious, which he would have thought everyone knew. "To protect the quality of our way of life and preserve our resources. They'll loot and strip Siberia, and when they've turned it into a waste, they'll come this way—first Europe, then us. Conserve now and be strong when the time comes. That's what the Consolidation means."

"Boy, you must have graduated top of the class," Paul said with mocking approval.

Jarrow expected to feel himself reddening, but somehow he seemed to have lost the reflex. "What do you mean?" he demanded stiffly.

Paul laid a hand on his shoulder for a moment. "Take it easy, eh? I know that's what everyone's told. But it's not the way it happened. The world could have been a great place when the smoke cleared after the Soviet empire fell apart. They wanted our products and we needed their materials. Everybody stood to be a winner."

"Hm. If turning the planet into a moonscape is what you mean by winning," Jarrow said coolly.

Paul shook his head. "That's just what the Green freaks who

took control of everything over on this side of the world think. But it doesn't have to be that way."

"I fail to see why trying to curb the reckless spread of industrial technology should be considered freakish," Jarrow retorted.

"They don't understand anything about it. See, you can't stand still. Better methods give you better solutions. When you stop growing and plateau out at some fixed level of technology, that's when you eat up its resource base and screw things. The Greens could only think in terms of control and restricting, shutting everything down—and the irony was that it happened just when the other half of the world was realizing that central controls don't work and discovering what free individuals can do. There was a massive flight of capital and talent to the east, a redirection of Asian investment, and the turkeys in charge of everything here responded, typically, in the only way they knew how and started closing the borders to preserve captive markets for what was left. They had no concept of competition. They tried to shut out what they saw as a threat and created an economic concentration camp." Paul took another drink and wiped his mouth with a cuff. "The whole way it's structured is unnatural. What it's aimed at is eventual world government. Then they could put a fence around everybody and cut the Offworlders out, who are the ones really running with the ball. But the FER isn't interested, won't buy the Consolidation line, and that's the flaw in the game plan."

Jarrow looked at Paul more fully. He was in his thirties, lean in the face, and had mild gray eyes that confronted Jarrow with a direct, unwavering stare, but laced with a humorous twinkle. As a rule Jarrow didn't like talking about such things. His job gave him access to enough sources to know what was what, and he had no crusading urge to rectify offbeat opinions. "So where do you get your information?" he challenged, yielding nothing but at the same time trying not to sound provocative.

"I'm a scientist, would you believe—or at least I used to be." Paul gestured up at the screen with his empty hand. "I mean a *real* scientist, not one of those house-trained hacks who play games on computers that they parade across there. In fact I used to work on what that dummy there is talking about, so I know it's a load of crap."

"What happened?" Jarrow asked.

"Oh, you know how it is. I was what you'd call pure and idealistic—I believed what all the books said about how science was supposed to be the honest pursuit of truth. I was going to go public and tell how it really is. Except nothing got published. So now I nail packing crates together. Happens all the time. The people who are running things want problems, not solutions. That's what keeps them in charge. . . . " Paul stared down at his drink. "Aw, who cares? It's all going to hell, anyhow. You have your turn, eat, get drunk, screw; and fifty years from now none of it'll matter a ratshit."

"Philosophy," Jarrow said, glad to put the subject to rest. "There you go—that's more my line. I'm no scientist."

Paul's face split into a grin, revealing white, even teeth through his beard. "You're okay." He thrust a hand out. "Name's Paul."

"I know. I heard. I'm . . . Dick."

"Hi. So what is your line?"

"I teach . . . " Jarrow hesitated again, then added, "history." In the light of Paul's earlier remarks, it seemed less risky than saying "social integration."

"Do you think I'm crazy, saying things like that to somebody in a bar?" Paul asked him. "I mean, you could have been anyone: FBI countersubversives, local watch committee? Who knows?"

"Well, I'm not, so don't worry about it."

"I guess what I'm trying to say is, what could they do to me if you were? See what I mean? I nail crates together. And if they busted me out of that I'd fix fences or shovel snow. I'm not a scientist anymore. I don't need their approvals, or their money, or their permission for anything now. See how *free* that makes me?"

"That's a good way of looking at it, I suppose." If Paul needed to rationalize his situation, it wasn't for Jarrow to disagree. "You see, I said you were a philosopher."

"So what's your philosophy of life?" Paul asked, sitting back and regarding him curiously.

"I'm not sure I've got one."

"They're like assholes. Everybody's got one."

Jarrow searched for something to oblige. "Just, keep it simple and try to stay out of trouble, I guess. Not a very exciting one, is it?"

"You live here in town?"

"I'm staying at a hotel a couple of blocks from here—the Lennox."

"I know it."

"And you?"

"Oh, I've got a place across the street. Wintertime, I like to stay in the city. When summer comes I'll head west and see what's going in the mountains. Maybe drift on up to Canada."

"Wouldn't you need a border pass? . . . I mean, if your name's been collecting penalty ratings in the Social Index computer . . ."

Paul gave Jarrow a conspiratorial wink. "There's ways. It's not like trying to get out of Consolidation territory into the FER or somewhere."

"What would you do there?"

"Hell, whatever's going. Swing a pick, lift a shovel. Anything where you don't have to give someone your life history before you can buy a meal or take a crap. Sometimes I think writing was the worst thing we ever invented. Once they can write your name down, you never get 'em off your back." Paul's gaze suddenly shifted from Jarrow's face to somewhere behind, in the direction of the door. "Hi," he said over Jarrow's shoulder. "Are you staying or just passing through?"

Jarrow turned and saw that two girls who must have just entered had joined them. One was tall and roundly filled out, with a heavy coat of brown suede and waves of black hair escaping from a tan bonnet. Her companion was smaller, a curly-headed blonde with an impish face and saucy blue eyes, dressed in an open gray parka and jeans. They were both in their mid to late twenties.

"What the hell, we'll stay for a couple," the taller one said. "You're better off in here than out there tonight, Paul, I'm telling you."

"Freeze your nuts off, eh?"

"You tell us," the blonde suggested.

Paul looked back at the other. "Did you talk to Harry?"

"Yes. He says he'll need another couple of days. Brian has to go out to St. Cloud to check the sizes."

"Jesus, I thought he already knew the sizes. Harry was out there on Thursday and he told me . . ."

As they carried on with whatever the matter was that needed to be cleared up, the blonde looked back at Jarrow with an interest that she didn't try to hide. Jarrow wasn't used to that kind of reaction from women and found it unnerving. "Hi," she said, smiling. She had freckles, and her cheeks dimpled.

"Er, hi."

"I'm Chris, since he hasn't bothered saying so. Who are you?"

"Dick."

"Another friend of Paul's? You'd think he owns this place."

"No. I only just met him."

"That's Paul—he talks to anyone. He's our resident intellectual."

Paul broke off in the middle of his conversation with the other girl. "Hey, I'm forgetting my manners here. These are Chris—you already know that—and Donna. Guys, this is Dick. He teaches." He indicated each of the girls in turn with nods of his head. "Groceries, post office."

"Well, now that we've traded résumés, do you think there might be any chance of a drink?" Chris suggested.

"Sure, I'll get 'em," Paul said. "Usuals?" He looked around. "We don't have enough seats here."

"There's a table there," Donna said, gesturing. The girls led the way over.

"Same again, Dick?" Paul said to Jarrow. This was the strangest evening Jarrow had ever had in his life. Normally two would have been his limit, but to his surprise his metabolism was generating no alarm signals. In fact, he was warming inside now, and could feel himself loosening up for the first time all day. It was almost as if his body were tuned to this and could use a little more.

"Sure," he said.

Paul waved toward the table. "Go on over. I'll take care of it." Jarrow took off his topcoat, sat down with the girls. Paul joined them after giving the order to the bartender.

They talked about the day the girls had had, debated whether the winters were getting worse or better, and compared Minneapolis with other cities they'd known. Chris was originally from Oklahoma, Donna a Minnesota native. Jarrow repeated that he was staying at the Lennox.

Chris seemed attracted to Jarrow, sitting close and looking at him a lot. Then Paul and Donna went off into a private dialogue about Paul's business with Harry again. Chris cocked her head to one side, regarding Jarrow quizzically for a moment, then asked in a confidential voice, "What happened, Dick? Wife throw you out?"

Jarrow frowned. "I don't understand."

Her eyes traveled down over him, then back up with a mischievous smile. "Quality suit, but staying at a place like that in this kind of neighborhood? Need a shave and a change of shirt. . . . It's either that or you rob banks." She winked in a way that said she didn't want to know which.

"Oh, you don't have to worry about that," Jarrow said. "I'm not exactly what you'd call adventurous. I hate any kind of violence."

"Good for you. That's what makes a real man," Donna said, catching the end of the conversation.

"Hey, me too," Paul put in. "Remember, I'm the intellectual."

"Right. And I could remind you of a few other things," Donna said.

"Hell, nobody's perfect."

Jarrow sat back. His glass was empty again, and he felt like another. "My turn," he announced. "Same again for everyone?" They affirmed. Jarrow caught the bartender's attention and signaled for another round.

"So, how did you handle being drafted?" Paul asked him, picking the thread up again.

Jarrow shook his head. "I disqualified on medical grounds." Then, through habit, he added, "Not exactly what you'd call a fighting physique, anyhow."

Chris looked him up and down again and shook her head. "Well, gee, Dick, you could have fooled me."

Jarrow became confused and talked on mechanically. "Although I think we have to have the draft. . . . I mean, the Consolidation's doing the right thing in setting the lead on restricting industry, and we've got to get the FER to follow. The Offworlders are going to outrun themselves one day, and then they'll be turning back in this direction." The expressions from around the table told him to forget all that for now. Then the bartender arrived with the drinks, and Jarrow gratefully let the subject drop.

Chris raised her glass before tasting from it. "Here's to you, Dick," she said. Donna followed suit.

"My pleasure," Jarrow said, and returned the gesture. Then he produced Gordon's wallet from his jacket and, still with his mind on what they had been saying, flipped it open carelessly to pay. In the shadows behind him a tall, hard-faced youth with cropped head, earring, and studded leather coat caught sight of the wad of hundreds and fifties and nudged his companion quietly. The other, pasty-faced but heavily built, with long, unkempt hair and tattooed knuckles, returned a faint nod.

"Good on ya," Paul acknowledged, raising a fresh beer toward Jarrow and taking a gulp.

"So, how long have you been in town now?" Chris asked. It seemed she just had to know all about him.

"Only today. I flew in from Atlanta this morning."

"How much longer will you be here?"

"I haven't made any plans yet."

"A real mystery guy," Donna commented.

"Chris, when will you ever learn to mind your own goddam business?" Paul said. "Can't you see the guy doesn't want to talk about it?"

Chris shrugged. "Well, I can't help being curious." She looked at Jarrow playfully. "Dick and I like each other . . . don't we?"

Jarrow's mouth twitched and he raised his glass hastily. He had never frequented such places and really didn't know the mores that were expected among people like these. Would acquiescence to Chris's overture be taken as confirmation that they were supposed to make a night of it? If so, what would be the best way to extricate himself cleanly? He had no inclination by temperament for any such liaison, and certainly no desire to complicate his situation further; on the other hand he was fearful of unwittingly giving offense.

But as the talk continued, he grew reassured that her teasing banter was intended as no more than that, and his apprehensions eased. Then some more acquaintances of Paul's arrived and began pulling up chairs to join them. Jarrow seized the opportunity to make his exit, pleading that he'd had a long day—which was no exaggeration—and left amid a profusion of customary "take care"s and "see you around"s.

Outside, he paused to check his bearings, pulling the scarf tight around his neck and zipping up his coat. Then he thrust his hands deep in his pockets and walked briskly away, his breath leaving a cloud in the cold night air. Above, the towers of the city stood dark and desolate.

Still to his surprise, the drink didn't seem to have affected him much, apart from dulling his fears and doubts to the point where he felt he could put off worrying about them until morning. First he would check the records to make sure he was officially dead. . . . Christ, how weird could this get? Then he'd begin trying to pick up the trail, starting with Larry. He'd need to come up with a plausible line of approach there, he told himself again. But for now, he felt pleasantly detached from it all. Enough, anyway, to get a decent night's sleep.

He wasn't aware of the two figures who had been quietly gaining on him until a hand grabbed his shoulder and spun him around, slamming him against a wall, and a knife was pushed up under his chin. A face contorted with malice, its hair cropped short and stark, thrust close and snarled at him. "Move and your throat spills. Where's the billfold?"

The other was already patting Jarrow's coat. "Okay, I've got it."

Jarrow had no awareness of reacting, no conscious knowledge of evaluating odds or deciding his action. What happened came out of nowhere. One hand twisted the knife away, and in the same movement his other shot upward, fingers curled, crashing the heel into the base of the punk's nose. Without missing a tempo, Jarrow seized the hand entering his coat and turned the wrist over savagely, forcing the second assailant's arm into a lever to double him over and jackknifing his face downward—straight into the foot flashing up to meet it. Three more lightning blows—each one delivered accurately and devastatingly enough to have finished matters on its own: edge-hand to the neck, fist to the hollow below the ear, elbow to the kidney—found their targets before the thug's knees had begun to buckle.

Jarrow, suddenly transformed into a totally dispassionate, high-precision, human-combat machine, wheeled as the crop-headed punk lunged back in, in the streetlight his lower face a mess of blood from his ruined nose, but still holding the knife. Jarrow evaded the slash and caught the punk's sleeve to draw him on, using his own weight and the other's momentum to whirl him around in an arc like a weight on a string, straight at a steel pole standing on the edge of the sidewalk. The punk's back hit it full force, snapping his head against the metal with a loud clang. Jarrow followed up with a kick to the groin and a straight-hand jab to the solar plexus as the form crumpled.

And then, just as quickly as the transformation had come over him, it left.

He stood bewildered, looking from one figure to another. The crop-headed thug was lying at the base of the pole, while the other, groaning feebly, was trying to pull himself up to his knees against the wall. A couple who had been walking along the other side of the street had stopped and were watching, petrified.

Jarrow stared back, as much at a loss as they were. The knife had nicked him below the chin. He took out a handkerchief, folded it into a pad, and held it to his neck.

"Are you okay?" the man called in a quavering voice. Hardly original; but it was more than Jarrow had managed.

It jerked Jarrow out of his state of shock. "You'd better call an ambulance," he retorted. Then, after feeling to make sure that the wallet was still in his jacket, he hurried away in the direction of his hotel.

When he got back to his room he was still shaking. He stripped for bed and stood looking at himself in the mirror. The cut under his chin didn't look serious, but it needed to be covered. He remembered the Band-Aids in the bathroom at the Hyatt in Atlanta and wished he'd had the presence of mind then to pick them up, along with the toilet articles and other things that he'd left there. Now, as things were, he would have to buy himself a new one of everything in the morning. Curiously, he removed the Band-Aid from the side of his neck, which had been there when he woke up. Underneath was a mild, pink swelling and what looked like a tiny puncture.

Looking at himself generally, he saw that Chris from the bar had been right: he *was* athletic and muscular. But strangely again, although he could retrieve no mental picture of ever having looked different, at an intellectual level he remembered always thinking of himself as puny.

And then another thing struck him that should have been obvious, surely, from the time he'd woken up and first caught sight of himself: How old was he? What kind of a question was that? Everyone knew how old they were. He was forty-six. He could produce memories from every one of those years.

But the reflection in the mirror was at least ten years younger.

Baffled and exhausted, he fell asleep straightaway. But not to the relaxed, undisturbed sleep that he had hoped for. He had strange dreams of being in uniform, adrift in a strange, distorted military environment that included a colonel with gold-tinted glasses, whose eyes were never seen. And mixed among them were persistent images of a girl with red hair.

eight

An Army truck with ridiculously huge wheels, like those of a giant earth-mover, was rolling through a field of tulips. The girl with the red hair was sitting on the hood, wearing an officer's cap and with her skirt hitched high, revealing long legs. The rear portion of the truck was a striped tent with tasseled ropes and pennants, like something from a carnival. A siren on the roof of the cab was blaring. . . .

The image dissolved, and the blaring became a car's horn outside in the street. Jarrow awoke sluggishly. His head ached, and there was a dry, acrid taste in his mouth. He opened his eyes, and then closed them again as the light coming through the cheap floral drapes turned the aching in his head into pain. He wished all the torments of the damned upon whoever was sounding the horn.

At last, mercifully, it stopped, and a void of quiet descended outside, only to be filled a moment later by the sound of two voices yelling an exchange of obscenities. It took Jarrow a few seconds to reassemble the fragmented recollection of where he was. For a while he just lay there, swallowing and working his mouth in an effort to wash away the sour taste, and trying to reconstruct his plan for the day. The air in the room felt chilly on his face. He remembered that there had been a sign on the desk downstairs yesterday, warning hotel residents to expect power cuts that morning.

He rose, rinsed his face in the sink by the bed, and checked himself in the mirror. By now his appearance was a source of total mystery to him. It looked familiar, yet what he saw clashed with everything he remembered about himself. Chris had mentioned last night that he needed a shave, and by now his chin was black with stubble. But he recalled being light-bearded—it had taken him a long time to grow his mustache. Now he didn't even have a mustache. Everything was crazy. And what had come over him that enabled him to demolish a couple of punk muggers as if they were pastry puffs?

The cut under his chin and the mark below his ear were doing fine, but still needed to be kept covered. Chris had been right about the shirt too, he saw when he held it up: the collar was grubby from a day's travel. He should have thought to buy a few more when he was in K mart. So, some shirts, Band-Aids, a razor, toothbrush, and some toilet gear were first on his list, and then to get himself cleaned up. After that, breakfast. And over breakfast, he could think about how he was going to approach Larry.

His first call when he returned to the hotel was to the Hennepin County coroner's office. A clerk there confirmed that Robert Jarrow, then residing at 703 Orchard Lea Court, Brooklyn Center, had died from a thrombosis of the brain on May 5. The body was cremated on May 8. Identification was made by the deceased's sister, Beatrice Ishen, from Duluth, who had taken care of the arrangements. Jarrow was referred to her for any further information. For a reverse-charge fee, the clerk faxed the details through to the hotel's receiver downstairs. Jarrow brought the copy up to his room and sat contemplating it for a long time with a curious mixture of emotions. He had read many literary allusions to people signing or reading their own death warrants. But never their own death certificate.

He thought of calling Betty—just to see if even his own sister didn't recognize him, he tried to tell himself, but he was just looking for somebody close to talk to, even for a few minutes. He already knew what the outcome would be. It would serve no purpose. He tucked the paper away in a pocket of the travel bag that he had bought to hold the things he was beginning to accumulate. Then he turned to the pad from the room in Atlanta, in which he had noted Larry's number.

Larry's girlfriend, Hilda, answered, but of course she didn't recognize Jarrow. He had moved the viewphone so that the window would be behind him, hiding the fact that he was calling from a hotel room.

"Hello, I'm trying to contact a Larry Banks. Do I have the right number?"

"Yes, you do. Who is it?"

"My name's Maurice Gordon. I'm an insurance investigator."

"I'll fetch him."

"Thanks."

That way Jarrow wouldn't be caught if Larry asked to see some ID. He was lucky that Larry wasn't at work, he reflected while he waited. That was something he should have thought of last night.

Larry appeared, rubbing his eyes and yawning, looking as if he had just gotten up, still much the same, yellow hair tumbling to his collar.

"Hello?"

"Mr. Banks?"

"Yes."

"I hope I'm not calling at an awkward time. My name's Gordon. I'm an insurance investigator. I'd like to talk to you, if I may, when you've got a few minutes."

"I don't need any insurance."

"No, you've got me wrong. I'm not selling. I said I was an investigator."

"I've heard it before."

"Believe me, Mr. Banks."

"Which company are you with?"

"No company. I'm an independent consultant."

"What's this about?"

"I believe you were a colleague of Richard Jarrow's, who died last May."

"Dick Jarrow? . . . Well, yes, that's right."

"We have reason to believe that the circumstances of his death might be part of a more widespread pattern that could affect insurance settlements. I'm helping some people who are putting some statistics together, and we'd like to know a little more about events just before he had his stroke. Somebody suggested I should talk to you."

Larry looked dubious. "I don't know much about that. I wasn't anyone particularly special, if you know what I mean. We worked in the same place, but I wouldn't say I knew any more about him than what anyone else there could tell you."

"I understand. But all the same, if you wouldn't mind, I do have some questions that I'd be interested in your answers to. Would you have a few minutes sometime today?"

"Can't we do it right now?"

"It's not quite that simple. And I don't think the subject is really suitable to discuss over the phone. I'd rather it were face-to-face."

Larry sighed, making it obvious that in his view it was already a waste of time. "Okay. But I'm going out about lunchtime and I don't know when I'll be back. Can you get here by then?"

"Sure."

"You know where to find us?"

"I can get it off the map."

"Look out for a gate with a big sign that says Farnstead. We're along the street practically opposite that."

"Thank you very much, Mr. Banks. I'll be there before lunch."

But how? Jarrow wondered after he had cleared down. An insurance investigator would look odd showing up on a bus. He shook his head and tutted at himself. His mind seemed to be functioning more coherently at last, but too slow. He paced across the room and stared down from the window at the traffic on the street.

Then he remembered the credit cards in Gordon's wallet. The obvious thing was to rent a car. True, the cards might have been reported as lost and invalidated . . . but there was only one way he was going to find out. If they were good, however, it would be an invaluable way of stretching out the remainder of the cash.

He sat down at the table by the window, took the cards from the wallet, and stared at them. The thought of illegality made him nervous, causing a queasy feeling in his stomach. But God, how often did anyone find themself in this kind of predicament? Surely no court on Earth would convict him in circumstances like these.

He selected the MasterCard and set it before him. Then he drew across the notepad again and turned it to a fresh sheet. He poised his pen over it and looked at the signature on the card again. In the stories he'd read about crooks and forgers, you were supposed to do it in one confident movement, the same way as the original had been written, without hesitating or breaking the rhythm. So telling himself, he lowered the point of the pen and wrote smoothly and deliberately: *Maurice J. Gordon*. And to his amazement, the match was perfect.

He held the pad and the card side by side and examined them in the light from the window. There was no doubt about it: he himself must have signed the card. So was he really Gordon after all, and not Jarrow? Of course he was, a panicky voice told him from somewhere inside. Wasn't the picture in Gordon's passport enough? He compared the top sheets of the pad—the mysterious message and phone numbers that he'd found when he awoke in Atlanta, the page he'd written yesterday with Larry's number, and his shopping list from first thing that morning. The writing on all of them was identical.

And then all of his doubts came flooding back. Who did he think he was, trying to act like some kind of police detective or private investigator? He needed help, not trivia answers from seven months ago. He threw the pad onto the bed and emitted a strangled sound, at the same time a moan of frustration and a despairing sob. Why him? Why couldn't he just be Richard Jarrow again and pick up the threads of his own life?

Because he wasn't. He was somebody else. . . . No, even that wasn't right. He was Jarrow *and* somebody else, two people mixed up together. So why not simply present himself to the authorities and say so? That was what they were there for, wasn't it, to look after citizens? They had people who would know what to do.

But as he thought it through further, more doubts assailed him. What would the likely reaction of the authorities be? As far as they were concerned, he would be Gordon—never mind how he felt about it inside. And from the little he knew of Gordon—the guns, the hotel-room woman, and the cash, the fleeting sample he'd seen last night of the kinds of things Gordon was capable of—their response might not be too friendly. They might even receive his story as an attempt on Gordon's part to concoct an excuse, an alibi . . . for what? God alone knew what he might have been involved in.

It was no good, he concluded. Until he knew more about who this other self of his was and what kind of business he was in, he could be walking into anything.

He waited ten minutes to calm himself down. Then, putting on his scarf and coat, he went down to the desk to find out about the nearest car rental office.

Jarrow sat on the couch by the window, his notebook opened on his knee. To look the part more, he had bought himself a stiff-backed one, legal size, and a plastic cover with pockets for pens and papers. Larry was sprawled in the easy chair by the woodstove, wearing old jeans and a sweater with frayed cuffs, and looking as if he had gone down a peg since Jarrow last saw him. The place was much the same as when Jarrow was here before—roomy but cluttered, a comfortably anarchic collection of scatter rugs and wood furnishings, lots of books and gadgets, shelves littered with domestic oddments and offbeat souvenirs. Hilda had let Jarrow in, said hello, then gone off discreetly to busy herself elsewhere.

Jarrow began. "Just to make sure we've got it right, you are Lawrence T. Banks, of this address?"

"Right."

Jarrow glanced at his pad again. "And you teach at Linden Junior High School?"

Larry snorted. "Well, you're some investigator. No, that's way out-of-date. I haven't worked there since June." Although Jarrow was used to Larry's cynicism, there was a bitterness in his tone that was new.

"When did you quit?"

"I didn't quit. I was asked to leave. They don't want teachers who show kids how to think anymore. They want rat trainers to condition them to run mazes. It's called eliciting desirable behavior."

"I see. . . . So what do you do now?"

"Look, are we talking about me or Dick Jarrow?"

"I'm sorry." Jarrow peered down at his pad and gave the mood a moment to lighten. "Let's see now, Jarrow died on May fifth."

"Did he? Okay, if you say so."

"As far as you recall, was he acting normally in the time leading up to that?"

Larry frowned and stared at the floor. "It's been a while now . . . but from what I can remember there was nothing especially strange. Like I tried to tell you on the phone, I wasn't especially a close kind of friend of his, you know."

"Was it sudden—did it come as a surprise to people? Or was it on the cards? Had he been hospitalized or taken away someplace before May fifth, for example?"

"Don't your records tell you that?"

"Er, there are some conflicting accounts that I'm trying to resolve."

"Accounts?" Larry's face wrinkled. "What do you need to go by accounts for? You've only got to look at admission records to see if he was hospitalized. What is this?"

"I'm just trying to reconstruct as much as I can of what Jarrow did in the month before his death, from independent sources. I've a note here that says that on April third you drove him to a doctor's off Groveland Avenue that he'd been attending, a Dr. Valdheim?"

"I dropped him off there a number of times—we used to ride-share into work. Was one of them April third? Okay."

"It was a Thursday."

"I'll take your word for it."

"Did he show up again at the school later that day, as he was supposed to?"

Larry tossed up his hands helplessly. "Look, I can't even remember which time that was. How do I know what he did later?"

Jarrow realized that the questions were becoming implausible, but he had to have answers. "Was April third the last time you took him to Valdheim's?"

"I just said, I *don't know!*"

"When was the last time you saw Jarrow?"

"Well, that's a bit easier. It was the day he fell over. He'd driven me to the school that morning."

For a moment Jarrow just stared. Obviously that was what he should have asked in the first place. That meant, then, that he'd been around and functioning normally, as Jarrow, for something like three weeks after that visit to Valdheim's. "So where did the stroke take place?" he asked unthinkingly. "Are you saying he died at work, at the school?"

"Are you saying you don't *know?*" Larry ceased trying to disguise the suspicion that had been building up inside. "Look, who are you? This insurance line smelled from the minute you walked in."

Jarrow spread his hands candidly. "Okay, I'm not in insurance. I—"

Larry stood up abruptly, his face paling with anger, and strode across the room. "Your people cost me my job and a lot of friends. So what have they sent you snooping around here for? If there's such a thing as rights left in this country, what I do now is my business.

Here's the door. On your way, mister. Tell 'em to waste their tax rake-offs on something else."

Jarrow stood up too, not wanting to let it go at this but flustered, and raised his arm in a way that was supposed to calm things. "Look, I didn't know how else to get to you, because this situation is crazy. This is going to be hard to accept, I know, but the fact is, *I'm* Dick Jarrow! Something that I don't understand has happened to me. That visit to Valdheim on April third is the last thing I remember. . . ."

Larry was staring at him in the way he might at a bomb likely to go off any second. "What kind of shit is this?"

Jarrow was desperate. The words babbled in an uncontrollable flow. "You drove me to Valdheim's that day. We were stopped at a traffic check on ninety-four. You talked about an engineer you knew, who said the pollution thing was misrepresented. You remember? How else would I know?"

"You know too damn much about me. That's all I'm hearing."

"You wanted a book that I'd borrowed from the library. You were going to pick it up that afternoon. . . ."

Larry leaned out through the door that he had been holding open and yelled toward the kitchen. "Hilda, call the cops. This guy's a nut."

"*No!* Don't do that. I just need five minutes to talk. Really, Larry, I *am* Dick. I woke up yesterday in Atlanta and—"

"Hilda! Do it now!"

Hilda's voice came distantly through the doorway. "Okay, I've got emergency on the line now. . . . Hello, yes. Send someone quick. We've got some kind of lunatic in the house here."

Jarrow panicked. "Okay, okay. I'm not here to make any trouble. I'll leave now. Just take it easy."

And he fled.

nine

Driving aimlessly, Jarrow found himself at an intersection of Interstate 52 and took the entry ramp. Originally, so he'd read, the highway system had been designed for hundred-mile-per-hour traffic. No wonder the world had started running out of everything. Since most of the cars these days were low-speed electric or gasohol metropolitan-area getabouts, regular traffic was restricted to the two inside lanes. Only official vehicles or holders of specially approved five-hundred-dollar-a-year licenses used the outside. Violators would be logged by buried sensors that read registration numbers.

Farther on, heading south back toward Minneapolis, he found himself driving along the same stretch of highway where he and Larry had been stopped at the checkpoint. It brought back memories of that day clearly. On impulse, instead of exiting into the city, Jarrow continued heading southward, the way they had gone then. After Larry, the only other thread available to him to pick up from that day was the one that had ended at Valdheim's place itself. And Valdheim's was just a few more miles ahead.

He wasn't sure what he was going to do when he got to Valdheim's. After his reception at the school yesterday and at Larry's today, the prospect was unnerving. But Valdheim was a medical man. He would be used to listening to strange stories. And then, after all, Jarrow told himself for consolation, there was nothing that said he *had* to do anything immediately. If inspiration failed him, he could sit in the car as long as he wanted and just think about it.

But when he left I-94 at Groveland and followed the familiar route to the green house with the laurel bushes, another problem awaited him: The green house was now yellow, and the plaque announcing the practice of DR. M. R. VALDHEIM, M.D., PH.D., M.A.P.A, M.I.P.N. CONSULTANT NEUROPHYSISOLOGIST had gone. Instead, a sign standing on the patch of grass outside the front door proclaimed: CHURCH OF THE TRANSCENDENTAL ONENESS.

Jarrow parked and contemplated the sign blankly for about five minutes. No obvious continuation from here suggested itself. Finally, reasoning that he might as well squeeze what he could out of the situation now he was here, he got out and walked up the path. The legend was repeated on the door in less glaring form with the added assurance: "Everyone Welcome." Otherwise, the door leered at him in smug inscrutability. He pressed the bell push set into the wall alongside, and waited.

A wraith opened the door. She couldn't have been more than eighteen, and was dressed in a flimsy white, chiffonous garment somewhere between a dress and a robe, reaching to her ankles. Straight, fair hair fell down her back almost to her waist. All that was missing were the wings. Her face, if not quite cadaverous, could have drawn color from most turkey cuts.

"Welcome to our Earthly harbor," she intoned expressionlessly. "Have you come in search of the Oneness?"

Jarrow groped for a response. Finally he said, "No. I was expecting to find something else. . . . How long have you been here?"

"When is 'being' 'been,' and where is 'here'?" she answered. "I am all and have always been, and everywhere that is, is here. All is one with the Cosmic Father and Void Mother. This is merely a short resting place on our voyage."

"Er, who's in charge?" Jarrow asked.

"You don't wish to regain knowledge of the Eternal Essence?"

"I just want to ask some questions about the building."

Although the face didn't change, the light in the eyes switched to a lower wattage. "I'll fetch Sister Ophelia."

She ushered Jarrow into a darkened anteroom and disappeared through a rear archway embellished with an ornate surround and screened by hanging beads. Her delicate wraith's tread receded, then came what sounded like the thud of part of a body striking something solid, and a muted but distinct hiss of *"Shit!"* floated from the sanctum.

Jarrow stood and looked around while he waited. There were heavy drapes on the walls, a couple of chairs piled with cushions, and a cane divider with recesses holding carved figures. An odor of incense wafted through from beyond the arch. Strategically placed by the door was a glass display case containing assorted books, pamphlets, crystals, charms, inscribed prayers, and other material aids to attaining nirvana, all with price tags.

Sister Ophelia swept in through the hanging beads in a flurry of taffeta and tinkling jewelry, accompanied by an aura of heady perfume. She was short, endomorphic, and hugely chested. Her hair hung on either side of her head in Wagnerian braids, the effect being offset somewhat by a pair of thick glasses with butterfly frames. "Can I be of assistance?" she warbled.

"I'm not sure. I wasn't expecting this. There used to be a medical practice here, a Dr. Valdheim's. Do you know what happened to him?"

"I don't know anything about that. It must have been before we took over."

"How long ago was that?"

"Let's see, now, around the middle of summer. The first of July, I think it was, when we moved in. . . . Yes, that's right, because they had the fireworks a few days later."

"And Valdheim wasn't here when you looked at the place?"

"No. Never heard of him. It was empty when we saw it. Not even a carpet or drapes."

Valdheim must have had a sudden change of plans, then, Jarrow reflected. He must have been gone less than two months after the last visit that Jarrow remembered—and less than a month after the date of Jarrow's death. And yet Valdheim had made no mention of such a possibility. It seemed strange.

"So you can't help me get in touch with him," Jarrow observed, as if it wasn't obvious.

"Never heard of him," Sister Ophelia said again. "You could try the real estate office that handled it: Bridger-Reece, in town."

"Yes, thanks. I'll try that."

Sister Ophelia stepped forward quickly to interpose herself as Jarrow turned toward the door. "How about some information that'll tell you more about us, before you leave? It could turn you into a different person."

Just what he needed, Jarrow thought. "No, really. I'm not into that kind of thing. Sorry."

She took one of several thick envelopes that were lying on top of the display case. "Then take this. It's our special introductory package at no charge. And there's twenty-five percent off the novice course if you enroll for the full twelve weeks."

"Sure. I'll think about it."

"We might see you again, then?"

"Maybe."

"Don't forget the name: Bridger-Reece."

"Right."

"Peace, Love, Joy, and may you arrive at the Oneness."

"Yes, er, thanks," Jarrow stammered, backing through the door. "You too. Good-bye now."

He called the real estate company as soon as he got back to his room in the Lennox, but they were unable to be of much help. They had not leased the property to Valdheim directly, but through an agent acting on his behalf, whom they knew only as J & F Associates, with the address of an office on Fourth Street, and a number. Jarrow tried the number, but as a rising suspicion had already forewarned him, he got nowhere. J & F Associates had packed up and gone last June, leaving no forwarding address or means of communication. From Jarrow's check with the city and state commercial directory, they had vanished without a trace.

His puzzlement growing, he tried the county and state health departments for a lead on the whereabouts of Dr. Valdheim, but nobody had a record of any such name. Finally, Jarrow was referred to the federal registry in Washington, where, after being bounced around from extension to extension until he felt like a Ping-Pong ball in a typhoon, he emerged none the wiser. Nobody had any information on a national program to field-test the QUIP neuro-analyzer; in fact, nobody had heard of QUIP. So, either Valdheim had been a fake, working for God knew who, for God knew what purpose; or, though it shook Jarrow's faith in the system to have to admit it to himself, Valdheim had been a fake set up by some department of officialdom for God knew what purpose, and officialdom wasn't telling. Either way, Jarrow was thankful that he'd refrained from rushing off to one of the organs of officialdom on the first impulse, to blurt out his story.

But what was he to do now, with the last of his leads having led nowhere? He stared blankly at the picture of the buffalo. They stared blankly back. Go west with Paul, the former scientist in the bar, and work in the woods? But without bothering to examine the thought, he knew there could be no question of it. It would mean leading a semifugitive existence, without papers or any properly established status, constantly having to guard against being too visible, never sure of who might be an informer of the local registration authorities. Paul might be cut out for that kind of thing, but Jarrow wasn't.

He sat by the bed and spread out his notes and papers, and the contents of Gordon's wallet: the total of information that he had available to him so far. It didn't amount to much. His eye roamed over the items again, looking for something new, some angle that he might have missed, and came to rest on the notepad from the Hyatt in Atlanta. He drew it across and read the message on the top sheet again: *Headman to ship out via J'ville, sometime Nov. 19. Check ref "Cop 3."* It still meant no more to him than it had when he first saw it. He didn't know anyone called Headman, or whom he'd have described as one. J'ville could have been Jacksonville, he supposed—not all that far from Atlanta. And what did Cop 3 refer to? Something connected with the police, maybe? If so, it reinforced his conviction that he was right to lie low until he knew more about what Maurice Gordon had been mixed up in.

He turned the page to uncover the one below, with the scrawled phone numbers that he had also found yesterday morning. They were the only unknown left.

He tried calling the first. It turned out to be a pizza restaurant in Atlanta. So, not surprisingly, Maurice Gordon had to eat too. Jarrow skipped the next couple, also Atlanta numbers, and studied the last, which he recognized from its area code as a Chicago number. That made him more curious. He reached over to the keypad and entered the number. The legend CALL RINGING appeared on the screen, and after about ten seconds was replaced by a head-and-shoulders view of a woman. Jarrow sat forward sharply in surprise as he experienced the immediate feeling of having seen her before somewhere.

Something was missing. . . . He took in her clear, finely lined features, firm but attractively feminine mouth, with a hint of a natural pout, light eyes, wavy red hair. . . . The red hair. The hair should have had a hat. No, a cap. The last time he'd seen her, she was wearing an Army general's cap. . . . And then he recognized her as the redheaded girl in the dream that he had awoken to that morning! But that was crazy. He didn't know anyone in Chicago, or a redhead that looked like that, anywhere.

And the even crazier part was that, from the way her expression changed, she evidently knew him.

"Well, hi," she said as Jarrow stared speechlessly. Her voice was dry and slightly husky. "I wondered when you'd call. I've been getting worried."

Somebody actually recognized him? After all that had been happening, it came as such a shock that for several seconds Jarrow could only gape. The woman's eyes flickered over him in a silent interrogation. Her face showed concern, but not surprise—he got the feeling that his confusion and strange behavior were not unexpected.

"You . . . you knew I'd call?" he managed finally, watching her face, searching for a hint of a memory. But apart from the fleeting parody from the dream, there was nothing.

"You just vanished into thin air," the woman said.

Jarrow swallowed and found himself shaking, hardly daring to believe it could be true. There was one other person in the world who didn't think he was going mad—either that, or the two of them alone were part of a peculiar reality that the rest of the world wasn't sharing.

"You recognize me?" he whispered. "You know who I am?"

Again the narrowing of the brows, signaling that she was worried, but still with the hint that she had been prepared for something like this. She nodded. "Of course I know who you are."

"So tell me." Inwardly Jarrow was on tenterhooks. Would it be the schoolteacher, Richard Jarrow, that no one else could see? Or the mysterious Maurice Gordon, who carried guns and hospitalized muggers?

"You're Tony Demiro," the woman said.

Jarrow slumped back in his chair and stared at her numbly.

"You don't remember?" she said.

He brought a hand up to massage his brow, then shook his head. "Who's Tony Demiro?"

"Warrant Officer Demiro? Of the Army?" She intoned the phrases like questions, as if trying to coax his memory.

Jarrow had thought that when she talked about his vanishing, she had meant last April or May. Now he wasn't so sure. "When did you last see me?" he asked.

"The night before last, in Atlanta. We were staying at the Hyatt. I went to freshen up in the pool before breakfast. When I got back to the room, you'd left. . . ." She paused, reading his expression of total bemusement. "You don't know who I am, do you?"

"I'm sorry. No, I don't."

"Rita. Rita Chilsen?"

Jarrow shook his head.

"You called me from Atlanta on Monday morning. You—"

"Wait a minute. Today's Wednesday, right?"

"Right. You said you had to see me. I managed to get a flight and joined you at the Hyatt on Monday evening."

Jarrow drew a long breath. He still had no recollection of anything that had happened before the previous day, Tuesday.

"I'm sorry," he said. "Some strange things have been happening to me."

"I know. You were pretty confused when I got there. But you knew who you were, then—and who I was. But you'd woken up that morning not knowing how you got to Atlanta at all. And the only clothes and ID you had were somebody else's."

On *Monday*? Jarrow was mystified. "Did they belong to somebody called Gordon, by any chance?" he asked.

"Yes." Rita nodded. So that much was hanging together, at least.

"How about the name Richard Jarrow?" Jarrow asked.

Rita shook her head. "Never heard of him."

It still wasn't making sense. But she obviously knew him. And if, as she claimed, he had known on Monday who she was, it would explain how her phone number came to be written on the pad. "And you're certain that I"—he gestured to indicate himself—"this person you're talking to now, am an Army officer called . . . What did you say his name was?"

"Tony Demiro." Rita gave a series of short, rapid nods. "Oh, yes, no question about it." Her voice caught. She bit her lip and brushed a hand quickly across her mouth.

"What is it?" Jarrow asked. "What's the matter?"

"You don't remember, do you?"

"What?"

"We talked about it . . . most of that evening in Atlanta."

He shook his head. "Sorry. It's like I said: I've had some pretty strange experiences lately. It's affected a lot of things. What's the problem?"

Rita swallowed audibly, and he could see her brace herself. "Tony Demiro was killed five months ago," she said.

ten

Colonel Rowan, commander, Third Battalion Supply & Support Depot, U.S. Army Materiel Command at Kankakee, south of Chicago, leaned back from his desk, his eyes impenetrable behind gold-tinted mirror glasses. Next to him, Major Kellend, who ran the logistics section, glanced over the file lying open in front of them. Warrant Officer Anthony Demiro stood at ease, waiting, watching them with dark, alert eyes.

Rowan, solid and thickset, square-chinned, with iron-gray hair and nicknamed "Yukon Jack"—after the liquor and because of his gold-shielded stare—never displayed humor. Major Kellend, blond and fresh-faced, with the youthful looks that make popular actors and doctors, but intelligent, straight, and a good officer, was Demiro's immediate chief. Between the two of them they got along well enough in the informal kind of way that develops when respect for competence is mutual. But in Yukon Jack's office, everyone had to keep things a little more formal.

"As far as your duties go, you've got a clean record," Rowan said, looking up. "You've got your act together and you know your job."

"Thank you, sir," Demiro acknowledged.

Rowan drew across one of the sheets that he had taken from the file and stared at it just long enough to let the tide retreat from that high point. "But unfortunately it doesn't stop there, does it? I have reports here that some of the views and opinions that you seem to be in the habit of expressing are not what I'd expect my officers to be airing, and especially not in the company of enlisted men."

"Sir?"

Rowan sighed. "This isn't the first time we've been through this, Demiro. You know damn well what I'm talking about. You've been heard on at least two occasions in the last week referring to our President as the 'Fuehrer' and to the Pentagon as the Kremlin. And yesterday, did you not make the remark that the reason there are no Communists left in the FER is that they're all running things over here? And the day before that, that the Consolidation is a game preserve for the white man, because he's made himself an endangered species?"

"I don't remember the context, sir. We could have been joking— you know how it is when guys get together. Maybe your source isn't strong in his sense of humor." Demiro's tone made the point without his having to use the word "spy."

"I don't buy that, Demiro. The contexts that I see here make it pretty plain to me that these constitute political statements; and not only that, but statements that could, by anyone of a mind to do so, be construed as being of subversive intent. Do I make myself clear? The United States Army isn't the place to be starting your own rebellion. You could end up in a lot of trouble. This is the last time I'm prepared to let it go with a warning."

"I understand. Thank you, sir."

Rowan set the paper down, paused for a moment, then turned to Kellend. "Warrant Officer Demiro was a volunteer, not a draftee?"

"That's correct," the major replied.

Rowan leaned forward to rest his elbows on the desk, and looked up again. His voice fell to a quieter note, signaling that the official business was over and he was speaking from personal curiosity. "What made you join?" he asked Demiro. "Your primary reason?"

"I didn't have a family, sir. I think, most of all it was the structure. Something to belong to."

Rowan nodded. "I appreciate your frankness. So we're not pretending that it was any motivation to dedicate yourself to the defense of the institutions and property of this country?"

"That's not quite true, sir," Demiro replied.

"Oh? How do you mean?"

"If the country was attacked or threatened, sure I'd want to help defend it."

"You don't consider that to be the case?"

The question put Demiro in an awkward position. He could agree, and in so doing deny his own last statement; or he could say, in effect, that the people were being routinely lied to. Finally, he replied, "With respect, aren't we getting into political opinions again, sir?"

"But this isn't a billet of enlisted men who might attach official authority to what you say. I'm simply curious, I'd like to hear your political view."

Demiro sensed an ulterior motive and answered guardedly. "Well . . . it just seems that we'd do better trying to get along a bit more with the Offworlders, instead of acting as if they're about to come after us all the time. I don't think they need anything we've got."

"What about this planet's material resources? Isn't it common knowledge that they'll be contested when the Offworld expansion overreaches itself, as it has to eventually?"

"That's what they tell us," Demiro agreed.

"And you have reason to disbelieve informed sources? In other words, we're all suffering from collective paranoia down here?"

"I didn't say that, sir."

Rowan stared up at the officer in silence for a few moments, seemingly pondering whether to draw this out any further. But his instructions had been simply to sound the applicants out on their politics, not engage them in a debate. He set the papers aside and picked up a thin sheaf of forms relating to a notice that had been put out inviting volunteers for a special assignment.

"I have your VR-1 application here, countersigned and completed. Are you still interested?"

"Yes, sir, I am."

"I can't tell you anything about it, because I don't know myself. But you do understand that it would involve transfer away from this unit, and possible absence of contact with the outside world for a considerable time?"

"Yes, sir."

"Out of curiosity, why do you want to do it?" Rowan asked.

"A chance for a change. To do something different." Demiro's olive, Mediterranean features, with their shaggy mat of black hair, softened into a faint grin that came easily and naturally. "I guess I get curious too, sir."

The colonel stared at him for a second or two longer, then nodded. "Very well. I'm putting it through. The application entitles you to a forty-eight-hour pass, which I'm making effective from sixteen hundred hours today since the people running this want to get started as quickly as possible. We'll see you back here on Sunday, and by that time we'll let you know their decision. If you're selected, you could be moving out Sunday night. So use the weekend to make any arrangements that you need to."

"Yes, sir."

"That's all. You're dismissed."

In a room on the floor below, the two visitors from Washington had been following the proceedings on a monitor screen hooked to the camera concealed in the Divisional crest mounted behind Colonel Rowan's desk. Colonel Wylvern, who believed with the conviction of a biblical prophet that the powers above knew what they were doing and that soldiers should preferably never have heard of politics, let alone hold political opinions, was tottering on the brink of apoplexy.

"That . . . man was as good as a goddam Communist!" he spluttered. He didn't know what this project in Georgia was all about, but he did know that it involved sensitive information and was highly classified. "A disruptive influence on everyone he comes in contact with. He ought to be discharged from the service."

The scientist who was with him keyed in a command for a replay and watched keenly through rimless bifocals as the sequence began again. Dr. Harold Nordens didn't agree at all.

"No, Colonel," he said in a voice that was only peripherally aware of the other's presence. "That's precisely what we're looking for. Warrant Officer Demiro, I suspect, would make an *ideal* subject."

The two girls that Rita commuted with dropped her at a convenience store off the Adlai E. Stevenson expressway at Hodgkins, twelve miles west of Chicago center. She collected some items of groceries that they were short of, a couple of magazines, a bottle of Gallo Dry Reserve, and some cigarettes—the store sold cigarettes under-the-counter to avoid hassles and picketing from neighborhood antismoking vigilantes. Then, taking her bags, she walked the two blocks to the mobile home park.

The unit that she shared with Tony was beginning to come apart at the seams; but it had meant an affordable cash outlay, instead of slow bloodletting by mortgage escalation clauses, or hemorrhaging to uncontrolled rents whose skyrocketing in response to vanishing supply was outdoing even the price for old-fashioned (and strictly illegal) freon-run refrigerators, whose pipes didn't rot away and release things that ate through the floor. Controlled places were fine, provided you didn't mind waiting for three years, and then the square footage was allocated through a points system and you took what was offered. Unless you got pregnant, were certified disabled, or qualified for criminal, mental stress, or drug-abuse rehabilitation, all of which came with the alternative complication of being required to let other people take charge of your life.

As she turned the last corner, she saw that the light in the house was on and there was a vehicle parked outside. Fifty yards nearer, and it revealed itself as an Army jeep. Great! Tony had fixed it for the weekend—and worked his charm with the transportation sergeant too, it seemed. She gripped the two bags more securely and quickened her pace.

"Hi!" she called to the house in general as she let herself in and closed the door with her back. "You made it, then."

Tony appeared from the living room, barefoot in his bathrobe and holding a beer. He took one of the bags and followed her through into the kitchen. "Free as a bird until Sunday night. I took a shower and called Sandy and Bruce. We're meeting them at the Admiral at eight. It seemed time we had a night out."

"Terrific." Rita put her bag down on the worktop by the refrigerator. As she turned, Tony moved close, slid an arm around her—the other was still holding the beer—and kissed her on the mouth. She responded, kissed back harder, putting her arms around his neck and drawing him close. His free hand fondled her neck, her back, her waist, then settled on her behind, squeezing the middles of their bodies together.

"You smell nice," he murmured. "Kind of outside-and-fresh-airy."

"I don't know so much about fresh. I had a hard day at work."

"It's animal."

"Most people call it sweat."

"It's you. I like it."

They kissed and rubbed and fondled.

"You're cool and clean," she said, loosening his robe and sliding her hands around his chest inside.

He drew her away from the worktop, turning them both around, and began steering her like a waltzing partner out of the kitchen and across the living room in the direction of the door to the bedroom. "Eight's a long time away," he said, his eyes laughing. "People who've had tough days ought to be relaxed. Relaxed all over."

"There's chocolate ice cream in the bag. It should go in the freezer."

"So, we'll have chocolate milk instead."

"Can't I get to shower first?"

"Shower after. I like you better the way you are."

"Sometimes I think you're perverted, you know that?"

"You only think? Honey, if you don't *know* by now . . .''

They lay together contentedly, he with an arm folded underneath his head, staring at the ceiling, she propped up against the pillows, smoking a cigarette and caressing his chest with her other hand.

"How long will this assignment last? Did they say?" she asked.

"Hey, hang on. I haven't even been told I've got it yet. I don't get to find out till Sunday."

"I thought you said you could be moving out Sunday."

"If I'm selected. I just need to be ready, that's all."

Rita would be going to Boston for a month on a training seminar to do with her government job, and Demiro had decided that he might as well volunteer for the special assignment as a way of keeping himself occupied and out of trouble. There was also a lot of truth in what he had told Colonel Rowan about needing a change of scene. And on top of that, naturally, there was the extra money, which would go toward getting them a better place that much sooner.

Rita drew at her cigarette quickly. "How much do you know about it?" she asked. "Is there much chance that it could be . . . well, you know, dangerous?"

Tony laughed and turned his head to kiss her on the hip. "Not a hope. It's probably one of them dumb psychological tests they dream up—you watch colored lights or something, and then fill in questionnaires for shrinks. At the end of it they figure out that some people always get things the wrong way around, and other people get bored and start making up answers—things that everyone except shrinks knew all along, anyway."

"Then why is it secret?"

"Because it's the Army. Everything about the Army has to be secret. You don't think they want people to know how they're spending their money, do you? Don't worry about it. I'll be back home before you are."

That night they met Sandy and Bruce for drinks, ran into some more friends, and all went together to eat Chinese. Then they found another bar and drank until the early hours. They talked about the trashy music that kid groups played and why vintage stuff from the nineties and two-ohs was better, traded reviews of new movies, rated the city's eating places and dance spots, argued about what ate up the value of money and whether people in the last century had been better off—anything to forget about the week.

By the time it was drawing near to closing, Terry, one of the others who had joined them, was describing a public-information documentary about the FER states and their Offworlder connections, which had been shown the previous night. "It's practically a crime-controlled empire out there," he said. "That's where all the generals and capos went after the fighting when the Red empire broke up: the Soviet Mafia—they run the lunar bases. If you go out there, it's a one-way trip. They run everything by what amounts to slave labor."

"And you really believe that?" Demiro asked.

Terry seemed taken aback. "Why not? I mean, look at the environment they have to deal with out there. There's nothing."

Demiro bunched his mouth and looked unconvinced. "People have always said things like that about anywhere new. Most places where people live now used to be nothing, just waste."

"They were gardens," Terry protested. "It was *us* who turned everywhere into wastes: people." He knew because everybody knew. They'd been told it since their school days.

"That's not what the books say," Demiro answered.

"What books?"

"Old books. Not the ones that you see these days. Ones that were written back when we're talking about. They're still around, if you know where to look. And they don't tell it the way you're saying."

Later, as they were leaving, Bruce drew Demiro and Rita to one side and asked, "Do you guys have any plans for tomorrow night?"

Demiro looked at Rita. She shrugged and shook her head. "Not really."

"Why?" Demiro asked. "What did you have in mind?"

"Oh, there's this place we go to sometimes, out near the university. There's music and you can dance, and they're not always careful about cards, so everyone can have a good time. And sometimes there's other things too—somebody talking or showing pictures maybe. It can be interesting."

"Different, anyhow," Sandy put in. "Give it a try."

"What kind of 'different'?" Demiro asked.

"Come and see," Bruce suggested. "From some of the things you say, I've got a feeling you'd like it."

"Why not?" Rita said, looking at Demiro.

He nodded. "Sure. Let's give it a try."

They stayed in bed until ten the next morning, making love and talking, got up for coffee and a breakfast of pancake, sausage, and egg, then went back to bed and started all over. The afternoon was a lazy affair of drinking the bottle of wine that Rita had bought the evening before, watching football, a movie, and other odds and ends on TV, eating chicken sandwiches with potato salad—and making love again, once on the couch in the living room and once, laughing inanely, entangled with the dishwasher and a window seat in the kitchen in a position that the compiler of the *Kama Sutra* had overlooked.

Evening found them at peace with the world again and in the frame of mind that international law should require all negotiators to attain before going off to discuss treaties. They showered, changed out of their house clothes, and left for the city to meet Sandy and Bruce.

eleven

Maisso's was located amid the jumble of aging tenements, crammed economy stores, and anything-to-go food shops squashed together along the streets of the West Side in the blocks north of the university campus. From piled windows and sagging shelves, the stores offered the city's most amazing variety of goods: clothes, shoes, electronics, knickknacks, all of it cheap—and untaxed to those who talked the right code words. More Poles once lived in the neighborhood than in any community outside Warsaw—drawn, perhaps, by nostalgia for Arctic-Siberian winters and the Windy City's fond evocations of homey breezes howling in from the steppes. As they dwindled, Puerto Ricans and Hispanics had taken over the area. Nowadays it was a general haven for refugees seeking relief from the increasing costs and restrictions of maintaining automobile lifelines to the suburbs.

The place itself was like a big, dark cavern, down creaking steps inside a dingy doorway on a side street—the kind of place that students everywhere liked to lose themselves in as a contrast to their visible aboveground existence during the day. There was a hole-in-the-wall serving as a bar on one side, a counter peddling sodas and snacks on the other, while from a raised stage at the far end a bizarrely clad rock group played to a floor crowded with shaking, gyrating bodies. The music was loud and brutal.

"See, a change," Sandy said. Demiro and Rita agreed.

"What'll it be—beer, beer, or beer?" Bruce called above the din.

"How about a beer?" Demiro answered.

"Are you staying on the soft stuff, same as last night?" Rita asked Sandy.

"I'd best," she replied, patting her tummy. She and Bruce had obtained a pregnancy approval, which meant they qualified for benefits. She was still excited about it and had talked about little else the night before.

"Sure you don't want to change your mind? You're drinking for two now, remember," Demiro quipped.

Sandy grinned. "Keep a tab. I'll make up for it after."

They quickly got into the swing of things and started dancing, changing partners for a while, then back again—Sandy taking things slow and easy, but enjoying herself. Then Bruce introduced them to Eric, who was into philosophy and classics at the university and looked the part: bespectacled, tall and gangling but with hefty shoulders, a mop of hair falling across his forehead, and wearing a baggy, roll-neck sweater, its color impossible to discern in the gloom and psychedelic lighting.

"Why classics?" Demiro asked him as they sat on a seat at the foot of a pillar, behind a bunch of people standing watching the action on the floor.

Eric swigged from a can. "Well, I'm not a tech, I don't do art, and nobody believes the history and politics they teach anymore. It's the only thing that's not doctored."

Demiro wasn't going to get into any of that tonight. He shook his head, smiling to himself, and looked away. Eric was with more of his own friends, and the two groups merged to find partners for more dancing, everyone mixing well.

The band took a break, and recorded music of a different style and tempo took over, slower, more structured, beginning quietly with a steady, driving rhythm, then rising to a pounding crescendo of brass and percussion. The kids seemed to enjoy it, responding with a lot of stamping, finger-snapping, and what looked like hands-on-hips, pseudo-Spanish dance motions. It was vaguely familiar, but Demiro couldn't place it.

"What's that?" he asked Eric, as Eric emerged from the throng, breathless and clammy, to down a mouthful from his drink.

"Ravel, Bolero."

"Is that what it's called? Not bad."

"It makes a change."

Eric seemed to change his mind about going back. Demiro shifted to make room for him to sit down. Demiro looked around and sipped his beer. "I guess they need to unwind, too, just like the rest of us, eh?"

Eric leaned forward, resting his elbows on his knees. His manner seemed serious for this kind of occasion, but Demiro had already figured him as one of those intense kinds of younger people. "Times are getting tense," he said. "I don't just mean here, in this city. All over. There have to be changes."

"How d'you mean?"

"The system has run out of credibility. Nobody believes the garbage that gets pumped out about anything anymore. And when they just keep cracking down harder, that's when you know they're losing their grip. Repression is always the last phase before things cave in. You see it all through history."

Demiro raised his eyebrows and looked up at Rita, who had moved over with Sandy to stand by them. "Repression? Do we have repression?"

"Don't tell me you never see it," Eric said. "What do you do, anyhow?"

"Me? I'm with the Army."

Eric looked away, shaking his head bleakly. "That's all we needed."

"Don't worry about it."

"Don't worry, he says."

"Come on, do you think I'd have said so if it made any difference? Go ahead. I'm interested."

"What they're telling people is an illusion. A make-believe reality that gives them a pretext for hanging on for as long as they can get away with it. But they don't even believe it themselves anymore—not privately. The public stuff is just pretense."

"How do you mean?" Demiro asked.

Eric waved a hand toward the now-empty stage, where some people were pulling back a set of curtains at the rear to uncover a large screen. "You'll see in a minute."

"Why? What's happening?"

"We're hooking into a pirate link that some hackers somewhere are going to try and crash through one of the comsats," Eric answered. He meant an illicit communications channel. By law, all publicly operated receiving equipment was required to embody a system of preset codes that denied access to unapproved transmis-

sions. Conceived and ordered by bureaucrats who were not engineers, the task was an impractical one, and pirate broadcasters were
always breaking in to make political statements, show foreign
program material, sell hard-core porn, or just for the hell of it. "If
they break in, they're going to get Daparras on the channel and spray
it all over the country. That would be a real gas."

"Isn't he some kind of anarchist, terrorist, something like that?"
Rita said.

"Who told you that?" Eric asked her, looking up.

"I've seen the name on subversives lists."

"Subversives lists? Where was that?" Eric's brow creased. "So
what in hell do *you* do?"

"Work for the government. I'm a clerk with the Economic
Coordination Board."

"Jesus! Who's letting these people *in* here?" Eric pleaded.

Bruce, who had been listening, grinned. "I brought 'em. Relax.
They're okay."

"That's just what they *tell* people, Tony," Eric said, turning back.
"It's part of the illusion. Daparras writes books on philosophy and
ethics—that you can buy legally anywhere except in Consolidation
countries. He talks to people. And he set up a string of homes for
kids who were orphaned in the fighting when the Soviet empire
broke up. What kind of terrorist is that?"

"Who are the hackers?" Demiro asked. "Are they around here
somewhere?"

Eric stretched back his elbows for a moment and returned a
you-should-know-better smile. "*That's* something we don't get to
find out. They could be anywhere from here to Texas."

Demiro turned to Bruce. "What are you getting us into now?"

"I told you it would be different," Bruce said.

"Interesting?" Sandy suggested.

And then a wave of cheering broke out all around. They looked
back at the stage and saw that the screen had come to life and was
showing the figure of an elderly man. He had a full head of white
hair beneath a black skullcap, and a wispy beard that hung in tufts
like a shortened version of a Chinese mandarin's. His face was
hollowed and parchmentlike, but with eyes that gleamed brightly,
and he held his frame upright, evidently with plenty of life left in it
yet.

"Yeah, I've seen him before." Demiro nodded.

"Of course you have," Eric muttered. A hush fell all around. Daparras was already talking.

". . . came back to this country because I wanted the truth to be known. They called me a tool of Offworlder propaganda, as I knew they would. They said I was a threat to law and order." The old man paused and looked down at his frail form, turning up his palms bemusedly to show the absurdity of the suggestion. Delighted laughter rippled around the room. "And yes, they put me under arrest, in my own house, where I'm supposed to be right now—but as you can see, I am not. So, they have not managed to shut me up just yet." The room registered its approval by another chorus of cheering.

"Since we probably won't have much time, let me tell you what life in the Federation of Eurasian Republics was really like. As most of you know, I was there through its inception, and I lived there for over twenty years as it emerged from its troubled beginnings and evolved into the unique social and political organism that it is today."

Daparras waved a hand briefly in front of his face. "It isn't the cesspool of anarchy and violence that you are told, with people being left to fend for themselves without care or compassion while others grow fat on vast fortunes. Yes, I admit that some of the several dozen republics, national congresses, ethnic provinces, and loosely federated territories that now extend from Poland to Kamchatka might be accused of permitting rough justice to those who transgress upon the rights of others; but if so, the fault is one of the states leaving its citizens too much freedom and independence, instead of stripping them, as is ever more the case here, of the ability and the right to defend themselves."

"Right on!" someone shouted.

"And, yes, it is true that some individuals are rewarded more than others. But it's the freedom of all to choose that decides those rewards—not a law passed by a few, which inevitably creates privileges that the few will have the power to sell. The FER provides opportunity for everybody, growth—without the phobias about resources running out and the imminence of collapse that have been paralyzing everyone over here since the end of the last century. For the people of the FER, everything is not all over; everything is only beginning! The space industries of the Consolidation states are bankrupt and languish under a deadweight of bureaucratic inertia. Meanwhile, the Offworlders have come to dominate near-Earth space, and the Siberian industries that are free to trade with them prosper. A Consolidation family loses its social benefits for an unlicensed birth—surely the ultimate in obscenity. FER children are welcomed as priceless assets—and what could be more natural?"

Sandy and Bruce smiled at each other and entwined hands. But there was a wistfulness on their faces as they listened.

"See what I was talking about earlier?" Eric whispered to Demiro.

Demiro nodded. All around, others were staring intently, hanging on every word. This was the kind of message they didn't hear every day. On the screen, Daparras made a brief, appealing gesture.

"It is not difficult to understand what makes this possible. For almost a century, the peoples of the lands that today make up most of the FER lived with the consequences of allowing a tyrannical minority enough power to literally steal an entire country—all its land, all its property—and to enslave its population. They *know* what happens when power becomes concentrated and is unaccountable to anyone.

"There is an irony in my talking to Americans like this, for most of the younger people here have never been taught about their country's origins. It is a sad fact that Russian schoolchildren know more about Western history than the graduates of many—"

The picture vanished suddenly to leave a random wash of colors flickering across the screen, and the voice cut out.

"That's it. It's been traced back," Eric said resignedly. "The beam's been cut."

The room registered its disapproval with a chorus of shouts, hisses, boos, and whistles.

Demiro wondered how common this kind of thing was becoming. From what he knew, such a gathering would be a prime target for infiltration by security agencies. Instinctively, he cast an uneasy eye around the place, and almost at once caught a glimpse of a shadowy figure on the far side of the room briefly raising what could have been a miniature camera—there were night-vision types that could snap a face in settings as dark as this. Just what Demiro needed in his file. And especially after his interview that afternoon with Colonel Rowan.

He leaned across and murmured in Rita's ear. "Come on. It's time we were leaving."

The next day was fine and warm for the end of September. Since they had the jeep for the weekend, Demiro and Rita decided to make the best of it. They packed a picnic lunch and drove up to the wooded, hilly country bordering Wisconsin, forty miles northwest. Leaving the road, they followed a dirt trail up among trees and boulders, and came to a shaded and secluded spot in a grassy grove by a small lake. They swam naked, dried off, and made love on a blanket in the sun. As she reached for her clothes to get dressed afterward, Rita saw a stag standing motionless, which had been watching them through the trees. Its expression could only be described as nonplussed, like that of a ten-beer-a-night redneck who had stumbled upon a gourmet wine-tasting ritual.

"I guess it never knew it was possible that way," Demiro surmised. Rita laughed.

Then they heard a low droning sound somewhere to the south, which after a few seconds became discernible as getting closer. Rita sat up, wrapping a blanket around herself. Demiro stood to pull on his pants. The rhythmic thwacking of rotor blades beating air resolved itself against the background drone, and moments later a helicopter, white with state police markings, appeared over a hilltop. It came lower, circling and banking to get a good look at the jeep and the figures beside it.

"Jesus, don't they ever leave you alone?" Demiro growled, watching it. Suddenly all the fun and laughter had evaporated out of the day.

"They probably check this area for drug growers," Rita said.

"It makes you feel like you're living in some kind of zoo. They can come and check you out, anytime they want."

"Don't let it bug you, Tony. Don't let them spoil our day."

The chopper straightened up and disappeared over a ridge to the west. Demiro watched it go, then turned back and forced a grin. "You're right, why should they? So . . . what have we got?"

Rita finished putting on her shorts and top and opened the picnic box. "Well, let's see now. Chicken salad in a sandwich, and there's cheese."

"Sounds good."

"A pie that I picked up, and some thick cream to go on it. And some fruit, juice, and a flask of coffee."

Demiro sat down again and tried to make talk, but his manner was still troubled and distant. Rita assumed he was brooding because it would be their last day together for some time. After she had put away the picnic things and collected the trash into a bag, she went over and sat next to him, resting her head against his shoulder.

"Don't get too down," she told him. "It'll only be a month."

For a moment it seemed as if he hadn't heard, then he said, "Do you think all those things are true—what that guy Daparras was talking about last night?" It was an odd question, since Demiro often said similar things himself. And Bruce was aware of it too—otherwise he wouldn't have invited them along. So Demiro wasn't really asking for an answer. It was just a way of raising the subject.

"Why? What are you—" Rita started to ask, but then they heard the sound of a vehicle approaching up the trail.

"I was wondering when they'd show up," Demiro said resignedly.

A state police Range Rover came around the bend and stopped behind the jeep. Demiro and Rita stood up. Two troopers climbed out of the Range Rover and sauntered across. One was heavily built, with a paunch sagging over his belt, florid-faced and fleshy, wearing sunglasses and a dark, baseball-style cap; the other was smaller, with plain, metal-rimmed glasses and a mustache, carrying a short-barreled shotgun.

"Well, what've we got here?" the larger of the two drawled with a leer. "Mr. Lover Boy himself an' a pretty cute piece of ass. Good fuckin' today, was it, folks?"

"It's none of your business, mister," Demiro said tightly.

"Oh, touchy, touchy. I think we have a case of offended sensibilities, Hank." Hank sniggered obligingly and moved forward to poke among the picnic things with the end of the shotgun.

"If you've got some business, state it," Demiro said.

The larger of the troopers turned toward the jeep and contemplated it. "Now that would appear to me to be an item of government property. I do suppose that your being here, in possession of it like this, is all legal and properly accountable for?"

Demiro sighed and walked over to the jeep to open the glove box. "Yes, everything's—"

"Real slow and easy," a voice warned as he reached inside. He heard the sound of a gun being cocked behind him.

Demiro turned back slowly, holding out the wallet containing his papers. "I'm with the Army at Kankakee," he said. "Warrant officer, Third Battalion Supply and Support. Everything's legit."

"Well, let's see about that, now." The trooper scanned the documents while the smaller one with the shotgun began checking the various recesses and compartments of the jeep. "Warrant Officer Anthony Demiro, huh?"

Rita clung to Demiro's arm, feeling his growing anger and frustration. "There's the requisition and approval, transport officer's clearance. It's all there," he said. "They let me use it for my two days off. Is that okay with you?"

"So why would you bring it to an area like this? You wouldn't be carrying any illegal substances, now, by any chance?"

"Look around. It's nice here. It's a change from the stinking city. Is that so strange?"

The big trooper looked across inquiringly at Hank. Hank shook his head. "It looks clean."

"Run an R7 on him and the vehicle," the larger one said, passing across the papers. Hank went back to the Range Rover, leaned inside, drew out a mike on a cord, and began talking to someone.

"What do you do?" the big trooper asked Rita.

"Bureau of Economic Coordination. In the city." The trooper's eyebrows rose a fraction. That seemed to carry some weight.

"Nothing. It's all clean," Hank called from the Range Rover. "Want them to run one on her too?"

"Nah. I guess they're okay. . . . As you were, soldier. You can get back to your basic training."

Demiro watched the trooper stride ponderously back to rejoin his companion—arrogant, unhurried, without care or apology. The Range Rover reversed onto the grass by the track and bumped away in the direction from which it came.

Demiro sat down and unscrewed the top of the flask with a

savage twist of his fingers to pour himself a coffee. "Suppose I found a way to get us into the FER. Would you go?" he asked suddenly.

It was so unexpected that for a moment Rita could only gape. "Defect to the East?" She sat down by him and raised a hand to her brow. "Tony, are you serious?"

"Why not? Maybe through Europe. Alaska's too risky. They've got it all sealed up with electronic fences."

"I don't know. I never . . ." Rita shrugged helplessly.

"How much longer could you put up with this kind of shit? Think about how Bruce and Sandy will have their baby: with somebody's permission, have to give it a number, be ordered around, insulted, treated like kids who can't take charge of their own lives. . . . I don't want us to be like that. I want to be *me*. The FER's got opportunities, a chance to make something worthwhile of ourselves. Here they just keep putting the squeezes on tighter and tighter until you can't breathe, and in the end you just rot away." He took a drink from the cup and looked at her. "You heard what Daparras said about kids. You don't need any license there. They *want* big families—like we always talked about. You can pick what kind of school you want for them, what things they do there, what kind of health care they get. . . . It isn't all spelled out to you by somebody you never see. What kind of place is this to raise a family?"

"You are . . . you are serious?"

"Sure, I'm serious. Maybe we could even go farther, to the Offworld independencies, maybe. Maybe what he said is true, and they're not militarized slave-labor camps. . . . What do you think?"

Rita slid an arm around his neck, kissed him, and held her face close. "I'll go wherever you go. That's all that matters."

Already the day was as it had been again, as if the troopers had never existed. "God," he sighed. "Do you know how much I love you?"

"Of course I do," she whispered. "It's as much as I love you."

Demiro returned to base on time that evening and found a message waiting for him to report to Major Kellend. Kellend informed him that he had been selected for the special assignment and should see Colonel Rowan for the details. Demiro would be shipping out first thing the next morning. His orders were to fly to Atlanta, Georgia, on a priority service ticket, where transportation would be waiting to take him to a place called the Pearse Psychological Research Laboratories, fifty-odd miles north of the city.

twelve

So now Jarrow was three people. Two of them were dead, and neither he nor the only person who seemed to know him had heard of the other. He was still bemused by it all when he boarded a flight for Chicago that same evening—his Maurice Gordon ID once again having proved effectual in jumping him to the head of the queue. If it wasn't for the fact that to himself he looked normal, he would have believed he was in the stock movie situation of somehow occupying another body. Whatever had happened was obviously not as simple, if that was an appropriate word. But Valdheim's abrupt disappearance removed any remaining doubt that, intentionally or otherwise, whatever had happened was a result of the process to which he had been subjecting Jarrow.

Could he, Jarrow asked himself, be the Warrant Officer Demiro that Rita had known, undergoing some kind of delusion of being Jarrow? Rita had never heard of Jarrow, but Demiro might have. The thought brought to mind accounts of hypnotic subjects who assumed personalities that they re-created in their minds from things they'd read or heard or imagined, possibly from childhood—in some cases sufficiently vivid to lead overcredulous researchers into believing that they were witnessing reincarnations.

On the other hand, how could Demiro be aware of things that only Jarrow could have known, such as what he and Larry Banks had talked about that day in the car on the way to Valdheim's, or things he'd talked about with the staff at the school? . . . Unless those things hadn't happened at all, but were simply fabrications of his—Demiro's—mind. The only way to find out would be to check such recollections against the accounts of the people actually involved, which meant that he still needed to find some way of approaching them without getting himself arrested or certified as insane.

Aside from all that, he was still none the wiser as to who Maurice Gordon was, whose clothes he was wearing, whose papers he was carrying, and in whose name he was obliged to travel, for it seemed that the name meant no more to Rita than it did to him. As he sat in his seat, turning over the possibilities and permutations in his mind, the disquieting realization unfolded that he really didn't know if he was Jarrow having somehow taken over Demiro, Demiro undergoing delusions that he was Jarrow, or really Maurice Gordon somehow endowed with different aspects of both of them.

Gordon with Demiro's body and Jarrow's persona? Surely that didn't make sense. If you replaced the handle of a hammer and then put on a new head, was it still the same hammer?

But who else could he be if Jarrow was dead, for Christ's sake, and now he'd just been told that Demiro was too?

Maybe Larry had been right, and Jarrow—or whoever—really was crazy. That thought didn't do much to gladden him, either.

Rita spotted him as he came off the jetway at Chicago's Midway Airport, before he recognized her. She had told him on the phone that it would be closer than O'Hare. She was wearing the same green coat that he'd seen in the room at the Atlanta Hyatt, with a white scarf wrapped around her neck and head. She moved toward him through the flurry of people, her step quickening when she saw the recognition on his face. An urge to throw out her arms to him telegraphed itself, causing Jarrow to stiffen, and she came to a confused halt, like a kitten suddenly wary of the reflection that it had been about to pounce on in a mirror.

They stood looking at each other for several seconds. From their conversation that afternoon, Rita seemed to know more than Jarrow did, and he had unconsciously come prepared to follow her lead on what to do next. On the other hand, he'd had longer to adjust to his own bizarre circumstances, and as the first full realization sunk into her that he was indeed a different person, he could see that she was at a loss.

He tried to force what he hoped would be a halfway reassuring smile, but it emerged as just a thin stretching of the month. "Er, I don't know what to say," he stammered. "It's all too insane."

Rita gave a quick nod. Her voice choked when she started to answer. She gulped and tried again. "I know. I don't meet bodies back from the dead at airports every day." Her eyes traveled down the length of him, then back up to find his again.

He said, not really thinking, "You're sure I'm this Demiro that you remember? It couldn't have been a mistake?"

She shook her head. "Oh, no. You're Tony. There's no question about it. Monday was enough to prove that—in Atlanta."

Jarrow flinched. Of course. "Oh, yes. . . . You realize that I don't remember anything about that? All I know is waking up the way I am now, on Tuesday."

"You told me that when you called. . . . What did you do to your chin?"

"Nothing. It's just a scratch."

She hesitated. "Nothing's changed?"

He shook his head. The hope that had flickered on her face for an instant vanished.

The crowd of arrivals and people who had been waiting to meet them was thinning, leaving them both feeling awkwardly unprepared and conspicuous. Jarrow looked around, searching for a way to inject some semblance of normality into this. "Have you eaten?" he asked. "I mean, would you like to get something here, before we go?"

"I'm not really hungry."

"I didn't—"

"Thanks. It's—"

"You—"

They stopped together, entangled in their own clumsiness. Then, for the first time, both managed thin smiles simultaneously at the absurdity of it. Rita recovered herself first.

"I borrowed someone's car—I haven't owned one since I moved into the city. I left it in an unloading area. It's a twenty-five-dollar hole in your budget if they tow it."

"Let's go then," Jarrow agreed. "Where to?"

Rita seemed surprised, as if it hadn't crossed her mind. It brought home to Jarrow once again that until just a few minutes ago, she really hadn't thought of him as anything else but Tony Demiro suffering from some kind of amnesia—returned unexpectedly from somewhere mysterious, to be sure, but very much alive. Indeed, from the little she had told him over the phone, three days ago he *had* been just that!

She shook her head and brushed a curl of red hair back under her scarf. "Back to my place, I guess," she said.

As they moved away in the direction of Baggage Claim and the exit, a mustached man in a fur-trimmed parka, who had been observing them from a position by a line of phone booths a short distance away across the concourse, spoke into a hand-held radio. "We've got him. The guy she met is Samurai, no question. They're heading for the exit."

A voice in the receiver acknowledged. "Got it. Follow them out front and wait there for Mac to pick you up. Are you reading, Jaybird Two?"

Another voice on the channel: "Two here."

"Positive identification of Samurai. They're coming out now. Stick with them when they leave."

"Gotcha."

"Jaybird Four, be standing by at the intersection with Cicero. Pick up the tail there, assuming they head back north and into the city."

"Moving out now."

The man in the fur-trimmed parka pocketed the radio and began strolling casually toward the main entrance of the terminal. So the longshot had paid off, and they'd found Samurai again: the girl had led them right back to him. Not that the party was quite over yet. They still had to bring Samurai in.

And they'd been warned by the people from Atlanta that Samurai could be dangerous.

thirteen

One result of travel restrictions was that the environs of airports were not as choked as they used to be in the days when anyone could go joyriding on planes whenever they wanted to. Jarrow and Rita soon cleared Midway—heading toward the city, Jarrow saw from the traffic signs—and then turned north onto an avenue posted as Cicero.

"Do you know Chicago?" Rita asked.

"Oh, I've visited from time to time. It's not that far from Minneapolis."

"Is Minneapolis where you're from originally?"

"Yes. . . . Well, close. Do you know a part called Brooklyn Center?"

"Not really."

"It's to the north, a little farther up the river."

"Oh."

"How about you? Is this where you're from?"

"No, from California originally."

"What do you do?"

"I'm with the state government. That's how I was able to get down to Atlanta so fast on Monday. I traded merit points with one of the other girls. You can redeem them for travel passes."

"That's handy."

A few seconds of uncomfortable silence fell. They were still evading the subject that eclipsed all else in both their minds.

Rita carried on, mainly to fill the void, "It's not right though, really. I hate the whole setup. That was why I got out of California—

because of the politics. They debit your taxes straight out of your bank there. It's always too much, so you have to file for a refund. All the returns come in right on time."

Jarrow didn't see anything especially wrong with that. "Sounds efficient," he replied. "Spreads out the burden and cuts costs. The state has to have revenue. It's probably cheaper for everyone that way."

"The drug squad can come into your house on suspicion, even if you're not there," Rita countered. They were both venting their frustrated expectations on each other. He had come looking for understanding. She had been half hoping to find Demiro. "I mean, no warrant or anything—just if they feel like it."

"It's a menace that has to be fought by its own rules. Would you rather live in the FER? Private armies of thugs shooting it out on the streets."

Rita emitted an exasperated sigh. "You don't believe all that stuff, do you? Those troubles were over years ago. It's all . . ." Her voice broke off. "Tony, I don't know if I'm going to be able to get used to this. You really do sound like a total stranger."

"But I am," Jarrow replied. "That's what I was trying to tell you on the phone."

She shook her head, tight-lipped. "No. . . . Look, I accept that it might seem that way to you, but things like that don't happen. You're Tony, with some kind of problem. You've been away, and something very strange has been going on. But you're back now, and I'm still here." She looked across the car and flashed him a look that was meant to say everything would straighten itself out now. "We can work on it together. Okay?"

Jarrow brought his hands up to his face and massaged his eyes wearily.

"Okay, Tony?"

"Please don't call me that."

Rita drew a long breath and exhaled it slowly, making it plain that it was his decision—but she'd tried to make it easy. "All right. What should I call you, then?"

"I said when we talked earlier, my name is Jarrow: Richard Jarrow." The tenseness between them crackled like the air around a power line. Jarrow didn't need a confrontation on top of everything else. He added, forcing a mellower tone into his voice, "'Dick' would be fine."

"Dick?"

"Yes."

Rita stared ahead, digesting it slowly with a long slow nod to herself. "Okay," she pronounced finally. "Let's talk some more about him, then."

"Go ahead."

"He's this teacher who woke up in Atlanta."

"Yes."

"On Tuesday."

"Right."

Rita bit her lip, hesitating. "Now don't get mad, because I'm only trying to understand and help. But I have to ask this. Is it possible— you know, in your opinion, if you take a totally open-minded attitude toward this—that this Richard Jarrow could be somebody you invented in your head? I mean, things like that have happened before. Sometimes, when a person—"

There was no point in continuing with that line. "No, he's not a figment of my imagination," Jarrow interrupted. "I'm a real person. Go to Minneapolis and check it out if you want. There are plenty of records, people I worked with."

Rita conceded with a nod. "Okay. Sometimes people think they're somebody else who's real too."

Jarrow couldn't contain a wry smile. "You mean it makes a change from Napoleon?"

"I didn't say you were crazy."

"You couldn't have come much closer."

"I'm sorry."

Jarrow tossed out a hand dismissively. "I've got memories, complete memories of personal things, little things. . . . It's not just a case of knowing a few facts. I've *lived* Jarrow's life. Hiking as a kid, around the lakes in Minnesota. Birthdays, Christmases, the house I grew up in. Other people in the family. How could Tony Demiro know about things like that?"

By unconsciously inventing them to fill in the gaps, he could see her thinking to herself—but she wasn't about to press the issue right now. Approaching it, instead, from a different angle, she said, "But if Jarrow doesn't look like Tony, then where's the person that he *does* look like? See what I mean? If this guy Jarrow is real, then the person who all these people in Minneapolis know must still be walking around somewhere. If you're him, then who's he? Where does he fit in?"

"He's not walking around," Jarrow said. "I tried talking to those people, but all I got was a hard time." He realized then, with a sinking feeling, that he could have an even tougher problem convincing Rita. She, after all, had her own explanation worked out. And it was irrefutable.

"Why?" Rita asked, glancing across at him again. Her tone was challenging, as if he had just made her point for her. "If they know the guy, how come they couldn't buy that they were talking to him?"

Jarrow sighed hopelessly. "Richard Jarrow died of a stroke in May," he replied.

After traveling a few miles north on Cicero they exited eastward, toward the upthrust of skyline massed behind the Sears Tower and the Federal Center. Relics from an age of bygone affluence, the monuments glittered like frosty cliffs in the last light of day against the sky darkening over Lake Michigan.

They entered an older part of the city, south of center and west of the Ship Canal and south branch of the Chicago River, from what Jarrow could remember. The streets were mainly of solid, high-built, stone and timber row houses, bearing the signs of transformation over the years as successive waves of fad or commercial promise came and went. There were cinemas that had been bowling alleys, then supermarkets, and had now become miniature malls of sandwich shops and oddments stalls, or capacious used-furniture emporiums piled with Brobdingnagian discards—symptomatic of a time when three-car-garage villas in Du Page and Lake counties were being traded for renovated duplexes within walking distance of the Loop. Brick-formed Carlsbads originally built as warehouses had been transformed first into light engineering factories; then later, as industry declined, into antique galleries to professional offices; and were now cellularized into studios and singles apartments. Like butchers who took pride in using everything from the ears to the hoof, it seemed that people loathed letting any part of their cities go to waste.

The street that Rita finally pulled into consisted of two rows of faded, four-floor brownstone walkups facing each other across a short length of pavement with snow heaped along the sides. A group of noisy, heavily muffled children who were playing halfway along moved aside as the car squelched past. Past them, a group of youths was standing around a fire burning in an oil drum by a wooden fence that closed off the far end of the street. Rita parked on the right almost at the end, and led Jarrow up one of the flights of wide, iron-railed steps leading to the front doors. She found her key and let them into a hallway that smelt of cats and musty carpet, from where they went up to one of what appeared to be two flats on the second floor. She shared with a girl called Margaret, she told him, more for the sake of saying something, as they went in.

Feeling more like an intruder than a guest, Jarrow followed her into the living room and looked around. The place was cramped, but cleanly kept and appealingly feminine, with fresh, warm colors, soft furnishings, and flowery decor. Before he had a chance to take off his coat, he was startled to see a picture of himself staring from a niche in the corner, in T-shirt and jeans, grinning and leaning with folded arms against a red pickup.

Then he remembered that, no, that was not *him*. It was Tony Demiro.

fourteen

Rita took off her scarf and coat and hung them behind the door, revealing a chunky beige sweater and black slacks. She shook her head, and her hair tumbled free in a bouncy red cascade, filling out the face that had seemed tight and strained outside. Her mouth still had the firmness that had struck Jarrow when he saw her on the phone that afternoon, although softened by an earthy femininity that was more pronounced at close quarters. Her eyes were a light greeny-gray, and her skin had a spattering of faint freckles that hadn't shown on the screen. Jarrow's impression was of a woman who would not be easily deflected from her opinions once she had formed them, and from their brief crossing of swords in the car it was evident that on some matters those opinions put her in a very different camp from his own.

But things like that didn't have to affect matters one way or the other. He was here for one reason only: so that Rita could tell him more about where Demiro fitted in. He had no interest in dragging this out any further than was necessary to learn whatever she knew. At the same time, he was under no illusions that all would be as simple as that. For it was already clear that Rita saw the situation in another light, and that she was motivated by very different hopes as to its outcome.

"I hate quiet," Rita said. "Mind if we have some noise?"

"I don't mind. It's your place."

She went over to a crystal-player—so called because the holo-plate cartridges looked like postage-stamp-size tiles of glass—and touched a button to start a preset selection of tunes. Then she moved to the window, which looked out over the rear of the house, and closed the drapes. "How about a coffee after that cold out there?"

"Do you have coylene?" He was referring to the soy-derived substitute that people were being encouraged to switch to.

"Coylene?" Rita looked surprised. More evidence that he wasn't Tony. "No, I'm afraid we don't. How about decaf?"

"That'll be fine."

She went over to the kitchen area that formed one corner of the living room and began filling the pot. "How do you take it?"

"A splash of cream, no sugar."

"You might as well take off your coat."

Jarrow hung his coat by hers and sat down on a couch by a low table near the window. While Rita busied herself with mugs, dishes, and spoons, using movement to keep herself occupied, his eyes roamed over the flat. There were two other doors, one open, obviously the bathroom, the other probably a bedroom. More pictures of Demiro adorned the walls, some showing him and Rita together, others of another girl whom he guessed was Margaret, fair and slightly pudgy-looking; a pile of women's magazines on a shelf, the kind that featured fashion, pop psychology, and sexual titillations disguised as advice; more shelves with racks holding music crystals, along with books, mainly fiction; posters from New York and the Grand Canyon; an old computer, which from the stuff piled around and on top of it was either seldom used or not working; a framed picture of Demiro in uniform, with an Army cap-badge fixed at the top of the frame.

"I, ah, I get the feeling you and Tony were kind of close," Jarrow said, looking back at Rita.

"We were planning on getting married, if that's what you mean."

"Oh, God. I really had no idea."

"How about a cookie as well?"

"Not really."

"Cheese or something? We've got potato chips and other munchies."

"No, thank you." Jarrow stared fixedly at the table, feeling his mind gluing in its search for a line to continue, as he had known would happen. His chronic discomfort with women had long ago become sufficiently a part of his life to have this self-fulfilling quality about it. The suspicion of possibly invading her private space, intimate surroundings that she might have shared with her dead fiancé, didn't help matters. He seized upon the thought for something to say and waved a hand vaguely at the surroundings. "Did you and Tony, I mean . . ."

"No. We had a mobile home out at Hodgkins. That's on the way to Kankakee, where he was based."

"So you've been here, how long?"

"Since August. I moved into the city after you . . ." Rita checked herself and picked up a pack of cigarettes that she had taken from her coat pocket, "after Tony was reported killed."

Jarrow stared down at his interlaced fingers, exhaled heavily, then looked up. "Listen, Rita . . . I know how you must feel. This has got to be a lot tougher for you than it is for me."

She stared at him for a moment; then her face softened, and she nodded to acknowledge that he was trying and she appreciated it. "I'm not too sure about that," she replied. "I don't wake up finding I'm someone else every morning."

They looked at each other, both feeling the first flicker of real communication. It seemed to say that in this much at least, they were on the same side. And with that, a part of the oppressiveness that had been hanging over the room since they came in lightened. Rita lit her cigarette and came over with two mugs to sit down in a cane chair facing the table. Jarrow reached out and pushed the ashtray closer to her.

"What are we going to do?" she sighed.

"All we can do: just keep sifting through what we know to see what comes out of it," he said. She nodded. Jarrow picked up his coffee and took a sip. "When was Tony supposed to have died, exactly?"

"June sixteenth. I was notified about a week later."

"By the Army?"

"Yes."

"They notified you, not his family?"

"Tony didn't have any family that he'd ever traced. He was an orphan. I was listed as his nearest relative-equivalent."

"What happened . . . as far as you were told?"

"Around a year ago—I think it was early last October—he volunteered for a special assignment. It was all secret. I didn't know what it was about, not then. But it seems it was something to do with a new technique for speeding up military training by transplanting whole patterns of things into somebody's head that other guys had already learned."

Jarrow looked up sharply. "How did you find out if it was so secret? Did he tell you?"

Rita drew quickly on her cigarette and shook her head. "Tony didn't blab about things he shouldn't, and I didn't press him to. *You* told me, on Monday—when we were in Atlanta."

Of course. That was when he was supposed to have *been* Demiro, Jarrow reminded himself. "Did you hear from him in all that time?"

"At first he used to come back on leave about once a month, but as I said he didn't talk then about what was going on. Later I got letters that had been censored." Rita sighed, shrugged, and took a drink of coffee in a way that said there really wasn't much more to tell. "Then this officer called at the place in Hodgkins one day and said Tony had been killed in a helicopter accident. Regrets and condolences and all that stuff. There was an official letter later, confirming it . . . and his things arrived in a plastic bag a couple of weeks later. That's what happens to your dreams." Rita's voice caught; her hand quivered as she set the mug down on the table. "And half a year later the phone rings, it's you . . . no, you *were* Tony on Monday . . . and you've just woken up in Atlanta."

At last Jarrow was getting information. He didn't want her going off into reminiscences right now. Another mystery that this might shed some light on was the change that had come over him the night before, after he left the bar in Minneapolis.

"What did Tony do in the Army?" he asked. "Was he involved in hand-to-hand combat, or with some elite fighting unit, maybe— anything like that?"

Rita looked surprised and shook her head. "Tony? Hell no. His whole idea of army life was that it would have been great if you didn't have to go and fight people sometimes."

"So what did he do?"

"He ran an office full of clerks in a transport depot."

"I see." Jarrow was perplexed. "How about hobbies and sports? Was he interested in martial arts, gymnastics . . . anything like that, athletic?"

Rita shook her head again. "He liked to enjoy life, sure, but that kind of hard work wasn't his idea of enjoyment. He partied a lot and had fun when he was in one kind of mood; then he'd maybe go off and like to be by himself and read when he was in another. He just wasn't a violent kind of person." She let her eyes flicker over Jarrow for a second, then added, "Although I have to say, you look as if you've been in training. That's a leaner, tougher body than the one I remember—and Tony wasn't exactly what you'd call flabby."

Jarrow blinked in surprise. He had never been described that way before. "What kind of things did Tony read?" he asked.

"Oh, science fiction, sports mags, westerns, sometimes. When he was in one of his serious moods, maybe history and politics. Arguing politics was the only kind of contest he got into with other guys. It got him into trouble sometimes at the base."

"What were his politics?"

Rita sighed. "I think you already have an idea. I don't think you and he would really have gotten along. I hear you as"—she made a we-are-being-frank-aren't-we, rocking motion with her head—"well, kind of straight and uptight, all for the system. That's what they'd want a teacher to be like, right?"

"Maybe."

"Well, Tony wasn't that way. He thought all this environmental stuff is crap, and the things you hear all the time about we've-got-to-control-this and we-have-to-regulate-that are just pretexts for keeping one bunch of people on top and the rest of us down here. But in the long run it can't last. It's just digging itself deeper into the ground. He figured the only way left to go was out."

"Out? You mean to somewhere else?"

Rita exhaled a stream of smoke away from him and stubbed her cigarette. "Right, FER. Offworld, maybe. Well, nobody's going to change down here, are they?"

Jarrow sat back. He didn't agree, but that kind of thing could wait until another time. Demiro couldn't have picked anyone more unlike himself to have transformed into; or Jarrow couldn't, to have taken over—whatever had happened. There was an ironic side to it all, he had to admit.

"I must sound like the perfect Jekyll and Hyde," he said. "Is that what you're thinking too? I bet you've got some kind of a theory that Jarrow is an opposite personality that Tony created in his head to resolve some kind of conflict or something." He saw the resigned look starting to form around her mouth. "Yes?"

A nod, accompanied by a slightly sheepish smile. "Something like that," she agreed.

The music stopped, marking a short pause before the next number. Rita didn't notice, but just at that instant a soft creak came from the landing outside the apartment door. That in itself wouldn't have been enough to make Jarrow's head whip around like that of a pointer catching a sudden scent, but the way the sound stopped abruptly a split second after the music ceased triggered deep-seated alarm responses, tuned and sensitized to stealth; responses that weren't his.

And then came a barely audible double click that would have meant nothing to Richard Jarrow . . . but which something inside him registered instantly as the slide-action of an automatic pistol, loading a round into the chamber.

He was at the door before Rita had even reacted to the first movement of his head. While his hands slammed home the security bolt and engaged the chain, his eyes raced over the room's contents, estimating sizes and weights. The door handle turned, there was an ineffective shove, then a series of loud raps. Jarrow heaved a bookcase over sideways to fall onto a hall table on the far side of the door, blocking it diagonally, then pushed an armchair behind it. Rita rose to her feet, knocking the table and spilling her coffee in her haste, her eyes wide.

"Tony, what the fuck do you think—"

The door rattled ineffectually, then a voice yelled from the other side. "Samurai, it's okay. It's us: Marty and Hank. It's okay, understand? We just want to talk. Open the door, willya?"

Jarrow moved the kitchen table behind the armchair, a cabinet behind that, and then turned the couch from the window around to form a chain of objects butting up against each other to the far wall. Rita watched, petrified.

The door shook under a louder thud, accompanied by a splintering noise. "Samurai, for Christ's sake, *it's okay!* Open the goddam door."

Jarrow snatched his coat and threw Rita's at her as he crossed to the door of the bedroom. He flung it open, and pertinent facts registered themselves like data being tagged in a computer: *one window, drapes open, facing rear from same wall as in living room; dark outside; recollection of street layout: elevated row houses with rear yards back-to-back; probable mode of approach: frontally up main stairs, with backup positioned halfway along street, rear of building staked out from the neighboring yards.*

He moved to the window and peered through, keeping himself in the dark to one side. The yards were separated by wooden fences, with toolsheds and garden structures in places, indistinct in the gloom. The row of houses on the far side of the intervening yards was split halfway along by a narrow alley. That was where he would have positioned the backup team at the rear, he decided: kept back to avoid setting all the dogs off. Possibly they'd have sent two men forward as stakeouts. His eyes scanned the layout like search radars, following the line that the stakeout pair would have taken from the end of the alley, picking out the patches of shadow that they would have made for. A few feet below the window was the smaller roof of an extension from the house. The crash came from the next room of the lock giving way and the door jamming into the barricade.

Rita was beside him, shaking with terror. "Who are they? What—"

He made a chopping motion with one hand: his manner, in contrast to that of the mild schoolteacher with whom she had entered, carrying such total authority that she fell silent at once. He looked up at the light: bedroom, probably low wattage. Better chances with something brighter. "Light bulbs," he snapped. "Where are they?"

"K-kitchen," she stammered.

"Fetch the biggest you've got." She nodded and disappeared back through the doorway. From beyond it, more splintering sounds came, of the front door being pried off its hinges. Jarrow took out the bulb in the room and tossed it onto one of the beds, then went to the window, released the catch, and checked that it moved freely.

Rita was back. "Hundred fifty. Biggest there is."

"Screw it in." While Rita complied, Jarrow locked the door and made another barricade from the beds and vanity, at the same time speaking rapidly. "Do exactly as I say. Turn the light on, then go to the window. Talk back into the room in a loud voice for five seconds, as if I'm behind you. Then go back to the switch and turn it off, but keep talking. Wait until I call, then get down onto that roof. If those guys get to this door, get out anyway."

She nodded tightly. Jarrow dropped to the floor and crawled to below the window. "Now," he told her.

Rita turned on the light and moved to stand silhouetted in the window frame. "What are you doing over there?" she called back. "Look, I don't know about you, but as far as I'm . . ." She went back to the door and flipped the switch.

As darkness filled the room again, Jarrow opened the window and flowed as if his body were liquid, silently over the sill and down onto the annex roof beneath, blending into its cover in the second or two that eyes watching from below would have taken to readjust from the brief glare. He wormed his way to a projecting corner cloaked in the shadows of a tree, and straightened up cautiously to explore around with his fingers. They found a down pipe, but to get to it he would have to stand on a sliver of roof only inches wide extending beyond the corner, and then make a long step to a pipe end sticking out of the wall. He made the move deftly and effortlessly with the ease of a Yosemite climber, lowered himself by the down pipe, and dropped noiselessly behind a fence skirting the rear patio.

In a patch of darkness in the yard of the house behind, agent Barney Costello of the Federal Security Service craned his neck trying to make out what was happening. First the light had come on in the window, and the Chilsen girl appeared, shouting to somebody else who had to be Samurai. Then the light had gone off again.

"She's still yelling at the window," Costello muttered into his radio. "I can't figure what it's about."

"Keep watching," came the reply. "Two of the guys from Pearse are in the front door, but there's nobody there. Samurai and the girl must be in the back room."

They're coming out this way, Costello thought to himself. All he had nearby was Kopel, posted in the adjacent yard. Better bring some of the backup guys forward from the alley on the next street . . .

And that was the last thing he thought for more than the next hour. Jarrow caught the limp form as it fell, frisking it quickly and taking the gun, ammunition clip, radio, and set of car keys on a ring with a remote button.

Fifty feet away in the next yard, Kopel, crouched behind a

toolshed, heard a muffled movement. "Barney?" he hissed. "Is everything okay over there? . . . Barney?"

An arm slid around his neck from behind, tightening like a steel band to cut off the main artery to the brain and causing him to slump senseless after a few seconds.

At the back of the house, Rita clambered out onto the annex roof as banging came from inside the window behind her. She moved warily to the edge and peered down into the darkness. "They're getting into the bedroom. Are you there?"

Jarrow materialized below her. "Turn around and let yourself drop," he hissed.

Across the way, drapes were parting in some of the windows. "What the hell's going on out there?" a voice yelled. Somebody else let out a dog, which erupted in a frenzy of barking.

Jarrow caught her as she dropped, and steered her to the fence separating the next yard. He guided her over, then vaulted after her, repeating the process a number of times to move them several houses along the row. Behind them, a figure appeared in the window of Rita's flat and leaned out, peering into the darkness. "They musta come out this way. Anybody down there?"

Jarrow and Rita were in the concrete yard of a house showing a light in the ground-floor rear window. Jarrow knocked sharply on the back door. A pause. Nothing. He knocked again. "Who is it?" a voice demanded inside. "What's going on out there?"

"Police," Jarrow snapped. "Open up. Emergency."

The door rattled and opened as far as the security chain would permit. "Got some ID?" the voice inquired.

"Right here."

A man's face appeared close to the crack. Jarrow shot one hand through, grabbing him by the shirtfront, and rammed the gun that he had taken hard up under his chin with the other. "We just need to come through, okay? Open the door and nobody gets hurt. We have to get to the street."

The door opened. Jarrow shoved the man back against the wall and sent Rita on through with a curt nod, ignoring the woman who was cowering against a countertop on the far side of a table with dishes and two half-eaten meals. "Just sit tight and enjoy the rest of your dinner," he murmured to the couple as he closed the door. Then he followed quickly through after Rita.

They emerged from a side door below the front steps of a house about halfway along the street. The car that Rita had borrowed was parked back outside the front of her place, which was where most of the backup squad would be, following the lead men inside or waiting. So they couldn't use that. The computer still working inside Jarrow's head told him that they didn't want to, anyway: her car had probably been bugged with a locator device ever since Rita left it at the airport. He looked the other way along the street and picked out the three cars that belonged to whoever was after them. Two were empty; the other had a couple of figures inside.

"Wait here," he murmured into Rita's ear. "Be ready to move fast."

He came out onto the sidewalk and walked rapidly toward the cars, at the same time taking out the keys he'd collected and pressing the remote button. The lights of one of the empty cars flashed in response, and Jarrow headed toward it. It was pointing the wrong way, toward the street's dead end, whereas the car with the two figures in was turned around. But he'd just have to take his chances.

He was inside and starting the motor before the two men in the other car realized what was happening. As Jarrow pulled away, one of them got out and called at him. "Hey! Who is that? What's going on?"

Jarrow whirled the wheel, sending the car skidding across the street into a snow mound, then back into reverse for a turn, wheels screeching.

"What the hell? *Hey, stop!*"

The agent just managed to leap clear as Jarrow came out of the turn. But the driver in the other car had thought quickly and was already moving. Jarrow cut in toward the sidewalk, throwing open the passenger door as Rita ran from the gate of the house they had come out of. As she tumbled in, the other car came up alongside and angled across their front to block them off, its front inside wheel plowing into the snowbank in the gutter. Front-wheel drive model, Jarrow registered. He slammed into reverse again, backed up, and changed to forward to go around the outside. As he'd figured, it took the other car a few vital seconds of wheel-spinning and lurching to unstick, which was all he needed to pull past it. But as they got to the end of the street he saw in his mirror that it was free and accelerating to follow them. Farther back behind it, figures were running out into the street from Rita's house.

"Hunch your back. Grip your neck hard with both hands," Jarrow ordered tersely.

Judging his moment, he hit the brakes and at the same time kicked into reverse again. The driver of the other car closing behind had no chance to avoid the impact. They hit with a loud rending crash that echoed along the short street. Leaving the other car immobilized with a stoved-in radiator, Jarrow accelerated forward once more, spinning the wheel first one way, then the other to take the corner like an unleashed rocket sleigh.

But a known car with a crumpled rear end wasn't exactly the most likely thing to have hopes of vanishing in for very long. They ditched it a half mile west, hailed the next passing cab, and Jarrow told the driver to take them to Union Station, which was the first place to come to mind in the opposite direction, toward the city. There, they changed to another cab, the driver of which would have no reason to connect them with the area where the ditched car would be found—if it hadn't been already.

"Where to?" the cabbie asked.

"Just go south on Lake Shore," Jarrow said.

Rita sank back in the seat and exhaled a long, quavering breath. Ever since Jarrow's first sudden move back at the flat, things had been happening too fast, and her mind had been in too much of a turmoil for a shred of coherent thought to form. Beside her, he was silent.

"Okay," she said, when her shaking had abated sufficiently for her to speak. "So, what kind of a school do you teach at? Tell me again that it's junior high."

But then to her surprise she saw in the passing streetlights that Jarrow too was trembling, and his face was wet with perspiration.

"I don't understand." His icy control and commanding manner were gone, and in their place his voice was barely a croak. "Something like this happened before. . . . Look, I can't explain now. We have to find somewhere to stay out of sight. Are there any people who you can trust?"

Rita thought for a moment, then nodded. "I think I know a place. Want me to take us there?"

"Drop us somewhere close. Don't give him the location."

Rita leaned forward and opened the driver's partition. "Driver, could we make that Clybourn, please?"

"You know that's completely the other way?"

"I know. We've had a change of plan."

The cabbie shrugged. "You're paying."

They turned at a gap in the center divider of the road and began heading back, toward the north end of Chicago. Jarrow now reverted once more to his "normal" self, and the first thing he did after the cab dropped them off was lose the gun and the other items that he had taken down a storm drain on the side of the road.

fifteen

They walked to a corner of a street of older redbrick houses standing opposite some shops, mostly closed by this time of night, and a bar standing beside a drab restaurant. It was quiet and deserted, with mist swirling in the glow of a few watery yellow streetlights.

"It's just along here, on this side," Rita said, pointing.

"Who are these people again?" Jarrow asked.

"Their names are Sandy and Bruce. They're old friends. Tony and I knew them for years."

"And you're sure they're reliable?" Jarrow was his normal hesitant self again. Just as in Minneapolis, the transformation had reversed itself as quickly as it had happened. Now, the knowledge that they were being hunted added more to his uncertainty and confusion.

"They're both okay," Rita assured him. She looked along the row of houses and thought for a moment. "Look, maybe it would be better if I go on ahead and talk to them first to give them some idea of what to expect. . . . I mean, this kind of thing doesn't happen every day. Can you wait here?"

Jarrow nodded.

"I'll be back in two minutes. Just give me a chance to explain first, okay?" She waited until he nodded again, then walked away and merged into the shadows of one of the doorways a short distance away in the gloom. Jarrow turned and moved a few paces away around the corner, exhaling white vapor into the chilly night air and stamping his feet against the cold seeping up through his shoes. That was something else he should have bought. Gordon's choice of footwear might have been fine in Georgia, but Chicago in November at this time of evening was something else.

What did it mean, this sudden change that had taken place in him twice now? It seemed to be triggered reflexively when danger threatened, as if from some depth of his being over which he had no voluntary control. And according to Rita, Demiro had been involved in a secret experimental program to transplant ready-learned behavior as an aid to military training. Furthermore, a conditioning to violence seemed to fit with the pointers that Jarrow had found in Atlanta to the kind of person Maurice Gordon was—or, more likely, he was beginning to suspect, had been a cover for. A cover for what? What had the men who had broken into Rita's called him?— "Samurai." It sounded like a code name. And they had acted as if they knew him. Jarrow pulled his coat tighter and stared at the murky outlines of the buildings across the street. As discomforting as he found the thought, there could be no denying that in a grisly but compelling kind of way that had to be faced, the pieces were starting to fit together.

Inside the house, Bruce, looking surprised but pleased, brought Rita into the kitchen, where Sandy was trying to introduce more baby cereal into their eight-month-old daughter, Alice, than was already plastered in her hair, ears, and nose and all over her hands and clothes. The piles of dishes, laundry, and food still not put away told of one of those days when entropy had won out.

"It's Rita," Bruce said unnecessarily. "Come on in. It's a hell of a cold night to take a walk. I thought it was one of those college kids from the welfare department, checking to make sure we know which end to put the diaper on."

"Hi," Sandy said. "Grab a chair if you can find one. Alice is having one of her frisky days. Isn't that right, Alice? . . . There, tastes good, huh? It might work better if I made this into pies and threw 'em at her. Bruce, put on some coffee for us, would you, hon?"

"Thanks," Rita said. "You'd better make it four."

At the clipped note in her voice, Bruce turned his head, then saw her face properly for the first time. "Hey, what's up?"

Sandy straightened up, forgetting her encrusted daughter for the moment. "Rita, what is it? What's happened?"

"Anybody got a cigarette?" Rita hadn't had one since she was at the flat, having left hers behind in the rush to get out. Bruce produced a pack from a drawer after some searching. He used them occasionally, and there were only a few left. Rita took one and held it steady with some effort while he lit it. "Thanks." She looked up at him, across at Sandy, and exhaled. "Tony isn't dead. He's come back." They stared incredulously. Bruce started to say something, but Rita stopped him with a quick motion of her hand. "I don't know where he's been or what's been going on. He arrived in town today from Minneapolis."

"Tony? Alive? But, but . . ." Sandy shook her head. "Is he okay?"

"Where is he?" Bruce asked, similarly astounded.

"That's the whole point. He's got some kind of amnesia . . . but not only that. It's not just that he doesn't know who he is. He thinks he's someone else completely. I mean it's total, a completely different personality. But apart from that he seems quite rational." Rita looked at Bruce. "He's outside, just along the street. . . . Look, we had some trouble back at the flat. There are some guys after him. I mean heavy stuff, with guns. I don't know who they are. They came busting into the place."

"Jesus Christ!" Bruce exclaimed.

"What happened to them?" Sandy asked, horrified.

"We got out and managed to lose them. That's another story. But we need to get inside off the streets, and we can't go back there tonight." Rita looked around at the room and gestured imploringly. "So what I'm saying is, is there any way we could . . ."

"Well, sure." Bruce's tone conveyed that she should have known better than to ask.

"It's so weird that I thought I ought to come in first and let you know how he is. And he agreed—I mean, he's not acting crazy or anything. But he's convinced he's somebody called Jarrow, Dick Jarrow. That's what I've been calling him. So just try and, kind of, go along with it for now, okay? Tomorrow will be a better time to figure out what to do."

"Get him inside," Sandy said. "He'll freeze out there."

Rita brought Jarrow in a few minutes later. There were some awkward preliminaries. Hard as they tried, Sandy and Bruce found it impossible to disguise the strangeness of being introduced to somebody they had known closely for years. "Don't feel too bad about it," Jarrow told them. "I know how this must feel. I've had a couple of days to get used to this, and I'm still having a problem."

They talked for a while over coffee, self-consciously at first, more or less repeating what Rita had already said in brief, but it gave Sandy and Bruce a chance to adapt. Then Sandy excused herself and went to get Alice washed and put to bed. Bruce began a brave attack upon the havoc of the kitchen and Rita rose to help, while Jarrow remained at the table, hands clasped around his mug.

"What were you doing in Minneapolis?" Bruce asked him as he moved to clear the table.

"It's where I live. I went back to where I'm from," Jarrow told him.

"Yeah. . . . Right," Bruce agreed, but still with detectable absence of conviction. "And you've no idea who these guys were who broke into Rita and Margaret's place?"

"No. They must have been watching either Rita or the place. The only thing I can think of is that they followed her from Atlanta."

"He called me from Atlanta on Monday," Rita explained.

"But there was no mention of any Dick Jarrow then," Rita said. "He was Tony, his old self. He'd woken up in a hotel there, and that was all he knew."

"But Georgia was where he transferred to last year, when he went on that special assignment," Bruce observed. "Where was it?"

"A place called Pearse," Rita said.

"Right. So there has to be some connection."

Rita went on, "The last thing he remembered was being at Pearse sometime last May. There was nothing then about anything that had to do with flying in helicopters."

Bruce turned toward Jarrow from the sink, where he had been stacking dishes. "Any idea what you were doing in Atlanta on Monday?"

Jarrow shook his head. "No."

The door opened and Sandy came back in. "Well, there's some justice in life after all. She went out like a light. Little snot—must run on some infinite energy source that science hasn't discovered yet. . . . Oh, thanks, Bruce."

"Needs a man's touch," Bruce grunted.

"How are we doing?" Sandy inquired, looking around.

"It's the strangest story I've heard for a long time," Bruce said. "No, wrong. It's the strangest story I've heard anytime. I don't know what to make of it. But I'm just an out-of-work machine operator. What do I know about any of it?"

"What happened to Margaret in all this?" Sandy asked.

Rita put a hand to her mouth. "Oh, Christ, I forgot about Margaret. She was out. What's she going to come back to? The place looked like it had been bombed."

"Will those guys still be around?" Bruce asked.

"How would I know?"

"Try giving her a call," Sandy suggested, indicating a traditional audio-only phone hanging over the half-height refrigerator.

Bruce lifted it off the hook and was about to tap in the number, then hesitated. "We don't know who they were," he said, looking at the others. "Do you think it might be tapped? Could they trace a calling number back to here?"

Rita glanced at Sandy. They both shrugged.

"I wouldn't risk it," Jarrow said from the table. "With computers they can do anything."

A few seconds of baffled silence ensued. Then Sandy said, "I guess we could always call from someplace else. Does that sound overdramatic, you know, too much like the movies?"

"Not to me it doesn't," Rita answered.

"I'll get Eric to call her," Bruce said. "He's on the other side of town."

"Who's Eric?" Jarrow asked.

"Another friend, student at University of Chicago," Bruce replied. "He's okay."

"Don't you call him, Bruce," Rita said. "Let me do it. If he hears from you, it'll be obvious where I've gone. If I call him, it could be from anywhere. People can't give away what they don't know."

Bruce nodded, picked up the phone again, and handed it to her.

"I just want him to let Margaret know that I'm okay, I know about the mess there, and I'll explain later," she said, taking it.

The others waited, keeping silent while Rita made the call. She kept it brief, told Eric that she'd call again in the morning, and hung up. The four of them exchanged looks that agreed there was nothing more that they could do now.

Sandy sighed and stretched out her arms to relieve aching muscles. "Whew, what a day. Well, now that the demolition machine's asleep, maybe we can get to eat too. Can I get you guys a sandwich or something? When did you last have a bite?"

"I don't know. It feels like sometime last week," Rita said. Now that her nerves were recovering, she was beginning to realize how much all the tension had taken out of her.

Jarrow had glimpsed how bare the refrigerator was while Bruce was putting the things away. "Is there a pizza place or anything like that near here?" he asked.

"A block and a half away," Sandy answered.

Jarrow felt inside his jacket for Gordon's wallet. "Then order a couple of big ones," he said. "And a six-pack or two to go with them. It's on me."

sixteen

Pearse Psychological Research Laboratories lay a little under fifty miles northwest of Atlanta, hidden among the wooded valleys forming the edge of the Dahlonega Plateau, the southern end of the Appalachians. What was now the Main Complex, containing the major laboratory and administration blocks, had been built originally as the research facility of private genetic engineering interests, closed down by animal-rights lobbying. Since its takeover as a military facility, a patchwork of more sprawling extensions had attached themselves in a succession of uncoordinated additions. The establishment oversaw and instituted programs connected with various aspects of military psychology and psychological warfare, stresses of combat environments, maintenance of morale, optimization of training methods, and a few other things that weren't publicly talked about.

Names only would be used for the volunteers, Demiro had been told; ranks would not be disclosed. He arrived with another soldier who gave his name as Schott, and a black called Lowe, who had been collected at the airport by the same shuttle bus. They had exchanged the usual basic data on the ride back to Pearse. Lowe was from Mississippi, had had postings in Venezuela and Alaska, had been a bugler, still played jazz trumpet, would lay odds on any sport, and thought that being in bed with a woman was the most natural thing in the world because he'd been born that way. Schott was more taciturn, but from the few things he said he came from New York State and thought that one thing to be said for army life as opposed to civilian was that at least you didn't have to choose who got to

push you around. Neither of them had any more idea than Demiro
did of what the assignment at Pearse was about. Lowe had volunteered to escape an amorous entanglement involving a sergeant's
wife; Schott said he was just curious to find out what kinds of things
happened on programs that volunteers were invited for.

They checked in at a guardhouse by the main gate, where IDs
and security clearances were verified, and were escorted to one of
several regular army-style billet huts in a compound on one side of
the Main Complex, which they were told would be their assigned
quarters. A number of other volunteers for the same program were
already unpacking kits into lockers and settling in, having picked the
best bunk spaces. A Sergeant Eades, from Pearse itself, was in
charge, standard Army product, stiff-backed, pressed and creased,
and would evidently be handling routine administrative and day-
to-day matters.

They had lunch, eleven of them, plus the sergeant and a couple
of other NCOs that they'd be working with, in a canteen located
outside an internal security perimeter that was designated the
Restricted Zone and included most of the Main Complex. That was
where the classified work went on, and anyone without high-level
clearance required escort at all times. This was when people com-
peted in the heats for first impressions, and the initial forays were
made to rough out whatever pecking order would finally assert
itself. Demiro tended to a lower-profile role, keeping eyes and ears
open. As an old cowhand turned bar owner had told him once when
he was a kid growing up in Denver, "Y' don't learn nuthin' while yer
talkin'."

After lunch the shuttle bus returned from another pickup at the
airport, bringing the total number of recruits up to twenty. When the
newcomers had been installed and given a chance to clean up, they
were all taken to a room in the Facilities Block, again still outside the
Restricted Zone, for a preliminary briefing.

The warm-up man was a Major Gleavey: a smiling Mr. Personality, everybody's friend—perhaps a frustrated talk-show host or
prime-time variety compere. He welcomed the company to the
establishment, enthusing about it as if it were a Boy Scout camp,
stressed the importance of team spirit and making the effort to fit in,
and promised them some "truly fascinating and exciting things" if

they stayed with it. He wanted this to be a happy place. The secret of success in anything was to learn to work together. And, of course, ". . . if you've got any problems, come to me, okay?"

He then introduced Colonel Wylvern, who, as most of the men present had already discerned for themselves, would be in ultimate charge of things while Gleavey did the legwork and fronting. He didn't make any especially spectacular impact: the kind of CO whom they'd all seen a dozen times before, square-set and solid, with wavy hair, a touch of floridness about the features, sufficiently aloof and remote to maintain a distance of militarily proper impartiality. He delivered a set-piece recitation on the importance of security, a warning that infractions of discipline would not be tolerated, and some words about the privilege of having an opportunity to serve the nation in this way. Nothing new or interesting there. Wylvern ended, "This may look like a small-time, backwater project from the scale of it and the limited number of you here, but I can assure you that it has national importance. In fact, it's under the personal direction of a general, who'll be making himself known in due course, after we've made some initial progress."

Then it was the turn of the civilian in a dark gray suit who had been sitting listening without change of expression through all this, and drawing curious looks from the troops. He was tight about the face and lean-jawed, which drew his mouth into a thin-lipped line that hinted of humorlessness, determination, or both, an impression strengthened by the narrow, tinily knotted necktie—constraining his person, as he perhaps did his emotions—and the cold eyes staring out through rimless bifocal spectacles. "Economy" was the word to summarize what everything about him seemed to project. He expended no unnecessary effort in his movements; there was no pointless expressiveness in his manner, nor sartorial elegances in his dress. Gleavey, whom Demiro had already dubbed inwardly as "Glee-show," introduced him as Dr. Nordens. And it quickly turned out that Nordens didn't waste anything in words, either.

"We'll be exploring a new territory of science, concerning the mind and how it functions. We are looking for a particular type of subject to help in these researches, and the first part of the program will consist of further testing and selection before we move on to the program itself. For obvious reasons I can't go into details at this stage. But I can say that those of you who remain can expect to acquire skills and abilities that you never thought possible. The rest of today is available for you to relax and settle in. We begin work tomorrow morning, at eight-thirty sharp. The schedule will be posted. Thank you." He sat down.

The official designation of the project they were now part of, the men learned, would be "Southside."

seventeen

The house had been subdivided into several family units, so space was limited. Bruce cleared away some junk and boxes in a small room that would eventually be Alice's and set up a folding bed there for Rita, while Jarrow made do with a couple of blankets on the living-room couch. It was comfortable enough, but he slept fitfully, unable to disengage his mind from continual replays of the things that had happened since his awakening in Atlanta. It didn't seem possible for it to have been only two days. What amazed him most was the uncanny way in which he knew just where the men who had come for him at Rita's would be and how they would react. It was almost as if he himself were one of them, and had known how people who did that kind of work would think. But he was unable to summon up any glimpse of a wider framework of associations, of which such knowledge would surely be a part.

The next morning Rita called Eric again while Sandy was scrambling eggs for breakfast. He had talked to Margaret the night before, who had sounded shaken but was otherwise all right. She had arrived home to find the street full of police, who had been called by the neighbors, taking statements everywhere. There was no sign by then of the men who had caused the disturbance. Whether that meant that they hadn't been from one of the law-enforcement agencies, or had, and were simply covering their tracks after a botched job, there was no way of telling. Eric had just called Margaret again that morning. The police had been keeping an eye on the street and there had been no further incidents. Apart from having the clearing up to do and some repairs to arrange with the landlord, Margaret was okay. Rita said she appreciated his help, promised to explain it all one day, and hung up before he could start pressing her with questions.

There was really nothing new to be said over breakfast. Rita and Jarrow must have been followed from the airport; it was obviously Jarrow that these people were interested in, since he was the one that all the strange things had been happening to; neither he nor Rita had any better notion than they'd had last night of what to do now. They couldn't go back to the flat now, Rita said. It would be exactly what the police would be waiting for, and once they got involved with them there'd be no end to it.

Sandy wanted to know why the police wouldn't be the *best* people *to* get involved with. If guys were breaking down doors and coming after her, that would be the first place she'd go. That was what police were for. Rita explained about the Maurice Gordon mystery, and the guns and other questionable items that Jarrow had been carrying in Atlanta—which she knew all about, since they'd been there when Jarrow was Tony and she was with him, the night before he woke up as Jarrow. Who knew what Gordon had been mixed up in?

"True," Sandy agreed.

And even more to the point, Jarrow reminded them, as far as the rest of the world seemed to be concerned, he was Tony Demiro. But Demiro was supposed to be dead. The official Army records said so. So something very strange and distinctly malodorous had been going on involving official departments.

"Do the police talk to the Army?" Sandy asked.

"They all talk to everybody," Rita said. "They've all got lines into each other's computers. Anything that carries what's called a general public service code can be fished out anywhere. That includes a summary listing of most routine police reports."

That settled it: they didn't want to get mixed up with official departments.

Bruce glanced at the clock. "Well," he announced, "it doesn't seem as if we're any nearer to settling anything. I have to go and see a guy in fifteen minutes about some part-time help that might bring in a few bucks."

"Oh, right. I'd forgotten about that," Sandy said. "We could sure use it."

"I should be back in under an hour."

"You go ahead," Jarrow told him. "Don't let us keep you. As you say, we aren't really any closer to settling anything."

Bruce got up and went to put on his coat. Just then the phone rang. "Ten to one it's Eric," he muttered. It was what they expected. Naturally, after Eric got the story from Margaret, he would be calling around, trying to find out where Rita had contacted him from.

"I'll get it," Sandy said, crossing the room. She picked up the receiver. "Hello? . . . Oh, Eric, hi. What's up? . . . No, why? . . . She did? . . . *You're kidding!* . . . Oh, my God, is she all right? . . ." The gist of the conversation was clear from Sandy's responses. Had she and Bruce seen or heard anything of Rita? Rita had called Eric last night and again just now, but wouldn't say from where. Eric then went on to relate the story, which Sandy of course had to listen through to be credible. She ended by assuring Eric that she'd let him know if they heard anything.

"The things I do for friends," Sandy sighed after she'd hung up.

"I won't forget it," Rita promised.

Bruce finished putting on his coat. "Anything you two need while I'm out?" he asked Rita and Jarrow. "I guess it would probably be better if you stayed inside."

"I could use some cigarettes," Rita replied. The few that Bruce had found hadn't lasted the previous evening.

"How about a paper?" Jarrow said. "There might be something about last night."

"I'll see to it," Sandy told them. "I've got to go out myself in a few minutes anyhow—do a few things and take the Wretch out for some air."

"Okay, take care." Bruce kissed her lightly and turned to the door. "See you later." He left, and they heard the front door close out in the hallway.

"You go ahead if you want," Rita told Sandy. "I can clear up in here."

Sandy grinned. "You're just jumpy for a cigarette, right?"

"Right."

Sandy hauled Alice out of the baby chair and wiped off the worst of the morning's devastations. "Okay. We shouldn't be more than half an hour. I need to stock up with a few groceries. Anything in particular you'd like?"

Jarrow took out a couple of twenties and held them out to her without asking. "Here's a contribution. We're not asking for a free hotel."

"What are you talking about?" Sandy protested. "I don't want that. You're friends of the family, for chrissakes."

"But I'm *not*," Jarrow reminded her.

Sandy and Rita caught each other's eye in a brief hiatus. Rita pursed her lips silently and looked down at the table. "Okay, we're not proud." Sandy took the bills and nodded appreciatively. "Thanks, Dick. It'll be a big help."

Sandy picked up Alice again and carried her out to the hallway, where she unfolded a stroller from its stowage space by the closet.

"Winston," Rita called after her, to remind her of the brand.

"Got it." Sandy closed the door and began the routine that she was sure she went through at least a thousand times every week of buttoning, buckling, and tying Alice into a panoply of quilted pants, coat, bonnet, furry boots, mittens, and restraining straps that would have defied Houdini.

In the kitchen, Jarrow refilled his mug and raised his eyebrows at Rita. She nodded, and he poured her another too.

"We didn't exactly get a chance to find out much about each other yesterday," he said.

Rita added a spoonful of sugar and stirred it in. "I can't imagine why not."

"You seem to know something about official data networks."

"Right, that's what I do."

"You said something about having a government job."

"I'm just a clerk—with the state Economic Coordination Bureau here. That's why I moved back into the city when you . . . when Tony disappeared. We process the permits that companies get, limiting production of indexed materials to conform to the quota assignments from the Resource Allocation Agency. I'm with a section called Petroleum-Derived Plastics. So it doesn't matter how much a customer's prepared to pay for, you can't ship more than our people say. Guess why Bruce doesn't have a job."

"You don't sound as if you approve," Jarrow commented.

"It started as part of what was supposed to change industry into putting service to the public good in place of private profit," Rita said.

"Well, that's a pretty desirable thing to strive for, isn't it?"

"I don't know, is it? Is that what you teach the kids?"

"I teach them what ought to be obvious to anyone: that industrial activity is basically damaging and polluting, and anything beyond the minimum that we have to put up with should be discouraged," Jarrow replied stiffly. He didn't like the undertone in her voice, which sounded mocking, nor did he like being cross-examined by somebody who still came across as half his age, however different it might look physically.

"But that isn't how it works," Rita said. "There's still a *lot* of profit to be made from giving out the permits. And I'm talking about private profit. When you can close down a billion-dollar plant, you make friends real easy."

"That would be illegal," Jarrow objected.

Rita laughed delightedly. "I don't believe this." Jarrow's face tightened defensively. Rita laid a restraining hand on his arm. "Sorry, don't get me wrong. You seem like a nice enough person, but you buy all this brainwashing that they pump out. Nobody down here in the real world—" The phone rang again and interrupted her.

She swung her head away to look at it. "Don't answer it," Jarrow murmured, lowering his voice instinctively, as if it might catch his voice even while still on the hook.

Rita looked back toward the door. "Has Sandy gone yet?"

She got up from her chair just as the door opened and Sandy reappeared. "Okay, I heard it." A wail went up from beyond the door. "Go and keep an eye on Wretch, or strangle her or something."

"Sure," Rita said, and hurried out. The wailing abated.

Sandy picked up the phone. "Hello? . . . Yes it is. Who's this?" She frowned as she listened. Then her eyes widened. Her expression changed suddenly, and she looked unconsciously at Jarrow with a confused, fearful expression. "No, I can't. He's dead. He was killed in an accident." Jarrow, startled, set down his mug and waited tensely. Sandy shook her head as she listened. "But, that's impossible. . . . I'm sorry, I can't help you." She listened some more, then nodded. "All right, if I do. One moment." She unhooked a tethered pen from its clip on the wall and pulled over the memo pad lying on top of the refrigerator. "Okay. . . . Yes, I said I would, if I hear anything. Good-bye." She hung up and stood staring down at what she had written.

"What is it?" Jarrow asked.

Sandy looked up bemusedly. "It was a woman—she didn't give any name. Said she wanted to get in touch with Tony Demiro. She understood we were friends of his. I told her he was dead. She said that was impossible, because she saw him two days ago in Atlanta. There's a number here to call if I hear anything."

Jarrow took the pad from her hand and looked at it. The number meant nothing to him.

"But there was more to it than that," Sandy said. "Something in her voice, I could tell. It wasn't just a casual inquiry. She *knew*."

Jarrow's main concern was that despite their precautions, they had been traced, somehow, to Bruce and Sandy's. He could only conclude ruefully that his ideas on how to lose tails left a lot to be desired.

"We have to get away from here," he said to Bruce and Sandy when they all talked things over after Bruce was back. "This isn't your problem. You've already done more than enough, and you've got other considerations to worry about. It'll be best all around if we just go now, and don't give any leads."

He was right, of course, and nobody went through the motions of arguing with him. "What are you going to do?" Sandy asked.

Jarrow spread his hands. "Call the number. It's the only way we're ever going to learn anything. Why else did that woman mention Atlanta than as a way of signaling that whoever she's with knows a lot that I'm interested in?"

But Bruce was still uneasy. "It has to be a trap," he insisted. "If they get you to a phone, they'll trace where you are. And we already know the kind of people we're talking about."

"What about public phones or vehicle phones?" Rita asked. "Can they trace those?"

"I don't know. I just know that if it were me, I wouldn't trust anything," Bruce replied.

"But they *must* know already where Rita and Dick are," Sandy said to him. "Why else would they call here?"

"Then why bother calling first at all?" Bruce said. "If they know, they could have sealed off the whole block by now."

"Maybe they're just not sure," Rita suggested. "They can't go around tearing the whole city apart on guesses—especially after last night."

"So if Rita and Tony . . . Dick, I mean . . . if they return the call, then it would confirm their location," Bruce said, feeling that it made his point.

Silence fell while everyone went over the same questions again in their minds, and came up again, inevitably, with the same answers. Finally Rita said, "There isn't any other way." Jarrow looked across, and she showed a hand imploringly. "Either we call the number and take whatever risk is involved; or we turn ourselves in to the cops and wait for whatever happens then; or we carry on hiding off the streets for the rest of time."

"I don't want to get involved with the police," Jarrow said. "Not until I know something more about who Gordon is and what he's been doing, anyway."

Rita was already nodding. "Exactly. I know. And option three isn't a way to spend a life. So we're left with option one. That's why I said there isn't any other way."

Jarrow nodded, resigning himself. They would have to deal with whoever the mysterious woman caller had spoken for. "But *you* don't have to get mixed up in this," he told Rita. "Whatever's been going on has had to do with me. I called your number from Atlanta, that's all."

The words needed saying, but he was unable to inject much conviction into them. He already knew what her answer would be.

"Look," she said. "Whatever else you may think, as far as I'm concerned you're Tony. And if you think I'm just going to let you walk out of my life again after you come back from being dead, you're out of your mind. So let's go."

They took the Howard/Englewood el into the city center and found an open shopping arcade off State Street with a line of nonscreen pay-phone booths. Jarrow made the call, while Rita stood watching from the door.

A gruff voice answered after a couple of rings. "Quincy's bar."

"Bar? Er, look, I don't know if I've got this right. I got a message. The name's Demiro. Somebody wanted me to call, but didn't give a name. She left this number."

"That's Tony, right?"

"Yes." Jarrow's eyebrows lifted in surprise. So he had got it right.

"Well, she ain't here, but I can get her to call you," the voice told him. "What's your number?"

"I'm not sure I want to say," Jarrow replied warily.

"What's up?" Rita hissed.

"It's just a bar," Jarrow whispered, raising a hand to stall her as the voice spoke again.

"Then I can't help ya. Look, I'm just doing the lady a favor, okay? I don't know what this is all about. If you want to talk to her, she'll call you. I got better things to do, you know. I run a bar, not a dating service."

"He wants this number so that she can call here," Jarrow whispered to Rita. "I'm not sure I like it."

"Tell him two minutes," Rita said.

"Just two minutes," Jarrow said into the phone. "Tell her I'll be here for two minutes, then I leave."

"Whatever you say," the voice answered in the kind of tone usually reserved for humoring psychotics. "I'll see what I can do." The line went dead.

"I don't understand it," Jarrow muttered as they waited, looking anxiously along the arcade and back at the entrance from the street. "If they had an idea we were at Bruce and Sandy's, they could have been waiting there. It's almost as if *they* are worried about being traced."

The call came in less than a minute later. But the voice was a man's. It had what sounded to Jarrow like an Eastern European accent, strengthened by the acoustics of the phone. He introduced himself as Josef.

"Where did you get our message?" Josef asked. Which meant that whoever they were, they had left it at a number of places and hence didn't know everything.

Jarrow wasn't about to reveal that it had been at Bruce and Sandy's. "I just heard it," he answered.

"Where are you? In the city?"

"Pretty central," Jarrow said vaguely.

"Are you anywhere near the Bismarck Hotel?"

"Wait a second." Jarrow covered the mouthpiece. "Where's the Bismarck Hotel?" he hissed at Rita.

"Not far. A couple of blocks."

"Pretty close," Jarrow said into the phone.

"Can you be there in fifteen minutes or so, say at ten-thirty?"

"Who is this? Why should I trust you?"

"I suspect that you are having some serious problems, and I think we might be able to help. Besides, who else can you trust? The people who nearly got to you last night won't give up."

"What do you want from me?" Jarrow asked.

"We need to find Ashling, urgently. I think you might be the key."

"I don't know anyone by that name," Jarrow said.

Josef seemed to have been half expecting it. "We need to talk," he said.

Jarrow drew a long breath. "Very well. I'll be at the Bismarck at ten-thirty."

"Come to the tenth floor. Somebody will meet you there."

"One more thing, I have somebody with me. Is that okay?"

"You mean Ms. Chilsen? Yes, bring her too, by all means."

There was nothing else for it, Jarrow decided. In those few sentences Josef had shown that he knew more than they had any hope of uncovering in weeks. And for some reason Jarrow believed him when he said that he wasn't connected with the men who had broken into Rita's the previous night.

They got to the Bismarck early and walked around the block to bring them back to the main doors at exactly ten-thirty. Inside, they crossed the lobby to the elevators. Jarrow glanced furtively around while they waited, feeling conspicuous and jittery like an amateur investigator on his first assignment, but nobody seemed to be paying them any attention. Just as the car arrived, a bearded man in a tweed hat and tan parka appeared from a side passage and got in with them. Jarrow pressed 10 and glanced inquiringly at the stranger.

"Two, please," the man said. Jarrow complied.

The three of them stared at the inside of the door in silence as the elevator ascended. It arrived at two, and the bearded man moved forward. Suddenly he turned and announced, "I am Josef. We get off here. Come with me, please."

Jarrow and Rita looked at each other uncertainly. But there was nothing else for it. They followed Josef out onto the landing and along one of the corridors, then through a door to a concrete stairway and back down to ground level. From there a service passage and rear door led out to a side yard where a closed van was waiting, aged and battered, painted a drab shade of brown. Josef thumped on the rear doors, which were opened from the inside by a man in a light overcoat. Another man appeared with him, and together they helped Jarrow and Rita up, and over to one of the wooden boards serving as bench seats along the sides. Up front of them, a woman was sitting in the driver's seat.

"Go," Josef said tersely. They moved off.

As the van turned onto the street, Josef peered out through the small windows set high in the doors, apparently worried about being followed. It reinforced the suspicion that Jarrow had already begun to form that these people were as nervous about trusting Jarrow as Jarrow and Rita were about them. The two men who had been in the van were sitting well apart on the seat opposite, watching them warily and, Jarrow couldn't help but notice, keeping their right hands very close to the fronts of their coats.

"See anything?" Josef called to the woman.

"Looks clean to me," she replied, checking her mirrors.

Josef seemed satisfied and sank down on the seat opposite, next to the man in the light overcoat. "Dear me. I'm getting too old for this. An unorthodox way of introducing oneself, but I'm sure you understand the necessity, sometimes, in this questionably sane world of ours." He indicated his companions. "You know my name already. These are Leon and Arnold." Jarrow nodded noncommittally. "The lady driving us is called Susan." At the front, Susan acknowledged by momentarily raising a hand. "And you, of course, are Warrant Officer Demiro."

Jarrow frowned, unsure of how to respond. If these people were going to be of any help, they might as well all get the situation straight right from the start. "I'm not sure," he replied.

"What do you mean?" Josef asked.

"I'm not sure who I am."

Josef seemed surprised, as if part of something that had been carefully planned and thought out was already coming apart. "Who do you think you are?" he asked cautiously.

"As far as I'm aware, my name is Richard Jarrow."

Josef looked taken aback. "Jarrow? I don't think I've ever heard the name. Who is Richard Jarrow?"

"I'm a schoolteacher, and I come from Minneapolis," Jarrow told him.

Josef stared at him for several seconds and seemed nonplussed. He had a ruddy, snub-nosed face with light-colored eyes that seemed to glitter, and was maybe in his late forties. Behind the eyes, Jarrow sensed a quick and adaptable mind, already racing to make sense out of a revelation that had been totally unexpected.

Finally Josef said, "Oh, dear. I have a suspicion that this could be even more complicated than we thought."

eighteen

They drove for a little under an hour. Josef moved up front to take the passenger seat beside Susan, where they talked intermittently in lowered voices. In the back, Arnold and Leon continued watching Jarrow and Rita vigilantly in silence. As far as Jarrow was concerned that was just as well; until he had more of an idea of what was going on, and in particular whether they had fallen into hands that were friendly or otherwise, he was in no mood for making conversation anyway. Rita evidently shared his sentiments.

When the van finally stopped, they got out to find themselves in the driveway of a typical small house in a neighborhood of mixed family dwellings spaced generously apart amid scattered pines. It could have been anywhere within fifty miles of the Chicago city limits. This place was painted a dark, ugly blue with white trim that was starting to flake. The yard was overgrown, and some of the clapboards needed replacing. Another car was parked ahead of them, alongside the porch.

"Not quite home, of course, but it does for now," Josef remarked, reading their expressions. "Shall we go inside?"

They followed him up the steps and across the porch, into a living room opening directly behind the front door, where another woman and a man were waiting. "Oh, just one thing," Josef said as Jarrow was about to move on into the room. He motioned with a hand for Jarrow to raise his arms. Jarrow did so, and Leon checked his person quickly but thoroughly for weapons. "Sorry, but one can't be too careful, as I'm sure you agree," Josef said. Susan did the same with Rita. "And now we can proceed with more customary civilities," Josef said.

The other woman had risen and come over to meet them. She was fortyish, Jarrow guessed, slender and fairly tall, with wavy blond hair and alert, inquisitive eyes that gave the impression of already having absorbed all there was to be learned about the newcomers from their appearance. Her face, though not unattractive, lacked color and showed traces of strain, which a straight, thin nose and high, hollow cheeks did nothing to disguise. She was wearing a heavy woolen sweater with jeans and ankle-high boots.

"This is Kay," Josef informed them, for what it was worth—from the melodramatics of the whole situation, Jarrow had already dismissed all the names as pseudonyms. The man that Kay had been with remained sitting in an armchair, one leg resting lazily on the other knee, seemingly not wanting to be sociable. He was hefty with hair cropped short, wearing a regular jacket over a black, crew-neck sweater. Josef didn't seem perturbed and left him alone. "Do you both take tea? Can we offer you something to eat?" he asked, looking at Jarrow and Rita.

Jarrow glanced at Rita. She nodded. "I could use something."

"Fine," Jarrow said.

"Get some tea on would you?" Josef called behind them. "And maybe a few sandwiches. I'll have one too, cheese—oh, and some of that canned ham if there's any left." Susan went out through another door, and Arnold went with her. Leon stayed in the living room, leaning against the wall by the front door to the porch, through which they had entered. Josef gestured for them to sit down. The room was drab and scantily furnished, with unadorned walls and the bareness that comes with an absence of ornaments. A woodstove standing in a brick surround halfway along one wall was putting out a good heat. Several chairs and a couch formed a rough semicircle facing it, one of the chairs being occupied by the silent man. There was another couch beneath a window, a table with several rough upright chairs, and a couple of small side tables and a cabinet. Jarrow and Rita sat on the couch by the stove, Kay took one of the chairs opposite them, while Josef paced over to a window, turned, and remained standing.

"Very well," Jarrow said. "We've trusted you. Now will someone tell us what's going on? But before we start I warn you that I don't think I'm going to be able to help much with whatever you want. I don't know anything."

"If you wouldn't mind, first, just answering some questions," Josef said from the window. "Don't wonder about them. Then we'll fill you in on as much as we know—which I admit isn't everything. Were it otherwise, you wouldn't be here."

"Okay," Jarrow agreed. That was what they had come here for. Kay reached over to where she had been sitting when they arrived and drew across a folder of papers. She opened it on her knee and stared down at the contents as if collecting her thoughts.

"I've already asked him about Ashling," Josef told her. "The name doesn't mean anything."

"We thought that might be the case," Kay said.

"Ah, but there's more. Apparently he hasn't reverted to Demiro. He's somebody else entirely. Who was it?" He looked across at Jarrow.

"Richard Jarrow," Jarrow supplied.

"Jarrow," Josef repeated. "He says he's a teacher and comes from Minneapolis."

Kay sat back in her chair. "You don't know Conrad Ashling?" she said again, as if to make sure.

"I've never heard of him."

Kay closed the folder slowly. "That does put a different light on things." She lapsed into thought, staring at Jarrow fixedly.

Josef resumed. "You were in Atlanta last weekend, isn't that correct? You stayed at the Hyatt there."

"Yes."

"Why did you go to Atlanta?"

"I don't know. I woke up on Tuesday morning with no memory of going there at all."

"You'd been there since Saturday."

"So I discovered when I checked out. I didn't know anything about it."

"What is the last thing you remember before that?" Josef asked.

Jarrow hesitated, looked at Kay, who was still watching him, then back at Josef again. "I'm not sure if you're going to believe this . . . but I don't remember anything since last April. You see, I'm supposed to be dead. I've even seen the certificate that was filed. I think I'm normal, but nobody recognizes me." He raised a hand to indicate Rita. "Except Rita here, who says I'm this person Tony

Demiro—which is what you seem to think. . . . I don't know what's happening." He shook his head helplessly.

Kay turned her head to look at Josef. There was still doubt on her face, as if she was of two minds as to whether to believe this.

"When did you leave Atlanta?" Josef asked Jarrow.

"Tuesday morning, first thing."

"Why?"

"Why? . . . I was confused. I didn't know what I was doing there. There was nobody around when I woke up. I just wanted to get out and go home."

Josef glanced at Rita. "I'd gone for an early swim while he was still asleep," she said in answer to his unasked question.

Josef nodded and looked back at Jarrow. "So you went back to Minneapolis?"

"Yes."

"Then what brought you to Chicago?"

"I found Rita's phone number on a pad I picked up in the hotel. Nothing else was making any sense, so I called it. Nobody else I'd talked to recognized me."

"But she did?"

"No."

"Yes."

Jarrow and Rita answered together, then stopped, confused.

"But not as anyone called Richard Jarrow," Rita said.

"As Warrant Officer Demiro, supposedly killed five months ago?" Josef said.

Rita swallowed visibly and gave a quick nod. "Yes."

Josef looked to Kay as if for a verdict. "It sounds like a complex reversion," she said. "Jarrow must be an original transfer source. Somehow the complete associative net has reactivated."

Josef chewed his lip for a moment. "And you've never heard of Ashling?" he asked again.

"Never," Jarrow said.

"How about a Maurice Gordon?"

Ah, so they did know something about that too. Jarrow reached inside his jacket and produced Gordon's wallet, opening it to show the ID. "I had this and other things with me when I woke up. None of it means a thing. I presume the clothes there were his as well."

Kay took the wallet and examined it, while Josef continued.

"Very well. So why did you go to Atlanta the day before, on Monday?" he asked, indicating Rita with a nod.

Rita replied, "He called me that morning. It was the same story: he'd woken up in the hotel and didn't know what he was doing there. But it was different. He *was* Tony then. And when I got there that evening he was Tony. Only Tony didn't remember anything since last May. I stayed, got up early the next morning to go for a swim as I said, and when I got back to the room he'd gone. Then I got this call from Minneapolis a day later"—she waved a hand—"only now he says he's this teacher."

"So I came to Chicago," Jarrow completed. "And then, last night . . ."

"Yes, we know about that," Josef told him.

"Were they anything to do with you?" Jarrow asked.

"No."

Jarrow sat back against the couch. So at least he didn't have to go through all that. A long silence followed. Kay folded the wallet and handed it back. "I think he's on the level," she pronounced. "We're not going to get anywhere by staying clammed up." The man in the jacket removed a hand that had been resting in his pocket and returned the gun he had been holding to a holster below his arm. Jarrow felt slightly pained as well as startled, not having realized that his word had been in question all the time.

"Sorry about that. One must take precautions, " Josef said matter-of-factly. He was in a different world, Jarrow told himself. He mustn't let himself get rattled by this kind of thing.

Josef gave a quick smile behind his beard and came forward a pace from the window, reversing one of the upright chairs and straddling it to regard them with his arms folded loosely along the back. "You have been very cooperative. Now, I think, we owe you something in the way of explanation.

"We are from an organization called Pipeline, which I hope you have never heard of. Its purpose is to recruit talent and ability for the Offworld enterprises, particularly skilled industrial personnel, engineers, and scientists. Our function is getting them out of here and the European Consolidation states, and offplanet via the FER. All strictly illegal here, of course, so I suppose you could call us an underground operation of sorts. Ashling is an important scientist who was about to be processed, but he has disappeared."

Rita was listening openmouthed. "Are you saying that you're from there? You're actually Offworlders, infiltrated down here?"

"Not all of us. But Kay and myself are, yes," Josef replied.

Jarrow frowned, trying to reconcile all this with the events of last night. There was still no hint of where Ashling fitted into anything.

"So who were those men who came to the flat?" he asked. "You said they weren't anything to do with you?" Hardly a necessary question. It would have been a strange way, to say the least, for an underground operation to have conducted itself.

"I can't say for certain," Josef replied. "But we're pretty certain that at least some of them were from a clandestine government research program, and had been sent to bring back one of their agents, a subject of the program, who had run amuck."

The code name, Jarrow thought. Didn't agents usually have code names in this kind of business? Another piece fell into place. "Was this agent known as Samurai?" he ventured.

Josef glanced briefly at Kay, who returned a shrug. "I've not heard that name before," he confessed. "But it seems possible. Where did you hear it?"

"They yelled it a couple of times before they started breaking down the door."

"That must be what he went by internally," Kay said.

Josef nodded. "Maurice Gordon was the name he was operating under," he told Jarrow. "That was what we had identified him as."

"Ah, yes, okay." Jarrow had suspected something similar himself. "So Maurice Gordon was Samurai's cover."

"So it seems."

Jarrow looked at Josef and Kay in turn. Now they were getting somewhere. "So far, so good, then," he said. "But what do we know about the person himself. Who *is* this Samurai?"

Josef gave him a long, penetrating look, as if inviting him to see the obvious. Jarrow frowned. The new revelations had come pouring in too quickly for him to have it all sorted out yet in his mind.

Josef gestured, indicating the side of Jarrow's coat to which he had returned the wallet. "But you've seen Gordon's ID," he said. "I don't think it could be any plainer than that. Why do you think we've been so nervous about you?" He nodded at the stunned look that came over Jarrow's face as the message finally percolated. "Yes, that's right. *You* are!"

nineteen

The first week at Pearse was devoted practically in its entirety to batteries of psychological tests, and a series of brain scans and physiological measurements to look for irregularities in neural functioning. Two of the original twenty volunteers were found unsuitable and returned to their units.

The second week consisted of protracted interviews held individually with the remainder, by Colonel Gleavey, Dr. Nordens, and several other civilians. The style of the interviews was free and rambling, ranging across a whole gamut of topics that covered hobbies, sports, personal lives, home backgrounds, ambitions and aspirations, and the men's views on everything from sex and religion to the political implications of the Western Consolidation, the nature of the FER, and the future of the Offworld expansion. Guessing the purpose of this was a continual subject of discussion and speculation back in the billet block during the evenings. The general consensus was that the range of subjects had been made wide and confusing deliberately, to obscure whatever it was that the program designers were really interested in.

Lowe dismissed the whole thing as a market-research exercise to find ways of increasing the appeal of service life, because the Europeans were allegedly losing a lot of defectors to the FER. Parker, a small, wiry tank man from Arizona, thought it might be a prelude to some kind of mood-altering-drug testing, aimed at restoring old-fashioned standards of discipline and dedication in an age when old-fashioned methods wouldn't work. Demiro didn't expound any theory. But there was one thing he'd noticed whenever the talk drifted into politics, which it tended to do more often than he'd have thought normal for a typical barracks-room mix: an underlying attitude, varying from vague disquiet to open cynicism toward the existing system, was something they all seemed to share.

Four of the group were rejected as unsuitable in this phase, and a further two as security risks, reducing the original twenty to a dozen. At the end of the second week, they assembled in the briefing room again, where Colonel Wylvern, Major Gleavey, and Dr. Nordens were waiting.

Nordens walked over to a metal shelf with a button panel underneath that hinged out from the wall on one side of the room to serve as a podium. The lights dimmed, and the screen facing the audience from behind him came to life. As usual, Nordens wasn't wasting any time on preliminaries. There was a shuffling and muttering of interest. After two weeks of interminable testing and talking, *this* was more like it.

The screen showed a chimpanzee squatting on one side of a barrier consisting of metal bars, like the side of a cage. The chimp was fiddling with some wooden rods, pushing them together end to end, watching them fall apart again, fingering its chin in growing exasperation, screeching, then trying again. Some distance away beyond the barrier was a bunch of bananas.

Nordens half turned to watch, commenting at the same time, "The rods are too short to reach the reward, but they can be joined together to form a single length that will. However, the ends are fitted with specially shaped keypieces that will mate only with the correct counterpart. Hence the rods must be assembled in the correct order, with the large hook—you can see it there—at the far end to retrieve the prize. This animal has not been trained to perform the task, but she has been allowed to observe others that have."

The chimp tried once again with several rods in turn, one at a time, got nowhere, and vented its frustration in a burst of screeching and whooping. Then it began vainly trying to join them together again. Nordens resumed, "As you can see, she hasn't a clue. She knows that the task is possible, but she has no idea of the detailed procedure necessary to accomplish it." This was confirmed a few moments later, when the chimp gave up, smashed all the rods in a rage, and proceeded to dance up and down on the pieces.

"Now, gentlemen, observe this," Nordens said.

The scene now was of a chimp lying apparently asleep, strapped to a couch with its head in the center of a complicated machine, surrounded by elaborate equipment. "The process you are observing is in no way harmful or uncomfortable," Nordens remarked, anticipating the unvoiced question of many of the audience. "Sedation is necessary simply because chimpanzees are not very good at following instructions. This is the same female as you saw before. Now let's see her again, shortly after this was taken."

Next they were back at the setup for the problem with the rods. But this time the chimp assembled the pieces deftly and unerringly, hooked the bananas, and settled down contentedly to enjoy the feast. Some murmurs of surprise and a whistle of appreciation came up from the watchers.

"I must stress that the recording was not doctored," Nordens went on. "The subject underwent no form of training whatsoever between the previous attempt that you saw, and the time we are observing here. Yet as you can see, she is now able to solve the problem easily." Nordens cut the screen, brought the lights up again, nodded curtly to Major Gleavey, and sat down.

Gleavey turned in the center of the room in front of the screen, his arms extended like a ringmaster announcing the star act. "When you input something to a computer, the electronic codes inside the computer are changed, right? The changes reflect the new information. Well, the same kind of thing holds true inside your head. When you learn something, something somewhere has to change. Something that's there after has to be different from what it was before." He looked around to check that they were all following, as if he were presenting quantum physics to ten-year-olds—not slow, but naturally new to this—and nodded. "Well, what you've just seen is that it's possible not only to identify what that 'something' is, but to *extract* it as a pattern, and *transfer* it into another brain."

A murmur of interest ran around the room. Lowe's voice came through above it, telling the man next to him, "And tomorrow somebody'll find it causes cancer."

Gleavey went on, "That's right. You can transfer it." He raised a warning finger. "Now, it's not quite the same as happens in a computer, but the principle's the same." He gestured briefly at the screen. "That's what the machine you saw does. First the monkey"—to one side, Nordens flinched visibly at the choice of word—"couldn't figure out how to get the bananas. Then the machine *transferred into its head* the patterns that it got from another monkey that had been taught how to do it. And then it could do it, no problem . . . *without* having to have any kind of regular training itself."

He held up a hand to stop anyone interrupting him there and breaking the flow. "Okay, well, I won't beat about the bush. This is what you're all here for. The next step is to take this to the human level. It has all kinds of potential benefits in all kinds of areas, and we—the Army, that is—have been asked to carry out the first tests. And it's something that the Army could be very interested in for its own reasons too. For instance, the modern Army is becoming increasingly labor and skills intensive. That means that compared to how things used to be, more and more time and effort and money goes into training soldiers to do their jobs. At one time it was good enough just to know how to shoot and strip a rifle, which part of the grenade you throw and which part you hold in your teeth, and the right way to clean your boots. Now you have to know all about battlefield computers, lasers, satellite grids, air coordination, as well as a hundred different kinds of ammunition and a different Barbie doll outfit for every kind of combat environment from chemical attack, to choppers, to digging in on glaciers. . . . Hell, you guys all know what I'm talking about.

"So . . . think what a difference it could make if what you saw with the monkey could be adapted for military training. For any skill that you need lots of people to have, you take just one person, one who's a natural, anyway, then trained until he's the best there is, and then what *he* can do gets copied into everyone else." Gleavey pointed randomly at several of the men one after another. "So suppose you're the best shot in the outfit—or the brigade, the division, or even the whole Army—you're a top radio man, you're an auto mechanic. . . . " An appealing gesture to the whole room. "Get the idea? We can combine all of that into every single person in a few sessions on the machine, without everyone having to spend hundreds of hours out on the range, going through communications school, or taking the same motors apart over and over, and still getting average grades. And think what that means if you extend it to the whole Army. . . . We're talking who-knows-how-many *millions* of man-hours every year—plus top performance all around."

He stood and waited, indicating that they were now free to respond. The pitch had had an effect. A buzz of excited muttering came up from the room. The men were impressed. In the back row of chairs, Demiro sat back and rubbed his chin. Yes: he was impressed too, he decided.

At the front, Gleavey raised his hands. "Well, that's what it's all about. Anyone who wants to opt out can do so now. But before anyone who might be thinking that way decides, let me suggest that you consider the benefits. During the program you'll learn a lot of good stuff the easy way, things that you maybe thought you'd never do because you're not made the right way to learn them, or things that you'd have to spend all your money and half your life finding out about at college. Well, you get to keep it all. And there's no charge. How could anyone turn down a deal like that?" He looked around. Nobody seemed about to drop out. "Questions?" he invited.

For a moment there was a confused exchange of mutterings and looks. Then Parker, the small, wiry tank man from Arizona, spoke up. "Yeah, I got one. You're talkin' 'bout switchin' what some other guy's learned, like bein' a crack shot, maybe?" Gleavey nodded. "Well, what happens if I don't happen to have the same good eye as he's got? Are you sayin' it'll still work just as good for me? If so, I can't see how."

"Good question," somebody else said. Gleavey looked to Nordens.

"That's one of the aspects that we intend to explore," Nordens answered.

"Next?" Gleavey said.

Lowe followed. "Just how safe is all this? I mean, that machine there looked pretty terrifying to me. Not sure I'd want to stick my head in that thing."

Again a look from Gleavey to Nordens. "Extensive animal tests give complete assurance that there are no adverse effects whatsoever," Nordens said.

"How long is this program scheduled to take?" someone else wanted to know.

Gleavey took that one himself. "We don't have a fixed limit on that as of this point in time. Our policy is to take things slowly, keep it careful, and get it right. So I'd be lying to you if I said it wasn't going to be a while."

Demiro stuck up a hand and got Gleavey's nod. "So what kind of leave allowances can we expect?" he asked.

"None for the first month at least. After that a weekend every two or three weeks, maybe more later." That didn't go down so well. Gleavey explained, "We don't want you attracting attention out there by showing off your new abilities until we've a better idea of what to expect. But I can tell you that the pay will be better than was indicated." That seemed to mollify them some.

"It sounds pretty great all around," Lowe said. "So why so much secrecy?"

"Prudence," Gleavey replied. "It sounds pretty weird, doesn't it? Imagine the version you'd get after the papers and the TV got ahold of it. There's enough objectors and protesters out there already, causing trouble for anything you can name. We just want to be left alone to concentrate on the work."

Lowe nodded that he was satisfied and looked back at Demiro. "Sounds to me like it could be fun. I'm sold. How about you?"

"You've got it," Demiro said.

twenty

"Conrad Ashling is a mathematical neurophysiologist. For many years he has specialized in the study of human memory and the mechanics of learned behavior. In fact, he's probably one of the world's top half-dozen authorities on the subject."

Jarrow had already got the feeling that Kay was some kind of scientist, whereas Josef came across more as an organizer and leader: the kind of person that most people would associate with an organization like Pipeline. They had eaten a lunch of cheese-and-ham sandwiches with strong tea, brewed European style in a pot. Kay was at last explaining some of the background to Jarrow and Rita around the woodstove in the room that they had first entered. Josef was with them. The silent man had left with Arnold in the van. Leon and Susan were in the kitchen.

Kay continued, "He was with MIT for a while, but when official interference in his work became intolerable he quit and set up a research company of his own, still in Massachusetts, called Memco."

Jarrow had read bits and pieces that sounded as if they related to that kind of thing. "I take it we're talking about the actual physical apparatus of learning?" he said. Kay nodded.

Rita thought she followed. "You mean that when you learn something new, it has to be stored somehow," she said.

"Exactly." Kay nodded. "Well, to put it shortly, Ashling developed a way of transferring that learning from the brain of one individual into the brain of another. So the second individual acquired the knowledge instantly, without having to go through the learning process itself."

In normal circumstances Jarrow would have been flabbergasted by such a suggestion. But after the things that he had been forced to come to terms with in the course of the last few days, he was already half prepared for something like this. He sat back in the chair, frowning, jumping ahead in his mind and trying to anticipate how a possibility like that might explain his present condition.

"You mean like the electronic codes in a computer? The way you can copy a file out of one machine and into another," Rita said.

"I thought some people were starting to say it's chemical," Jarrow murmured distantly. "Coded into complex molecules. . . . Don't ask me how, though."

"You've got the general idea," Kay told them. "In fact, both processes enter into it. But the way the brain works can't be thought of in the same way as computers—which is what sent most mainstream research up the wrong path for a number of years. No two human brains contain the same configuration of neural connections. Therefore the same information isn't stored in the same way, as it would be in different computers that are designed the same way to handle the same data representations. What happens is that genetic directions lay down a general pattern that has certain commonalities in the embryonic nervous systems, but the actual configuration that's realized is a result of selection and reinforcement between competing neural subnets as they develop, guided by experiences and to a certain degree by chance. Then, later, after a unique connectivity is established at the physical level, a secondary process of adaptive modification is superposed on it, essentially in the form of selective reinforcement of preferred pathways, based on the variable sensitivity of synaptic receptors."

Jarrow looked away, shaking his head. "Sorry. I teach social adaptability, not biology." Rita just stared glazedly.

"It means that the computer model of the brain isn't really accurate," Kay said. "Brains aren't wired to any preexisting design that's stored somehow in the chromosomes. They develop through a process of competition and selection among complex neuronal groups, and they're all different. So you can't just take the same pattern out of here and put it in there."

At least Rita followed that part. "Okay," she accepted. "So what do you do?"

"I think of it in terms of high-level languages," Josef offered. "They let you move the functionality of a program between machines, in other words what the program does, even though the machines are different and might operate in different ways. But you still get the same results, which is what matters."

"Yes," Kay agreed. "And the concepts that people think and communicate in are indeed high-level constructs. What Ashling did was find a way of reprogramming the synaptic pathways to emulate the mode of high-level symbolic synthesis derived from another brain, even though the underlying micro-operations supporting it are quite different. You could think of it as emulating a part of one person's mind inside another, with the wiring that's already there."

To Rita, that sounded pretty much like what she'd said in the first place. If scientists wrote cookbooks it would take a hundred pages to tell you how to make a pancake.

Jarrow was seized by a sinking feeling. Did that mean that he really *was* Demiro, somehow emulating Jarrow? That *he* was really dead? . . . But what else did the facts of the last two days tell him, if he faced up to them? Weren't the records in Minneapolis enough? Or the physical discrepancies between the person he remembered being and the one who stared back at him from a mirror now?

But until now, there had been the hope, however irrational and unsupportable, that somehow there might be a different answer. He hadn't realized how much he had been hiding from himself until now. Rita understood it too, but with her the effect was different. He could see it shining in her eyes.

Kay didn't want to dwell at this point, and went on, "Ashling's thought was of the commercial potential. He saw Memco as the forerunner of a whole new industry, as one day becoming the IBM of a new technological field. Imagine what it would mean to become an instant chess player, musician, speak a new language overnight, or become a skier and really do something different this vacation—as long as you remember to tone up the muscles first. Probably all kinds of things you'd never think of. Who knows?"

Kay shrugged and emitted one of those sighs with which people dismiss a daydream. "But the corporate empire and personal fortune that Ashling envisaged never happened. Certain agencies of the government began showing an interest in all this, and soon afterward his operation was taken over and classified."

Josef interjected, "They persuaded him of the defense implications, its potential as an aid to military training, for example, and painted a specter of what would happen if something like this became the object of an arms race with the Offworlders. Better to keep it out of sight, under control. . . . And, of course, they could tempt him with the thought of virtually unlimited funding and resources. Ashling was a more or less loyal and patriotic kind of person—then, anyway—and he agreed to continue working for them secretly, under government direction."

"In any case, he was under no illusions about the kind of harassment he'd be inviting if he wouldn't cooperate," Kay added. "So his private venture was finished either way."

Rita lit a cigarette. "You talked about that in Atlanta," she said, nodding toward Jarrow.

"You mean when I was Tony?"

"Yes. About some of the things you'd found you could do after you went on the program. . . . I guess I should say 'Tony' could. He'd never talked about any of that before—when he came back on leave, I mean. He just used to say he was involved with new training methods. Nothing at all about mind implants, or whatever you'd call them."

"A good soldier, observing security," Josef commented. "A bit of a rebel underneath, maybe, but not irresponsible."

"That was Tony," Rita agreed.

"What kinds of things did he tell you about in Atlanta?" Jarrow asked her curiously. By now he had gotten used to using the third person when they talked about Demiro.

"He could strip down weapons he'd never seen before, and put them together again. He found he could work all kinds of equipment that he'd never been trained in. Understood all kinds of mathematical stuff—and that wasn't Tony's thing at all. But he said it seemed to work. What else was there?"

"I think we know the kind of thing you mean," Josef said. "But it doesn't really matter much, because that was all just a cover." Jarrow and Rita looked surprised. Josef explained, "The real aim of the project, code-named Southside, was political. You see, what somebody, somewhere, had glimpsed when they looked into this new technology of Ashling's was the possibility of being able to reprogram somebody's *political* beliefs." He gave them a moment or two to think about that. Jarrow found it hard to accept. Surely governments wouldn't do something like that? . . . Anyway, not *our* government?

Kay picked it up again from there. "People in this society aren't repressed by overt force, or any of the other cruder methods of days gone by."

Jarrow's face tightened as he listened. He didn't accept that this was a repressive society at all, and didn't think the presumption should go unchallenged, but at the same time he didn't want to go making a fuss about it right now. Who did these Offworld people think they were, running what amounted to a spy network and now making insinuations like this?

Kay went on, "It's done by control and manipulation of information. And it follows that the main threats to such a regime come not from traditional bullets-and-barricades revolutionaries, but from effective purveyors of counterinformation: public figures, celebrities, trendsetters, and so on, who challenge the conventional wisdoms that 'everyone knows' to be true. They become the nuclei from which waves of undesirable thought are likely to spread, and therefore where any destabilization would begin."

"Somebody like Daparras for instance?" Rita said.

"Good example," Josef agreed. "And look where he ended up." It should have been jail, Jarrow thought to himself. The man was a menace, a cult hero among half his students, and an out-and-out terrorist.

Kay continued, "But suppose that instead of making martyrs out of such people, you could *convert* them?" She paused to let them reflect on the proposition. "By changing the underlying belief structure that was responsible for their views. . . . Slowly, a little at a time, so that it would look like a process of deeper insight and enlightenment taking root, rather than smack of their being 'got at,' as would be the case if it happened too suddenly. You'd be able not only to eliminate such inconvenient people as problems, but actually transform them into assets who'd bring their followers around with them as their own conversion progressed. No fuss. No ugly confrontations. Just what governments like."

"And Ashling's system could really do that?" Rita said. Her face looked pained, as if she were having trouble accepting the enormity of it.

"That was what they wanted to find out," Kay answered. "And the even nicer thing was that if just the beliefs that were of concern could be modified, leaving the rest of the personality intact, outward appearances would remain normal. So your former adversary could continue exerting his or her own brand of charisma, only working this time in your interests instead of against them."

"Neat, eh?" Josef commented.

"Are you sure you're not imagining a lot of this?" Jarrow challenged, unable any longer to prevent himself from putting up some defense.

Josef waved a hand casually in his direction. "What about you? Do you think you've been imagining things?" he countered. Jarrow subsided disconsolately.

Kay moved on more briskly, before they could bog down on such issues. "The project was set up under the code name Southside at the Pearse military psychological labs in Georgia, about fifty miles from Atlanta. Demiro was one of the volunteers selected. But something very strange happened in his case. It must have been somewhere around six months ago. Exactly what went wrong, we don't know. But it was enough to warrant a faked death certificate as a cover-up."

Jarrow looked suspiciously at her and Josef in turn. "You seem to know a hell of a lot, all the same," he remarked. "How come?"

"And where does this scientist, Ashling, fit in?" Rita asked.

"Advance neuroresearch is also being conducted Offworld," Kay replied. "In fact, I'm connected with it myself, part of a group headed by a man you've probably not heard of: a Russian called Ulkanov. Science usually works that way—if different people are heading along the same road, you'd expect them to get to the same place, though not necessarily at the same time. In fact, Ulkanov and Ashling got to know each other quite well during Ashling's MIT days—before the restrictions on scientific exchange visits were tightened up. Ashling was ahead, though. There's no question he's a genius. That's why we were more than interested when Josef's people contacted us with the news that Ashling wanted out." She turned to Josef. "Why don't you tell your side of it from there."

Josef leaned forward to toss a couple more logs into the stove, closed the iron door on the front, and settled back again. "Ashling was told that the purpose of Southside was to assess the feasibility of using his technique as a way of accelerating military training. He agreed to cooperate on that basis. However, he's one of those methodical people who believe in knowing everything thoroughly. He did his own quiet probing around at Pearse, and in the process discovered that the training story was just a cover for the political objectives that Kay described a moment ago. That side of it was being handled by another scientist, called Nordens, who supposedly was there to assist Ashling."

Kay looked inquiringly at Rita. "Out of curiosity, did Tony seem different in any way sometimes, when he came back on leave?"

Rita looked uncertain. "Different? . . . How? I'm not sure what you mean."

"Was Tony what you'd call a political kind of person? Did he talk about things like that? Have strong opinions?"

"Well . . . yes, in some ways I guess you could say he did. It used to get him into trouble at the base sometimes—at Kankakee, before he went to Georgia."

"Did any of those views seem to have changed at all, in the later months, after he'd been there for some time?"

Rita tried to think back, but shook her head. "It's been so long. Such a lot's happened. I really can't remember."

"It doesn't matter," Kay said.

"But you can see why he'd be an ideal subject," Josef said.

"You see, to maintain the cover, they did experiment with all the volunteers on implanting some genuine technical and other skills, of the kind that the program was supposed to be about. But the real work went on behind that. All of the volunteers were picked for having strong, offbeat political opinions, to see if they could be modified. Ashling found out, and was horrified. That was when he decided that he wanted nothing more to do with it. He knew of Pipeline—there is an amazing network of jungle drums among scientists—and through means that I have no intention of revealing was able to make contact with us and indicate that he wanted to defect. As a sign of good faith, he provided us with copies of some of the secret records from Pearse on the subjects who were undergoing political processing."

"How long ago did he contact you?" Jarrow asked.

"Early in September, I think it was." Josef glanced across at Kay. She returned an affirmative nod. He went on, "We fed the information back through the system, and as Kay said, the Offworlders were very interested. News found its way to Ulkanov, and he was behind the decision to bring Ashling out. All that took time, of course, and then there were the arrangements to make, but by last Saturday all was ready. With some help from us, Ashling slipped the surveillance that he was kept under all the time, and we installed him in a room at the Hyatt in Atlanta with three of our men to await a courier who would arrive the next day to take him through. But something went wrong. Early the next morning we received a message from Ashling on a number that we had given him to be used in emergencies." Josef glanced at Kay. "Do you have it there?"

Kay produced a message text and handed it to Jarrow. It read:

Unforeseen developments have resulted in drastic change of situation. Regret am unable to proceed with plan. Imperative you clear your suite at Hyatt immediately. Also convey following to Ulkanov. Will explain all when opportunity permits. Grateful for your efforts. Ashling.

"What was with it?" Jarrow inquired, passing the text to Rita.

Kay handed him several sheets packed with mnemonics and scientific jargon that conveyed absolutely nothing. "I've seen this kind of thing before, when I was with Ulkanov on Luna," she commented. "It's an encryption technique that some scientists have developed among themselves for getting things past censors in the Consolidation countries."

"So you don't know what it means, either?" Jarrow checked. Kay shook her head.

Rita handed back the message text. "So what did you find at the Hyatt?" she asked Josef.

"Ashling was gone. Our three guards were all unconscious, knocked out with a drug. Whoever did it had come in via a shaft in the bathroom from the room upstairs. We got our people out, cleared everything up, and vacated the room. That was on Sunday, the day after Ashling disappeared."

"Was this the room I woke up in?" Jarrow asked. But even as he said it, he realized that it couldn't have been. The desk clerk said he'd been checked in since Saturday.

Josef shook his head. "No. It was in another part of the hotel."

"So where do I fit in?" Jarrow asked.

"Obviously we'd been blown," Josef replied. "We just took

everything out through a side door and decided to stay out of sight for the rest of that day. Then on Monday, when we figured things would have blown over, I went back with Leon, who was one of the three men who had been there on Saturday, to settle with the hotel. And to our amazement, he recognized the agent who had broken in and knocked them out—and who had presumably taken Ashling— still there, walking around the hotel. Leon got out of sight quickly, and we moved in a couple of our other people that the agent hadn't seen before, to see what he did." Josef looked at Jarrow, and although Jarrow knew what was coming next, still he could only stare back disbelievingly. Josef confirmed, "He turned out to be staying in room 1406, and was registered as Maurice Gordon.

"We watched him, hoping for a lead back to Ashling. Then on Monday evening he was joined by a woman." Josef nodded at Rita. "Yourself, of course. But early on Tuesday morning Gordon took us by surprise and vanished himself."

Rita was shaking her head in bewilderment. "Are you saying that Tony was turned into some kind of secret agent or something? Was that part of this training? I can't believe it. It's just not him."

"We don't know," Josef replied frankly. "The only other lead we had was you. We traced you back to Chicago, and watched your house there in the hope that Gordon, our only lead to Ashling, would show up. But it turned out that we were not the only ones. Federal Security Service agents were staking the place too, presumably also having tracked you back from Atlanta. They watched the house and we watched them, and while this was going on, some of our other people were trying to establish who you were and what connection you had with Southside. Your name didn't mean anything until we found it mentioned in the records that Ashling had from Pearse, given as the former fiancée and nearest relative-equivalent of Warrant Officer Demiro, since listed as killed in an accident." Josef showed his palms briefly. "That was intriguing enough. But what did it mean? What was Maurice Gordon doing there?" He glanced at Rita, then Jarrow. "The real shock came when I looked at the pictures from the Southside files and found that Gordon *was* Demiro!"

Josef stared at Jarrow, as if to invite comment. Jarrow just stared back, now wanting only to hear whatever might be left to tell.

"Then you appeared suddenly in Chicago. We observed the

attempt by the FSS men to grab you at the house, how you dealt with them, and we saw you get away. But get away to where, we didn't know."

Kay came in again at that point. "That was when we concluded that something very serious had gone wrong with the Southside project. We speculated that maybe Gordon-Demiro, whoever—the agent who had been chasing Ashling in Atlanta—might be having second thoughts about where he stood in all this. Why else would he quit, go back to his girl in Chicago, and be chased by the FSS? If so, we reasoned that he might be approachable. That was where Josef and his people helped again. They really are amazing."

Josef permitted a quick grin. "You'd be surprised how many contacts who have Offworlder sympathies we have been able to cultivate in this country," he replied. "We compiled a list of Demiro and Rita's known friends, and short-listed a half dozen or so that we thought they'd be likely to head for. That was a long night's work. In the morning we called each of them, leaving a message that we hoped Demiro-Gordon would respond to. And the rest you both know."

Which brought them all up to the present. Except for one thing. Jarrow was the obvious one to ask it. "So . . . where do *I* appear in all this—Richard Jarrow?"

"That's the part that's still missing," Kay said. "Now it's your turn to do the talking. I want you to go over your story again, from the beginning, in detail. Don't leave anything out."

Jarrow gave her a long, uncertain stare. In this new light, the business of his visits to Valdheim was starting to take on a whole new significance. "Okay," Jarrow agreed.

"So, let's go back to the last thing you remember, before you woke up in Atlanta on Tuesday."

Jarrow described his last visit to Valdheim's, giving as much detail about the machine there as he could recall. Kay listened intently, evidently very interested. Very interested indeed.

twenty-one

It was late evening in the billet block at Pearse, and the troops were relaxing. Niderinsky, Jones, Halliman, and Zwinny had got the poker school going at the end table as usual. Thorben was on his bunk, writing a letter. Polk, Yerks, and Irvine were by the TV, arguing politics, which was also getting to be pretty usual. Schott was reading, and Demiro and Lowe, the black PFC that Demiro had met on the first day, were watching Parker fan out a deck of cards while Major Gleavey, who had stopped by in one of his social visits, looked on with interest.

"The darnedest thing is that I never used to be able to pick up an egg without crackin' it," Parker told them. "Now watch this." He ripple-shuffled the deck in midair, extended a forearm and spread the cards out in a smooth run from elbow to palm, flipped the end one over with his fingers, causing the whole line to flip in a wave motion that flowed back to the first, dropped his arm vertically to let the cards fall into a neat stack in his hand, and then spread it one-handed into a perfect fan. "Pick one, somebody. I'll show you sump'n else."

Demiro obliged, showed it to Lowe, and returned it to the deck. Parker mixed it into the deck. Gave the deck to each of them to shuffle in turn, then executed a deft series of cuts and passes, resulting in the card being materialized magically out of thin air. Lowe whooped appreciatively.

The scientists—mainly Nordens, but also another called Ashling, who seemed to be more a theoretician in the background and only appeared from time to time—had been looking into the transference of complex motor skills that week. The cardsharping routine was a "something extra" that they'd included in Parker's program that day, on top of the officially scheduled items. The men enjoyed this kind of unexpected bonus, and keeping up their enthusiasm was an important part of the work.

"Hey, guys," Lowe called across to the poker game. "Get a load of this. You wanna deal Parker in over there? He'll take your shirts, an' I'm ready to place bets."

"Shove it," Halliman muttered back, studying his cards.

"You see, guys," Gleavey told them, beaming. "I told you on the first day you'd be doing things you never thought possible. Never say we don't deliver, eh?" He nodded at Parker. "The man that came from is a stage magician. He had to practice four hours a day for five years to do what you're doing now."

Demiro had to admit that he was impressed. That same day, after a session on the machine, he himself had been introduced to a new, joint-services logistics-processing computer program. He'd been able to work effortlessly through complicated materials and parts scheduling routines that would previously have taken weeks of operator training and poring over manuals to master. He could also, to his astonishment, pick a pretty good tune out of a guitar.

Lowe turned to regard the major with a thoughtful look. "Say, do you think we could get to bring a friend or two in on this?"

"What do you mean?" Gleavey asked suspiciously.

"Well, I was just thinking. See, I've got this chick back home who's okay in a lot o' ways, but she ain't been around too much, if you know what I mean. Could use a little more, what you might call, 'worldly education.' Well, see, there's this place in L.A. called Pussy in Boots, and man, what it'd do for Nancy if she could pick up a few tips from some of the girls in there. I'd be set for life."

Gleavey shook his head in mock despair. "I guess that's a bit further down the line. I've got things to do. I'll see you men tomorrow." He left.

Lowe shrugged. "Sounded like a great idea to me. Don't you reckon so, Tony?"

Demiro, who was in the process of standing up to leave the group, stopped to think about it for the moment. "I think I'd pick the brains of whoever runs that place," he said. "Find out what he knows that I don't know. Then I could make lots of money, *and* have a good time."

"You can't take money with you, man," Lowe said as Demiro turned away.

"Where can you get to without it?" Demiro threw back.

He went back to his bunk and sat down on the edge to look for something in a magazine he'd left there. Schott was lying reading on the adjacent one. He regarded Demiro over the top of his book for a while, then murmured, "I like your thinking. That's what I'd do too, if I had the choice: learn about making money. Then I'd take it to a place where business isn't a crime, the way it's getting to be here. Know what I mean? Someplace where people might actually be appreciated for doing something worthwhile."

"Not a lot of that around these days," Demiro agreed.

Schott set his book aside and leaned on an elbow. His voice fell to a more confidential note. "No wonder the ones who are really smart get out. You know what I'm talking about?—out of this whole mess."

Demiro frowned. "Out? . . . You mean to the FER?"

"And more than that. Offworld. That's where it's all happening."

"Is it?" Demiro said guardedly. "I never really thought about it."

"It's not like some garden lawn out there, where all the grass has to be the same height. Down here they say we all have to be the same. You stick your head up, and someone comes along with a lawn mower. But there, they let everybody grow to whatever they can. That's how it oughta be."

"I don't know. Maybe." Demiro settled back and opened the magazine, not wanting to be drawn into this. On the other bunk, Schott picked up his book again and resumed reading.

Talking about things like that with people you didn't really know wasn't smart. For all he knew, Schott could be a plant, put there to sound out hidden loyalties. Demiro would have been surprised if there weren't at least one in a group like this.

In fact he had been thinking a lot more about defecting, and had talked to Rita about it again during his last leave. Their dream wasn't of anything really farfetched or ambitious. Demiro had always wanted to run his own bookstore—with lots of offbeat titles that you couldn't find in the regular chains, and a section for used books. Rita wanted a coffee shop, one with a feel of quality instead of the usual noisy, plastic-and-glass goldfish bowl, always filled with sloppy-mannered kids—with a score of different blends of coffee, and Viennese pastries, she'd said, and maybe playing classical music. Their latest thought had been to combine the two into one venture. Nothing really fancy. It would just be a way of making a living. And leave enough time to raise a family—a large one, without needing anyone's permission.

But you didn't talk about such things in a place like this. The way was to keep a clean nose and a straight record, make your plans quietly, and wait for the right opportunities.

Dr. Nordens had followed Schott and Demiro's brief exchange on a screen in a monitor room in part of the Main Complex. He'd have to talk to Schott a bit more, he decided. Schott's job was to bring out the men's political opinions and get them to talk about them, not go probing for possible subversiveness or tendencies to defect. Nordens was interested in identifying optimum subjects, not purging the service. But he had already tagged Demiro as one of the first candidates. His very wariness at being drawn into such matters showed that he had the intelligence.

Nordens thought some more, and then summoned a file onto another screen and entered his decision. So now they'd be able to make a start on the real business at hand. There was no indication that Ashling suspected anything. But they'd have to watch him. Ashling was no fool.

He switched the screen to communications mode and entered a Minneapolis number. Ten seconds later he was talking to Dr. Valdheim. "I've selected the first subject," Nordens advised. "So we're practically ready to go. What's the situation there?"

The gaunt, bespectacled face on the screen nodded. "Everything is looking well. Jarrow is responding successfully. We should have some extracts processed and sent down to you by tomorrow."

"Let's hope so," Nordens replied.

twenty-two

Josef said they had to wait for more Pipeline people to join them before they could make any further plans. These people had some distance to travel, so it would take time. Jarrow thought it probable that they were involved in the scheme to extract Ashling, and would therefore be coming up from Atlanta, but it didn't seem the place or time to be inquisitive.

He and Rita were given rooms to use for the night, which like the rest of the house were bare and on the drab side, but adequate. Although they weren't captives as such, Josef made it plain that they were to stay out of sight and not go wandering around the neighborhood—which was fine by both of them, in any case. Jarrow had no incentive to go anywhere else, and Rita was reluctant to go back to her apartment. Susan went out to do some shopping, returning with changes of clothes for both of them. There were books to read, a collection of movies, and the evening passed with pleasant uneventfulness.

The tensions of the past twenty-four hours must have exhausted both of them more than they realized, for Josef and his companions were all up and about and had eaten by the time Jarrow and Rita surfaced. They had a late breakfast alone together in the kitchen.

"You mightn't believe it, but I wanted to be a biochemist once," Rita said over the table. "I even started a degree. But it got to be disheartening. Everybody these days seems to think that anything in that line has to be involved with engineering viruses that might escape, or putting things into food that cause cancer—which is stupid anyway, because natural pesticides that plants make themselves are thousands of times stronger. We've got so many laws now protecting the rights of malaria viruses that making a career fighting disease seemed pointless."

"Oh, come on. Aren't you exaggerating?" Jarrow said.

"Am I? There are people dying today from malaria and viral encephalitis in California. And don't tell me I read too many campus propaganda sheets, because I had a cousin who was one of them. Things like that were wiped out once in this country." Rita tossed salt liberally over her plate of eggs, hash browns, and bacon and poured a glass of orange juice. "So, I went and worked for a company that made coolants for power transformers. Then they got banned, the owner closed down, sold everything, and moved out to Malaysia." She paused, looking oddly at Jarrow as the sight of him across the breakfast table triggered old memories. "Know what I'd really like to do?"

"What?" he asked.

"We used to talk about it: run a coffee shop. Have a family and run a coffee shop. I don't know why, especially. I think maybe it's the thought of having lots of people stopping by, who you'd get to know and never be short of friends. I just like people, I guess. I hate all these restrictions, as if humans were pollution or something. It shouldn't be that way."

"Well, now, I'm not so sure," Jarrow replied. "You have to admit that overpopulation is a real problem. And if the Southern World and the FER states don't fall into line pretty soon, it's going to turn into a real catastrophe."

Rita shook her head. "I don't believe it. . . . Oh, sure, I agree there are places that have got local problems. But most of the world's still empty. People produce more than they use—at least they can, if they're let. They solve problems. Having more of them around ought to make things better, not worse."

"Surely it's elementary," Jarrow said, feeling more like a teacher for the moment. "More people use up more resources. Therefore they'll run out sooner."

"But they *make* resources too," Rita objected. "Foxes and people both eat chickens. With foxes it means less chickens, but with people you get more chickens. See what I mean? It's the same with everything else." She stared down at the muesli and fruit on his plate and smiled faintly to herself.

"What's funny?" Jarrow asked.

"Oh, I'm sorry. . . . It just seems strange to watch you—sorry, but I can't help thinking of Tony—eating that kind of food. He was always meat, potatoes, and everything fried."

Jarrow maintained a cold, defensive look. "Why? Didn't he believe in keeping healthy?"

"Look," Rita said, gesturing at him generally. "How does it feel? Looks okay to me. From the way you talk, it sounds as if *you're* the one who had problems. He didn't believe any of that garbage. I don't either."

"It's all been scientifically proved," Jarrow assured her loftily.

Rita snorted. "Stuff a rat till it bursts, then wonder why it got sick? You don't call *that* science. It'd be like testing a piano with a sledgehammer and saying it's equal to ten years of playing. I mean, you just can't do that. . . . Those people aren't scientists, not *real* scientists. They're paid propaganda hacks. They start out with the answers they want to prove. Science doesn't work like that."

It seemed they were about to get into another of their arguments, when Josef came into the room and rescued the situation. "Oh, you're still eating," he said.

"That's okay. What is it?" Jarrow answered.

"I thought you'd like to know, Rita's place is still under surveillance by federal security agents," he informed them. Which meant they had done the right thing at Sandy and Bruce's by deciding not to risk going back there. All the same, Sandy and Bruce would no doubt be wondering what had happened to them, Jarrow thought. The same thing evidently occurred to Rita.

"Could I call the people that we stayed with, just to let them know we're okay?" she asked, looking at Josef. There was a phone upstairs somewhere that Jarrow and Rita didn't have ready access to, doubtless intentionally. They hadn't seen any reason to disclose which of the names, from the list of possibilities that the Pipeline people had compiled and called, they had sought refuge with after fleeing the apartment, and Josef hadn't asked them.

"The number could have been tagged," Josef cautioned. "If we were able to come up with some likely guesses, so could the FSS."

"I wasn't going to call them direct," Rita told him. "There's another friend who'll pass it on," meaning Eric.

Josef smiled. "I see you're starting to think like a professional.

We'll end up recruiting you yet. Very well. Come this way." He glanced at Jarrow. "Excuse us for a moment."

"Go ahead."

Josef and Rita left the room. Jarrow finished his meal, rose, and sauntered back into the living room. Kay was alone by the wood-stove, pondering over her notes. She had spent a lot of time the day before talking to him about his background and views, and made innumerable trips up and down the stairs, calling and taking calls from mysterious people, probably the ones who were on their way.

"Feeling better?" she asked, glancing up.

"Much."

"That's good."

He moved over toward the warmth and ran an eye over the files and papers strewn around her. "Are we getting anywhere?"

"Maybe," Kay said. She put down the pad she'd been jotting in and sat back. "The Jarrow side of all this makes sense. It's the Gordon part that doesn't fit."

"How come?"

"We know that the primary object of Southside was political reprogramming, not military training. And Tony Demiro would have been an ideal test subject—deep-rooted, anti-Establishment radicalism like his would be exactly the kind of thing they'd want to see if they could change. But not only that. He was an orphan, without close family connections, who joined the Army basically to have something to belong to. What was going on at Pearse was a shady, underhanded business. . . . You see what I'm getting at. If anything went wrong, he could quietly be made to disappear without fuss and complications—as in fact seems to have happened."

Jarrow sat down slowly in one of the other chairs. That much made sense, certainly. "Yes, I see."

"And that's where you come into it," Kay said.

He didn't see how immediately. "Go on," he said.

Kay made a tossing motion with her fingers. "The new patterns that were implanted had to be extracted from a suitable *source*." She gestured toward Jarrow briefly. "Well, wouldn't Richard Jarrow, the respectable, conservative schoolteacher—I'm not being impolite or offensive, am I? Is that how you'd describe yourself?"

"Well, yes, I can't say I'd disagree," Jarrow said, not really seeing what there was to be impolite or offensive about in that.

"Wouldn't somebody like you have been the perfect original for the kinds of patterns they'd need to reprogram somebody like Demiro?" Kay completed.

Jarrow blinked. Now that she had spelled it out, it seemed so obvious. "Of course," he murmured. "Of course. That's what Valdheim was doing, wasn't it?"

"Yes. That whole setup was a fake. Why would the Health Service use private practices to test a new technique? They've got enough places of their own, which they have far more control over. In any case, they're trying to phase out private practice, not encourage it."

Jarrow put a hand to his brow and shook his head as he strove to piece together what that meant. "So what are you saying?" he asked finally. "That something went wrong. Instead of just extracting the . . . the codes, patterns, whatever you call them, that they wanted, my entire . . . 'personality' got dumped somehow, instead?" He stared incredulously at her, not wanting to believe it; but there was no other explanation.

"Yes, something like that." Suddenly Kay sounded weary.

Jarrow slumped back in the chair. "So Rita's right? I am really Demiro, just suffering from the delusion of being Jarrow?"

Kay sighed. "I don't know if that's the right way to put it," she said, endeavoring to soften the impact. "After all, what *is* a person? If a personality is defined by a dynamic configuration of neural activity, then you're Richard Jarrow. Is there more of Demiro underneath as well, somewhere? We have no way of knowing. And what about those strange manifestations of an alter ego that you say have happened twice now?—Rita says that Tony Demiro was nothing like that. All we can conclude is that more went on at Pearse than we're able to account for right now."

It didn't help Jarrow's discomfort. From outside there came the sound of a vehicle pulling up in the driveway. He looked away for a moment as footsteps sounded, going around to the side door of the house. Josef came down from upstairs and went through into the kitchen. They heard the back door open and close, and then voices talking indistinctly.

Jarrow faced back toward Kay. "What I don't understand about it all is why I find nothing abnormal in my appearance," he said. "If I think I'm Jarrow, but physically this is Demiro, then why don't I see any clash?"

"I've been wondering about that too," Kay admitted. "It's impossible to be certain. There's never been a case like this before."

"But you do have an idea?" Jarrow persisted. "You said you were involved with similar work Offworld on Luna with this—what was his name, the Russian?—Ulkanov."

"Well, possibly. . . . This is all very crude and speculative, you understand. But basically, it's pretty established these days that the mind contains two distinct operating levels. First, there's what we call the 'data' level, which processes fact-based information handled by the intellectual faculties: all the things that you 'know' and remember as representative of the real world. Then, below that, is the 'associative' level, which contains the structures and relation-ships that are invoked unconsciously by the operations of those faculties."

It made a sort of sense. Jarrow nodded for her to continue.

"Okay. Well, what I suspect is that the patterns that Ashling's process implants only modify the recipient's neurochemical struc-ture at the data level. That would mean, for example, that your intellectual personality knows itself to be Richard Jarrow, and remembers factually related details that come with that knowledge—for example, that Jarrow is forty-six and has a mus-tache." Jarrow nodded again. Kay went on, "But the associative-level correlates have remained unaltered. So when the data-level Jarrow reaches down, as it were, to access the deeper associative substrate supporting that identity, the pictures that are returned to consciousness derive from the associative level of Demiro. That's why you're unable to recall any visual images other than the younger, darker complexioned, clean-shaven face that you see in the mirror, and you find nothing amiss."

Jarrow swallowed visibly. "So there's no question, then. . . . The person who was originally me . . ." He couldn't finish it. But it really didn't need saying.

Then he realized that Josef was at the kitchen door and had been listening to the tail end of the conversation. He came forward into the room and was followed by the new arrival, wearing a hooded, red overjacket on top of a white sweater. He was tall, bronzed, and athletically built, with curly blond hair and clear eyes. Whereas, previously, Jarrow had classed Josef as "leader" among the group at the house, the presence that the newcomer brought into the room was commanding. Here, he knew at once, instinctively, was the person who would produce a decision on where they went next.

Kay obviously knew him and was about to say something, but he raised a hand. "No, that's all right. Please carry on."

Kay looked at Jarrow again. "Can there really be any doubt? The records that you saw in Minneapolis are about as conclusive as you can get." She hesitated. "We can see what must have happened. You used to see Valdheim about once a month, yes? Your last recollection is from the visit on April third. Everything was normal. Those must have been the occasions when Valdheim obtained the implants to send down to Pearse. But the visit on April third turned out to be the last, when Jarrow died unexpectedly from a stroke on May fifth—corresponding to a time about six months into the program at Pearse, which had begun in earnest the previous October.

"Then something went wrong down at Pearse, and Demiro was overwritten with an entire transplant of the Jarrow identity at its data level. To cover up what had been going on and prevent awkward questions being asked, Demiro was officially eliminated from the picture."

And Demiro, in effect, became Jarrow. There was no point in trying to deny it any longer. Jarrow exhaled a heavy sigh. Kay showed an empty palm, indicating that there was nothing more she could say.

"But this is November," Jarrow said. "Demiro was listed as killed in June. So what's been happening in these last five months? Where do Samurai and Gordon come into it?"

Josef spoke for the first time since entering the room. "We don't know. But we need to find out. Furthermore, what connection did it have with Ashling and his disappearance?"

"And we think that you, Mr. Jarrow, can enable us to find the answers to both questions," the newcomer said.

Kay motioned toward him as he came forward to look down at where Jarrow was sitting. "Richard, this is Scipio, another of our team."

Jarrow nodded in acknowledgment, but was too startled by the statement to let it go just then. "Me?" he said uncomprehendingly. "How can I help?"

"From the inside," Scipio replied. "Where none of us can penetrate. But that's where the answers are, and only you can get there."

Jarrow's bewilderment only increased further. "How?" he asked again. "What do you want me to do?"

"We want you to let the FSS agents who are looking for you find you, and go back to Pearse with them as Samurai," Scipio said. "Which shouldn't be too difficult to accomplish. After all, that's who they seem to think you are."

Jarrow looked from one to another of them in sudden alarm. "Now wait a minute. Whatever else you or those people at Pearse may think, I'm a schoolteacher. I don't know anything about what Samurai was doing. I couldn't hope to pass myself off as him. I wouldn't last five minutes."

Scipio sat down on an arm of one of the chairs and gazed at him intently. "It mightn't be as bad as you assume. Think about it for a minute. The people at Pearse were tampering with minds, and they know that something strange happened in Demiro's case. They know that he was acting unstably in Chicago. They won't know what to expect next. They'll be prepared for anything. You go in pleading amnesia, confusion, reversion to past personality types—whatever suits the situation. I think there's a good chance of pulling it off. You're the key to uncovering what's been going on in this whole business."

What Scipio was saying carried an implication that their problem was automatically Jarrow's problem, and that they all saw things from the same viewpoint. But Jarrow was far from accepting that such was the case.

"No," he said, shaking his head. His voice had a tight edge. "I don't think it's that simple at all. I'm sorry, but this kind of thing isn't my line." He stood up and turned, making a sweeping motion with his hand that took in the whole company. "You . . . you come up with this story about sinister brainwashing plots, then presume that I should want to get involved to elaborate it further—as if it were some duty I owe. . . . It could all be a paranoid invention for all I know. I mean, how do any of *you* know? Have you checked it? How?"

"That's precisely what we're asking you to help us do, Mr. Jarrow," Scipio pointed out.

"Why should *I* help your subversions against my own government?" Jarrow retorted. "*You* are the aliens here, not me. This kind of notion might be credible where you come from, but it isn't here. This isn't that kind of country. We have a Constitution that gives our citizens certain rights protected by laws. I don't suppose anybody from Offworld could comprehend things like that."

That was too much for Kay. "*Rights!*" she exploded. "*You* talk to us about rights? What right could be more basic than the freedom to become whatever you're capable of? And that's just what the Offworld culture means: room for everyone to grow, and achieve, and become; with unlimited room to do it in and unlimited means to do it with, because new technologies create their own resources out of things that weren't resources before. We're already building industries that will make Earth's as obsolete as the windmills and waterwheels of the Middle Ages."

She too got up, walked over to a window, then turned to face the room again. "And what's happening down here? This idiocy that you call the Consolidation is the final expression of closed minds and a closed system. It's driven by this obsession with limits that exist only in its own collective imagination, dangers magnified out of all proportion until the fear of them paralyzes everything, even the capacity to think. There was a time when the West believed in itself, in reason, in its ability to carry on creating better futures. Now it's having to put up fences to keep its people in and the truth out. How much longer do you think something like that can last? It has to cave in under its own self-doubts and superstitions. The younger people are starting to reject it already. You try to indoctrinate them with defeatism and negativism, but their instincts tell them it's wrong. . . . And you talk to us about rights?"

Jarrow looked back at her stonily. "I teach reality," he replied coldly. "Not simple-minded pipe dreams. When your bubbles burst, then you'll be coming back, expecting us to take you back in. Don't think we won't be prepared."

"Oh, God, surely nobody really believes that," Kay groaned tiredly.

Josef made an appealing gesture at Jarrow, trying in turn. "But surely you can't deny the erosion of freedoms that used to be taken as basic. Even travel is restricted. Ashling had to approach us, an underground organization, to get himself out of the country."

"Regrettable, I agree, but necessary," Jarrow maintained unyieldingly. "Crime grows with population: vice, drugs. Terrorism is rampant everywhere. Do you think such people can be allowed to come and go whenever they please? We *have* to have controls."

"What terrorism?" Josef scoffed. "Show me where it exists as anything beyond an occasional nuisance, apart from in official propaganda and in the world created by mass media."

"Ask your friend Daparras," Jarrow retorted.

"He's a writer, for heaven's sake," Kay pleaded. "And the Offworld population centers are far more densely crowded. But their society is open. People can live their lives as they please."

"Reckless and irresponsible," Jarrow opined. "You've got uncontrolled anarchy in the making. A workable society has to be structured and directed."

"You mean as with this environmentalist fascism that's out of control down here, bankrupting practically the entire West?" Josef said.

"I'd call it responsible stewardship of a legacy that Offworlder mentalities are either unable to comprehend or have forgotten," Jarrow said.

Scipio could see that this wasn't going to get them anywhere, and held up a hand. "Maybe so, maybe not," he said. "We're not going to resolve any of that right now. But look at the actions of Valdheim and Nordens and whoever was behind them, and how the thing at Pearse was set up. It was hardly done in a way that you could call ethical, was it? Doesn't that say something about the powers that are running things here?"

"And I still say you're prejudging an issue that you know nothing about," Jarrow replied. "I don't know what really happened, and neither do you." He advanced a step and pointed a finger. "But I'll tell you one thing I do know, and that is that if whatever it was hadn't happened, I wouldn't be standing here now. So you three can intellectualize all you want, but that *fact* happens to mean a lot to me!"

"But that's what we're asking you to do: to *help us find out!*" Kay said again, her voice rising uncontrollably.

Jarrow had heard as much as he was prepared to listen to. His voice rose too, and his color deepened. "Oh, is that so? Well, now let me tell you something: I too would be curious to know how I got to be this way. But it's a lot to get mixed up in just to satisfy curiosity. I feel like an integrated, functioning person, and this body I've inherited seems a great improvement over what I remember. I figure that *I* can live with the complications. If you people want to know what went on down there in Pearse, well, that's fine by me but it's your problem. After being told twice in the last week that I'm dead, I'm quite starting to like the idea of being alive after all, and I'd prefer to stay that way. Who do you think you are to assume that I'm available for the asking to promote *your* ends? I've got my own. If you want to go messing with the FSS and the military, then go ahead. But I can live with the situation."

And with that, Jarrow marched stiffly and tight-mouthed from the room.

After a silence Kay said with a sigh, "I guess we blew it."

Scipio stared at the stove. "There must be a way," he insisted. "We have to find one. He's the only link we have to Ashling."

twenty-three

Kay was in the kitchen talking to Susan, who was making coffee, when Rita came back downstairs. Josef and Scipio were still talking by the stove in the next room. There was no sign of Jarrow or Leon.

"What was that all about?" Rita asked. "It sounded like tempers were getting frayed, so I stayed out of it."

"Very wise," Kay said. She sat down on one of the stools at the breakfast bar. "Oh, I got a bit carried away about some things that Jarrow takes seriously. It was a mistake. I find it difficult to stay calm about matters I feel strongly about, and he's no different. People are never more irrational than when their prejudices are under attack."

"Welcome to the human race," Susan murmured, setting mugs down on a piece of board to use as a tray. Kay sent her a tired smile of thanks. Susan indicated the coffees and raised her eyebrows at Rita. "You want one too?"

"Thanks, I'll fix myself one."

"It's all there." Susan picked up the board and disappeared with it back out to the living room. Rita moved over to the worktop to fill another mug.

"So where is he now?" she asked Kay over her shoulder.

"Gone out for a walk to get some air, and hopefully cool down a little. Josef sent Leon with him."

Rita finished making her drink and sat down with it at the table. "You really are from Offworld, then?" she said, changing the subject. "You live out there?"

"Yes. Not born there, of course, although a generation is growing up now that's genuine Offworld native."

"Where were you from originally?" Rita asked, intrigued.

"Germany. It used to be divided once. I don't know if you'd remember anything about that."

"It got split up after some war, didn't it? Was that the big war over resources, that the demands of industrializing made inevitable?"

"It wasn't quite like that," Kay said.

Rita shrugged. "I only know what they said at school."

"I studied computer science at first," Kay resumed. "I wanted to get into Artificial Intelligence and understand how the mind works. That was the latest explanation then, you see. It's funny how people are always finding that the mind works like their latest technology. It never does, of course, but it shows how they always think that the latest technology must be the ultimate. At one time the brain was an elaborate telephone exchange of nerves going in and out. Then, after servomechanisms were developed, it worked by feedback loops and error signals. And then after that, naturally, it had to be a computer."

"Which turned out not to be true either," Rita said.

Kay shook her head. "It's based on the selective training of neuronal groupings, not information storage. A brain isn't so much a receptacle of programs as an *expression* of them." She sipped her coffee. "Anyway, so I moved from computers into neurophysiological research. But everything was starting to get political by then. The Consolidation had formed and was closing its eastern borders to enforce sanctions against the FER states that weren't following the Green initiatives, and ideological factors were hampering all fields of research. So I crossed over with some friends in the aftermath of the final Soviet breakup . . . probably as much from curiosity and the hope of excitement as for any reason that made sense, I suppose." Kay smiled distantly at the far wall. "People called it the Wild East, in those days. There were so many conflicting stories coming back that no one knew what to believe. We were all young, thirsty for change and adventure. In the years that followed, I was swept along with the thrust offplanet that began from there . . . and now if anyone asked me where home is, I'd have to say Tycho."

"You've actually been to the Moon," Rita said dreamily.

Kay gave a short laugh. "People probably said the same kind of thing about America once."

"What made you come back?"

"I thought that was pretty obvious. I finally did get to work in the field I'd always wanted to, and ended up associated with Professor Ulkanov, whom you heard about. He already knew that some of the things Ashling was doing were revolutionary—I told you about the communications grapevine that scientists use to evade the Consolidation controls. Ulkanov had already got Ashling's name put on Pipeline's target list, so when the news came through that Ashling had contacted Pipeline independently and wanted to get out, it was given top priority. I agreed to come down and help out."

"I thought Tycho was supposed to be some kind of militarized base up there," Rita said. "Isn't it like an industrial gold-rush camp? You know, all violence and lawlessness. People being exploited for high pay in hazardous conditions, and that kind of thing?"

Kay laughed again, with open amusement this time. "I know that's what people are told," she said. "But why do you think communications are controlled here? Ours aren't. There are over fifty thousand people at Tycho now. Three times as many at Copernicus. The Newton and Aristotle colonies are being expanded further. There are pilot bases on Mars."

"Those are colonies, not military platforms? It said on TV the other week that they're building a beam-gun on one of them that could incinerate Chicago."

"They're space habitats," Kay assured her. "Do I look like a comic-book scientist who wants to rule the world? I've got three children who go to school at Tycho. They live in a warm, comfortable house below the surface"—she gestured with a hand, indicating the place they were in—"not like this box, sticking up into the cold, with wind blowing through the clapboard and bugs in the walls—which is part of a complex that includes a mall, small but it has everything, pool, leisure center all outside the door. Their friends are just a walk away, and there's a dome with a park in it two levels up. It's our place, and we chose it. It wasn't allocated or assigned, we can sell it for whatever we can get, anytime we choose, without needing a transfer approval, price clearance, or certificate of paid-up taxes. Does that sound like a shack by the Klondike to you?"

"I wouldn't have thought you had children, somehow," Rita said, propping her chin on a hand and staring. "How old are they?"

"Oh, Max is fifteen. He's into all things electronic. And there are two girls, Maria, who's twelve and wants to do the same as me, and

Annette, who's a year younger and hasn't a clue yet. But there's plenty of time. I'm an old relic, though, by today's standards."

"Oh, listen to her. Don't say that," Rita protested.

"Offworlders have children early. Teenage parenthood is common; in fact it's encouraged. So I'll probably be a granny before very much longer."

"Who's your husband?" Rita asked.

"His name is Joao. He is from Brazil. We met in the Ukrainian Republic."

"What does he do?"

"He's a mathematician, involved in plasma dynamics. When the Consolidation barriers went up, it created havoc in what used to be called the Third World. The South American dictatorships fell apart, and Africa and the Islamic areas were economic shambles with the collapse of investments. The productive elements from everywhere flocked into the new FER states, and that was where the momentum came from that created a new renaissance. The irony of it all was that what drove them together were the Green policies that the West was trying to foist on the rest of the world to keep the Third World backward and stop it becoming an industrial competitor. But the frauds and hoaxes that were manufactured as pretexts for imposing political controls got out of hand, and the fanatics who believed it all ended up in charge. So while the West was shutting itself in with its own delusions, capital from East Asia and Japan was launching the expansion offplanet, from the FER. That's why the Offworld links today are to there and not here."

"Tony used to talk about defecting to the FER," Rita said, staring down at her mug. "It's funny, listening to you and thinking of some of the things he used to say. Maybe he knew more about what was going on than I realized. We always wanted a large family. He always wanted to open a bookstore. . . ." She looked up at Kay and hesitated. "Do you think there's a chance that he really is still there somewhere—in Jarrow, I mean? Could he be revived somehow? Is it possible?"

"You were very fond of each other, weren't you?" Kay said. Rita nodded mutely. Kay sighed. "I really can't say. I wouldn't want to raise your hopes unduly. . . . But if you're looking for a way to help, then find a way of getting him to cooperate in finding Ashling. If it is possible at all, Ashling is the one who'd know how."

"Why should he?" Rita asked. "Why should Jarrow want to do that? He'd be wiping himself out."

Which Rita could see; so why hadn't she been able to see it too, before she went shooting her mouth off? Kay asked herself glumly. Why was it that the most obvious things in life were always the last ones you saw?

Jarrow went straight up to his room when he returned. He was still in a sullen mood ten minutes later when a knock sounded on the door.

"Who is it?" he called gruffly.

"Rita."

"What do you want?"

"To talk for a minute."

He opened the door. She came in, and sat down on the edge of the bed, staring at him.

"I assume they've sent you up here to have a go at me too," Jarrow said, sounding not particularly friendly.

"Somebody has to do something if we're ever going to get out of this," Rita replied evenly, refusing to be put on the defensive.

"That's easy. They can simply disappear."

"And leave you to do what?" she said, bordering on sounding derisive. "Report back to Kankakee and say you're not dead, it was just a small case of AWOL?"

"You still think of me as Demiro, don't you?" Jarrow said. "Well, I'm not. Why won't you get it into your head that I'm a different person? The Army has listed him as dead. It would be a lot easier if you accepted it as meaning just that, and went back to picking up your own life the way you were. I'm sorry I intruded into it as I did, just when you were finding your feet again, but you know how it was, and I can't change that now." Rita said nothing. Jarrow looked across at her sourly. "Or isn't that good enough? Have you still got hopes that I'll revert back to being Demiro, somehow? Is that why you want me to go back to Pearse? That's what you think might happen there? It would suit you nicely, wouldn't it. Never mind how *I* might feel about it."

Rita ignored the barbs. "They would hardly reinstate Tony, even if they could, would they? He's officially dead. Why would they want to complicate everything by bringing him back? If they reinstated anyone, it would be Gordon, Samurai—whichever one you call him. He's the one who showed up at the Hyatt to begin with."

"No, they wouldn't," Jarrow agreed. "But Ashling might know how to do it. You'd like that, wouldn't you. You want them to find Ashling."

For the first time, Rita's voice took on an angry note. "And why not? What do you expect? Look, I've just about had enough of hearing about your problems all the time, and how *you* feel about everything. Now how do you think I feel, for a change? Look, mister, I'm sorry and all that, but Richard Jarrow died last May. Naturally. He had his run, and it was over. In Tony's case it was different. *His* certificate had to be faked. Yours didn't. *You* don't belong here. You're living in a stolen body."

Jarrow's jaw tightened obstinately. "Maybe, but it wasn't my doing. Stolen or whatever, it happens to be the only one I've got. I can't change that now, either. Do you really expect me to give it up?"

"I'm not expecting anything. I'm just asking you to help find out what the facts are. I'll take the risk that it might mean losing Tony for good. Those people downstairs obviously believe in the things they say, and they're prepared to back them. Why can't you show the same conviction about the things you say you believe in? I mean, I can't see what your problem is. If what you say is right, you don't have anything to lose."

Jarrow frowned at her. "What do you mean?" he asked.

"Look at it this way," Rita said. "Scipio and the others are prepared to let you go back into Pearse, thinking the way you do now. But to be any use to them, you'll have to stay in touch, won't you? In other words, they'll have to set up some channel for you to communicate back to them. But once you're among your friends, there'd be nothing to stop you from setting Pipeline up and sending them straight to the FSS. But Scipio's saying he'll risk that, which is another way of saying he's pretty sure that when you find out what they're really up to there—these people that you have so much trust in and defend so touchingly—you'll change your mind. So what do you have to lose? How come you can't match it?"

Jarrow stared steadily at her. Clearly this was a line of thinking that he hadn't pursued himself.

"And anyhow, what alternative do you have?" Rita tossed in as a final word.

But although her words had made an impression, Jarrow still wasn't of a mood to be pliable. "I'm sick of all of you," he snapped. "I'd like to be thought of as something other than a laboratory rat for once. For your information I do have alternatives. I have contacts, back in Minneapolis. I can go west, to the mountains. I can take care of my own life without anyone at Pearse, and without you. Now please leave me alone."

But later, after turning the thought over in his mind for some time, he had to concede that Rita had a valid point. Seriously, what alternative did he have? He obviously couldn't stay here forever. And if he refused to cooperate and Pipeline gave up and ditched him, what then? He'd be left on the streets with some cash that would soon run out, a few credit cards that could be invalidated at any time, no job, and no ID apart from a couple of scraps relating to someone who didn't exist. He didn't really believe his line himself about going to the mountains with Paul—he'd met Paul only once, in a bar. At the bottom of it all, despite his talk, he was, inside, still a timid, not very adventurous schoolteacher.

Unwittingly, driven by her own misguided hopes, Rita had given him his answer. Obviously the thing to do was go back to Pearse and get among the people who had the real power to change things. Then he could forget all about Pipeline and their fantasies. There really was no immediate conflict of interests. If Kay and the others hadn't been more interested in peddling their infantile ideals and getting him excited, instead of concentrating on the matter at hand, he'd have seen it for himself in the first place.

Very well, he told himself. So let's get on with it.

He went back downstairs and sought out Scipio. "Tell me again how this would work?" he said.

"Very simply," Scipio replied. "All you do is go back to the people who sent you and tell them you've been having blackouts and amnesia. We'll give you details of a means of getting in touch with us later, should you wish to do so. I'm sorry if we made it sound like an elaborate espionage undertaking of some kind. I don't really see what the problem is."

"There isn't any," Jarrow told him. "Very well, I'll do it."

twenty-four

What was needed next was a believable way of making Jarrow visible again. Kay's suggestion was to use Rita. How, Kay asked, would a woman react if her supposedly dead fiancé reappeared suddenly not knowing where he had been, and then promptly forgot who he was? Eventually, whether she liked it or not, she might be forced to take it to the authorities. That, then, would bring Jarrow to the attention of the people who wanted him back.

Rita's story would describe his worsening condition of confusion and amnesia, and how she had come to the realization within days that this wasn't going to be something she could cope with. Unwilling to simply abandon him, she had decided that her only choice was to seek help. She accepted that it would mean getting involved with officialdom and having to answer endless questions. Jarrow concurred readily with whatever was said, since he was only playing along, anyway. When he got free of them and back to Pearse, his intention was to tell the whole story straight and let the experts there sort it out.

Josef, with Susan and Leon, drove Jarrow and Rita back into the city. To create a false trail to account for their movements in the past forty-eight hours, Josef gave Jarrow a collection of meal tabs, subway and bus tickets, and shopping receipts from various parts of Chicago that he had assembled, to be found on Jarrow's person when he was picked up. Gordon's credit card, it turned out, was still valid— probably deliberately so, to provide a means of locating him. Later that night, Jarrow and Rita checked into one of the smaller downtown hotels, again to leave a verifiable trail. Jarrow remained there the next morning, while Rita went alone to the police station of the local precinct.

"Morning, ma'am. What can we do for you?" the desk sergeant inquired. She looked haggard, he noted—as if she had a lot on her mind.

"There's a guy who's sick," Rita replied. "It's a really strange situation. I can't deal with it. He's back in a hotel about three blocks from here, right now. It's called the Griffin. You need to get somebody down there right away."

The sergeant drew across a pad. "Is he okay?"

"I think so. But he wasn't making any sense. I was scared he might get violent."

"What's his name?"

"Demiro. Tony Demiro. . . . We were engaged. He needs help."

The sergeant went over to a desk at the rear and used a screen to check the current list of hot names, then paused and glanced at her. "Would you excuse me for one moment?" he said, and went through to a back room to notify the captain. The captain checked a number he had been given and made a call.

In an office elsewhere in Chicago, an agent of the Federal Security Service turned from his desk. "It's the Chilsen girl. She's just walked in off the street at the police station on Monroe to turn Samurai in. He's at the Griffin."

The chief stood up and reached for his jacket. "Get the team moving," he snapped. "I want all of them over there with full backup. And nobody lets those jerks from Pearse near it, understand? There isn't gonna be another screwup this time."

Three agents sealed off the hotel lobby, supported by a six-man detachment of the city police. Two more agents with more police secured the rear approach, while one agent and two men were posted at each end of the corridor leading to Jarrow's room. Three agents, guns drawn and cocked, went with the manager to open the door, followed by a police detective and four men.

They went in like Marines hitting the beach on Okinawa. *"Police. Freeze!"* the captain in the lead shouted.

Jarrow sat on the edge of the bed and watched indifferently.

There was a moment of anticlimactic uncertainty as the adrenaline highs dissipated.

"Are you Maurice Gordon, resident of Philadelphia, Pennsylvania?" the captain asked, producing a set of handcuffs while the others spread out around the room and covered.

"I don't know," Jarrow replied.

In the drab brown van, Josef and Scipio watched from halfway back along the block as the procession emerged from the Griffin and a cavalcade of unmarked cars and police cruisers formed up to move off. People on the sidewalks were stopping to stare, and faces peered from windows on both sides of the street.

"I'm not convinced that he's genuine," Josef muttered, shaking his head.

"Oh, of course he's not genuine," Scipio agreed breezily. "He'll spill the whole story the moment he gets back. We can only hope that what he finds out later will make him come to see things differently. That makes it doubly important that every link back to Pipeline is thoroughly erased."

Apart, of course, from a channel for Jarrow to communicate through, which couldn't be traced. But Josef had a lot of experience in handling requirements like that. They would use a commercial answering service. The number they had given Jarrow would connect him to an answering and recording machine that could be remote-accessed from anywhere. That way, it wouldn't matter much if he divulged the number when he got back to Pearse.

And if he did change his mind later and decided to leave a message, the security people at Pearse wouldn't be able to call in to check, because to interrogate the machine one would need to know the right code, and every time that happened, the code would change to a new one. And only Josef had the list giving the sequence. You couldn't be much more careful than that.

Jerry Tierney, Director of Internal Security at the Pearse Psychological Research Laboratories, took a call from the FSS agent in charge of operations in Chicago, advising that Samurai had been taken without offering resistance. First reports were that he seemed disoriented and had only fragmented recollections of events over the previous few days.

The news wasn't especially a cause for elation. Tierney's original hope when he sent Wesserman and the others to Chicago had been that with the help of the local FSS office, they'd be able to lift Samurai quietly and get him back down to Georgia without anyone who didn't need to know being any the wiser. But Wesserman, or the FSS, or all of them together, had bungled it and been traced through the car that Samurai had ditched, and now the city police were involved, along with the state authorities, God alone knew who else, and the fan was about to receive a shovelful. True, they would doubtless be able to spirit Samurai away under the secrecy protection provisions, but that didn't alter the fact that they had suffered a lot of visibility where it wasn't needed, and some important people weren't going to be pleased. He cleared down, stared reluctantly at the blank screen while he mentally prepared his line, then sighed and touched a button to call Fairfax, the establishment's director.

Raymond Fairfax was in his office with Dr. Nordens, waiting for news. They listened silently while Tierney summarized what had happened, Fairfax sitting erect like some frosty Olympian with his crown of white hair, his mouth clamped in a grim line across his florid features; Nordens watching expressionlessly through his rimless spectacles.

Tierney concluded: "He's being taken to police headquarters up there right now. Wesserman is waiting for them, and will take him in charge immediately under Section 36. But there's still the problem of the girl. Obviously she's going to be blabbing all over the place that Demiro is supposed to be dead, if she hasn't started already. We need a line that'll tie in with it."

Fairfax was aware of that. He should have let Tierney go to Chicago himself and handle things on the spot, the way Tierney had wanted, he told himself bitterly—although it was the last thing he was going to admit now. "We're working on that," he replied. "Stall them for now. Tell Wesserman to say that he knows the subject only by a code name; his job is simply to return him to military custody. So either the girl's crazy, or there must have been a mixup in the records department. Then make sure that Wesserman gets him out without leaving tracks. And I want *you* to monitor every move personally. After that, work out a clean way for getting Wesserman and his whole bunch off the case. We can't risk any more incompetence."

Fairfax cleared down without waiting for Tierney to reply, and looked at Nordens. "I don't like it," he muttered darkly. "The whole business was illicit. It was a mistake ever to have got involved with it. And the others will all be bailing out with emergency chutes when this gets around. It's us that'll be left carrying it. I say the best thing would be to get rid of Samurai as soon as he's back here. Then it'll just be the girl's word against everyone else's that it was Demiro at all. It wouldn't be too difficult to put some holes in her story. . . . Clear up the whole mess. What do you think?"

Nordens remained motionless for several seconds. Finally he said, "I'm not so sure. Samurai is still our best hope for finding Ashling, and if Ashling's loose it could sink all of them, not just you and me. So it would pay them to sit tight in their seats for a little longer yet."

"If Ashling hasn't already slipped the country," Fairfax said.

Nordens gave a barely perceptible shake of his head. "I don't think so. If he had, then Pipeline wouldn't be showing so much interest. . . . And besides, Samurai might be the ideal means for getting rid of the Chilsen girl and putting a stop to any story of hers permanently. We wouldn't want to involve Tierney's people in something like that. Too much risk of it getting messy—especially with all the attention that they've attracted now. Then Samurai can be eliminated without leaving any traces. That would be the best course, for everybody."

Fairfax took a long breath and nodded reluctantly. "All right. Let's get Jerry over here when he's off the line from Chicago. This time I want us both to be in on all the details, every step of the way."

twenty-five

Jarrow was flown south to a military airbase that he took to be in Georgia, where a helicopter was waiting to collect him, along with the three men whom the police had handed him over to in Chicago. They flew at a modest height for about twenty minutes over wooded, hilly terrain and an occasional river valley. Then, a broken area between the trees ahead unfolded into a cluster of white and brown office blocks and other structures several stories high, standing amid a sprawl of outbuildings and parking lots, a tower with a water tank and another carrying communications antennae, all geometrically segmented and enclosed by lines of wire fences. As the helicopter descended, the central complex of buildings rose up and took on solid form to look for a moment like the superstructure of a ship sailing on a sea of green . . . and then they were landing on a pad in front of a five-story frontage of polished stone panels and copper-tinted glass. They got out to the scent of pines and a breeze pleasantly mild after the wintriness of Illinois. Everything about the surroundings suggested efficiency, organization, authority, and order, from the military emblem painted on the helicopter's fuselage to the smartly turned-out uniformed guards in the post ahead of them beside the door. Jarrow felt the reassurance of being on the right side and in capable hands at last. His problems, he was sure, would soon be resolved.

They took him up to the top floor, where wood-paneled doors opened off carpeted corridors, and secretaries sat at desks with terminals and screens outside glass-partitioned offices. He waited in a small room with chairs and a table set conference style, and a woman in a pastel blue two-piece and blouse brought him a snack with a cup of coylene. Then he was shown into a spacious office with a leather-topped desk standing before a wall of tinted windows looking out over the Georgia hills. A man with white hair and a pinkish, tight-mouthed countenance, wearing a dark suit, was sitting behind the desk. With him were a sallow-faced man with dark curly hair, dressed in a light tan suit, and a smaller man with rimless spectacles and an intense expression, who, from the description that Josef had obtained from Ashling, had to be Dr. Nordens. Jarrow guessed the man behind the desk to be the director, Raymond Fairfax, whose name Josef had supplied in the course of briefing Jarrow with as much as he knew about the setup at Pearse. Jarrow didn't know who the third man was.

Jarrow sat down, and the assistant who had shown him in withdrew, closing the door. Fairfax stared at him fixedly for several seconds. It was a troubled look, the look of somebody trapped into something he'd rather not have to deal with, and at the same time wary of an unknown.

Finally he said, "Why did you decide to run? What did you think you were doing?"

Jarrow shrugged and did his best to look mystified but composed. The fastest way to getting this whole business resolved would be to tell them everything candidly.

"I don't know," he replied simply. "I don't remember anything about it."

The news didn't seem to take Fairfax by surprise. But of course he would already have known enough to have expected that. "Do you know who I am?" he asked, looking at Jarrow strangely. He raised a hand in a brief, dismissive gesture. "Do you know these people . . . or these surroundings, where you are?"

"From what I've been told, I presume this is the Pearse military psychological laboratories," Jarrow replied. "I don't know if I've been in this office before. I imagine that you're the director here, Raymond Fairfax." Jarrow inclined his head to indicate the others. "This looks like Dr. Nordens, whom I know I've dealt with. . . . I'm sorry, I can't place you."

"This is Jerry Tierney," Fairfax said. "He's in charge of security operations here." Tierney returned a faint nod.

Nordens shifted his posture and looked at Jarrow, intrigued. "Who told you these things?" he asked. "What's the last thing you do remember?"

Jarrow took a moment to collect his words, and then began relating his story. He described his last recollection of visiting Valdheim in April, then told of waking up in Atlanta with no idea of how he got there; his journey back to Minneapolis, discovery that it was November, and confusion on learning that Richard Jarrow was dead; of going to Chicago and the subsequent events there after meeting Rita. "I realize now that what happened was a misunderstanding," he said. "Your people were merely taking precautions, as they had to in the circumstances. There wasn't any violence or shooting or anything like that. The problem was my doing, for overreacting."

"Where did you go after you evaded them?" Nordens asked curiously.

"Some friends of Rita's put us up for the night, in another part of Chicago."

"Do you have their names or the address?" Tierney asked.

Jarrow hesitated. He didn't see how that could be useful. "No, I'm afraid I don't. It didn't seem important."

"Carry on," Fairfax said.

Jarrow told how he had learned from Rita that the day before he awoke in Atlanta he had apparently been functioning as Warrant Officer Tony Demiro, who had been connected with certain work going on at Pearse, and that this was Demiro's physical body. Finally, he described how they were contacted by Pipeline, the meeting with Josef, and the two days that followed in the house somewhere outside the city. The people from Pipeline were looking for a scientist called Ashling, who had apparently disappeared from Pearse, and they thought that Jarrow would be able to help. In response to Tierney's further questioning, Jarrow described the Pipeline agents whom he had met and outlined their apparent functions. He concluded, managing a hint of a wry smile, "They hoped they could recruit me as a spy to work for them on the inside, here at Pearse. I played along with it because it seemed the only way to get away. So here I am. . . . And now you know as much as I do."

He waited. There was a drawn-out silence. Jarrow looked from

182 James P. Hogan

one to the other expectantly, but their expressions remained unreadable. At length Nordens asked him, "Do you recall anything at all
about Ashling?"

Jarrow shook his head. "Apart from what they told me, no,
nothing."

"Nothing about Ashling's intending to leave the country,
maybe? About where he might be going?"

"Nothing," Jarrow said again. "But they were anxious to find
him too, so I imagine he's still here."

Nordens nodded. He seemed relieved.

"You don't actually remember anything about being Demiro the
day before you woke up as you are now?" Tierney checked once
again.

"No."

"Anything at all prior to waking up on November seventeenth."

"Nothing since the visit to Valdheim on April third. Up to that
point everything was normal."

"Does the name Samurai mean anything?" Nordens asked.

"Your agents called me that when they tried to intervene in
Chicago. I assume it was some kind of code designation associated
with whatever Demiro was involved in here."

Nordens gave a noncommittal nod. "I see."

Again there was silence. Jarrow looked from one to the other,
puzzled and feeling increasingly disturbed now. "Look, I've been as
frank as I can," he said at last. "I was hoping for some answers
myself."

Which of course was only reasonable. Nordens took off his
spectacles, squinted through one of the lenses, then removed a speck
of something and replaced them again. "We're not sure of all the
answers ourselves yet," he replied. "We'll need to perform some
tests, check our facts. This is an extremely complicated matter. I'm
sure you understand."

It seemed very vague. Jarrow conceded the point with a nod, but
holding his ground in the manner of one who was still entitled to
something. "Of course. But at least give me an outline of what's been
going on, even if you can't explain all of it just at this moment."

Nordens glanced at Fairfax, who nodded a quick assent. Nordens looked at Jarrow and replied, "Demiro was part of a volunteer
program that we've been running here to investigate a new method

of training military personnel—and eventually we hope it will have many other applications too. Essentially it involves extracting encoded skills from the brains of existing experts, and implanting them into novices. The results have been quite remarkable."

"Yes." Jarrow was aware of that much, which tied in with the things that Josef and Kay had said. What he wasn't ready to accept was the further account of sinister political agendas and deliberate use of unwitting subjects that they had tried to draw from it.

Nordens went on, "Dr. Valdheim's work was also in a new area of physiological research that involved deriving the codes of certain neural patterns, but in his case for pathological diagnosis and treatment. That was why you were referred to him. Well, to cut a long story short, we reached an agreement with the department sponsoring Valdheim's work, under which he could transmit his data here for processing. We possess a large array of computing and other equipment, together with appropriate software, that is already developed to perform precisely the kind of tasks that Valdheim required." Nordens sighed and raised a hand briefly. "As far as we can make out, one of those files from Valdheim—it was still stored here, you understand, after Jarrow's unfortunate death—was somehow mixed up with our own experimental training files, and implanted into Demiro. How it happened, we don't know. And even more perplexing is the fact that the entire Jarrow personality seems to have established itself. By all our models and theories that shouldn't have been possible. And that, of course, is why we're so anxious to find Ashling: an intellect of his caliber will be essential to help us resolve your problem."

"Where's Valdheim now?" Jarrow asked. He had already told of his attempts to locate the doctor when he was in Minneapolis.

"Back in Washington. After the unfortunate setback involving yourself, naturally his program was suspended. As far as I know, the department responsible has ruled to keep details out of the public domain until they have more facts to go on. Premature release of information in cases like this always causes misunderstandings and needless alarm."

There, it all had an innocent explanation, as Jarrow had known all along that it would. "And Samurai?" he inquired lightly, as if just filling in a missing detail. "Where did he come in?"

Nordens tossed up a hand carelessly. "Oh, Samurai and Gordon were pseudonyms connected with some tests we were carrying out on Demiro."

Jarrow was already nodding. He felt like laughing aloud with relief and gratitude. The situation was a bizarre one, no question about that. But the world could be a strange place. The fantasies that Kay and Josef had spun were typical of the delusions of subversive mentalities everywhere, resentful at not having what they thought should be their say in running things, who would say anything to derogate what they couldn't become part of.

"There's just one more thing that I'm not clear on," he said. "How could Demiro have been the subject of all this if he was killed five months ago in June?"

Nordens made a good job of looking puzzled. "Killed? What do you mean, killed?" he asked, taking off his spectacles again.

Jarrow gestured uncertainly. "I told you just now. . . . The girl, Rita Chilsen. She said that Demiro was killed in June, in a helicopter accident."

"Oh, that!" Nordens scoffed, dismissing the suggestion with a wave. "A hysterical woman, maybe wanting to rationalize breaking up with her fiancé or something. Who knows? People do the oddest things all the time, Mr. Jarrow. Sometimes I wonder if half the world is sane at all."

Jarrow was incredulous. "Surely you're not saying that she made it up?"

Nordens allowed his mouth to bend in a rare hint of humor and motioned in Jarrow's direction. "Consider the evidence for yourself. You don't look very dead to me. Do you feel dead, Mr. Jarrow?"

Jarrow saw that the others were smiling thinly too. It was reassuring. *This* was where the power lay, and they were on his side. He smiled in turn, and then broke into a quick laugh that he found impossible to suppress. "No," he told them. "I don't feel dead at all."

Nordens and Tierney took him on a tour of parts of the establishment. He learned that the cluster of larger buildings that they were in was called the Main Complex, which contained the administrative section and much of the laboratory space. The major projects were located within a Restricted Zone, outside which were various ancillary buildings and outstations. One of these was the

Facilities Block, housing such general amenities as the dining hall and cafeteria, medical center, recreational provisions, and a social club. None of it meant anything to Jarrow. They took him out to a fenced compound behind the primary establishment buildings and showed him around inside a military-style billet hut with dormitory area, washrooms, staff room, and kitchen, all very clean, bare, and deserted. Jarrow got the feeling that it was an attempt to trigger his recollections of something by means of association. But it didn't succeed.

Finally they left the main compound and drove around to a wooded area on one side of the establishment, hidden from the main approach road and secluded, where a smaller side gate with its own guardpost gave access to a separate annex area. It consisted of low, bungalow-style chalets and what looked like apartment units, jumbled together around an irregular arrangement of interconnecting parking areas and forecourts. Some effort had been made here to relieve the uniform, military-scientific austerity of the larger adjoining compound, with its faceless walls of concrete, storage tanks, and pipes. The designs of the buildings were colorful and varied, and the outlines broken up with screens of greenery interspersed with pines. This, Jarrow was informed, was the Permanent Quarters Annex, or PQA. It backed onto one side of where Jarrow thought the Restricted Zone perimeter lay inside the Main Complex.

"Do you recognize this place?" Nordens asked him.

This had become a familiar routine by now. Jarrow shook his head. "Sorry. It could be off a street in any town. Should I?"

"Yes, you should," Nordens told him. "It's where you've been living. Come on, we'll show you."

They walked along a path behind several parked vehicles, then up a short flight of stone steps flanked by a grassy mound and a wall masked by shrubbery to a covered walkway that brought them to a door. "Try your keys here," Nordens said.

For a moment Jarrow didn't know what he meant. Then he remembered the keys that he'd taken from the hotel room in Atlanta—which had been no good for his own former apartment in Minneapolis. He took them from his pocket, selected one that looked right, and the door opened on the first try. He withdrew the key and entered. Nordens and Tierney followed.

It was a residential apartment. But not any kind of apartment that Jarrow would have chosen for himself. His first impression was of one of those ultra-contemporary galleries intended to display avant-garde art forms. The floor was of mottled gray, polished marble, the walls stark white, and the furnishings sleek and streamlined, unrelieved harshness, in black leather curves with chrome and steel supports, glass surfaces, ceramic inlays, and tiles. The fittings were contrasting black and white or metal; the framed designs and sculptures adorning the walls and alcoves were angular and sharp; the lighting bright, hard, penetrating, precise. A terminal with several screens and an entertainment selector panel, black and silver, with aluminum controls, formed a cornerpiece between a black-upholstered recliner and a glass-sided, slender-legged desk. Everything was well spaced, positioned exactly, selected for function. Every ornament, even, was there for a purpose. It was all hard, cold, unyielding, without blemish of any wavering to the seductions of softness or color; no admission of the weakness that succumbing to warmth and frivolity betrays.

To Jarrow it was daunting. *He* had lived here? He could no more picture himself inhabiting such surroundings than a piece of sterilized packaging enlarged to room size. If gleaming robots with metal faces and compound-lens eyes ever took over the world in the way the movies depicted, this was where they would come home to.

"We'll leave you on your own for a while to adjust and find your feet," Nordens said. "You'll find all your possessions untouched. There is a domestic staff who look after the Annex and take care of things like housekeeping, catering, and laundry. Seven-seven will get them on the terminal. Is there anything else that you need for now?"

Jarrow was too disoriented by this latest turn of events to think of anything. "No, I don't think so," he said. "You're probably right. Just let me rest up for a while."

Nordens nodded. "Best. It's late afternoon now. I'll be around for a few more hours. If you need to contact me for anything, the terminal will give you my code. Otherwise we'll see you again tomorrow."

After they had left, Jarrow explored the rest of the apartment and found it to consist of a bedroom, kitchen and breakfast area, and bathroom in addition to the living room that he had already seen. In keeping with his first impressions, all of it was harshly etched in black, white, metal, and glass, tile, and ceramic; sheer drapes, maroon-and-black bed linen; suits and jackets of black, light gray, charcoal, and subdued blue in the closet; tailored shirts, silk ties; all dispassionately severe, coldly masculine.

He took off the crumpled clothes of Gordon's that he was wearing again and dropped them into the laundry basket provided. Then he shaved, using a new, manual razor, and after that spent twenty minutes soaping and rinsing away several days of grime, perspiration, travel, and tensions in the shower. He selected some clean clothes and shoes from the closet and drawers in the bedroom, stretched out on the bed, and relaxed totally and luxuriously for almost the next hour. By that time he was feeling hungry. He called the service number from the bedside unit, switched to audio only. A man's voice answered, sounding courteous and obliging. After some questions and answers, Jarrow ordered a cheese-and-mushroom omelette with potatoes, side salad, whole-grain bread with butter, orange juice, followed by milk pudding and fruit desert, cheese with crackers, pot of coylene. He was told it would be there in fifteen minutes.

Shortly afterward, a chime sounded from the front door. Jarrow went out to the living room and opened it. The woman standing there could have been a model for one of the magazines that some of his students occasionally showed up at school with. She had long, straight, ebony-black hair sweeping down to her shoulders, sultry eyes, emphasized with shadowed lids and mascara, and full, heavily made-up lips. Her outfit could have been chosen to match the decor of the apartment, and comprised a black leather skirt, cut at half-thigh length to reveal well-shaped legs in net stockings, a white top embroidered with silver thread, which squeezed and exposed the tops of her breasts, and a light, silver-gray jacket thrown back at the shoulders. She exuded a voluptuous perfume and wore a silver pendant at her throat, bracelets, rings on several of her fingers, and a jeweled broach on one lapel.

To Jarrow the sight was totally unnerving. All he could do was stare, incapable of speech.

"So you're back," she said. Her voice was low, soft, intimately familiar. "Could you use some company over dinner? From your choice, your tastes seem to have changed toward what might be called the more conservative." She reached out a hand with slender fingers tipped by long, red-lacquered nails and undid the top button of his shirt. "Then later, I thought maybe a little . . . 'relaxation' might be a good idea? Kind of, like a welcome home?" Her eyes flickered quickly across his face, but without losing their mischievous half smile. "You don't remember me, do you?"

Jarrow gulped and shook his head. No home comforts were spared for the volunteers here, it seemed. She had evidently been briefed since his arrival.

"I'm Vera," she said.

Confusion came boiling up uncontrollably inside him. "No. . . . Not now, really," he stammered. "I've been affected by some kind of amnesia or something. They must have told you. . . . I just need to rest."

"Sure," she said lightly. She was unperturbed and unfazed, evidently prepared for something like that. "I just wanted to let you know that I'm still around. There'll be plenty of time for reunions later. They say that waiting makes it that much better. I'll see how you're feeling in the morning." She smiled, winked at him, and walked away.

"Yes. . . . Do." Jarrow closed the door shakily and sat down.

He went to bed shortly after finishing his meal. But the feeling of self-congratulatory satisfaction that he had anticipated wasn't there. He thought of Rita, Sandy and Bruce—he was glad now that he'd chosen not to remember their names—of Josef, Kay, and Scipio, and while he could never condone what they stood for, somehow he couldn't bring himself to think of them as "enemy." And while by no stretch of the imagination could he accept that denouncing self-proclaimed saboteurs and subversives qualified as "betrayal" . . . somewhere deep down, he wasn't comfortable about what he had done.

twenty-six

Again Jarrow's sleep was troubled by strange, yet vividly real, dreams. He was one of a group of men who lived in the empty billet hut that Nordens and Tierney had taken him to. They were all military people, he knew somehow, although in the dream everyone wore a green, one-piece smock, something like a surgeon's. They moved with jerky, zombielike motions and their features were distorted like the faces of rubber bendy-dolls. There were mirrors on the walls, which Jarrow continually avoided confronting, because he was terrified of seeing that he might be the same as the others, although he knew all along, anyway, that it was true.

He woke up feeling panicky, and shook while the images faded away. But even when he was fully conscious again, he still felt acutely disturbed. He was unable to pinpoint why.

As his mental gears slowly reengaged, the events of the previous day replayed themselves through his mind, leading him to experience again the vague but firmly rooted dissatisfaction that he had felt just before falling asleep. Something felt very wrong about this whole business. Something was trying to stare him in the face, but the conscious part of him that was in control kept looking the other way.

He got up, showered, and dressed slowly, moving around as he did so and taking in the mood and feeling of the place he was in. These had been his quarters for several months at least, seemingly. Yet nothing was familiar; nothing evoked any flicker of recognition or touched a sympathetic chord of some buried memory. And even more than that, every bit as much as yesterday, it was all so unlike him, so uncharacteristic of anything he could have wished to be a part of, so . . . *alien.*

Several months here—of doing what? How did it tie in with appearing one day at the Atlanta Hyatt as Maurice Gordon, carrying weapons and strange equipment that looked like the kinds of things that secret agents in movies used? Josef had told him that he had arrived there looking for Ashling. Why would Demiro, a volunteer subject for a research program intended to explore a new military training method, know anything about a defecting scientist or be involved with attempts to find him? Could Josef have been simply grasping at a straw in the wild hope that anyone from Pearse might know something about Ashling? . . . No, that didn't ring true, Jarrow told himself. Josef wouldn't act that way. He'd had a reason for saying what he had. Jarrow stopped in the living room and stared at the window looking out over the shrubs screening the parking area below. He had to find out more about those missing months and the connection with Ashling.

The sound of a woman's footsteps approaching came from the walkway below the shrubbery and the steps leading up to the door. Jarrow moved forward, expecting to see Vera again, but it was a dark-skinned girl in a white tunic. She was carrying a plastic bag containing the clothes that Jarrow had left for laundering the evening before. Jarrow opened the door before she could ring.

"Good morning," he said, extending an arm to accept them.

"Good morning, sir. That's all right, I'll take care of it." She had a Hispanic voice. "There were these things as well." She handed him some scraps of paper, ticket stubs, a few receipts, and the memo pad from the Hyatt, all from the pockets of Gordon's gray suit, which he had been wearing yesterday. The girl went through to the bedroom to hang the jacket, shirts, and pants, and put the other items away. Jarrow moved over to the desk and opened one of the drawers to get rid of the things that she had given him. He paused when he saw the note that he had found in the pad on the morning that he first awoke:

Headman to ship out via J'ville, sometime Nov 19. Check ref "Cop 3."

Somebody shipping out? From the things he knew now, he guessed that it was probably a reference to Ashling. Had Samurai known something, then? Yesterday he would have taken this straight to Dr. Nordens. Now, with these new doubts assailing him, he was less sure.

His gaze came to the phone unit standing to one side of the desk. He thought of Vera again. There was somebody who could probably tell him a lot about those crucial missing months. He had no delusions that she had reappeared simply by courtesy of the management to let Samurai have his plaything back; she was on the payroll to watch Jarrow, and doubtless briefed to try to help him jog his memory. In other words she'd be more than ready to talk. . . .

But he'd never learn anything if he wouldn't let her near him. He put the pad in the drawer with the other things and closed it. The girl came back into the living room and began crossing toward the door. "What do I call you?" Jarrow asked, turning his head.

"My name is Maria." A puzzled look crossed her face, as if he should have known that.

"Do you know the lady called Vera, who comes here?"

"Of course, sir."

Jarrow gestured toward the desk. "How would I contact her?"

"Seven-oh will get you the general directory. You should have a personal section indexed from there. I think she would be in that somewhere."

"Thank you."

"You're welcome." Maria smiled a little nervously, gave him a strange look again, and left. Jarrow activated the terminal, tapped in 70, and after a little experimentation found himself looking at Vera's feline-eyed features, framed by the sweep of black hair.

"Well, hello there," she greeted. "Sleep well?"

"Not too bad. Look, I'm just about to order breakfast. How would you like to join me?"

"I'd love it. . . . Why? Changed your mind about needing some company?"

Jarrow fought to try to suppress the flush of color that he could feel rising around his ears. "I'd like to talk some more, anyway," he replied.

Jarrow tried a few guesses based on the two strange regressions that he had experienced, which he presumed were flashes of the mysterious Samurai.

"Are there any recreational facilities here?" he asked Vera as they picked at iced melon and fruit slices across the table in the dining area of the apartment. "A gymnasium, training room, something like that?"

"Why?" Vera asked, raising an eyebrow and looking interested.

"I get the feeling of having been in a place like that here. With a soft mat floor, the kind they do martial arts in."

"Were you doing anything like that yourself?"

"I'm not sure." Jarrow saw the look of anticipation on her face. "Yes, I think I was." He'd read somewhere about how so-called psychics achieved their results by leading their clients into telling them what they were later supposed to have divined. Maybe he could manage something similar too. He sat back and took on a distant expression. "There was a kind of teacher, or maybe sparring partner. He had an odd face, something different about it . . ."

"You mean Oriental, maybe?" Vera said.

"Yes, that was it. He had dark hair. I can see him."

Vera leaned forward encouragingly. "What else?"

"Guns. I did things with guns."

"Where?"

"I don't know."

"Was it outside or inside."

"Er, outside."

"You're sure?"

"Wait. No, maybe it was inside. There were bright lights overhead."

"You mean like in a shooting range?"

"Exactly."

Vera affirmed with a nod. "Yes, there is a range here. You used to use it."

"Right." Jarrow frowned and tried a long shot. "Wasn't there a group of us? We were in one of the huts over the other side."

"That must go back to some earlier days, before I was around."

"Oh. So how long have we known each other?" Jarrow asked.

"Since around early September: a couple of months."

"What happened to the others?"

"As I said, that must have been before my time. I gather you were something special. Anyhow, there weren't any others around by then."

"So how did you appear on the scene?"

"You don't remember anything about that?"

Jarrow had nothing to go on here and could only shake his head. "Not really."

"Maybe we should take another trip to Philadelphia," Vera said, smiling suggestively.

"Another? Were we in Philadelphia?"

"We went there to set up your cover."

Jarrow spooned scrambled eggs onto a plate and gave her a long, contemplative look. They were alone for now, and she was being cooperative. He didn't know what might happen once Nordens reappeared and began unrolling whatever schedule he'd prepared for the day. If Jarrow had one chance of finding out anything on the side, it was now.

"Look, why don't we save ourselves a lot of time and be frank," he suggested. "Obviously you're aware that I'm undergoing a severe loss of memory. And, just as obviously, you're not here to add to the decorations. So why not simply fill me in with as much as you know? For instance, I believe that I was known here as Samurai, is that right?"

Vera frowned, for the first time showing uneasiness. "I'm not sure that it's supposed to work like that. The whole idea is for *you* to try and remember."

"But all I'm asking is my own name," Jarrow said. "Just tell me if Samurai is what you call me. That's hardly giving any state secrets away." Vera hesitated, then nodded. "So what did I do?" Jarrow asked.

"I didn't go into that," Vera said, speaking just a shade hastily. "Politics isn't my thing." She relaxed again with an effort and switched on her seductive smile. "I'm more concerned with, shall we say, the off-duty side of things."

"So what does that make you?" Jarrow asked. "Some kind of a . . ." He trailed off, lost for a word.

"You could think of it as a personal companion," Vera said. "The on-duty side could be stressful. The management believes in looking after a specially selected asset."

Jarrow was about to say something more, when a tone sounded from the phone on the wall. "Excuse me." He got up to answer it and found himself looking at a man in an Army major's uniform. He had one of those mobile, expressive, smiling faces that exuded trust and bonhomie, adding instantly to Jarrow's growing feeling of distrust.

"Hi. My name's Gleavey. You may not be too sure of your

bearings yet, but I'm the guy who used to take care of things for you and make sure that everything was just the way you like. Right now, I just wanted to touch base and go over the items that we've got scheduled for today.''

From the way that Gleavey had just happened to call as soon as Jarrow began pressing Vera for information, the suspicion rooted itself in Jarrow's mind that the conversation had probably been monitored.

Gleavey appeared in person ten minutes or so later with a schedule for the day. First on the list was a visit to the medical department, where Jarrow was subjected to a thorough physical check. He was pronounced to be in good shape, with the bruise on his face having practically disappeared. The inflamed area around the tiny puncture on the side of his neck, which had been there when he awoke in Atlanta, had also nearly healed. The doctors showed more interest in this, but they volunteered no information about it.

Then came another round of debriefing with Nordens and Gleavey, again with the emphasis on probing Jarrow's memory: Had anything further come together in his mind overnight? Had talking to Vera helped? Did he remember going with her to Philadelphia? Had he managed to recall anything about Ashling yet?

Through it all, Jarrow, despite himself, found his mind going back to Josef and the others from Pipeline whom he had met in Chicago. There was no evading the contrast that he saw between them and the people he was dealing with now. The assurance that he had felt only yesterday, of being in safe hands and among experts who had his best interests at heart, was already dimming. Josef had been blunt and candid in his answers, while Scipio hadn't even tried to conceal that he didn't expect Jarrow to believe him. Gleavey, on the other hand, came across as being about as sincere as his unremitting smile, which was beginning to have the same effect on Jarrow's nerves as a coarse sock on a blistered toe. Everything that Nordens said sounded secretive and devious, as if hiding his true motives about anything had become second nature in whatever world of ubiquitous mistrust and paranoia he moved in. Jarrow found himself doubting everything. The story that he had swallowed so readily yesterday about his medical file having been mixed up with Demiro's now seemed absurd. And when he thought of Rita's honest directness, and Kay, with her calm, reasoned competence, and compared them to the polished whore who was presumably supposed to complete his existence, his disillusionment turned to outrage.

He lunched with Nordens in a private dining room on the floor below Nordens's office in the Main Complex, where Tierney joined them. The same atmosphere of wariness and double-talk pervaded. They weren't concerned for Jarrow's interests at all. It was all a pretense. They only wanted to find Ashling. Jarrow grew increasingly perturbed and morose. When they were finished, he said that he needed time on his own to rest some more.

Back in his apartment of black and white and gleaming metal, he prowled agitatedly from room to room, going back over everything yet again in his mind. There were certain things that Vera had let slip that morning: snippets that he had barely noticed at the time, but which took on new perspective from the changing view that he found himself slipping inexorably into.

He had been "something special," she'd said. What did that mean? It no longer smacked of the crude personal allusion that he'd taken it to be at the time. There had been no others around by then, she'd said. What others? He thought back. . . . It had been when he asked her about being one of a group of men in the hut that Nordens and Tierney had shown him on the far side of the complex—the men from his dream. But if that had been before Vera's appearance on the scene, maybe it was before Samurai's time too—in other words nearer the time that Tony Demiro had first arrived here. And that made sense, since Demiro had been an Army volunteer. Who else could the rest of the group in a military hut be but other volunteers who had arrived with him?

So Demiro had been picked for some reason. . . . Which also tied in. Somewhere else, Vera had talked about his being a "specially selected asset." Selected for what? . . . He stopped, staring hard at the wall in the living room. Hadn't Kay already told him?

And then another little phrase of Vera's came back to him and clinched it: "Politics isn't my thing," she had said.

Politics!

That was what they had been looking for. It wasn't any coincidence that Jarrow's own political views were diametrically opposed to what Demiro's had been. Nordens had needed originals to extract the transfer codes from. The real purpose of what had been going on was to experiment with methods of political reprogramming.

Jarrow turned and stared at the window in a daze. For that was precisely what Josef and Kay had been trying to tell him. But it wasn't what Fairfax and Nordens had told him. So the whole official line that he had been given was a lie. They had lied to Demiro and the others; they had lied about Demiro's death; they were lying to Jarrow still about Valdheim. The "subversives" whom he'd scorned had been correct all along. The realization surged through Jarrow like a tidal wave.

He stifled the anger that he could feel boiling up inside and forced himself to think it through further.

Suppose, then, that Kay had been right also in her theory about Jarrow's whole personality having been transferred into Demiro inadvertently, instead of just the target patterns containing Jarrow's political convictions. . . . And then Jarrow had died unexpectedly. Nordens and his group found themselves with an experimental subject walking around thinking he was somebody who was dead. Clearly an intolerable situation. So they had simplified things by officially getting Demiro out of the picture—cynically, callously, and with lies.

But despite what the rest of the world might have been told, they still had the actual "Demiro," alive and well, inside Pearse. What might they have done with him then? A cold feeling of revulsion slithered up Jarrow's spine as the glimmerings came to him of the answer. The people at Pearse—maybe just a close inner group of those connected with the original program—had found themselves in possession of a healthy, militarily trained body that had lost all recollection of its identity and which officially didn't exist; also, they had at their disposal the unique new technology commandeered from Ashling, no doubt with many unanswered questions as to what it could accomplish.

And so they had suppressed the implanted Jarrow psyche, and in its place created a synthetic personality of their own devising, optimized for their own purposes: a "super agent" for employment in the most demanding assignments, formed by combining the best skills available from experts in every specialty that circumstances might require.

Jarrow moved across the room and stared numbly at his

reflection in a mirror. He was a freak. A psychological Frankenstein monster, pieced together from the parts of scores of unknown minds. Code name Samurai. Meanwhile, Ashling had found out about the true political goals of Southside, decided that he wanted out, and approached Pipeline. After Ashling's disappearance, Nordens and his group had no way of knowing how much Ashling had uncovered. Threatened with exposure, they sent their super agent out under the cover identity of Maurice Gordon to find Ashling and bring him back. Everything fitted now.

Unable to contain himself, Jarrow drove a fist into the other palm and paced about the room, slamming his fist and his hand together repeatedly. He stood for perhaps half a minute, breathing heavily and composing himself, then strode to the desk and hammered Nordens's number into the viewphone with savage jabs of his finger. The assistant in Nordens's outer office answered a moment later. "Dr. Nordens's office. Is it—"

"Put me through! I want to talk to him *now!*"

Nordens and Tierney had observed Jarrow's eruption via a monitor in another part of the building. "It's as I've been saying all along," Nordens said, swinging away from the screen. "He knows. There's no hope of finding out anything this way. We can't waste any more time on it. The only chance is to try and reactivate Samurai. Ashling must still be in the country somewhere, otherwise Pipeline wouldn't be looking for him."

In Jarrow's quarters Vera had appeared, seemingly concerned. "It's all right," she told him. "They're trying to locate Dr. Nordens for you now. Sit down. It's just a relapse after all the tension you've been through. Everything will be all right."

Jarrow felt an impulse to rage at her, but checked himself. Getting excited wasn't going to do him any good. It would only give the game away. He needed time to get to an outside phone somehow and contact Pipeline. Vera took his arm and steered him to one of the armchairs. He allowed himself to sink into it. "Maybe you're right," he said.

Vera smiled. "That's better. Take it easy for a day or two. But right now you look as if you could use a drink."

Jarrow nodded, content to let things follow their course now. "Sure," he agreed.

Vera went to a cabinet and began spooning ice into two glasses. "Usual?" she asked over her shoulder.

"Why not?"

She paused. "Does that mean that you remember what the usual is?"

"I haven't a clue," Jarrow said. Vera carried on pouring. He watched her from the chair. "You know, maybe that trip to Philadelphia wouldn't be a bad idea. How soon could we fix it?"

She came over to him and held out a glass of something amber. "Not too long. It's something to talk about, anyway. Here."

"Thanks." He took the glass and drank, then looked back up to find her watching him with an odd intensity. Only then did he realize how he'd been lulled off his guard. He started to rise, but whatever she'd used was taking effect already. The glass fell from his fingers as numbness came over his body. He collapsed back into the chair, still conscious in a fragmented kind of way of what was going on, but unable to resist the paralysis that was taking hold of him.

Vera, her face cold and clinical suddenly, stooped to lift one of his eyelids with a thumb and peer at him. Then she turned away, and Jarrow felt himself fading as he watched her move quickly across the room and open the door. He just had time to recognize Dr. Valdheim entering before he passed out.

Nordens was close behind, followed by several attendants. "Get him to the machine right away and power up the system," he instructed. "We should have done it from the beginning. This whole nonsense has been nothing but a waste of time."

Samurai
Samurai
Samurai
Samurai
Samurai
Samurai
Samurai
Samurai

twenty-seven

The guard at the Pearse main gate signaled for the barrier to be raised and waved the car through. Conrad Ashling followed the concrete approach road by its wire fence to the main highway and turned southward toward Atlanta.

It was a relief to be out among the trees and hills again, after too many late nights cooped up under bright lights between laboratory walls. He had been warned that with his work being taken under an official wing and security classified, there would be restrictions on his privacy and freedom of movement, and reluctantly he had agreed; but this was almost like being some kind of political prisoner under open arrest. He glanced at his mirror as he speeded up along the ramp and merged into the through lane. Sure enough, the surveillance car from Pearse security was just turning out from the end of the approach road to take up station a hundred yards behind him.

He hadn't liked the notion of his work being confined and adopted for military training purposes from the beginning. His original vision had been of possibilities that would enrich the lives of millions by eliminating the drudgery from learning, and multiplying enormously the amount and variety of knowledge and skills that anyone would be able to amass in a lifetime. But the political realities of the times had not permitted that to happen, and he had been left with only one avenue open to him by which his theories might be tested—and the chance of access to equipment that he could never have obtained through his own resources, and funding that appeared unlimited. So he had gone along with it and accepted the restrictions.

However, the experience had left him distrustful of the people whom he found himself dealing with and the power they represented. His suspicion grew that there was more to the Southside project than he had been told. He began quietly investigating, and in the process discovered that the story about revolutionizing military training was just a cover. The real aim was to determine the feasibility of political reprogramming.

Ashling's first thought had been to take the whole matter to higher authority. But on reflection he doubted that there would be much point. From what he had seen, he wouldn't have been surprised to find that it went all the way to the top. So he had decided to get out.

There were hidden networks of communications that scientists in various disciplines maintained among themselves. Through such a channel he had regained contact with an old colleague from the days before the Green Curtain had slammed down around the West, the Russian professor, Ulkanov, who was now on Luna, equipped by a consortium of unfettered public and private interests with a research team of his own, and by the sound of things on the same track as Ashling himself had been before state intervention put an end to his plans. That was where he must go, Ashling had decided. To the Offworld independencies, where knowledge could be pursued for its own sake, without direction to political purposes, and the spirit of discovery ran free.

If he could survive the stress . . .

He was turning sixty now, and feeling the worse for wear with every new day of awakening. A lifetime of compulsive overwork, too little distraction and relaxation, an attempt at marriage that had never had a hope, and unceasing battles with meddling intellectual dwarfs whose only purpose in life seemed to be to frustrate his goals had left him with a Damoclean blood pressure that threatened to smite him at any time, and an accompanying heart condition that made any excitement an invitation to a terminal attack. But there was nothing left for him here, and so he was determined to go through with it. Even so, the thought of what lay ahead in the next few hours in Atlanta was enough to give him palpitations—never mind getting out of the country, across to the FER, and from there up and off the planet. He fumbled the container of Panacyn from his jacket pocket as he drove, and popped one of the capsules into his mouth, washing it down with a swig of orange juice from the bottle that he kept in the car. Everything, now, depended on Josef having his end of things organized. Ashling prayed that there had been no slipups.

It was important not to break the pattern of movement that he typically followed in his visits to Atlanta. North of the city, he left I-75/85 and parked in a lot off Peachtree Plaza. Taking only his briefcase, he browsed for an hour or so in several of the nearby bookshops, then spent the rest of the morning leafing through scientific journals and making notes in the library of the Institute of Technology. Ostensibly the briefcase contained only routine notes and papers. But in addition, he had concealed inside the lining a high-density holographic storage film carrying details of his most important work.

After that he had lunch in an Italian restaurant that he often used when in town, across the street from the campus. While he ate, he ignored the two agents from Pearse, who took up station over cups of coffee and a sandwich apiece at a table near the door. Instead he thought about the Offworld culture that was coming into being in defiance of all the expert predictions, and the prospect of his living there—which, if it came about, would probably be for the remainder of his years.

Nobody was sure exactly what the phenomenon exploding outward into space to the Moon and beyond meant, or what coming together of happenstance, opportunity, and the realization of human vision was impelling it. Some spoke of it as a new renaissance, others as a next phase of industrial revolution stemming from new, nuclear-based alchemies that would yield bulk transmutation of matter with energy as a by-product on a scale undreamed of, in the same way that Nature did in the stars. But although whatever was happening out there undoubtedly included aspects comparable to both those past upheavals, its true commonality with them lay in its uniqueness. As had been the case with each of the preceding epochs, the significant thing that it shared was that nobody really under-stood it, for nothing like it had happened before. But, as seemed to have been the pattern of history when Rome began as an outer colony of the Greeks, the nations that gave rise to the West sprang from the periphery of the Roman world, and America grew from an outpost of Western empire, the new, emergent culture was budding from the fringes of the old, while the core stagnated and died. And this latest thrust, Ashling believed, was the one that would carry mankind out of the Solar System.

After lunch he went to a small mall across from the institute and did some shopping, after which he made a phone call. The response that he got told him that everything was still set to go as arranged. Ashling's hand trembled as he replaced the receiver. He could feel himself breaking out in a sweat. There was a painful constriction about his chest, as if it were bound with chains.

The mall's principal business was a department store that the lesser shops and kiosks clustered around—a smaller affair now than it had been originally, with about half its space closed for economy and leased off for warehousing. Ashling entered through the main doors and went first to the men's room, where he took a long drink of water and swallowed another Panacyn capsule to calm himself. Even if he did manage to make it to Luna, the days, maybe weeks, of this kind of thing that still lay ahead of him before then could do nothing to prolong what he could realistically expect would be his time there. His image stared back at him from the mirror: the white hair, the lined features, the ailing frame, and the tired eyes. He was under no illusions as to what it portended. If he could just hold together long enough for his work not to have been wasted . . .

He emerged from the rest room and went through the fashion department to the menswear section. Every step of the way he was acutely conscious of the two agents sauntering casually after him a short distance back along the adjacent aisle. He stopped at a rack displaying cord and twill pants and began rummaging among the hangers, trying to make his movements natural but seized by an uncontrollable awkwardness that he was convinced was signaling his intent to the whole world as surely as a flashing neon sign hanging over his head. The plan depended on the agents being off guard, with no reason to be suspicious of an aging scientist doing a little shopping on a routine trip into town. All he had to do was act normally. No sooner had he reaffirmed that determination to himself, when one of the hangers came off the rail and dropped to the floor. He picked it up hastily and tried to replace it, but the pants twisted with the ones next to them somehow and wouldn't hang straight. Then those came away too, and Ashling was left clutching an armful of both.

"Is there something I can help you with?" a voice said from

behind him. Ashling turned, startled. An assistant had seen his predicament and come over.

"Oh. . . . This." Ashling held the tangle up, and the assistant relieved him of it.

"Sure, I'll take care of that."

"And these." Ashling grabbed two pairs at random from the section labeled thirty-eight. "Where can I try them on?"

The assistant nodded toward a doorway at the rear as he replaced the hangers. "The fitting rooms are that way."

"Can I leave these here?" Ashling put down the packages that he had been carrying, but kept hold of the briefcase. As he walked through to the fitting cubicles he stole a quick glance back. One of the two agents was on the far side of the menswear area, looking bored and studying shirts; the other was not in sight.

Through the door was a short corridor with louvered doors of changing cubicles on both sides, and at the far end another door leading to a staff washroom. All exactly as he had been told.

He went into one of the cubicles and hung the two pairs of pants on one of the hooks. Then he emerged into the corridor again, but instead of going back the way he had come, he went on through into the washroom and found the emergency door to the outside unlocked as planned.

Josef was waiting for him in the unloading bay outside. He had a car standing around the corner with another man waiting at the wheel, and in a matter of moments Ashling was being whisked on his way.

Employed by the Federal Security Service's training center for new recruits at Frederick, Maryland, was a former CIA instructor by the name of Lorenzo, whose specialty was lock picking. Over years of experience gained in occupations that predated his hiring by the Agency and not detailed in his personnel record, Lorenzo had built up an extensive knowledge of all the areas pertinent to his craft: all the locks that he might encounter, who designed them and which firms made them, how they worked, the tricks and traps that might be utilized to foil an assailant, how long each type should take to pick. He owned several models of each type in order to practice his picking techniques, which in some cases required the patience of a cryptologist and the delicacy of touch of a surgeon. Locks weren't just popped open in a matter of seconds in the way invariably depicted in the movies.

For Lorenzo, the simple ward lock, where the correct positions for cutting a blank could be read from a pattern transferred into lighter or candle soot, was child's play. The feel for tensioning a regular pin-tumbler lock—just hard enough for the pins to stick, but not such as to cause them to jam—came as naturally to him as breathing, after which he could lift each pin to its shear point as deftly as a watchmaker mounting balances, enabling the core to turn inside the shell. He knew how to rake or ease tension gradually to overcome mushroom pins, the quick ways to nudge disk tumblers or wafer tumblers into line, the pressures to apply when tackling lever tumblers, and at precisely which point to forget the niceties and resort to brute-force drilling. His knowledge had been amassed meticulously and carefully over a period that had spanned more than twenty years.

That knowledge was incorporated into the composite, synthetic personality that had been designated "Samurai" in less than fifteen minutes of machine time. An aide brought the message from Nordens, requesting Samurai's immediate presence, while Samurai was confounding experts in one of the Pearse laboratories by opening a series of test locks in minutes that theoretically should have been impregnable. Shortly afterward, Samurai arrived on the top floor of the Main Complex to find Nordens with Tierney. They were both in an extremely anxious state.

"Ashling has disappeared," Nordens informed Samurai tightly. "He slipped surveillance earlier today in Atlanta. We think it was prearranged." He went on to summarize as much as could be pieced together of what had happened.

The news didn't come as any particular surprise to Samurai. He had been briefed previously to make Ashling a special object for attention, and in keeping with the cynical nature that came with his emerging personality, he had never trusted the competence of Tierney's security operatives, whom he dismissed with unconcealed contempt as amateurs.

"Don't worry about it," Samurai told them. "It was obvious that something like this was going to happen sooner or later. So I took my own precautions."

Nordens stared at him uncertainly. "How?" he asked. "What precautions? What are you talking about?"

Samurai smiled humorlessly. "Back in my apartment in the Annex is an electronic homing device that's tuned to a bug that I hid in Ashling's briefcase several weeks ago. I figured that if he decided to defect he'd take his papers, and the briefcase would be one thing that would be certain to go with him. The bug has a range of over two miles. He has to be in the Atlanta area somewhere. I'll find him for you before the night's out."

Nordens and Tierney exchanged relieved looks. "Go to it, then," Nordens said. "You can consider this your first test mission."

Samurai arrived in Atlanta a little over an hour later, and picked up the transmission less than thirty minutes after commencing to cruise the city center. The homing device led him to the Atlanta Hyatt hotel. His cover identity had already been arranged. He parked in front of the Hyatt and went in to register for a room, presenting the ID and credentials of one Maurice Gordon, visiting from Philadelphia. The date was November 14.

twenty-eight

Samurai closed the door of room 1406 and put down the black briefcase and leather travel bag that he had brought with him from the car. He inspected the surroundings and the bathroom and put his spare clothes in the closet to hang. Then he sat down at the bureau-vanity and opened the briefcase to lay out the contents and check them item by item, moving with the unhurried purposefulness that comes with total confidence. He set aside the electronic homer, which was still registering the transmission from the bug that he had planted on Ashling, loaded the two weapons that he had selected for the job—one a regular 9mm automatic, the other a compressed-gas pistol that fired up to four nonlethal knockout darts tipped with a neurotoxin, effective in seconds—and replaced them in the briefcase. He stowed the briefcase out of sight in a drawer, and picking up the homer again, he let himself back out into the corridor.

The signal led him through the hotel's central block into another wing, then up to the eighth floor, partway along a corridor, and finally back down a level via the emergency stairs to pinpoint the source as room 7319. He spent some time surveying the approaches from all directions, noting the locations of fire exits and elevators, and familiarizing himself with the layout from the floor plan displayed at the end of the corridor. The floor plan also told him that 7319 was a two-room suite consisting of a living room with bathroom opening off inside the main door, and a bedroom with a second bathroom through another door at the rear. He walked the floors above and below one more time, took a look around the outside, and then returned to his own room to consider his options.

Almost certainly, Ashling had contacted Pipeline and was being hidden here as a prelude to being moved out of the country. Pipeline would have at least one, probably more, of their people in there with him constantly. They would be on guard, naturally, against anyone's approaching via the door, which ruled out impersonating the likes of hotel staff or outside delivery carriers. Samurai's reconnaissance outside had eliminated the windows as a practicable means of entry, also.

He got up and moved around the room, examining the ceilings, flooring, and the wall at the rear of the closet. The building was of fairly recent construction, incorporating a low-cost, highly modular design that enabled maximum use to be made of preformed sections fabricated off-site. The heating and air-conditioning outlet was high in the wall to one side of the closet. The inside of the closet stopped short in that direction, indicating that the space beyond might house the ducting to the outlet—in which case it possibly passed between floors. Also, the bathroom backed onto the closet, making it logical to suppose that the same shaft might carry the plumbing, also. Samurai tapped along the end wall on the inside of the closet. It sounded hollow, sure enough, but offered no ready way of gaining access.

He went around into the bathroom and found an enclosed space beside the shower stall, walled in by screw-down panels, just where such a shaft would be. He brought a multipurpose tool that included a screwdriver bit from his briefcase, and in less than a minute lifted the lowermost of the panels away. Inside was a vertical shaft carrying ducts and various sizes of pipes. There was little room to spare, but it would take him at a squeeze. A probe upward and down with his penlight confirmed that the shaft continued to the adjacent floors without serious obstacles. The screws went into hollow-wall anchors that could be cut from the inside. Satisfied, and with the outline of a plan now taking shape in his mind, he replaced the panel and left once more for the other wing of the hotel.

Back on the eighth floor, he found as he had expected that room 8319 was situated immediately above 7319. The floor plan there also confirmed that 8319 was identical in layout. Samurai went to the door of 8319 and tapped lightly, with a prepared excuse should someone answer. Nobody did. It was a Saturday, not yet evening. There seemed to be no convention or major function being held in the hotel that weekend, and he was banking that the chances of the room's being unoccupied were high. As a final check, he went back to his own room and called the hotel on an outside line.

"Atlanta Hyatt. Can I help you?"

"Yes. Could I have room 8319 please?"

There was a pause, then, "I'm sorry, but there doesn't appear to be anyone answering. Would you like to leave a message?"

"Could you tell me if they've checked in yet?" Samurai said.

"One moment, I'll check." He waited. Then the clerk came back on the line. "That room is empty, sir, and we don't show any reservation for tonight. What was the name?"

"Carrel. Ms. Judy Carrel."

Another pause. "I don't see any reservation here under that name. Are you sure it was for tonight."

"Yes, I am. Isn't this the Hilton?"

"No, sir. We're the Hyatt."

"Oh, excuse me. My mistake."

"Would you like the number of the Hilton?"

"It's all right. I have it here. I'm sorry to have troubled you."

So, the suite above the one that Ashling was hiding out in would be empty for a while at least. That was all that Samurai needed to know.

Taking the briefcase, he went out to the front and moved his car around to the parking area outside the door at the rear of the other wing. The inside of the trunk was virtually a mobile larceny, homicide, and espionage laboratory. From its contents Samurai selected a basic kit of tools and drills, several microphone probes along with amplifier and earpiece, and transferred them to the briefcase. Fifteen minutes later he let himself quietly into suite 8319 with a master magnetic passcard stolen from Housekeeping. A quick check of the bathroom confirmed that the hotel's construction was uniform—it was the same as in his room.

He opened an inch or two of seam in the carpet in the center of the living room. Then, working carefully and silently, he bored a hole through the floor panel, and after that a finer hole almost through the ceiling slab below, into which he inserted one of the audio probes. Through the earpiece he was able to pick up the voices in the suite below, which, although muffled and only semi-intelligible, gave him the number of people down there and a feel for their whereabouts and movements. After repeating the procedure in the bedroom and by the doorway to the living room bathroom, he established that there were three others present besides Ashling. One of them was always in the outer room near the door, which was to be expected, while the others moved around haphazardly. Ashling himself tended to remain in the bedroom at the rear. Also, the TV was on—which was good.

Samurai checked his watch. It was still early evening. Plenty of time. He collected his tools and equipment together in the bathroom and removed the bottom panel by the shower. Inside was a shaft similar to the one he'd found in his own room. There were no nasty surprises. Taking some cutters for the screws below, a couple of other basic tools, the 9mm automatic, and the dart pistol, he eased himself in between the largest of the ducts and a pipe run and lowered himself carefully and noiselessly to the corresponding part of suite 7319 below.

Twenty minutes went by before one of the guards came in to use the bathroom . . . and went out without a murmur. Samurai lowered the limp form into the shower stall and took out the dart pistol. He flushed the toilet and shot a needlelike projectile into the guard's neck that would keep him out until the next morning, afterward dissolving in the body fluids to leave just a tiny puncture. Then Samurai sauntered casually out into the living room and shot a second guard before anyone out there realized that the person coming out of the bathroom was not the one who had gone in.

But the third's reactions were fast. Even as the second guard was falling, he crossed the living room and was through the door leading into the bedroom. Samurai's reflexes were as quick, however, and before the guard could close the door behind him, Samurai hurled one of the chairs with enough momentum to send the guard staggering back, then followed on through to deliver a sidekick into the midriff that sent the guard reeling backward over one of the beds. While Ashling, who had risen to his feet from a chair by the window, watched, horrified, Samurai leveled the pistol again and shot the guard in the chest through his shirt. The guard stiffened, and fell back onto the bed, senseless.

"Oh, my God!" Ashling whispered.

Samurai turned and laughed derisively at the expression on the scientist's face. "Don't worry. We don't want killings. Too many complications. It'll keep them out until I get back here to tidy things up."

Ashling stared at him in confusion. "But you're one of the volunteers, Demiro, isn't it? . . . I thought you'd been transferred away. What's going on? I don't understand."

"Let's just say for now that there's more going on than you know about. There isn't time now. Ask Nordens to tell you about it when we get back." Samurai made a curt wave with a hand, and Ashling followed him back into the living room. Suddenly he clutched at his chest and fell against the side of the doorway, his face contorted in a grimace. Samurai looked back at him.

"What is it?"

Ashling made a gurgling noise and held on to the doorjamb, his face white. "Pill," he croaked. "White jar . . . other bathroom."

Samurai steered him to the nearest chair, sat him down, and went swiftly through to the bathroom opening off from the living room. Among the articles strewn over the sink top was a white pill container with a label bearing Ashling's name. Samurai picked it up, filled a glass with water, and went back to Ashling.

Ashling took one of the capsules, downed it with a drink of water, and sat weakly, waiting for his breathing to recover. Samurai waited perhaps half a minute. The TV in the room was on. A program was just beginning about tropical insects. Finally he asked, "Okay? Can you move now?" Ashling didn't respond, but continued panting, staring down at the floor. "Come on," Samurai said, straightening up. "We have to get your briefcase. What else do you need?"

And that was the last thing that Samurai remembered.

With no sensation of time having passed, he woke up to find himself covered by a blanket on a rubber-topped couch in clinical surroundings. After a few seconds he recognized it as the recovery room in the experimental wing at Pearse.

twenty-nine

A monitoring system that had been tracking Samurai's condition registered his return to consciousness and activated a staff alert. Moments later, Dr. Valdheim appeared. Samurai rubbed his eyes, shook his head to clear it, and lifted himself up on his elbows to gaze around. Valdheim stacked pillows behind his head and looked down at him gravely.

"How are you feeling?" he asked. There was a curiously uncharacteristic anxiety in his voice.

Samurai took stock of himself. His head felt heavy and muzzy, as if his brain were permeated by a viscous fluid. Such sluggishness of thought was not normal for him. "I'm not sure. . . . How did I get back here?"

Valdheim ignored the question and raised a hand with the index and little fingers extended. "Just a few answers, please. How many fingers do you see?"

"Two." Valdheim opened his full hand. "Four." Valdheim straightened his thumb. "Five."

An attendant appeared in the doorway. Valdheim continued, "You know who I am?"

"Of course."

"Tell me."

"Valdheim."

"And where is this place?"

"Pearse laboratories, experimental wing inside the Restricted Zone. Recovery room adjoining the machine bay, Southside project."

Valdheim nodded. "And who are you?"

"Special agent, code name Samurai."

"What was your last mission?"

"To find and apprehend the scientist Ashling, believed to be attempting to defect with the aid of the subversive organization Pipeline," Samurai replied.

Valdheim seemed satisfied. "Fetch Dr. Nordens," he instructed the attendant. "Say that Samurai appears to be fully reactivated."

Although Samurai's head was already clearing, the implication of the term didn't strike him immediately. "How did I get here?" he asked again.

"What is the last thing you remember?" Valdheim asked in turn.

"I was at the Hyatt in Atlanta."

"More detail, please. What were you doing at the Hyatt?"

Samurai propped himself higher against the pillows and took a moment to recollect. "I'd traced Ashling there, by means of the bug in his briefcase. I ascertained the room that Pipeline was keeping him in and evaluated the situation as involving three others in addition to the target. Entry was effected successfully and the opposition neutralized. The target was apprehended. Preparations for delivery and eradication of traces were complete."

"Go on," Valdheim said.

Samurai replied expressionlessly, "Recollection ends at that point. Indicated conclusion is that another party was present, undetected, or that somebody entered unobserved. Unable to offer explanation in either case."

"And you remember nothing else since then?" Valdheim said. Once again, his voice carried a strangely ominous note.

Samurai could only shake his head. "No. Why?" Valdheim said nothing but moved a step closer and tilted Samurai's head lightly to one side. He stared at a spot below Samurai's ear and explored it lightly with a fingertip. The area felt slightly sore. Samurai brought his own hand up and felt the fading traces of some kind of lesion. "What is this?" he asked. "What's been happening?"

Before Valdheim could say anything, Nordens came in with Tierney.

"It's true?" Nordens said without preliminaries. "We have full reactivation?"

"So it would appear," Valdheim murmured, nodding, still looking at Samurai. "As far as it's possible to say initially, anyway."

He went on to summarize briefly what he had learned from Samurai, and concluded, "He seems to be himself again."

Samurai looked sharply at Nordens. "Why shouldn't I be? What has been going on?"

Nordens settled himself on a stool by the door and lifted one heel onto the circular bar bracing the legs. "Tell me, Samurai," he said, "does the name Jarrow mean anything to you? Richard Jarrow?"

"Nothing. Should it?"

Nordens peered intently through his spectacles. "What about Minneapolis, or Chicago? Do you have any recent associations with those places, for any reason?"

Samurai shook his head, by now completely mystified. "No, I don't."

"What was the date, when you tracked Ashling to the Hyatt?"

Samurai thought for a second and replied, "A Saturday, November fourteenth."

"After which you remember nothing?" Nordens checked.

"I've already said, no."

Nordens glanced at Tierney, then looked back at Samurai. "The following day, Sunday, you made a call here, to Pearse, and left a message for me saying that you knew how Ashling was to be got out of the country. You intended giving us full details when you got back here . . . but you never did. It's vital that we retrieve that information. You have no knowledge of leaving that message?"

Samurai shook his head, trying to make sense of it. "I must have been jumped somehow . . . and they got Ashling away again," he said. "But you're saying that I picked up his trail again. . . . But no, I don't remember it." He looked from Nordens to Tierney to Valdheim and asked again, "Will somebody tell me what in hell has been going on?"

"I wish we knew," Nordens replied. "Saturday the fourteenth was some time ago now. A lot of strange things have been happening since then. You see, Samurai, today is Monday the twenty-third."

Later that day, a helicopter bearing government insignia arrived at Pearse from Washington, D.C. A tall, square-built man with smooth, tanned features, hard eyes, and straight gray hair, wearing a hat and dark overcoat, alighted and was shown straight up to Director Fairfax's office. He was Roland Circo, deputy head of the Federal Security Service. The look on his face was not a happy one. Nordens, Tierney, and Valdheim joined them shortly afterward.

Circo was wishing he'd never heard of this insane Samurai experiment, which hadn't been authorized officially and which the President didn't know about. The President! Washington's daily soap offering to distract the electorate and foster the illusion that they had a say in anything that mattered. The real power game took place behind the facade, and one group of the adversaries involved in it was *very* interested in the possibility of being able to transform, or even create, political personalities to specification. Circo's place, if that became the winning side, was assured. And not just his: Fairfax, Nordens, Tierney—they were all in it for the same thing. The screwup that had led them into having to fake the record of Demiro's death should have been warning enough, he could now reflect wryly. Now Ashling had turned and was loose, and the Samurai agent who was supposed to be proof of the concept couldn't remember what he'd found out and didn't know what day it was. The whole thing was a mess of worms.

"So what have we got?" Circo said after Nordens had gone through the details. "Ashling took off over a week ago now. You got word from Samurai that he knew where and when and how Pipeline were getting him out, but now Samurai's been through a couple of identity flips and doesn't remember anything about it. Is that it? I've got it right so far?"

"That's about how it is," Fairfax agreed gloomily.

"Except that he doesn't remember *consciously*," Valdheim put in. "The information is in there, inside his head. With the facilities we have we can get it out. We just need a little time."

"Time!" Circo threw the word out derisively and looked in despair at the ceiling. "After a week? Are you trying to tell me that Ashling will still be sitting there in Atlanta, waiting for us to get our act together? If he's not in the FER already, he's halfway there."

"We have to use whatever overseas help we can," Fairfax urged. "Alert them for leads on anybody of Ashling's description being concealed or smuggled in that direction." He glanced quickly at the others in turn. It was a lame suggestion to have to fall back on, as he knew and their expressions affirmed. He added, to make it fractionally more credible, "Keep a special watch on medical contacts. He'll need a supply of that drug that he has to take all the time because of his heart condition. What was it called?"

"Panacyn," Valdheim said, seeming to only half hear.

They all knew they needed something a lot better than that. Nordens gnawed pensively at a knuckle, then said finally, "Valdheim's right. We have to get a lead on the route that Ashling took, even if he's already left."

"Then what?" Circo asked him.

Nordens paused just long enough to suggest an appropriate shade of regret and delicacy, then shrugged. "We go after him. Either he's brought back here, or . . ." He left the obvious unsaid. The others all found places to stare at that avoided meeting anyone else's gaze.

After several seconds, Circo emitted a heavy sigh and shook his head. "I can't have our field men implicated in this. We're already in for enough. I'm not prepared to risk it getting messier. This is a pig's ass as it is."

"I didn't say to use your field men," Nordens answered. He waited until the faces turning sharply one by one told him that the others had caught what he was saying. "We already have the ideal person to go after him."

Circo frowned. "Do you mean Samurai?"

Nordens nodded. "Of course."

"But—"

"Oh, he's functioning quite normally now, I can assure you of that." Nordens glanced around at the others again. "In terms of professional abilities to carry out the job, you won't find an equal. . . . And then, of course, there is the additional advantage that as far as the rest of the world is concerned, Samurai doesn't exist."

Which meant, as everyone in the room understood, that once it was done, Circo's agents would be used to get rid of Samurai. After which, all traces of the entire affair could be quietly eradicated.

All they needed was a lead to set them on Ashling's trail.

Throughout it all, Jerry Tierney remained silent. Inwardly he was growing increasingly uncomfortable.

Samurai stood naked, facing one of the mirrors in the bedroom of his apartment in the PQ Annex, regarding his reflection with satisfaction. He raised his arms to chest height, and went through a slow sequence of formalized karate attack and defense movements, his muscles outlining themselves and rippling like cables with every feigned jab, punch, change of posture, and kick. Two lines of fresh fingernail gouges stood red against the skin of his back.

Vera, covered as far as her pubic mound by a sheet, watched from the bed. A redness still smarted on one side of her face, but her eyes showed excitement in spite of it—or maybe in part because of it. Samurai's lovemaking was brutal and harsh, the compulsive expression of domination and the will to subdue, forged from a synthesis of human drives that had been fashioned to know no other context for relationship. His function was to observe, to analyze, to kill, and to destroy. He had no other purpose. Vera's was to react, to provide, to comply; to be used—and, if necessary, abused. That was what the government paid her for.

"Welcome back," she commented approvingly.

Samurai extended an arm horizontally, fingers flattened, the other arm guarding, and returned to a formal defensive pose. "Not all back," he replied, still looking in the mirror. "This week is still mostly a blank."

"You're making good progress."

"Maybe."

"You still don't remember anything about the cars?"

"No."

After Samurai's disappearance in Atlanta, his car was found to be still parked in the Annex at Pearse, its windshield shattered. A pickup truck belonging to the Maintenance Department, which Samurai had a spare set of keys to and sometimes borrowed to go on recreational trips into the hills in the area, was missing, which was presumably how he had gotten into Atlanta. This had been confirmed when two of Tierney's security staff, sent to check, found the pickup in the parking lot of the Hyatt. Samurai could offer no explanation.

Samurai's briefcase, leather traveling bag, and the clothes left at the Hyatt had been returned via the Philadelphia address given for Gordon, after Jarrow walked out and left them. But still, Samurai's memory of the circumstances surrounding his actions was a complete blank.

"How about a swim to cool off?" Vera suggested. "Then I thought we'd find something relaxing to do this evening, maybe. Valdheim wants to run some more tests later."

"I don't need to relax. I want a challenge. Something that stretches nerves and tests abilities."

"That would sound a bit too much like work for most men," Vera remarked.

Samurai snorted contemptuously. "Worms. I could crush them." He drew back into a disengagement posture, held it for a second, then turned and reached for his robe. "The world drowns itself in words that achieve nothing. Action alone has meaning. Nothing else."

Vera leaned across to open the drawer in the bedside unit. "Well, there's one small action I'd appreciate right now. We're out of joints. I think there are some in the desk."

"A weakness," Samurai said.

"Guilty."

Samurai tied the belt of the robe and went out into the living room. He crossed to the desk, opened the center drawer, and checked over the items inside. Some pieces of paper caught his eye that he didn't recall putting there. He picked them up and examined them curiously.

Headman to ship out via J'ville, sometime Nov. 19. Check ref "Cop 3."

"Headman"?

Who else could that be a reference to but Ashling?

Shipping out via J'ville—which had to be Jacksonville, Florida—on November 19? That was four days ago. Cop 3? Maybe something to do with police, but that wasn't the important thing right now.

Samurai activated the desk terminal and punched in Nordens's number. Nordens's assistant answered.

"Samurai. Put me through."

"Hey, what's up out there?" Vera's voice called from the bedroom.

Nordens appeared on the screen. "What?"

Samurai spoke rapidly and urgently. "I've found it. He shipped out by sea from Jacksonville four days ago, on the nineteenth. If he's going in via Europe, that means he won't be there for probably another seven days. There can't be many ships going there from Jacksonville. If we can identify the one he's on, we can intercept him at the other end."

thirty

In a brothel in the nightclub district of the German city-port of Hamburg, the girl who called herself Dagmar steered her unsteady client across the landing and into her room at the top of the second flight of stairs. It was a snug, warm-looking room with chintz draperies, red wallpaper and lighting, and a king-size, brass-railed bed. Dagmar was petite, blue-eyed, and blond with an urchin-cut fringe. The client was cheerful, merry, and drunk.

"Come on, in here. Don't make so much noise or the madam will come and throw you out early."

"Ah, and you are the pretty Dag-Dagmar, yes? I like that name. Yes, it's a very pretty name. You're a pretty lady."

"I'm glad you think so," she said, closing the door.

"And this is where Dagmar lives, eh?"

"It's where I work."

"I think I would like to live here too. Can I come an' live here with you?"

"You haven't paid for that long."

He threw up his arms and beamed at her. "Oh, well, too bad."

Dagmar kicked off her shoes and began unfastening her dress. "Aren't you going to get undressed?" she suggested. The man took off his jacket. She hung it over a chair. He fumbled with the knot of his tie, which was pulled several inches down below the open neck of his shirt and had tightened. "Here," she said. "I'll do it."

"And I like the perfume," the man said.

"You're easy to please, I can see. So what should I call you?"

"People who like me call me Nicolaus. Others think of other things. But I don't care about them."

"You're from farther east somewhere, aren't you?"

"That's right. I'm Estonian. Ever been there?"

"It's not so easy these days for us to get over into the FER states." Dagmar was suddenly more attentive. "Are you visiting Hamburg?"

"Oh, yes." Nicolaus put a fingertip to his lips and swayed. "An important international assignment," he whispered.

"Oh, really?"

"You don't believe me."

"How could you possibly think that?" Dagmar steered him to the bed, and he collapsed down onto it. He looked up at her as she removed her underwear and joined him.

"I'll have you know that you are p-privileged to be en'taining a very important person," he mumbled.

This was going to take time, she could see. If he wanted to talk a bit first, that was fine by her and would probably help him relax. He had bought plenty of time.

"Don't tell me," she said. "You're here to negotiate Germany out of the Consolidation and get us into the FER."

"Those are nice tits."

"Hm . . . that feels good. Really, I'm interested. What brings you here?"

Nicolaus bunched his mouth tight and shook his head knowingly.

"You're right, then. I don't believe you," Dagmar told him.

He focused on her with an effort and looked pained. "Promise you won't tell?"

"Not a soul."

Nicolaus looked from side to side over each shoulder and leaned closer. "I'm meeting a very special illegal who's arriving here tomorrow from America. A scientist, no less."

"A scientist!" Dagmar looked impressed. "What does he do?"

"Ah, that's a secret." Nicolaus shook his head firmly, in a way that said hot irons and pliers would never get that out of him.

Dagmar traced fingers over his chest. "Where are you staying in Hamburg?" she inquired lightly.

"Oh, what's it called? . . . The Harbor Light Bar, down by the water. Sort of a pub. But they let a few rooms."

"Yes, I know it."

"Why?"

She shrugged. "Oh, I do outcalls too. I just thought that this scientist might enjoy a little native hospitality . . . some relaxation after the journey, maybe?"

"Unlikely," Nicolaus said. "I'm told he's getting old. In any case, we'll be gone by tomorrow night. Anyhow, I'm fed up talking about him. Let's do something about me."

Later that night, Dagmar made her routine call to a number at the local police headquarters to report the snippets she had collected that evening. It was amazing how interested they were in even the most trivial-sounding gossip. Besides ensuring that she always had friends in the right places, the extra money came in useful. She was learning to cultivate some refined and expensive tastes.

The foreign liaison officer at police headquarters traded information with a contact at the U.S. consulate who had put out a priority request for anything on a defecting scientist, aged sixty, possibly sailing from Jacksonville, known to have a heart condition for which he was prescribed Panacyn, and thought to be using the code name "Headman." The details from the hooker's account were delivered to Circo in Washington less than thirty minutes later, at what was still 5:00 P.M. local time.

Circo had already established that three ships had sailed from Jacksonville for Europe on November 19: one bound for London, one for Naples, and one for Hamburg. The one going to Hamburg, the *Auriga*, also registered there, was due to arrive on December 1—which was the following day. It all fitted. The "Cop 3" reference in Samurai's message was thought to mean the Offworld colony at Copernicus, on Luna. A scientific group there was known to be working in the same field of research as Ashling. That, then, would be the destination that Ashling was making for.

Circo called Fairfax at Pearse on a secure channel and announced, "We've got the break!"

Samurai hadn't incurred any physical or psychological impairment that the formidable battery of tests, which he had been subjected to through the past week, could detect. On all fitness and reflex scales he scored well above average, his mental acuity rated superbly, and there was no measurable loss of performance in any of the skills that had been combined into his persona. These had been further extended and now included marksmanship and expertise in all weapons categories as well as hand-to-hand combat; gymnastics, swimming-diving, climbing, and parachuting; survival and stunt driving; fixed and rotary-wing aircraft piloting; codes and communications; familiarity with subversive organizations and enemies of the state, their methods, ideologies, and sympathizers; expertise in electronics, chemistry, forgery, explosives, vehicle mechanics, and computer techniques; and fluency in French, German, Spanish, and Russian.

After an hour of tests on breaking computer access codes, then a shower followed by a light dinner, he was sitting at the kitchen table in the apartment, confronting Vera across a chessboard.

Vera frowned down at the pieces while Samurai watched indifferently, still playing in his mind with decision trees and probability matches. Finally she moved a knight.

"You lose in three," Samurai said. "Rook takes pawn, check, followed by bishop to bishop six if you block it, or pawn takes pawn if you move the king. Either way, the queen mates."

"Hm. What if I exchange rooks?"

"The same thing, after rook to bishop one. You're dead."

Vera pushed the board aside with a sigh. "Oh, this isn't fair. They've downloaded a tape. How am I supposed to compete against that?"

She said the right thing instinctively. It all nurtured the feeling of his own dominance and invincibility, which Samurai seemed to need. He got up and moved out into the living room.

"Any plans for this evening?" Vera asked, rising and following.

He scowled, seemingly morose and restless. "I don't know. Maybe I'll work out on the mat. Find out for me if Nagaoko is available. He's good."

"I thought Valdheim wanted to stage some retentivity tests tonight."

Samurai's expression darkened. "Tests, tests. I'm tired of their tests. It's time to get out of here."

"The NSA are doing what they can. They don't exactly have a lot to go on."

"The NSA are imbeciles. I could do it better myself. Give me a day to go through their intercepts and I'd—"

A call tone sounded from the desk unit. He strode over and stabbed a button to accept. It was Nordens, for once looking excited.

"Get packing. You're on your way," he announced. "They've found him."

"Where?" Samurai snapped.

"Hamburg. It's as well that we made one of your test languages German, because there wouldn't be time to add it in now. Ashling arrives aboard a German ship called the *Auriga,* due to dock at two-thirty tomorrow afternoon. There's a flight out of Dulles to Frankfurt tonight. You're booked through as Sam Harris." Since the Gordon identity was compromised, a new cover for Samurai had already been created. "Circo is arranging entry papers now. His people from the consulate will meet you at Hamburg when you arrive tomorrow morning. You leave right away."

thirty-one

Nordens stood with Jerry Tierney by the landing pad at Pearse, watching the helicopter that would take Samurai to Dulles rise into the night sky. The helicopter turned onto a northeast heading and sped away to lose itself among the stars. Nordens stared after the receding speck, moonlight glinting from his spectacles. Tierney looked disconsolately at the ground.

"We can do no more," Nordens said. "Everything depends on Samurai now."

"If you say so," Tierney replied neutrally.

They turned and began walking toward the experimental wing. "I don't get the impression that you quite understand the full ramifications of the project, Jerry," Nordens said, as if reading his thoughts.

"Explain it to me, then," Tierney said.

"We are constrained to the service of fools. Those people in Washington are too dull-witted to grasp the opportunity for real power when it presents itself to them. They live their overcautious lives paralyzed by their own indecision and half measures."

Tierney looked at him uncertainly. Nordens seemed not to notice, and expounded as they passed the security post and went on into the ground-level reception area, "Reprogramming the opposition's political beliefs is only the tip of what can be achieved. It's too limited—limited by the necessity of concentrating on just a few key individuals—people like Daparras, for instance. The targets that we could hope for would be too few, and the time required for each too much for the whole thing to be really effective. It's not a practicable way to go about things if you want to shape a society."

They stopped in front of the elevators. It wasn't the first time that Tierney had heard Nordens talking in this fashion.

"Have you read Plato, Jerry?" Nordens asked.

"Can't say it's something that I ever got around to," Tierney replied.

"Do so. It will clarify your understanding of the importance of the state, and the duty of the citizen to subordinate individual interests to those of the whole. And who is to decide what are the better interests of the whole? That's where what we in this part of the world called democracy was bound to fail, leading us to the predicament that we now find ourselves in. Sheep can't rule themselves. They're not capable of determining in which direction their true interests lie. Society will produce an elite whose natural role is to know and decide, just as the place of the rest is to follow. But discipline and firmness are essential for such an order to prevail—and, if need be, ruthlessness."

The elevator arrived, and the door opened. Tierney was going on through to the security office and had intended leaving Nordens here, but Nordens ignored the waiting car and continued, "That truth was glimpsed by many thinkers in history, but the ideals that they aspired to were always thwarted by the perverseness of raw human material, which was all they ever had to work with. Even Plato himself failed, when he went as adviser to Dionysius and attempted to guide the formation of a model state in Sicily. The ideal society has always been unattainable because the material to build it with was unsuitable. Until now." Nordens's eyes gleamed behind his spectacles. "Now we can change the material!"

Tierney looked at him uncertainly. "*The* material? You mean all of it? You're not talking about just a few individuals?"

Nordens shook his head. "Test cases. Mere beginnings. You might alter the population's disposition slightly by influencing a few individuals like Daparras, but you won't change it radically. What a paucity of result for the effort expended. . . . But suppose we had the ability to *predispose* an entire population to exhibiting more desirable and compliant attitudes, say by introducing suitable chemical agents on a mass scale—which could be accomplished by any of several means. Because I think that could be the next step in this—provided we can learn enough about the relevant transfer patterns to encode them into molecular form." Nordens was visibly excited by the prospect. He grasped Tierney by the arm. "And who knows. Maybe, one day, we could actually fuse it into the genome and make it hereditable. So once society was conditioned into being untroublesome, its traits would automatically be passed on, which would enable us, its rightful rulers, to govern unthreatened and effectively, without the inconvenience of having to indoctrinate every generation afresh. In other words, we are standing on the threshold of a whole new age. But Ashling could give the Off-worlders the key to unlocking the information that will enable it to be realized. And that's why he must be stopped. *That* is what this is all about."

Tierney looked away, at the concrete-walled passages and doors leading to the lab areas. Or to prevent the rest of the world from finding out, he thought to himself.

Nordens, carried away now by his vision, went on, "We've shown that we can shape an individual to our needs. Next is to shape a whole population. That's where the people who are backing this are heading. I'm talking about powerful people, Jerry. There's no better security in life than making sure you're on the right side."

Clearly, Nordens had no hesitation in ranking himself among the elite who would plan and guide the shaping of this utopia. Tierney was less happy about where those such as himself were likely to end up in the eventual scheme of things.

After Nordens finally entered the elevator, Tierney continued on his way to the security office. It led through the bio-assay section, where various animals were kept. Tierney walked between the cages of rats, hamsters, and rabbits, all laid out in neat rows according to what people like Nordens viewed as a desirable pattern of order and tidiness, suited to their own convenience. That's how they would organize all of us, Tierney thought.

His mood had grown very troubled by the time he got back to his office. Somebody was going to have to do something before this got out of hand, he decided. Nordens and Circo were already taking it upon themselves effectively to formulate their own foreign policy. What would be next if that kind of megalomania went unchecked?

thirty-two

Samurai was met at Hamburg's Fuhlsbüttel airport by the local CIA station chief, Ambrose Chame, who was based at the U.S. consulate ostensibly as a member of a trade delegation, and a younger man whom he introduced as William Litherland, one of his agents. A black Mercedes waited for them outside the terminal. As they sped south into the city preceded by a Hamburg police car flashing a blue light, Chame briefed Samurai on the measures that had been put in place. Circo had called somebody at the Berlin embassy the night before, requesting police cooperation but declining to give details on grounds of national security, and the German federal authorities had cleared things with Hamburg.

Chame was a solid, heavily built man in his fifties, who moved ponderously and wheezily, with shaggy hair, ample, ruddy features, and a ragged mustache. He was wearing an open raincoat and scarf with a Tyrolean hat against the north German winter cold, and talked in a blunt, forthright manner that said he'd been doing this for years, it was as lousy as any other job, and anyone who didn't like his manners should be looking for a different line of work.

"The latest is that the boat's on time. The kraut honcho running this end is a guy called Weyel. He's down at the docks now, getting set up. They'll be checking out everyone who comes down the plank."

"How many men does he have? Where has he deployed them?" Samurai asked.

"That's his bag. We'll find out when we get there."

"How will they identify Ashling?"

"We got pictures through the wire first thing this morning."

"These men of Weyel's, I assume they are reliable?" Samurai fired the questions in a clipped, authoritative voice, conveying more than a hint of presumption that he already regarded this as *his* operation.

Chame eyed him undecidedly for a second before replying. "Relax. Yeah, they're as good as you're gonna get, okay?"

"We can't afford any mistakes," Samurai insisted.

"We're just gonna grab a guy who's coming off a fuckin' ship, for chrissakes," Chame pointed out. "You wanna call out the whole army?"

"I'm used to perfection, and I expect nothing less," Samurai informed him curtly.

Chame caught Litherland's look, turned his eyes upward briefly, and looked away out the window at the outskirts of the city. Desk cowboy from inside the Beltway. This was going to be one of those pain-in-the-ass jobs that he just loved.

Inspector Weyel, in contrast to Chame, was small and dapper, clad in a gray overcoat over a suit, with checkered vest and a crisp white shirt. Also, to begin with anyway, he was impressed by, and approving of, Samurai's display of professional thoroughness.

The *Auriga* was a medium-tonnage freighter that carried maybe a dozen passengers in addition to cargo. It would moor at the Baltic-Pacific Line berths on a quay backed by warehouses and the company's offices in the north-shore docks. Weyel had the full cooperation of the owners, and had spread out a plan of the berthing area on a table in the loading manager's office, which looked out over the quay. Three gangplanks were usually used, one forward, one stern, and one amidships. The passengers disembarked via the last. Nevertheless, Samurai had insisted on having one of Weyel's men at every gate, each of them backed by two uniformed men.

"What happens after they come ashore?" Samurai asked, studying the plan. "Which way do they leave?"

An official of the company pointed. "The luggage is brought through to there, where they clear immigration and customs. Then along that corridor past the trucking bays to the exit. The roadway there connects out through gates to the street."

"Place another man in the customs hall there, with two uniformed men by the door out," Samurai directed. "Also, keep a car standing by outside that gate." Weyel nodded and passed the instructions to an assistant, who said *"Ja"* and hurried away.

Samurai went to the window and surveyed the berth where the *Auriga* would dock. "There is the chance that they could take him off the far side in a boat," he said. "Contact the harbor police and have a launch patrolling about five hundred meters out there."

Weyel thought that was getting a bit melodramatic, but he complied.

"I assume we have direct contact from here to all your units?" Samurai said.

Weyel indicated the radio on the table beside the plans.

"The sets have all been tested?"

"They are quite reliable," Weyel assured him. For the first time, a discernible edge of irritation crept into his voice.

"Test them," Samurai said.

Chame and Litherland were watching from inside the doorway. "Think we need the Navy too, in case he tries to get away in a submarine?" Litherland murmured from the side of his mouth, his face deadpan.

Chame snorted beneath his breath and shook his head. "That guy's got a fuckin' cattle prod stuck up his ass. Where are they getting 'em from these days, Bill?"

The harbor police launch duly appeared and began circling slowly offshore in the estuary. The phone rang and was answered by the company official, who announced that the *Auriga* was less than a kilometer away along the channel. The ship came into sight shortly afterward under the overcast sky, an unremarkable container ship with a stern superstructure, hull lime-green showing a few streaks of rust, and an orange stack. It turned at one of the outer buoys, came in on an approach course to align gradually with the dock, reversed screws, and nudged gently against the quay. Hawsers were pulled across and secured fore and aft. The gangways went up, shouted orders and replies sounded back and forth, and a few minutes later figures began filing down.

But nothing came from the policemen watching the midships ramp to report anybody resembling Ashling. Nor from neither of the other two ramps, where crewmen had also started coming off.

"Stop them all at the customs point," Samurai instructed, looking strained. "I'm going down there myself."

He did so, and observed personally while each of the ten listed passengers was interviewed by an immigration agent. None of them was Ashling.

"Seal off this whole area," Samurai said. "None of the crew are to be let out without being checked. He could be disguised."

Everyone who had come ashore was cleared. The delay was affecting operations aboard the ship, and the captain was getting annoyed, demanding to know what in hell was going on. Chame stayed out of it, smoking cigarettes, and seemed to find it amusing.

"There is no way they could have been tipped off," Samurai fumed. "He *must* be here somewhere. Inspector, organize a search of the ship."

But by now Weyel had had enough. "Look, I think it's about time you realized that *you* don't have the authority to give orders here," he retorted.

"Just do it, dammit!"

"My instructions were to assist you in apprehending a passenger," Weyel reminded him. "The passengers have all been accounted for, and the man you're looking for was not among them. Therefore I have no further obligation. I suggest you recheck with your sources of information."

Samurai looked across in exasperation to Chame, who was smirking over a plastic cup of coffee. "Can you explain to this idiot that this is important?"

"You're the hot shit from the top, who knows what's going on. You explain it to him."

At that moment, hurrying footsteps sounded from the corridor leading out to the street entrance. The policemen by the door into the customs hall parted to let through a man in a raincoat, who came straight over to Weyel.

"What is it, Gustav?" Weyel said, reading the urgency on his face.

"We've just got news from the Harbor Light Bar, sir. The Estonian who calls himself Nicolaus was seen there within the last hour, accompanied by a man answering to Ashling's description. They left through the rear entrance when our men arrived who were sent to check."

Samurai put a hand to his brow. "You mean you didn't have the back of the place covered?" he grated.

"Let's get over there," Weyel snapped. Chame gulped down the last of his coffee, crumpled the cup, and tossed it at a bin. Samurai was already following Weyel out, while the other policemen around the room converged toward the doorway behind them.

The Harbor Light Bar was little more than a glorified pub down on the waterfront, with a couple of drinking lounges, one of which also served as the restaurant, and a few rooms that were let out upstairs.

"Yes, he left that way, the Estonian," the proprietor confirmed, indicating a passageway leading to the back of the premises. He nodded and stabbed a finger up and down on the photograph of Ashling that was lying on the bartop. "The man who was with him looked like that. They sneaked out with their bags as if they were in a hurry. It was when your police came in this way and started asking questions."

"You're sure?" Weyel said, sounding as if he found it hard to believe.

"Of course he's sure," Samurai seethed. "Does he look like one of those incompetents that you've got working for you?"

"I'd suggest that language like that is hardly likely to prove constructive," Weyel said stiffly.

"What kind of language do you expect, Inspector?" Samurai demanded. "Why not face the facts? Hell, you screwed up."

Weyel wasn't used to having this kind of difference aired in public. "How can you say that?" he retorted. "We did everything exactly as *you* specified."

"On the contrary, you did everything wrong. Am I expected to be everywhere at once?"

"What else did you want?" Weyel demanded angrily.

Samurai enumerated on his fingers, his eyes blazing. "You let him slip through somewhere, off the ship. You didn't have this place staked out from the start, which allowed them to get back here. You sent uniformed men blundering in the front to alert them. You hadn't secured the rear. Do you want me to go on? . . . Should I take over running whatever passes for a training school in this city?"

Weyel colored visibly and whirled upon him, whereupon

Chame interjected, "Why don't we check out the room? It might tell us something."

Which averted a row for the time being. The policemen, Chame and Litherland, and Samurai followed the proprietor up a flight of stairs behind the living room, and along a passage adorned with nautical decor and paintings of ships.

The room was a plain but bright and cleanly kept single, with closet doors open, a half-empty bottle of schnapps left on the vanity, and other signs of having been hurriedly vacated. There were some oddments of food, discarded wrappings, and a couple of used bus and train tickets lying around, but nothing immediately useful. Litherland touched a fingertip to a trace of white crystalline powder on the vanity top near the bottle and tested it experimentally with his tongue. "Salt," he informed the others simply.

Chame, meanwhile, had straightened up from the waste bin, holding an empty, cylindrical, plastic container.

Samurai took it from him and turned it to show the label. It read *"Panacyn,"* and had Ashling's name, along with directions.

"It's his," Samurai announced grimly. "He *was* here." He held the container out, as if offering evidence that he was inviting any of the others to challenge. None of them did.

The implication was clear. Germany was part of the Consolidation, and hence its security and police forces cooperated closely with U.S. and other Western agencies, and maintained strict frontier controls. But if Ashling nevertheless managed to cross over into Poland or the states that had once constituted Czechoslovakia, he would be virtually unstoppable. After half a century of the delights of communism, those countries took a more relaxed attitude toward such matters, making passage onward into the FER little more than a formality. In fact, some said that Eastern Europe was already as good as a part of the FER. And once there, in the chaos and anarchy that now prevailed where tsars and commissars had once ruled, he could vanish without effort.

Samurai looked from one to another of the faces confronting him, as if expecting somebody to voice the obvious. They stared back, waiting. "He must be stopped before he gets out of Hamburg," he said finally.

"Very well. *You're* the perfectionist. What would you suggest?" Weyel replied, sounding sarcastic and relishing it.

For once Samurai's resourcefulness failed him. After a final check around the room, which turned up nothing new, the party went back downstairs and split up to depart in several vehicles. Weyel accompanied Chame, Litherland, and Samurai back to the U.S. consulate to make sure that his version of the story was incorporated into the record there. Samurai said nothing, but sat glowering with suppressed rage throughout the drive.

Chame, in between popping peanuts into his mouth and studying the city passing by, sent occasional, curiously thoughtful glances in his direction as they drove. For somebody who seemed to be exceptional in a lot of ways, this Sam Harris was astoundingly inept at handling the human side of the business, Chame thought. And in Chame's experience, the people side was what it was all about. Somehow he got chilly passings of a feeling that Harris didn't have a human side to him at all. Either that, or something inside the hotshot from Washington was starting to come apart.

The news waiting when they got to the consulate changed the whole picture, however. Following a priority-one request from Circo, search keywords relating to Ashling's defection had been watchlisted in the National Security Agency computers at Fort Meade, the final repository and clearinghouse of the nation's prolific industry in global communications tapping and eavesdropping. A satellite intercept that morning had picked up an item in a microwaved message stream of telephone conversations emanating from an unidentified source inside the FER. The extract, routed to the consulate in Hamburg via the U.S. embassy in Berlin, had come in only minutes previously. It read:

"There's been a change of plan. We've got a place reserved for Headman on a December 6 launch from Semipalatinsk. Have you got that?" . . . There was a gap to indicate a reply, which the satellite hadn't recorded since it would have been carried in a transmission going the other way. Then: *"Yuri won't be able to make it tonight to collect him in Berlin. So can you put him up somewhere overnight, and Yuri will meet you for breakfast instead."* . . . Another gap, followed by, *"Okay, then. That's the Brandenburger on Heerstrasse, ten o'clock sharp. Yuri will be there. . . ."* The route-back code contained in the transmission indicated that the call had originated from Volgograd, in what was now the Kalmyk Republic.

And that suddenly answered everything. Semipalatinsk, formerly a center of the Soviet space program, was now one of the principal Earthports to Offworld, located in the Kazakh Free State. Pipeline's intention was clearly to ship Ashling up from there, launching off in five days' time. Yuri was evidently a courier being sent to collect Ashling and take him across the frontier. And they weren't due to meet until tomorrow!

Samurai departed for Berlin less than an hour later, having made arrangements with his U.S. embassy contact to be met there, and for police cooperation and backup to be available.

This was going to be Berlin district's problem now! Inspector Weyel obligingly agreed to provide Samurai with a car. He even supplied him with a police driver. Just to make sure he got there.

thirty-three

Circo's boss, the head of the Federal Security Service, was a man called Andrew Grazin. The FSS was essentially his own creation. Introduced to begin with—ostensibly, at least—as an exclusive intelligence arm of the Executive Branch, it had swiftly expanded its role to supplant the FBI in the investigation and prosecution of domestic matters deemed "political"; it could also intervene in situations outside the home borders when directed, which the CIA resented but found itself powerless to change. In practice this meant having virtually a free hand to pursue and suppress any organization, critic, or other focus of opposition that was considered to be sufficiently inconvenient, and that the ordinary constraints on search, privacy invasion, and seizure made it difficult to deal with. This, of course, had been the original intention. The service had been modeled on lessons drawn from experiments in drug and environmental-law enforcement conducted in earlier years to test just what degree of constitutional circumvention it was possible to get away with. The answer turned out to be "practically as much as you like," since the bulk of the population was long past being able to distinguish between mass-media-created make-believe and reality, anyway.

By its very nature, the FSS was an organization that attracted people who were ambitious, adversatively disposed, unlikely to be impressed by legal or ethical impediments to getting results, and who presumed ulterior motives in everything, suspected anything that came too easily, and trusted nobody. Grazin, therefore, took it for granted that all of his subordinates were potential rivals for his job. Accordingly, he considered it no more than an elementary precaution to divulge nothing unnecessarily, while expecting everything to be reported to him, thus exploiting their insecurity and bolstering his own. Since nothing in life had caused him to conceive otherwise, he assumed that, whatever else their public images and pretensions, all organizations that had demonstrated the wherewithal for survival worked the same way.

It didn't strike him as surprising or unfitting, therefore, when Jerry Tierney, head of internal security at Pearse, contacted him late at night on a personal line with something urgent to discuss. Grazin had been informed of Southside over a year ago when the project was conceived, his brief being to render support and cooperation, if requested, while keeping a low profile. A week ago some of Circo's men had been mixed up in the fiasco in Chicago, when three of Tierney's men had gone after a subject from Pearse who had gone off the rails and needed to be brought back. Grazin assumed that Tierney's request had something to do with that—although why he hadn't gone through Circo, who handled Southside, or why, if it was really a top-level matter, it hadn't come through Fairfax, was a good question.

They met early the following morning. In view of the irregularity of the situation, and since, in any case, Grazin generally preferred not to advertise whom he was talking to and when, they talked from the windows of their cars in a parking lot outside Union Station, a quarter mile from the Capitol.

"Sure, of course I know that the business about military personnel training was just a cover," Grazin said when Tierney went back to the origins of the project. "The real object is ideological reprogramming." He shrugged in a so-what kind of way. "It's a changing world. You can't just keep freaks who want to change the system off the streets anymore. So you change how they think, instead."

"That was how it started out," Tierney agreed. "But then things got more complicated."

Grazin frowned. "I thought everything was okay. The first phase was wrapped up. Now they're evaluating results out in the field. Isn't that how it is?" As far as he was aware, the volunteers who hadn't been screened out had each been implanted with a test set of reorientation patterns, and then returned to their normal working environments so that the results could be observed.

Tierney shook his head, however. "There's more to it. One of the subjects wasn't returned. There was some kind of screwup, and he ended up with the donor's complete personality in his head, not just the target patterns. In other words, he thought he *was* the donor. Only, in the meantime, the guy'd had a stroke and fallen over up in Minneapolis. It was all a mess. So an accident record was faked to write the subject off in a helicopter accident—to clear the picture."

"Shit." Grazin covered his eyes. "Who arranged this?"

Tierney sighed resignedly. "Fairfax, Nordens. . . ."

"You're telling me you weren't a part of it?"

"I knew there was something odd going on, but I didn't realize how much at the time."

Grazin didn't believe that, but this wasn't the time to worry about it. "And Circo?" he guessed.

Tierney nodded heavily. "Sure. Circo was in it up to his ass. He fixed things with the military."

Grazin nodded curtly. "So why are you telling me now?"

"Because of the way it's gone since. You see, they could have come clean with the people who'd need to know, and simply told them that they'd screwed up and were stuck with this guy who thinks he's someone else who's dead. But they didn't do that. They've been using him for a different kind of experiment that nobody knows about—that goes a lot further than Southside."

Grazin frowned again. "Further? . . . What are you talking about?"

"Something that Nordens dreamed up—about not just changing parts of a person, but *creating* a whole new one, to order."

"Creating a person?"

"Right. Synthetic. Purpose-built to be anything you want. Think what the right people could do with that."

"What people? Who else are you saying knows about this?"

"Fairfax and Circo have got the backing of some group somewhere, who are worth a lot of bread and think they can run the system better. I don't have names yet. . . . But there's a crazy note starting to sound all through this. To try and check out this idea, they turned this volunteer they were left with into a kind of super field man: a composite of everything, physical skills, tech know-how, knowledge base, you name it. His code designation is Samurai. There were a few problems—"

"Wait. Wasn't he the loose cannon that Fairfax wanted Circo's people to bring back from Chicago?"

"Right. Only, recently it's gotten worse. The scientist who started the whole business off, the one they thought they had by the balls, who was working down at Pearse, opted out and blew the country through Pipeline. Right now he's in Germany, offplanet-bound via the FER, obviously to spill the works. Fairfax and the others have panicked and sent Samurai after him. Circo has requested official cooperation locally through the embassy. They've—"

"What!" Grazin paled. "You mean they've sent him to Europe, on their own authority? . . . Obtained unsanctioned involvement of foreign government agencies. This is insane."

"That's what I'm saying. They're out of control down there. He's briefed to assassinate if necessary."

"Jesus Christ!"

"They—"

"Taking out a dissident scientist on foreign territory? Getting foreign authorities mixed up in it? He's got to be called off. This is a fuse leading straight to an international situation."

Tierney shook his head. "No chance. You don't understand."

"Understand what?"

"You can't call him off. Samurai won't stop."

Grazin's expression hardened. "Then he'll have to *be* stopped," he declared grimly.

Tierney bit his lip. "That mightn't be so easy," he replied.

thirty-four

This time there would be no mistake. The Brandenburger restaurant was being staked out from unmarked cars placed in both directions from the entrance; the only other exit at the rear was covered; a plainclothes policeman and policewoman had been inside, posing as customers, since 9:30; and the arrest squad was with Samurai in the temporary headquarters that he had set up in a hairdresser's on the other side of the street, with an open line to police headquarters. It had all been arranged smoothly and without hitches since Samurai's arrival from Hamburg the previous evening: a paradigm of German thoroughness, exemplifying the kind of discipline and concern for detail that the rest of the Consolidation needed. Samurai was well satisfied.

Tension rose as 10:00 drew nearer, peaking expectantly as the hour came. . . . But nothing happened. By 10:30 the watchers were growing anxious and puzzled. Chief Inspector Gelhardt of the Berlin Police tapped a code into his communicator to activate the unit contained in the purse that the woman inside had placed on the table in front of her. It emitted a low beep, inaudible beyond a few feet.

"Go ahead," the woman's voice acknowledged, indicating that it was clear for him to speak.

"Anything?"

"No. There has been nobody resembling either of them." They had Ashling's picture and knew what Nicolaus looked like from the description furnished by the girl in the Hamburg brothel. Yuri's appearance, of course, was unknown.

When it got to 11:00, Samurai had had enough. Followed by

Gelhardt and two of his men, he crossed the street and entered the restaurant. The plainclothes policeman shook his head almost imperceptibly. Samurai marched up to the cash desk and confronted the manager with an ID card.

"International security. These men with me are police." He produced a print of the picture of Ashling sent through from Washington. "Have you seen this man in here this morning?"

The manager looked at the picture. "Yes," he replied simply. "He was here with two other men. They had breakfast together."

"*What!*" Samurai nearly choked. "When was this? How long ago?"

The manager looked across at a clock on the far wall. "Let me see, a while ago now—the early rush was still on. They sat at that table over there. . . . I'd say about eight, eight-thirty, something like that. A quarter to nine at the latest, anyway."

Samurai stared at him, speechless. It was sickening. There must have been another call from Volgograd later, changing the time, which had either been missed by the NSA or hadn't got through yet. Or maybe the first message had been in a code, where "ten" meant "eight," or something equally simple. But if that was the case, why hadn't the name of the location been coded? . . . Whatever the answer, it wouldn't help now.

"How did they leave?" Gelhardt inquired.

"By taxi."

"Were they carrying anything?"

"I'm sorry, I don't remember."

"Have you any idea where they were heading?"

The manager spread his hands and smiled apologetically. "Again, I am sorry, gentlemen. I don't know where our customers go when they leave. What else can I say?"

The operation was called off forthwith. The cavalcade formed up and proceeded back to the local police headquarters. It wasn't long before Samurai was upsetting people again.

"Absolutely out of the question!" Gelhardt threw up his hands, turned away toward the window to compose himself, then wheeled back again and planted his knuckles on the top of the desk in his office. "Look, Mr. Harris, I don't think you quite appreciate what you're asking. Close all crossing points through the eastern frontier? I don't have the authority to do that. Nobody in this department does. Nobody in this building does. It's not even under police jurisdiction. It's a matter for border security, and they—"

"And I don't think that *you* appreciate that what we're talking about here has ramifications of the utmost importance," Samurai countered. "National and international. The outcome of this could affect the political stability of your country and mine . . . of the whole Consolidation."

"That's as may be, but if so it's a matter for international authorities, not us."

"Then I strongly suggest that you—" A phone on Gelhardt's desk interrupted.

"Excuse me." He touched a button to accept. The screen showed the face of an aide in the general office outside—Gelhardt had closed the door when his exchange with Samurai started getting heated. "I thought I said we weren't to be interrupted," Gelhardt said.

"I know, sir, but we've just had some news that appears pertinent. The desk sergeant at Third Precinct station is on the line. A taxi driver has just walked in there, saying he has information concerning three men that he understands you were looking for at the Brandenburger. Apparently he took them to Friedrichstrasse."

"Third Precinct?" Samurai queried.

Gelhardt glanced at him. "Off Heerstrasse, a few blocks from the Brandenburger." Samurai didn't need to be told that Friedrichstrasse was one of the city's principal railroad stations.

Gelhardt looked back at the screen. "Tell them to keep him there. We're on our way over."

Another break, straight out of the blue, just when Samurai had been hard put to know which way to go next. It was almost as if Fate was determined to lead him on. Lucky coincidences, he concluded gratefully, didn't only happen in second-rate fiction.

He drove with Gelhardt and several other officers to the Third Precinct station, where a small and scruffily clad man with a day's growth of razor stubble and yellow teeth confirmed that he had picked up two men fitting Ashling's and Nicolaus's descriptions, along with a third man, pinkish in complexion, from the Brandenburger at eight-forty according to his log, and driven them to Friedrichstrasse. He had returned to the Brandenburger later for another fare and been told by the manager that the police were looking for his previous passengers.

"Did they say where they were going?" Gelhardt asked the taxi driver.

"Not to me, sir. But on the way I overheard one of them grumbling about having to spend half the day in Zittau. Then the pink-faced one said that he hoped that this person would get them across tonight. I didn't really catch the name. It sounded like Rosky, Rosesky, or something like that. Then one of the others hushed him up—you know, as if he shouldn't have been talking about it."

There was no guarantee, of course, that all three men would actually be traveling together, which would have been conspicuous. From the wording of the telephone call picked up by NSA, it seemed more likely that Nicolaus would have handed Ashling over to Yuri and seen them onto the train, and then gone his own way.

A check of the railway timetables showed that a train had departed at 9:35 from Friedrichstrasse going through Cottbus, a rail interchange town to the east, roughly halfway down to the southern tip of the country. There was a regular service through Cottbus down to Görlitz, farther south and east, situated on the Lausitzer Neisse River, opposite the Polish town of Zgorzelec. There was a rail connection from there to Zittau, the town mentioned by the taxi driver, which lay yet farther south in the extreme southeastern tip of Germany.

"Why go all the way to Zittau?" Samurai asked Gelhardt after digesting this much from maps.

"It's just past the point where the three frontiers meet," Gelhardt replied. "The crossing is into Bohemia, not Poland. Controls are easier. From Bohemia they could either go north again into Poland, or eastward, through Moravia and Slovakia into FER territory. Either way would be easy, since outside the Consolidation everything gets lax. Zittau is the kind of place that Pipeline would use."

Samurai departed for Zittau shortly after lunch. Gelhardt, suddenly undergoing the same kind of miraculous transformation into a model of cooperation as had overcome Inspector Weyel in Hamburg, phoned ahead to have the local agents there check into possible leads on anyone called Rosky, Rosesky, or anything similar, who might be connected with border crossing procedures. As an afterthought, he told the desk sergeant to slip the taxi driver an extra fifty marks from the grease fund the next time he came in.

While Samurai was on his way to Zittau it was still morning in Washington, where a dumbfounded Circo was being blasted by Grazin after being wakened and flown up from Pearse in the middle of the night.

"I don't have any time for bullshit. The war's over for you, buddy," Grazin stormed. "There's only one thing left for you to do now to make it easier on yourself when you go through the wringer, and that's come clean. I want a full disclosure of what's been going on and who's been involved. But before we get into that, we've got this situation over in Europe. Now, I want to know where this Samurai is, exactly what he's doing over there, and who his contacts are." He flipped a switch to start the recorder built into the desk's comms unit. "So sing."

thirty-five

There was something odd about Captain Erenthaller, Samurai had decided.

It was early evening in the border town of Zittau. Snow had fallen during the day, and against the heavy sky the outlines of factories stood out starkly behind rows of drab, slate-roofed houses huddled in the pale light from the street lamps. In the yellow-painted, austere local offices of the Dresden district border police, Samurai sat making notes and watching as the staff searched records and dossiers for possible leads to the names that the taxi driver had given in Berlin. The commissioner was standing behind a clerk at a computer screen, checking the "Rovikossky" who was listed as working at the passport office in Dresden, but it appeared that he had retired some years ago. A policeman was going through one of a pile of files, while another was on the line to verify an address. They were all working methodically, if a little tensely in view of the urgency that Samurai had stressed. But the captain, Erenthaller, seemed deeply ill at ease. Samurai had been observing him surreptitiously for some time.

He was heavily built but out of shape, late thirties, with black hair cropped close above a creased bull neck, a slack but pugnacious mouth set in a blue-shadowed chin, and furtive eyes that betrayed slyness but little intelligence. For the past hour he had been in constant nervous motion about the room, unable to keep still, and had flinched visibly every time an incoming call sounded, then watched when somebody took it, as if on tenterhooks over what it might be about. And there was a pallor about his face that Samurai sensed not to be normal, and a dampness that could almost be felt, emanating from his skin.

He knew something, Samurai was certain. His reaction had started as soon as the commissioner gave them the brief on Rosky/ Rosesky and introduced Samurai as a "special agent from Washington, cleared by Berlin." He knew something. At any moment the checks could turn up something that he was involved in and that would incriminate him, and he was scared. And being scared meant being vulnerable, as Samurai was well aware.

The policeman who had been on the phone cleared down, shaking his head. "Nothing there. He did have a boat, but he got rid of it six months ago and now lives with his daughter in Leipzig."

"Cross him off," the commissioner said. He looked at the policeman who was checking the files. "What about this Rosinsky?"

"Well . . . yes, he's still here in town. But at fifty-five, a night watchman at a shunting yard? What's the connection?"

The commissioner pulled a face. "Railroads, eh? Put him down as a possible."

Across the room, Erenthaller started to move, changed his mind, then stood up. "Er, I'll be back in a minute," he muttered, and left. Samurai set down his pen and sat back in the chair. Through the doorway, which had been left slightly open, he tracked Erenthaller's footsteps and movements: away a short distance to the right along the corridor outside, a turn, several more steps, then the wary opening, as if making sure that nobody was inside, and then even more careful closing, of a door.

A tone rang for an incoming call. One of the policemen turned to a screen and activated it. The commissioner looked at a sheet of paper that he was holding and moved over to compare something written on it with an item showing on another screen. "What the hell's this name doing here, Carl?" he grumbled. "It's a woman."

"Oh, sorry. My mistake."

Samurai moved his chair and stood up. "Excuse me for a moment," he murmured softly, and vanished.

To the left, the corridor opened into a main office; there was nobody in the part of it that was visible. In the other direction it passed a wide alcove a few yards away on one side, across which two doors faced each other, and continued beyond. Samurai moved quietly to the alcove and listened at one of the doors, but could hear nothing. He tried the other. Inside, a lowered voice was speaking hurriedly, the words too indistinct to make out. He tried the handle gently. The door was locked. Drawing a long breath to concentrate his strength, he drew back a short distance, then launched himself at it, at the same time half turning his body to impact with full force focused on a line from the shoulder to the hip. The lockplate tore out of the jamb with a sharp *crack*; without breaking his movement, Samurai pivoted inside, wheeled to face the room, and closed the door behind him.

Erenthaller was standing beside a desk with a phone in his hand, guilt etched all over his face. Samurai took the phone from his hand before he had reacted to what was happening and hung it up.

"Okay, let's hear it," he hissed.

Erenthaller looked confused for a moment, and then took a swing. It was clumsy and inexpert. Samurai rode the blow easily with an arm and went in low and fast with a straight-hand jab to the solar plexus and punch to the kidney, following through by locking an arm across Erenthaller's throat and slamming him down into the chair. He banged the side of the German's head hard against the wall and drove a thumb into the cavity beneath his other ear. Erenthaller grimaced and writhed with the pain, but the blow to his middle had paralyzed his breathing and the arm across his throat stifled any sound.

"You know something," Samurai growled. "What have you been hiding?"

Erenthaller clutched at his chest, gasped, puffed, and shook his head. "You're mad. . . . I don't know . . . what you're talking about. Who do you think—"

Samurai palm-heeled his chin, forcing his head back over the top of the chair, and brought a knee up hard into his testicles. Erenthaller shrieked noiselessly. Samurai slapped him several times forehand and backhand across the face. "I don't have time for games. Who were you calling?" Erenthaller's head lolled drunkenly to one side in a daze. Samurai seized one of his little fingers and began forcing it back over the hand. Erenthaller could feel it on the verge of cracking.

"Okay, okay. . . . Don't."

"Talk. What's the name?"

"For God's sake ease up!" Samurai relaxed the pressure a fraction. Erenthaller licked his lips and swallowed for breath, his head still jammed against the back of the chair and his face running with perspiration.

"Rostiescki. . . . We have an arrangement."

"Who is he?"

"Local undercover contact in Zittau. . . . Arranges crossings for people without papers. Pipeline uses him. . . ." Erenthaller hesitated. Samurai could see he was holding something back and began increasing the pressure on the finger again.

"*Aghhh. All right!* . . . But he's also a spy. I get tip-offs from him on who's due to go across. We work it between us. Know what I mean?"

Samurai released him contemptuously. Erenthaller massaged his bruised finger, wheezing erratically, then felt his throat. Samurai understood all too well. Rostiescki betrayed the people who trusted him for favors that Erenthaller could arrange, and Erenthaller took a cut of the fees that Rostiescki was paid. Erenthaller would let enough smaller fish through not to arouse suspicion, but he could make his record look good when an important catch came along. But he wouldn't be averse to looking the other way if Rostiescki could secure a further payment on top of the original deal. A shabby operation, worked by a pretty shabby pair of operators.

"What do you know about these two men I'm interested in?" Samurai demanded. "These two men coming from Berlin."

"I don't know anything about them. You must have made a mistake."

"There has been no mistake."

"It they were coming here to go across with Rostiescki, I'd know about it," Erenthaller insisted.

Samurai remained unimpressed. "Then let's ask Rostiescki, shall we? Where can he be found?"

Erenthaller stared up and seemed about to say something, then saw the look in Samurai's eyes and changed his mind. "He has a room in town, but he won't be there now. There are a couple of places that he hangs around in."

"Let's go, then," Samurai said.

Erenthaller looked startled. "But . . ." He gestured in the direction of the room they had come from.

"Never mind about them. We'll get our coats on the way out. Move."

They stopped at the cloakroom by the entrance for the coats. Samurai also took the briefcase that he carried on assignment, but left the bag with his clothes and personal effects. They slipped out of a side door into an alley and followed it to the street, with Erenthaller slithering on the snow in his attempt to keep up the pace, uncomfortably conscious of the gun that Samurai was holding in his overcoat pocket.

Minutes after they rounded the corner at the end of the street, a black Mercedes drew up at the front door from the opposite direction. Muffled figures emerged, hurried up the steps, and disappeared inside.

The third bar they tried was as drab as the others, with a low door beneath a wooden sign unreadable in the gloom, and yellow light showing through a window of small dirty panes set high in the wall. It lay between a few shops, all closed, and what looked like some kind of commercial premises, looming solid and featureless in the night. Samurai said he'd wait outside. Erenthaller ducked his head and went. Samurai stamped his feet, then moved away a short distance along the street and back again, swinging his arms to keep up the circulation. The street remained deserted. After a minute or two, Erenthaller emerged clutching the sleeve of a weasely looking man in a flat cap and black overcoat, who was protesting vehemently, but in a low voice.

"What are you doing? I told you not to talk to me in public places. Haven't you got . . ." His mouth closed like a trap when he saw Samurai waiting. "Who's he?"

"It's complicated," Erenthaller began. "There have been rumors of a consignment due through here tonight. It seems there's a lot of interest in high places. Do you know anything about it?"

Rostiescki shook his head violently. "Not me! No, I don't know anything." The fearful look that he shot Erenthaller in the wan light from the bar window told Samurai that he was lying. In a movement that all but lifted Rostiescki off his feet, Samurai seized his coat front and banged him back against the wall.

"Two of them, coming from Berlin," Samurai said crisply.

"I don't know anything, I swear. On my mother's holy—"

Samurai produced his automatic and thrust the barrel up under

Rostiescki's chin. The click sounded of the safety catch disengaging. "You've got five seconds."

"You can't. I'm a—"

"Four."

"For God's sake, he doesn't kn—" Erenthaller pleaded.

"Three."

"*All right, all right!* . . . They're here. I was scared. Honest, I thought they'd kill me."

"What names were you given?"

"One was Yuri, the other Oleg."

"Their full names."

"That's all I was told, I swear—"

"Don't treat me like a fool. If you were getting them out, you'd be arranging their papers. You'd need their full names."

Rostiescki swallowed. "Yuri Baselyavin. Oleg Kubalov. Honest, I don't know any more." Samurai released him with a contemptuous shove.

Erenthaller moved forward a step, tensing. "What? Why wasn't I told about this? When was it arranged?"

"I was going to," Rostiescki whined. "I didn't know myself until this afternoon. It all happened too fast."

"They're here somewhere now—right at this moment?" Samurai checked, repocketing the gun. "You can take us to them?"

Rostiescki looked at Erenthaller. The captain nodded. "Tell him."

"They're holed up in a boardinghouse on Kelenstrasse. The sergeant on the north bridge checkpoint until midnight will pass them through if I'm with them." Rostiescki looked at Erenthaller pleadingly. "You would have got your cut, slit my throat if it isn't true. There wasn't time to tell you about it."

"We'll see about that. How many more times has this happened?"

"Save your squabbling until later," Samurai told them curtly. He gestured at Erenthaller. "I'm going there with him right now. You get some of your men and follow. Meet us at the boardinghouse."

"Which is it?" Erenthaller asked Rostiescki.

"Number nine. It has a wooden gate. They should be in the back room. I was to collect them."

"I'll see you there," Erenthaller said, and hastened away.

Samurai and Rostiescki walked in silence through narrow, ill-lit streets, passing only the occasional shuffling figure and seeing little traffic. The air had a feel about it of more snow before morning. As far as Samurai was concerned, it was better this way. With treachery working both ways, and people to whom lying and double-crossing came as naturally as breathing, he would trust only what he had control over himself. That meant getting to Ashling first, before anyone else was even close.

They came to the end of a street of nondescript row houses. Rostiescki placed a restraining hand on Samurai's arm and nodded. "It's along there on the other side," he murmured. "Opposite the lamp."

"Who else is there?" Samurai asked.

"Just regular lodgers in the other rooms, and the woman who runs it."

"Who'll let us in?"

"I have a key."

"We'll go inside first and make sure that we've got them, then wait for the others," Samurai said. He took out his gun again and fitted a silencer to the end.

Rostiescki watched apprehensively. "What are you going to do?"

"Just a precaution," Samurai said.

They walked along the street to the door that Rostiescki had indicated. Rostiescki produced a key and pushed the door open. Samurai shoved him in ahead, keeping the gun in the other hand out of sight inside his coat. The passageway was dark and narrow, with stairs going up on one side, lit only by the light from a bare bulb on the first landing. They went past the stairs to a door in an even darker continuation of the passage at the rear, where only the light from an uncurtained window guided them. Rostiescki glanced at Samurai inquiringly. Samurai nodded. Rostiescki tapped on the door. "Hello," he called quietly. " I am the one who has been sent to fetch you. Open the door." There was no response. He tapped again, waited some more, then looked around.

"I don't understand it."

"Open it," Samurai muttered. Holding his gun cocked and ready, he flattened himself against the wall on one side of the doorway.

Rostiescki took out his keys, fumbled for a while in the dim light, and eventually the lock clicked. He pushed the door open cautiously. "Hello?" No sound or movement came from inside. Samurai nodded for him to go in. Rostiescki reached inside for the light switch, flipped it on, and went through. "There's nobody here," his puzzled voice called back after a few seconds. Samurai came out into the light and joined him.

It was a charmless room with a blanked-off fireplace, a double bed and a few pieces of old-fashioned furniture, dusty drapes still open, and smelling damp. There were no clothes, bags, or other signs of occupancy. Samurai moved around, nonplussed. He opened the doors of the ponderous, freestanding oak wardrobe and looked inside the chest of drawers. Had this loathsome little man been lying all along about this as well? He started to turn toward Rostiescki accusingly, but his eye caught something lying on the mantelpiece. He picked it up. It was an empty matchbook cover from the Atlanta Hyatt hotel.

"They've been here," he snapped. "Where have they gone?"

Rostiescki shook his head wildly. "I don't know. I was supposed to collect them here. They were supposed to wait. On my mother's grave I don't know."

Samurai stalked over to the window and stared out at the shadows of the tiny rear yard. Now he thought he could see what had happened. Pipeline was smarter than he'd given them credit for. They knew that the operation here was corrupt and unreliable, and had made the arrangements with Rostiescki as a decoy, to mislead him and his contact in the border police, while the real escape was effected by other means. So Ashling was very possibly over the border already. . . .

And then again, maybe Pipeline wasn't so smart after all, Samurai reflected as he thought further. For Rostiescki had given one of the names as "Yuri," which Samurai knew to be correct, since it had been obtained from Pipeline's own intercepted communication to Nicolaus. Therefore "Oleg Kubalov" was probably correct too, which meant that Samurai knew the name that Ashling was traveling under. And he already knew Ashling's destination, Semipalatinsk, and that he had to be there on December 6. Tomorrow would be December 3. That would give Samurai the best part of three days to stop him. Ample, he decided with satisfaction as he turned back from the window.

"I could talk to the landlady," Rostiescki offered.

Samurai shook his head. "She won't know anything. Turn out the light. We're going to the north bridge checkpoint."

As they came back outside, vehicle headlights approached from the direction of the town center. It was a Mercedes. But instead of the detachment of police that Samurai had expected, three men in raincoats and overcoats, all wearing hats, got out, leaving the rear doors open. Another man in civilian clothes was driving, with Erenthaller in the passenger seat beside him.

The three drew up around Samurai, backing him against the wall and ignoring Rostiescki. One of them showed a badge that was invisible in the dark. "You are Sam Harris, on a U.S. military assignment?"

"Yes."

"Federal Republic State Security. Our instructions are to terminate your mission forthwith. You are to accompany us back to Berlin immediately."

Samurai thought of the people he'd crossed in Hamburg and Berlin, and decided that this had been instigated out of malice to thwart him. "I'm not under Federal Security orders," he told them. "My assignment was cleared through the embassy. You don't give me instructions."

"Mr. Harris, I must insist. We are authorized to use whatever force may be necessary, should you compel us to do so." More headlights had appeared at the far end of the street: the backup squad, no doubt.

"Is that so?" Samurai said, planting his briefcase in the unresisting hands of Rostiescki, who looked on incredulously as in rapid succession one overcoated figured was catapulted over the wall by the gate, the second was felled where he stood, and the third ended up tumbling heels over head in the gutter behind the Mercedes. Before the form had stopped skidding in the snow, Samurai yanked open the door, hauled the driver out by the collar, and sent him sprawling with a cuff to the side of the head. He jammed Rostiescki, still clutching the briefcase, into the rear seat and slammed the door behind him.

Erenthaller, still in the front passenger seat, could have opened the door and jumped. Instead he pulled his gun. But Samurai fired first as he slid into the driver's seat, wounding Erenthaller in the side, and pushed him out the other side with one arm as he steered the car away. Erenthaller fell in the path of the backup car closing in from behind, causing it to brake and swerve. By the time the driver had sorted himself out again, the Mercedes was away along the street.

"Which way is the bridge?" Samurai yelled over his shoulder to the terrified Rostiescki.

"Ahead, but over to the left." Samurai went in the other direction to draw the followers away for a distance, then lost them without much trouble in some high-speed skidding and cornering around the suburbs, ending when the police car went out of control and fell into a canal. Then he doubled back and drove to within a few hundred yards of the bridge, from which point he and Rostiescki walked.

The turn of events had reinforced his decision to follow Ashling into the FER. After all, he reasoned, he wasn't about to get any more help here in Germany. The car would have been nice to keep, but it would have attracted too much attention, and getting it over would need all kinds of special papers.

"I'll be going across tonight, instead of the two you were expecting," Samurai told Rostiescki as they approached the floodlit gate area with its barriers and uniformed sentries.

"What about papers?"

"Would Headman and Yuri have had papers? You said you'd fixed things."

"It costs money," Rostiescki said.

"You've already been paid by Pipeline," Samurai reminded him. "For two. I'm only one."

"You weren't scheduled," Rostiescki persisted, still holding out. "That's different."

"Let's put it this way. Either I walk off the other end of this bridge tonight. Or you never get to walk off it at all."

On the far side, Samurai hitched a ride in an oil delivery truck a few miles to the town of Liberec, in Bohemia, one of the states that had previously formed Czechoslovakia. The driver dropped him off a block from a hotel that looked comfortable. After everything that had happened that day, Samurai was content to think simply of sleeping, and let the question of how to get farther wait until tomorrow.

thirty-six

The Federal Security Service preferred to stay out of the public eye and maintain low visibility in the pursuit of its varied objectives. The official lists and guides to government departments made minimal reference to it, and the people who ran it would have preferred not to be mentioned at all. In keeping with this habit of professional shyness, the organization shunned the kind of prestigious headquarters that Washington agencies usually built for themselves to flaunt their success in having made it to the big league. Instead, the FSS operated from an unassuming, unadvertised office block tucked away in a side street near the tiny green rectangle of Marion Park on the south side of town. Such unobtrusiveness symbolized a new management style. In other times and other cultures, the organs of state had cultivated awe-inspiring, intimidating images to impress the populace with its power and authority. Modest, low-profile externals, by contrast, elbowed aside by media-network skyscrapers and ever-vaster football stadiums, offered tangible reassurance that ultimately the people's temples prevailed and *they* were in charge.

Some hours after news came in of Samurai's disappearance across the Lausitzer Neisse River, a Colonel Hautz arrived at FSS HQ to meet with Grazin. Hautz commanded a unit of dirty-work specialists that all armies keep in the background like the shovels at a horse show, officially described as a Flexible Response Team, attached to the Special Forces. Hautz knew of the Southside project through its official relevance to the training of military personnel. He didn't know, or need to know, about its true political purpose. Grazin presented the Samurai episode as an aberration by a local scientific group at Pearse who had gone too far, and on their own authority produced a military prodigy that went way past all the rules, and who was now out of control.

Grazin gestured at the sheet of computer printout lying in front of him on the desk. "Look at this. We've got police departments pissed from one end of Germany to the other—how he got them involved in the first place is a mystery." Hardly true, but total candor was seldom practicable in life. "He's hospitalized three of their federal agents. There's a police captain shot and on the critical list, a car totaled and the crew almost drowned, and now we're heading for a political assassination that the world will see as officially instigated, no matter what we say. He's got to be stopped. The President agrees. Tackle it any way you want, as long as we come out clean, with no pointers and no mess."

Hautz nodded that he understood. It wasn't clear to him what these scientists down at Pearse had thought they were doing. He had no doubt that others were involved as well, and that there was more to the story than Grazin was telling. But that wasn't Hautz's business.

"How sure are we that he's heading for Semipalatinsk?" he asked.

Grazin pushed across a folder lying on the desk and showed the satellite intercept from two days previously. "It's right there, in the call that NSA picked up. His target's due to make a launch out of there on the sixth."

"Has there been any coordination with the Kazakhskij government—to get the launch port secured and have Ashling put under protective custody when he shows up?"

Grazin snorted and tossed up a hand. "What government? It's practically anarchy out there. I doubt if they'd have the machinery to do it. Anyhow, Harris could still get to him first."

Hautz nodded. It was as he'd hoped: a free hand. The squad that he had in mind would also appreciate the informality and the opportunity to operate invisibly. They were overdue for some excitement in life.

"What do we do about the target, Ashling?" Hautz asked.

"If you can bring him back without precipitating an incident, then do so," Grazin replied. "Otherwise leave him. This is complicated enough already." He had already discussed it with Fairfax.

There was no way around having to face the fact that Ashling would probably get away to tell his story. If it turned out that he knew about the Samurai experiment—and it was by no means established that he did—then the only thing to do would be to eliminate the evidence and dismiss the whole thing as Offworld propaganda.

"He's got less than three days," Hautz mused. "It means catching a plane somewhere. He'd have to use the regular airports. There can't be too many routes that would get him there."

"Right. That's what we figured."

"We've got military aircraft on standby, with preclearance codes fixed with the Consolidation states," Hautz said. "I could have the team over there in eight hours."

"How about infiltration into the FER?" Grazin asked.

"No problem. Like you said, their security isn't exactly what you'd call the last word. In fact, from what I've seen of it, nobody seems to give much of a shit."

"You can go after him for us, then, eh, Colonel?"

"He's as good as in the bag."

Grazin frowned. "Don't underestimate this guy. You can see the havoc he's caused in two days already. This scientist he's after seems to be becoming some kind of personal obsession with him. He won't stop. Pick good men."

"The best," Hautz assured him.

thirty-seven

Samurai studied the breakfast menu dubiously. Full of cholesterol, sugar, fat, starch; it wasn't the kind of thing he was used to seeing being blatantly encouraged—and without warnings. The people behind him were smoking shamelessly in public, and the staff took no notice. He was only a few miles past the border, and already standards were beginning to revert to primitive. Yet his destination lay nearly three thousand miles farther east. Why would people voluntarily forgo the security of ordered lives and the fulfillment of dedicating themselves to a duty, in favor of such places? . . . Freedom? Most of them wouldn't know what to do with it. Responsibility would terrify them far more than anything the state could ever impose. No wonder psychiatric wards were full. The counselors and analysts were right: anyone who found things at home dissatisfying had to be a victim of serious maladjustment problems.

He hadn't risen especially early, and there were only a few people left in the hotel restaurant. A couple was sitting in the far corner, a woman on her own was behind him, two men who looked like travelers were eating alone, and there was a party of two men and a woman together. Samurai's first thought was to get away from this area as quickly as possible, since he wasn't sure of the situation concerning possible cooperation between the German and local police. Maybe it was unwise to have remained this close to the border for as long as he had, but that was irrelevant now. The most obvious place to make for would be the capital, Prague, roughly fifty miles away, where the options for further travel onward would be greatest.

The waitress came over and asked something in Czech, which wasn't among the languages that Samurai was equipped with. He asked if she could repeat it in German, which seemed not unlikely since this was a border town. "Would you like coffee?" she complied.

"Do you have coylene?"

"In the kitchen. I'll get them to make you some."

Samurai ordered rolls with an egg dish and sausage that didn't sound too red. "How could I get to Prague from here?" he asked before she left.

"Are you driving?"

"Of course not. If I were, I'd simply look at a map."

"Well, excuse me. You can get a bus to Jablonec, or a cab if you're in a hurry. And another bus or the train from there. They'll have details at the desk."

"Thanks."

"Do I detect German with a trace of an American accent there?" a voice said genially behind him, in English. He turned. The woman who was alone was looking at him. She was approaching middle age, rounding out and showing the beginnings of a second chin. All the same she was not unattractive, with clear, bright eyes, dark hair cut straight across at the neckline, and fresh makeup. She was wearing a navy top with a flimsy orange scarf tied at her throat, which added a mischievous, carefree touch.

"Yes. That's right," Samurai said.

"Great! It isn't exactly what you'd call crawling with us around here."

"I guess not." Samurai had a lot of thinking to do. He didn't have time for chatter, nor any inclination, and tried not to show any reaction that might encourage her.

She gave him a moment to reciprocate, but he turned back to pour himself a glass of water. Then she said, "I heard you asking about getting to Prague. I'm driving there myself, if you'd like a ride."

Samurai's head turned back around. "When?"

"As soon as I've finished this."

That changed everything. Samurai grinned and received a pleased smile in return. "That's very good of you," he said. "The name's Sam, Sam Harris. Maybe I could join you? Breakfast is on me."

The snow in the night had confined itself to the higher reaches of the hills, standing white against a sky that had cleared to misty blue, streaked with furrows of cloud high up. Even so, the road was frosty and treacherous, calling for careful driving.

She had arrived sometime in the middle of the night. Her name, she said, was Roxy, originally from Montana, but that had been quite a few years ago. Although easygoing and convivial, she was vague about what she did these days. Samurai got the impression of some kind of businesswoman or free-lancing adventuress who went with whatever opportunities life decided to cast her way at the moment. She seemed to travel a lot and knew the FER, which promised much useful information in the course of the journey and made Samurai doubly glad that he had changed his mind.

"How about you?" she inquired finally.

"What about me?"

"Quit stalling. Where are you from? What do you do?"

"Does it matter?"

"Hell, why not get to know each other a little for the duration, even if it's not going to be a lifelong affair? I like talking to people. I'm just curious."

"Oh . . . I'm based out of Philadelphia right now." Which was what Sam Harris's documents said. It saved having to invent a whole new background after Maurice Gordon was deactivated. "I import stuff mostly. This and that. Not anything in particular. Spend a lot of time all over the States."

"So what brings you here?"

"Some possible lines that I might get an exclusive on. Anyhow, new places are interesting. Like you, curious maybe."

"This and that, eh?"

Samurai didn't like the cross-examining and looked away out the window. "Whatever."

"Now why not come clean?" Roxy suggested.

"What are you talking about?"

"Oh, come on." Roxy's voice was softly chiding, in a way that said she wasn't really trying to pry, but it was too obvious. "A town near the border, first thing in the morning. No transport. No bags, just a briefcase. No real plans." She glanced across pointedly. "You're defecting, right? You want to get through into FER territory."

"Look, I just agreed to accept a ride to Prague, okay?"

"Hey, don't worry about it. There's no need to be so touchy. How do you think I got here? I said Montana was a long time ago now."

He was being touchy, he told himself. She could be useful, and she sounded as if she wanted to help. "I'm sorry. . . . Okay, so I'm just out. It does things to your nerves."

"I know. Like I said, don't worry about it. So where are you heading, out east?"

"Yep. I've got contacts in a couple of places that I can follow up."

"So you want a connection from Prague. Do you like driving? I'm going to Budapest. Not FER, but it's closer."

"It's a nice thought, but I have to be a long way from here in two days."

"Do you have cash?"

"Oh, enough, I'd think."

"Be careful budgeting. Consolidation currency probably isn't worth as much as you think. Train or plane, then? I can drop you at either." Samurai didn't reply immediately. He needed to find out about how his being a fugitive on the other side of the border might affect things here. "You've gone quiet," Roxy said, looking across. "Is there some kind of problem?"

"I don't know too much about this country," Samurai said. "I ended up here . . . I guess you could call it kind of 'unintentionally.'"

Roxy's eyes wrinkled with amusement. "Okay."

"How closely do the police here cooperate with the Germans? If you were being chased over there, would they be watching for you here?"

She answered matter-of-factly, almost as if expecting it. "A lot of the old system is still intact here at the western end of what used to be Czechoslovakia. In Moravia it gets easier, and Slovakia is FER. But here where we are, yes, the police across the border tend to work together. It depends how bad it is. If it's a parking ticket, don't lose too much sleep about it. But if you've just assassinated the German chancellor or something . . ."

"No." Samurai hesitated, but decided that his best chance was to be straight. Roxy could hardly tell him what he needed to know without knowing the situation herself. He drew a long breath and sighed. "But there was a mess with their border police last night. One of them stopped a bullet."

"Oh, shit."

"Don't worry. He'll live."

"Did you do that?"

"Somebody I was with, but does it matter? . . . There were Berlin federal agents involved too."

"Terrific. . . . Boy, do I pick me some company for breakfast."

"So, what would you do?"

Roxy thought for a few seconds, then shook her head. "If you're hot, I wouldn't risk the airport. You want to keep your name off the passenger lists. In the FER it gets easier, but here you're too close. Train would be better."

"I don't have the time. It's too far. I need to fly."

Roxy fell silent again for a short while, then said, "Maybe there's another way. The airport at Ruzyne has a flying club attached, where the small stuff is based: private planes, company planes, choppers, that kind of thing."

"Do they lease planes out?" Samurai asked, seeing the possibility. "I am a pilot, fixed wing and helicopters."

"To someone they've never heard of, who just walks in off the street? That could be difficult. I was thinking more that you might be able to work a deal with somebody—you know, make it worth their while. That's how things tend to work here. There's all kinds of commercial activity going on in places like Slovenia, Croatia, Serbia. It shouldn't be hard to find someone who's heading that way."

"Do you know anybody at this airport?" Samurai asked.

"Not really. But I know how to talk to people."

"Why should you do that for me?"

"Well, I assumed you'd be making it worth my while too." She flashed him a mock-seductive, pouty look. "What's wrong with helping a guy out for a little money? Maybe I missed out when I was younger."

They passed through some snow that had been recently plowed, and descended out of the hills to the north of Prague, with the landscape taking on a recognizably Wenceslasian flavor. Lower down, they passed a baroque mansion, solid and immutable amid high-walled grounds, washed up from the ocean of a time long gone.

"You say it should be easier once I'm in the FER," Samurai checked.

"So long as you mind your manners and don't go trying to rip too many people off. They call it the Wild East, didn't you know?"

She seemed to approve of such a state of affairs, and that provoked him. "Don't they have any law there?" he said acidly. "Is everyone a criminal?"

Roxy laughed delightedly. "Boy, did they put you through school. Look, don't believe everything you heard back home. It's the gateway off the planet out there in the FER, the new frontier. That's where it's all happening. Oh, sure, it can be kind of rough and ready at times. People who mess other people around tend to get dealt with pretty abruptly. But it works the other way too: people don't bother you too much. Just don't try and push them around; and be straight, because they're sharp. . . . So, yes, there the law is pretty straightforward in most of the territories, even if some people might say it's a bit basic. It protects rights. But it doesn't concern itself all that much with the rest of the world's politics."

"Well, maybe it should," Samurai suggested. "Politics is the science of maintaining order, which makes it necessary that people obey the same rules. And the only way they can be made to do that is through force and through fear."

"They're obeying something else inside them, which they believe in," Roxy said. "Maybe fifty years from now academics will invent a word for it. Meanwhile, it seems to be working a lot better than the things you're talking about ever did."

They stopped for a snack and a shared pot of tea, after which the surroundings became more suburban, with townships, industrial and office parks, and newish-looking road systems. To Samurai, it all suggested a playpen for overindulged children. The cars were gaudy, and there were too many of them in too many needless varieties, spread unnecessarily over multiple lanes that wasted fuel as well as space by encouraging uneconomical speeds. The buildings were flimsily built and inefficient, with too much glass. Roxy said it was because they ran on fusion-generated electricity fed into the grid from the FER, which was cheap enough to make the building codes that were mandatory back in the States not worth the hassle. Samurai doubted it, since the technical problems had caused the U.S. fusion program to stagnate years ago. It was inevitable that when this kind of extravagance had run its course, these people would be coming bowl-in-hand to the West like prodigals returning to the family estate, in the way the experts were predicting. Only this time, there would be no bailouts. If they had listened, they would have known that a finite world imposes its own harsh realities. That was when the reckoning would come.

They skirted the western outskirts of Prague and joined a wide highway that brought them to Ruzyne by early afternoon. Roxy followed signs into the airport complex, and after a couple of wrong turns, doublings back, and a stop to ask directions, they found their way to the terminal and outbuildings of the club and flying school, located at a remote end away from the main facilities. They went inside, and after a brief look around sat down with two cups of coffee—there was no coylene this time—at a window booth in a cafeteria lounge situated on one side of the reception area. The place was filled with a colorful mix of people, talking, laughing, arguing, some sitting alone; wearing business clothes, casual gear, flying suits, others in working jeans and mechanic's coveralls.

The window looked out over the parking apron for private aircraft, beyond which lay a taxiing area and the main airport runways. There was a steady traffic of international and regular domestic flights, most of the aircraft types being one or other of various Siberian makes. Samurai hadn't realized that they were so widely used. In the immediate vicinity there seemed to be a fairly continuous coming and going of smaller machines, also—as Roxy had said would be the case.

She looked across at him and raised her eyebrows. "Well, want me to give it a shot?"

"Why? It's my problem."

Roxy pursed her lips for an instant, then smiled. "Nothing personal, Sam, okay? But you fly the planes. I think I might be better at handling the people." She stood up before he could respond, squeezed his shoulder good-naturedly, and sauntered over to a group of men and a woman in a mixture of flying clothes, who were talking loudly around a table.

"Hi, guys, how're you doing today?" he heard her say. Then her voice fell and some muted conversation followed, marked after a while by several curious glances thrown in Samurai's direction. Then one of the men called over two others who were sitting together a short distance away. More talking ensued, and then the two came with Roxy over to the booth where Samurai was sitting. One was tall and swarthy, with a lazy stride, an easygoing face that seemed to smile easily, and a walrus mustache. He was wearing a fleece-lined leather jacket, woolen cap, and jeans tucked into calf-length boots. The man with him was short and pale, with a fur-trimmed parka and cossack cap. Samurai's first thought was of flying cowboys.

"I hear you're looking to hitch a ride east," the tall one said without preamble, perching himself on the end of the seat opposite.

"Where are you going?" Samurai asked him.

"We'll be taking some parts for a turbine to Cluj. They're being loaded outside there now."

"How far's that?"

"About two hours' flight time. But we gain an hour because of the time zone."

"Cluj-Napoca," Roxy supplied. "It's FER, in Transylvania—part of what used to be called Romania."

"Where do you want to get to?" the smaller of the two asked Samurai.

"East, into Siberia. Could I connect from Cluj?"

The one who was sitting showed a palm casually. "Sure. Straight into Odessa. There should be something going there tonight, but if not there's definitely a couple in the morning. From there you're in the trans-Siberian trunk net, with flights round the clock."

Samurai regarded him cautiously. It sounded too easy. "There are no exit formalities for leaving Bohemia?" he queried.

The flier with the mustache grinned. "Why? Did you want to ask someone if it's okay?"

"What about getting into Transylvania at the other end? I don't have any entry permit or visa, you understand."

The smaller one gave a short laugh and looked at his companion. "He hasn't been in the FER before," he said.

The other shrugged and showed his palms to indicate that he had no more to say. "So, we've got a spare seat. Does that sound good?"

Samurai still felt uneasy, mainly because of the unfamiliarity of the situation, he had to admit. But really he had no choice. "Okay," he agreed.

The flier gave one of his easy smiles. "Good. Now let's talk about money. . . ."

But when Samurai tried to settle up with Roxy, she would have none of it. "Let's make it a way of saying welcome to somebody else from home," she told him. "Always be the first to do the other guy a favor—it's a saying they've got in Siberia. Remember it. That's the way you get along in the FER." She smiled and gripped his hand. "So long, Sam Harris. Good luck."

They took off later in the afternoon in a small cargo plane with twin turboprops. Samurai sat by a window in one of several seats in the forward cabin behind the pilots. The seat next to him was empty, the two behind piled with baggage, and the only other passengers were two Asiatics opposite, who talked between themselves in a dialect he didn't understand. Apart from offering him a swig of a potent-smelling drink from a flask that they kept passing back and forth, which he declined, they paid him no attention.

The plane flew south of the Carpathian Mountains across Bohemia and Moravia, which like Poland were in a halfway state between the West and the FER. Then, above lengthening winter shadows, the plane entered FER airspace over the northern part of Hungary. By the time the pilot announced the commencement of their descent, the ground was getting dark. On the approach, Samurai was surprised to see a bustling city with lots of tall buildings, bridges, and lights spread out below, and enormous floodlit structures of steelwork and engineering that appeared to be under construction beyond the perimeter of the airfield. For some reason he'd expected Cluj to be some kind of shantytown, neglected and decayed.

After landing, they taxied to a parking area in front of a hangar away from the main terminal. The three passengers and two-man crew climbed down to the tarmac and walked to an entrance in a row of small buildings housing workshops and a cargo bay. Inside was a small reception office with seats and a counter. For a moment it seemed to Samurai that he could simply walk through, but the pilot indicated for him to wait at the counter.

"We'll get you a ride over to the terminal," he explained.

"I'll be okay."

"No chance. They make changes to this airport so fast that even I get lost in it." Just then, a man came out of the office behind the counter. "Marek, can we get this guy a ride to the terminal? He just came in with me."

"Sure." Marek turned and called back through the door. "Is the wagon out front? We got somebody who needs to go across to main arrivals, international."

Samurai resigned himself to accepting that he wasn't going to have much option. An old man with a grizzled beard drove him along the side of the tarmac behind a line of parked aircraft, across part of the airfield, and deposited him at a glass door with stairs leading up inside. Samurai followed the corridor and ramp at the top and found himself on the route through to the main arrivals concourse. Ahead, he could see, he would have to pass a desk where an official in a white shirt was sitting. There was no way around. Samurai thrust across his passport, and having nothing else to offer, his German visa and U.S. exit papers.

The official pushed them back again. "I don't need those. You're in the Free World now." He stamped the passport without giving it a second glance and handed it back. "Welcome to the Federation of Eurasian Republics."

Samurai stared about him. There was no obvious continuation from there on, no indicators for the next stage of processing, no guards, no signs instructing anyone what to do.

He looked back uncertainly. "Where do I go now?"

The official shrugged. "Anywhere you want."

thirty-eight

The first thing that Samurai checked while still in the airport was on getting the rest of the way to Semipalatinsk. The last flight that evening to Odessa, shown on an illuminated map by the ticketing desks as the capital of the Independent State of Moldavskaja, was full, but there would be two the next morning and another in the afternoon. From Odessa, as the cargo pilot had said, he would be in the trans-Siberian trunk net, and the rest was straightforward.

Samurai hadn't realized that in their race to lay waste the planet, the Eurasians were flying SSTs. If he took the early flight to Odessa, he could get an SST connection direct into Semipalatinsk by early afternoon, even with the four-hour time difference; but the fare was high compared to the subsonic alternatives, and Roxy hadn't been kidding when she warned him that Western currency wouldn't stretch very far. He didn't want to use his credit cards because of the risk of giving anyone with the right contacts or access procedures an audit trail of his movements—despite superficial East-West differences, he didn't know what arrangements might exist between security agencies. And it was still only December 3. The launch that Ashling was scheduled on wasn't until the sixth. Samurai still had plenty of time.

The Air Moldavskaja flight tomorrow afternoon would get him into Odessa at 5:00 P.M. local time, with a connection later that evening to Volgograd. From there, a long Aerospaceflot night flight would arrive in Novosibirsk at the ungodly hour of 4:40 A.M., from where an early morning flight south to the Kazachskij Republic got into Semipalatinsk at 8:30. That would be on the morning of the fifth, still giving him a full day to locate Ashling. Of the two morning flights to Odessa, the first was too early, and a quick study of the connections showed that the second wouldn't gain him anything. Accordingly, he booked a seat on the afternoon flight. Any misgivings that he might still have had about being traceable from passenger lists were quickly dispelled: the ticket carried flight details only, without requiring a name. Tomorrow morning, he decided, could usefully be spent shopping to replace the clothes and other things that he'd left with his bag in the police building at Zittau.

A branch of the local rapid transit system, running every two minutes through a glass-walled flyover, connected the terminal to a hotel complex by the airport approaches. From the view out of the car as it passed above traffic ramps and parking lots, much of the surroundings seemed to be still under construction, with concrete being poured under arc lights into huge steel and timber forms, and cranes working into the evening. But the hotel section itself, when he got there, was more or less complete, even if still lacking in some of the finishing touches of comfort and decor, and Samurai had no trouble getting a room for the night.

The room came with bathrobe, disposable slippers, and a complimentary kit of toilet articles, he discovered, so at least he would be comfortable until morning. On a less salubrious note, an automatic dispenser offered candy, alcohol, coffee, tobacco, and a selection of drugs, right there in the room. The local business and entertainments directory included with the hotel guide listed sexual companionship—straight, gay, male, female, or both—alongside where to shop, places to eat, music and shows, and the old city's museums and medieval churches. Guns were advertised openly, and there was a school of erotic moviemaking. The police even ran an ad giving a get-you-home-safe number that drunks could call to avoid driving. Farther on, Samurai was astounded to read that a private investigative agency in the city included "legally sanctioned homicides" in its list of professional services.

But at least there was some comfort in the thought that self-destruction would inevitably overtake such a society before it could proceed too far with the destruction of everything else. He could see why many of the West's analysts had concluded that eventually the solution would have to be a military one.

He ate later in the hotel restaurant. The food was ample and varied, but irresponsibly nonselective. Service, although efficient, was performed with a presumptuous familiarity that bordered on insolence. The host who showed Samurai to a table joked about American "neurotics" as if there were something wrong with being educated about dietary risks, and then added insult by referring to the U.S. Bureau of Environmental Control as the Green Gestapo.

Later, the waitress, as she was clearing the dishes, asked Samurai if he was on his own here. When he replied that he was, she murmured that she finished her shift at ten and could stay an extra hour "for half the rate you'll get in town."

A big, bearded man dining at the next table overheard and cautioned Samurai not to have anything to do with it. "It's a rip-off. She'll talk the money out of you ahead of time, then no-show. By the time she gets back on her next shift you'll be a thousand miles away. She wouldn't try it on us, but Westerners get taken every time."

Samurai was outraged. "Why doesn't someone tell the management about it?" he demanded.

"They already know."

"What! And they don't do anything?"

"What should they do?"

"Well, get it stopped. Fire her or something."

"Why? Whose rights are being violated?"

Samurai gestured helplessly with a hand and shook his head. "But hell, their staff, their room?"

"She's not 'theirs.' She works the hours for them that she contracts to, that's all. And so long as you're paying the charge, it's *your* room."

It still didn't sound right to Samurai. "Well, if it's a rip-off, doesn't the hotel figure its customers have a right to be protected?" he said.

The bearded man thought about it. "Maybe," he conceded. "But they probably figure they're doing them a bigger favor by letting them learn not to be stupid."

After dinner, Samurai wandered into the bar and permitted himself a vodka with tonic. The place was raucous and noisy with what looked like engineers and construction crew from the work going on all around the area, and a lot of what Samurai assumed were local women. He left and wandered around a few more parts of the complex that were sufficiently finished to be open for business, but found them much the same. The atmosphere didn't appeal to him, so he returned to his room and retired early.

More of the vicinity was visible the next morning. The airport adjoined what was virtually a new industrial city springing up separate from the older, historic capital of Transylvania, which dated from fortifications first recorded in the thirteenth century and had been largely preserved as a cultural center. The constructions that Samurai had seen from the plane lay beyond the far edge of the airfield, and revealed themselves now as just one end of a line of massive structures in various stages of completion extending away for what must have been one to two miles, with tangles of service roads, pipe runs, and latticeworks taking shape between them.

He asked about it at the hotel information desk and learned that the new city was being developed as a spaceport and would become the region's principal link to the Offworld independencies. Similar things were going on in Latvia and the Belorussian Republic. The Eurasians, it seemed, regarded the Consolidation as a temporary affair that was destined to fall apart, and the westernmost FER states were vying for the Western European space business that they expected to materialize when the Green Curtain came down.

Samurai didn't bother disagreeing. It was depressing enough to watch so much effort and material being misdirected into pipe dreams. But the more chilling thought was the ease with which such facilities could be converted for military use when the orgy of profligacy ended and the FER was forced to turn upon the West. Or maybe the Eurasians weren't the simpletons they seemed. Could that be the real intent, he wondered, and the talk about spaceports mere camouflage?

He took the transit shuttle into a nearby part of the city to buy the things he needed, and found it to be pretty much as he'd expected: superficially glittery and affluent, but underneath it all the kind of mindless gaudiness that inevitably accompanied preoccupation with the material and the banal. There were too many colors and styles of everything on the shelves, too many overproduced, overadvertised gimmicks that consumed resources to no useful purpose, and that no half-effective planning committee would ever have allowed. The automobiles were huge and criminally wasteful, many of them carrying only the driver. Every conceivable type of electronic and computing device was on open sale, with no evidence of proof-of-need or licensing requirements.

He was in a sober and reflective mood by the time he returned to join the flight for Odessa. There were no security checks on boarding. Half the people on the plane were smoking and drinking. Segregation was nonexistent, and he had to share the cabin with plebs.

At Odessa everything was as bad, but on an even vaster scale, with hypersonic, suborbital transports leaving for Tokyo, Singapore, and Capetown. During the flight from Odessa to Volgograd, two couples across the aisle were playing a card game that involved brazen gambling, and the flight attendants didn't even seem to notice.

Everywhere was degeneracy, recklessness, profligacy, corruption, all on its way to going out of control. Samurai didn't think that these people would ever find it within themselves to put a stop to it. That meant the West would have to, before everyone was dragged down.

Previously known as Stalingrad, the easternmost limit of advance reached by Hitler's armies in 1942, Volgograd had been completely rebuilt from rubble after World War II. It suffered further damage in the turbulent years following the final breakup of the Soviet empires—though nothing like the devastation wrought previously—and was again restored to become one of the FER's most ambitious metropolises. Samurai had neither the time nor reason—nor, for that matter, any particular inclination—to leave the airport to see the city at close hand, but as the plane came in late in the afternoon, it presented a full view of the integrated central area, with towers, terraces, and glass-walled cliffs, all flowing together and interpenetrated by elevated roads and rail tubes like arteries feeding a single sprawling organism.

One of the major Siberian spacegates already operating to support the Offworld expansion was located several miles to the north. Shortly after Samurai emerged into the elevated level of the airport transfer lounge, with high observation windows stretching the length of the building, a squat delta shape rose up above the skyline, balanced on a pencil of violet light, and accelerated rapidly to vanish into the high cloud cover.

"Heavy-lift surface shuttle going up on a ground laser," he overheard a man nearby saying to a boy, who looked like his son. "Could be heading for a lunar-transfer orbit."

"That's three in the last hour," the boy said.

"Gonna be a lot more'n that before much longer too."

Samurai turned away and began heading toward the departure gate for his flight. Just then, an unusual sound, like that from an approaching train still in a tunnel, came from outside, and several people began pointing. He stopped and looked back. A craft unlike anything he had seen before had broken through the cloud canopy and was coming down toward the field at an angle steeper than any conventional airplane. It was disk-shaped, black and featureless in silhouette against the sky, although there seemed to be a bluish radiance emanating from parts of the rim. As it came lower over the far boundary fence, it revealed a humped upper part, the shape of a flattened bell. And most puzzling of all, it seemed to be hanging on the end of a faint beam of pinkish light, like a barely visible rod supporting it at its center, coming down through the clouds.

"That's an IRH pulsejet lifter," a voice mused next to him. "What's it doing here? I thought they were still experimental."

Samurai turned and saw that it was a man in a jacket and tie with an overcoat, addressing a companion.

The other shook his head. "Maybe they're trying out a few prototypes." He noticed Samurai looking at them and inclined his head to indicate the vessel outside. "Do you know anything about it?"

Samurai shook his head. "I've never even heard of it."

The man caught the accent and smiled elusively. "Canadian? American? I can tell it's not British."

"U.S.," Samurai said.

"Ah, yes. . . . We're engineers, you see. That uses what's called IRH: Internal Radiation Heating. It's an air breather, but using external laser energy to heat it instead of onboard fuel. The beam comes from a nuclear generator satellite in a two-thousand-mile-high orbit."

Samurai looked out across the airfield again. The disk was just coming down behind some conventionally shaped craft on the far side of the main runways and appeared a little smaller than them, making it maybe fifty to a hundred feet across. "I've never seen anything like that," he said.

"No, probably not," the first of the two engineers said. "Your countries won't let them fly over because they think the risks of down-pointing lasers are too high. There was a big political thing about it a few years ago. But I don't suppose they told you about that."

A part of Samurai's implanted nature had been designed to make him an instinctive combatant. Alertness to danger was his natural condition, causing him to scan and scrutinize everything around him constantly and automatically.

As soon as he entered the departure lounge, he read something suspicious in the manner of the two men sitting together among the passengers awaiting the Aerospaceflot night flight to Novosibirsk. Their body language betrayed tenseness, and they shifted their eyes away too suddenly when Samurai entered, yet at the same time their altering of postures signaled an unnatural interest in him. Without changing his step, he ambled across to a bookshop on the far side of the area and observed them through the window while turning idly through a magazine from one of the racks. Their clothes were of American style and cut, marking them as recent arrivals. One of them was watching him and trying not to show it.

Samurai bought the magazine and tucked it under his arm, then came out of the shop and began walking toward them, noting the involuntary stiffening of their postures as he approached. He stopped several yards away from them and reached suddenly inside his coat. One of the men began moving a hand reflexively toward his jacket, checking himself with a conscious effort when Samurai produced his ticket.

They were armed.

Samurai studied his ticket nonchalantly for a few seconds and then walked away without looking at them. Why anyone from the States should be after him was a question that could wait till later. The important thing for now was that somebody was trying to interfere with his mission. If it were anyone legitimately connected with it, they would have simply contacted him openly. When he was out of sight around a corner he bought himself a cup of tea and sat down to think what he was going to do.

Meanwhile, one of the two Americans had gone to a booth to make a phone call. "Identification positive," he said into the receiver. "We'll be shadowing him all the way on the same flight. Get the welcoming party ready at Novosibirsk. We'll grab him there."

thirty-nine

During the flight a movie was shown depicting ordinary citizens taking up weapons and violently resisting representatives of the state's authority. Most of the passengers seemed to enjoy it.

The two men who had attracted Samurai's attention at Volgograd had boarded also, and were sitting together several rows behind him. He was now certain that their presence was no accident; they were keeping him under observation.

He reflected on their probable plans. The flight was due to arrive at Novosibirsk at 4:40 A.M., after a long haul from Volgograd. At that time of the morning, in the cold and dark of midwinter, airport activity would be at its lowest, with relatively few staff on duty and those at a reduced level of alertness. Response times by the local authorities in the case of a possible hitch would be greatest. There, Samurai concluded, was where the reception for him was being prepared. What, then, would be his plan?

His best strategy would be to reduce the odds against him by eliminating the two who were on the plane from the equation before having to tackle the rest. That much seemed eminently simple and basic. However, it would be better to avoid killing people from his own side if he could help it, he decided. Besides being a messy way to go about things in a foreign country, it was likely to create complications when he got back. He sat quietly, staring at a magazine and considering his options.

When the movie ended, the lights remained dim and most of the passengers settled back with pillows and blankets to snatch a few hours sleep. Samurai took down his briefcase, ostensibly to put back the magazine he had been reading and to take out a few others; but while doing so, he removed a pack containing another of his specialized devices: a spring-operated syringe with an assortment of needles and nozzles, which among other things could inject various lethal or incapacitating substances. Slipping the pack in his jacket pocket, he strolled back to the toilet, noting on the way that one of the two agents seemed to be asleep and the other was reading. There were some empty places in the row behind them, and the people in the occupied seats were asleep.

On emerging again, instead of returning to his own seat, Samurai went to another, farther back, from where he could observe. When the agent who was awake began turning his head curiously to see what had become of him, he saw Samurai stretched out with a blanket about him, apparently having moved to be by some empty seats in order to sleep more comfortably. The agent returned to his book, but seemed restless. Samurai carried on watching him. Eventually the agent put down the book and went back to use the toilet.

In the shadows, Samurai sat up and looked around. Of the few people awake, no one was paying any attention. The only visible flight attendant was back at the far end of the next cabin, talking to a colleague. Samurai fitted a long, large-bore needle to the syringe, which he had already loaded while he was in the toilet. He folded the blanket aside, rose, and, taking one of the magazines, moved into the aisle. A couple of steps brought him behind the agent who was asleep. Nobody in the row behind stirred. For the benefit of anyone who might be watching, Samurai dropped the magazine and, in the process of going down to retrieve it, moved into an empty space in the row behind the sleeping agent. He positioned the needle carefully behind the soft backrest, slightly to the left of the spine, then quickly slipped a hand around and cupped it over the agent's mouth while he drove the needle home. The spring trigger did the rest, and he felt the body go limp after four or five seconds. He straightened up again, holding the syringe under cover of the magazine, then continued forward to return the items to his briefcase in the overhead bin above his original seat. By the time the agent in the toilet came out, Samurai was back once again in the seat that he had moved to before, with the blanket pulled over him.

When the lights brightened and the cabin staff began moving around to awaken the passengers in preparation for landing at

Novosibirsk, Samurai got up and returned to his original seat. Behind him, the efforts of the agent to rouse his companion drew the attention of the flight attendant. She tried, equally unsuccessfully, and called a companion. The agent was still out cold when the plane touched down. When the doors were opened, Samurai collected his things and began moving nonchalantly to the forward door with the other deplaning passengers. Behind him, the agent who was left assessed the situation frantically while three of the cabin crew fussed over the unconscious form next to him. Whatever was wrong with him, there was nothing to be done that would add to what was being done already, he decided. The important thing was to maintain contact with the target.

"No, we're not together," he said in answer to one of the flight attendants. "I just got talking to him, that's all. I guess he'll be okay, eh? You'll take good care of him." With that he grabbed his coat and carry-on bag and hastened after Samurai, who by now had disappeared from the aircraft.

By the time he reached the exit ramp, the last of the passengers were out of sight. He hurried along after them, and on the way passed a service doorway leading to a cupola where an external stairway went down to the tarmac outside. Samurai stepped out behind him and pulled him back into the cupola without a sound. He emerged alone ten seconds later with his coat and briefcase, checked that nobody had observed, and resumed walking toward the arrival gate. As he did so, he put on a pair of heavy dark glasses.

Two down, but an unknown number to go.

When Samurai came through the gate, the gaggle of arrivals and the few people out to meet them at that hour of the morning were already thinning. The three men still scanning the jetway anxiously from the far side of the hall gave themselves away instantly. Samurai ignored them and walked on by, following the other passengers. The three exchanged puzzled looks when the two who were supposed to be following him failed to materialize. But then, after a moment's hesitation, the leader gave a curt nod; they turned and followed at a quickening pace.

A long corridor led toward the arrivals concourse. Halfway along it, two of them moved up alongside Samurai while the third closed in behind. Guns pressed into Samurai's ribs from both sides.

"One wrong move and you're Swiss cheese, buddy," a voice

muttered. "Just make for the door in front there on the right, and we'll all be okay." They steered him through the straggle of people to a door with a STAFF ONLY sign. Inside was a storage room of some kind, with a passage and stairway leading down. The last of the three closed the door.

"Now reach high, nice and easy."

As Samurai brought his right hand out of his pocket to obey, he let go the flash grenade that he had been holding primed, and closed his eyes tight. Even behind his dark glasses, the four-million-candlepower detonation was blinding. For the other three, it was devastating—a couple of days was usually necessary for vision to return to normal. It was an easy matter to dispose of them in such a condition, after which he checked their pockets, in the process finding the means of relieving his cash situation appreciably. Then he paused to reflect on what their intentions might have been.

Why had they brought him in here? Most likely, it led to an exit that would have enabled them to get him away without risking a public spectacle. He followed the stairs down and found a passage leading past more rooms to, sure enough, what looked like an outside door. One of the rooms to the side had a window. Samurai moved over to it cautiously in the darkness and peered out. There were two cars outside, one empty, the other with a man standing by the open driver's door. It was a service road, deserted and dark except for a few orange lamps. That suited Samurai just fine: if whoever was trying to stop him had the airports covered, it wouldn't be a good idea to carry on any farther by air.

He explored along the building until he came to another door, well beyond where the cars were, in the shadows. It was locked, and took him a few minutes to open. By then, the man waiting by the car was getting worried. He stood anxiously, directing all his attention toward the building . . . and oblivious to the shadow stealing up through the night from behind him.

The keys were in the car. Samurai hauled the unconscious form inside the door that the others were supposed to have come out of, and was on his way less than a minute later. He found his way to the main airport exit and stopped in a parking area to check the glove box for maps. He found some, and the tank was not far off full. It was not yet 5:30 in the morning; the distance to Semipalatinsk was roughly 400 miles. Depending on driving conditions and assuming that whoever was responsible did a reasonable job of keeping the main road clear, he should still be able to make it by late afternoon or evening, he estimated. That didn't give him as much time as he'd hoped to figure out how he was going to deal with Ashling. But having gotten this far, he wasn't about to quit now.

News of the debacle didn't reach Washington until a couple of hours later, by which time it was midnight and Grazin was just about to go to bed. He called Colonel Hautz at once on an emergency circuit.

"He wiped out your whole squad," Grazin fumed. "Now will you believe what I told you about this guy? How many more people do you have out there?"

Hautz was stunned by the news. "The rest of the group at Novosibirsk are still functional. And we've got the backup team arriving in Semipalatinsk in the next eight hours."

"Well, amend your field orders," Grazin instructed. "Forget any notion of trying to apprehend or immobilize. A lot of people over here would be more than happy if he never set foot in the country again, anyhow. Kill him on sight, then get your men out."

forty

The car was absurdly large, even if it could hold five people. The upholstery was plush and pretentiously ornate, with padded trim inside the doors and seats that felt like armchairs. The controls had a section labeled "Autodrive" that included a switch with a "Wireguide" position, and an electronic device tagged as a "Nav-grid Locator," neither of which Samurai understood. But they were both evidently optional, for the conventional systems that he was familiar with all responded normally. It fairly surged with power and handled amazingly well. And although there was snow on the rooftops, highway shoulders, central divisions, and other unused areas, the roadways and sidewalks themselves were actually dry! Surely not even Eurasians could be sufficiently out of their minds to heat them. But what other explanation was there?

As he had come to expect by now, everything was built on a scale that was big, brash, gaudily flaunting its imagined grandeur. Huge buildings flanked the highways like mountains of luminescent crystal towering in the night. Lurid signs proclaimed the presence of hotels, business corporations, the Berdsk Plasma Physics Institute, the South Sub-City, whatever that was; others advertised everything from brands of hashish and vodka to dance schools and performances of orchestral music. There was a rainbow-lit fountain throwing water hundreds of feet into the air. He passed some kind of enormous glass enclosure with domes, illuminated inside and containing an artificial beach and palm trees.

Farther on, the roadway merged alongside several rail lines, some regular, others monotrack supported by pylons, to follow the top of a huge dam at one end of a lake, which, from the lights stretching away along its shore, receded as far as it was possible to see. The far shore was lined with floodlit industrial installations: tanks and towers braced by latticeworks, domes and spheres, concrete massifs wreathed in power lines and pipes. The lights of an aircraft rose up from among it all and vanished into the far sky over the lake.

There was a modest amount of other traffic about. A train and several unattached cars on the monotracks sped past him while he was negotiating the dam. Some distance past the end of it, the rail lines went off in their own separate directions. He passed what looked like an all-night restaurant and service area where several hopefuls were trying to hitch rides. Past the dam, the artificially dry road ended; but the continuation had been effectively plowed and the surface treated, enabling him to keep up a better speed than he had hoped. As the route began climbing into the hills south of Novosibirsk, his hopes for the mission rose with it.

By the time daylight arrived, he was descending again. The surroundings now were more sparsely inhabited, but the traffic increased steadily. An hour later he passed through another urban area, which his map showed to be the city of Barnaut—almost a quarter of the way to Semipalatinsk already. As the morning traffic got into its swing, he was astonished to see swarms of what had to be tiny personal aircraft taking to the skies in orderly, well-defined traffic corridors.

Eurasians doing something orderly? It didn't seem possible. Maybe if their necks were on the line, even they were capable of some measure of rationality, he reflected. Or maybe all the ones who weren't up to it had self-selected themselves out of the population by now.

In his own mind, Samurai had far from written off the opposition who were out looking for him. The sight of the personal flyers made him think of them again, and left no guessing what their next move was likely to be. From the NSA intercept they knew where he was heading; there was only one route for getting there; and they knew what car he was driving, since he'd stolen it from them. There were no doubt as few restrictions on hiring private aircraft here as on everything else. As he continued southward from Barnaut, the surroundings became bleaker and more deserted; the traffic thinned down to occasional heavy commercial rigs. Perfect surroundings for an interception. Having concluded that much, Samurai began taking a greater interest in the hitchhikers out on the road, whom he was still passing from time to time.

He raised and then dashed several hopes by slowing down promisingly, then speeding up again and driving on by. But eventually he saw what he was looking for: a man of reasonably presentable appearance, around thirty, dark-haired, with olive features—not unlike Samurai himself. He was wearing a blue parka and woolen hat, and had a black leather carryall by his feet. The man grinned and made a face to say it was cold out here. Samurai pulled over.

"Going as far as Semipalatinsk?"

"All the way."

"Great. Can I put this in the back?"

"Go ahead." The man heaved the carryall inside. "You might want to throw that coat in there as well," Samurai said. "It's warm in the car."

"Good idea. I'll do that."

His name was Rudi, from a province in the central Urals. He was heading south for the winter after working on a land drainage project farther north, which was now frozen. He was jovial and talkative, and especially curious when he learned that Samurai was a recently arrived American.

"Are you going back, or will you be staying here now?" he asked.

"Why shouldn't I want to go back?" Samurai said. He was preoccupied with keeping an eye on the mirror and trying to watch the skyline behind them, happy to let Rudi carry on doing most of the talking.

"Is it true what they say about the repression over there? All the censorship, and everything they say on the news being distorted? A friend of mine told me that communications equipment can only pick up approved channels, by law. Is that right?"

"We don't like anybody who wants to be able to pump whatever they like into people's minds," Samurai said shortly. "Is that so bad?"

"Well, can't the people have a say in it? They don't have to listen."

"People are like sheep. Most of them have never had a worthwhile thought in their lives. They'll believe anything they're told."

"Maybe not, if they're allowed to learn how to think. Instead of being told what to think."

"Look, if you must talk, why not find a different subject? I'm not criticizing your country. Otherwise you might end up hiking it to Semipalatinsk."

Rudi grinned unrepentantly and raised a hand in mock submission. "You're absolutely right! How ungracious of me. You are our guest. Not another word, I promise."

They drove on in silence for a mile or so. The road followed the base of a line of low, rounded hills, with desolation stretching away on the opposite side. "Do they really think we're running out of room?" Rudi said. "I mean, look at that. And it's nothing. I read somewhere that Americans have to move into smaller houses when their children leave home. Is that right? Do you really need licenses to have children there?"

"Do you drive, Rudi?" Samurai asked.

"I'm doing it again, aren't I?"

"Don't worry about it."

"Sure, everyone drives. Why?"

"I've been traveling all night. I could use an hour's sleep in the back. How would you like to take over for a spell?"

"Okay, if you trust me with it."

"Just don't talk so much, and watch the road."

They pulled over onto the verge and got out. The air outside was cold, with a mild but biting wind. Rudi got into the driver's side and adjusted the mirrors and seats. Samurai climbed in the back and settled down among his and Rudi's coats, his briefcase, Rudi's bag, and a couple of bags belonging to the Americans, which had been there when Samurai took the car. As they came back onto the roadway, he scanned the sky behind through the rear window. There was no local air traffic now, and anything approaching would stand out easily.

"I grew up in a place as dismal as this," Rudi said. "Sometimes it got so waterlogged in the thaw that we went to school in a boat."

"Really?"

"Yes. . . . I heard that over there they teach children in the schools that nobody should be different," Rudi said over his shoulder. "Is that really true?"

It was about a half hour later when Samurai spotted what he had been expecting: a dot flying low, following the road behind them. It gained rapidly, swooping even lower, circled, then passed immediately overhead for a close look as it overhauled the car. Rudi peered in his mirror and turned his head to look up at it through the window, muttering to himself but not bothering Samurai, who he believed was asleep. Samurai slid the automatic from his briefcase and squeezed himself down behind the seat, covering himself with the coats and bags to make it look as if the car had only one occupant. Then the aircraft rose and sped away ahead of them— checking that the road was free of approaching traffic from that direction, Samurai had no doubt. As it receded, he raised his head and saw that it was a rotorless hoverjet, about the size of a six-seat chopper.

Minutes later it was back again. Samurai didn't expect for a moment that its occupants would simply open fire; besides its being a messy and needlessly overdramatic way of going about things, there was always the risk that they might have latched on to the wrong car. They would check it out first.

The machine came in close to fly just above the car, slightly back and to one side, the noise from its turbines drowning out the car's engine. Rudi, clearly alarmed by now, was turning his head frantically from side to side as he drove.

"Don't look back. Just keep driving and do as I say," Samurai instructed. His tone was harsh and authoritative suddenly, leaving no room for argument.

"What the hell's going on?" Rudi demanded. "Who are they? Look, I don't know what—"

"Shut up!"

Ahead, a wide expanse of flat, open ground lay to one side of the road, churned up by tire marks. It looked like a rest area that trucks used. A door in the side of the hoverjet opened, and a figure inside made pointing motions toward it. He was also holding a submachine gun.

"Slow down," Samurai ordered.

"But shit, that guy's got a gun! This doesn't have anything to do with me. I don't want to get mixed up in it."

"You are mixed up in it, so just do as I say. Pull over and stop." Rudi did so, and sat, shaking visibly. The flyer came down and hovered a few yards behind him, probably checking the registration. "Now get out, leave your door open, and move well away from the car with your hands raised," Samurai said. *"Don't look back at me!"*

Rudi's voice was choking with fear. "They'll k-kill me. This hasn't got anything to do with me."

"They might," Samurai agreed. "But I will for sure if you don't get out. Do it." Rudi opened the door with trembling hands and got out. "Hands high. Away from the car," Samurai repeated. Rudi raised his hands and stumbled away dazedly. Samurai stayed low, watching motionless through the chink beside the driver's headrest.

The flyer came down in a flurry of snow about thirty feet from the car, facing where Rudi was standing. The engine note dropped, and two armed men jumped out, leaving a third still in the pilot's seat. All attention was on Rudi, standing ahead of them in the snow with his arms high. Samurai eased himself up a fraction, his eyes moving rapidly, assessing distances and angles. The two who had got out approached Rudi warily from different sides, their guns leveled. Then the voice of the one who had remained in the cabin sounded over a loud hailer. "Don't fuck with this guy. You heard the order. Drop him."

Very well. They had made the rules. . . .

And then one of the two on foot moved a pace closer and peered at Rudi quizzically. "Wait. That isn't—"

From the car, Samurai took out the pilot with a head shot through the open door of the hoverjet; the other two started to turn, but were dispatched before they had registered what was happening. Rudi, still with his hands in the air, watched horrified as Samurai got out. But Samurai gave him no time for wondering.

"Come on. You can't stand there like a tree all day. Help me move them." They dragged the bodies to the car and heaved them inside. Then Samurai told Rudi to move the car over to the far side of the open area, away from the road. While Rudi was doing that, Samurai loaded their coats and bags into the flyer.

"Now get in," Samurai said, waving toward the passenger-side door when Rudi came back.

Rudi, still white-faced and feeling nauseous, shook his head fearfully. "I've seen enough. I don't want any part of this."

"Do you want to stay here and freeze? Look, you wanted a ride to Semipalatinsk, didn't you? If I wanted to kill you, you'd be with those three in the car already, wouldn't you? So get in and stop looking like that. It's over."

Rudi obeyed, moving as if in a trance. Samurai spent some time going over the controls and checking the instruments. Satisfied that he understood the basics, he increased power and lifted off cautiously. Everything felt right. "It goes without saying that you don't mention anything to anyone," Samurai said as they rose. Rudi had seen what Samurai was capable of, and didn't argue. Soon they were high over the road and heading south once more.

Being in motion again seemed to snap Rudi out of his stupor. He looked at Samurai with a new interest. "Who are you?" he asked. His voice was genuinely curious. "I mean, whatever you do, there has to be money in it, right?"

"I get by," Samurai replied neutrally.

There was a short silence, as if Rudi was weighing his chances. Then he said, "Whatever you're here for, you're a stranger in the FER. I know my way around, how things work here. . . . You know, Sam, I could be a useful guy to have around."

Samurai looked across at him. That was certainly a thought. He was glad now that he hadn't eliminated Rudi along with the other three. That had puzzled him, since it would have been the correct and logical thing to do.

Perhaps a little something had rubbed off on him from Roxy.

forty-one

Semipalatinsk was one of the Siberian space cities, a major gateway to the baffling outthrust of humanity nobody could quite explain that was bursting spaceward beyond Earth. The shuttles and orbital lifters stood on their pads among launch complexes, beam ground-stations, support installations, and freight-handling bays that extended for miles outside the city. Samurai contacted local control for directions on flight procedures, and was diverted to a landing pad for private flying vehicles not far from the regular airport, on the opposite side of the Irtysh River. From there, he and Rudi, who was by this time a fully recruited accomplice, took a transit tube into the city and arrived not long after noon. Ashling's launch was scheduled for 10:00 A.M. the next day. Therefore it was very likely that he was already in the city somewhere. So Samurai still had the best part of a day to track him down. And if he failed to intercept Ashling before the launch, he now had the wherewithal for buying a shuttle ticket himself to go after him.

After they had eaten lunch together, Samurai sent Rudi off to find them a hotel for the night, with instructions to reserve Samurai's room under the name, dreamed up on a whim, of Abraham Washington. They arranged to meet up again later at four o'clock. That would keep Rudi usefully occupied for a while and allow Samurai some free time to consider how to go about tracing Ashling. The other problem, of course, would be to avoid whoever the people were who were pursuing him. They had known where he was heading, and it wouldn't be long before somebody realized that the group dispatched to take care of him on the road from Novosibirsk wasn't going to be reporting in. Knowing the way such people operated, Samurai guessed that there would be a backup group here in Semipalatinsk as well. In any case, the only prudent course would be to assume that there was.

What, he asked himself, would they expect him to do?

Since they knew the contents of the NSA intercept, they would also know the time of Ashling's flight. Also, they knew that he knew it. From that, it wouldn't be difficult for either them or him to establish which particular shuttle Ashling would be departing on. By this time, also, the authorities in Zittau would no doubt have obtained from Rostiescki the information he had given Samurai—that Ashling was traveling under the pseudonym of Oleg Kubalov—and passed it back via Berlin. Therefore the people pursuing Samurai would know that he was on the trail of somebody called Kubalov.

But they would have no reason to think that he knew where Kubalov was staying in the city—any more than they did themselves. Therefore they would be expecting him to try to find out. And the way to do that would be to get at the spaceline's records, which would almost certainly show phone numbers at which passengers could be contacted, to notify of any schedule changes, confirm bookings, and so forth. If Samurai could get access to the record for Oleg Kubalov, he would be able to trace Ashling's whereabouts.

That, Samurai decided, was what they would expect him to do. Thus they would be on the lookout for anyone showing an undue interest in the name Kubalov and the passenger list for that particular shuttle flight. And that gave Samurai the beginnings of a notion of how Rudi might begin his apprenticeship. . . .

He found some phone booths in a commercial and shopping precinct, and called up the directory listing of local Aerospaceflot branches and offices. A quick call to one of the numbers established that the only candidate was one of their own shuttles, flight LTR-7, due off the pad at 10:00 the next morning for an orbital transfer to an LLL transporter, which, he discovered, stood for Lunar Link Lines, an Offworld operation based at Copernicus.

After establishing that much, he went on, "I'm trying to contact one of the passengers on that flight. It is very urgent. His name is Oleg Kubalov. Do you have a number or something, by any chance, or some other way I can get in touch with him?"

"Sorry, sir. I can't give you the hotel's number," the clerk replied. "But I can have them get Mr. Kubalov to call you. Where can you be reached?"

"Oh, I see. Well, I haven't checked in anywhere myself yet. Why don't I give you a call again as soon as I'm fixed up?"

"Very well, sir. Thanks for calling."

"Thank you."

Which was what Samurai had expected. But it had confirmed his hope that Ashling was in a *hotel*, which made things a lot simpler. So, Samurai could more confidently proceed to the next stage of what he had in mind.

He browsed around a little, and after making inquiries located a theatrical supply shop that sold wigs, hairpieces, dyes, face paints, and other aids to disguise. After selecting several items there, he bought himself a change of clothes to complete the transformation. Then he found a small hotel called the Kestrel. He took a room there as George Lincoln and left the things he had purchased.

From there, he went to a travel agent and checked the booking situation for tomorrow's Aerospaceflot flight LTR-7 and connection to Luna Copernicus. There were a few places left but they were filling fast. He made a reservation in the name of Carl Zimmer and left a deposit, arranging to pay the balance and collect the ticket when he checked in the next morning. Finally he went back to meet Rudi at four as arranged, in the same restaurant where they'd had lunch.

"I got us into a place called the Hotel Marko," Rudi said. "It's small, and a bit on the bare side, but out of the way. I assumed you didn't want to be too visible. Anyhow, here's the address. You're booked in as Abraham Washington, like you said."

"It sounds fine," Samurai said, taking the hotel's card that Rudi had picked up.

"Is it true that in your country, hotels have to report their guest lists to the police?"

"You know, you really are going to have to quit this," Samurai told him.

Rudi held up his hands in apology. "Not another word, I promise."

Samurai sat forward over the table and lowered his voice. "Look, there's something I want you to do."

"If I can."

"How's your charm with women? You strike me as the kind who could probably talk acid into being sweet if you had a mind to."

Rudi grinned at the compliment. "I have my days," he agreed. "What do you want?"

"I'm being watched, and I can't move too openly. There's a person leaving tomorrow on a lunar transfer shuttle that I need to get in touch with. His name is Oleg Kubalov. He should be out at the spaceport later today. What I want you to do is go to the Aerospaceflot desk there at about six and get them to put out a call for him. If he's there, give him the Hotel Marko's number and get him to call me there. If he's not, see if you can find out from the desk where he's staying."

Rudi looked doubtful. "Will they tell me?"

"They're not supposed to. That's where the charm comes in. They won't give it over the phone, but they might if you go in person. I can't risk being seen there myself. Will you give it a try?"

Rudi thought, then turned up his hands. "It can't hurt, I guess. What happens if they won't buy it?"

"Then we'll have to think of something else."

Rudi drummed his fingers on the table and eyed Samurai obliquely. "Can I ask what this is about?"

"Sure."

Rudi waited. Samurai remained impassive. Finally Rudi asked, "Okay, what's it about?"

"It's none of your business."

Rudi sighed and nodded resignedly. "Okay, I'll give it a shot. What about you?"

"I've got some other things to do, so I have to go now. I'll see you back at the Marko at . . . oh, it should be sometime around midnight."

"I'll see you then," Rudi said.

"Let's hope you have some luck."

By 6:00 Samurai, with blond hair, mustache, glasses, and wearing the change of clothes he had bought, was inconspicuously reading a newspaper in the back row of some seats near the Aerospaceflot desk in the main spaceport terminal building. Rudi appeared on time and approached one of the clerks. She nodded after listening to him for a moment and scribbling down a note, then picked up a phone and called somebody. Shortly afterward a message came over the public-address system:

"Would Oleg Kubalov, traveling tomorrow to Luna Copernicus, contact the Aerospaceflot desk, please. Mr. Oleg Kubalov."

Obviously, before Rudi could credibly pester the clerk for information connected with a name, he would need to have tried paging the name first. And if he was supposed to be trying to trace Ashling, he would have to give, and therefore have paged, the name that Ashling was going under—as anybody looking out for such behavior would already have figured.

Nobody responded to the call. After waiting a few minutes, Rudi went back to the desk and said something to the clerk. She checked on her terminal and nodded, Samurai saw with satisfaction: yes, there was an Oleg Kubalov booked on the flight. Rudi leaned closer and started talking. Samurai also saw another man in a tan suit, who had been hanging around in the general area, draw nearer behind Rudi, apparently trying to catch the conversation.

Rudi became more earnest, coaxing, beguiling, then finally throwing up his arms and demanding. But it did no good. The clerk shook her head insistently, and when that failed to deter him, she called a man in a red blazer out from the doorway behind. The man listened as Rudi remonstrated, shook his head, and ended up thumping the countertop and making a dismissive gesture. Well, nobody could have tried harder than that. Rudi finally gave up and walked away.

So did the man in the tan suit, along with a couple of others who had been moving closer. They recognized a setup when they saw it. It meant that Samurai was here and testing the water to see who was about.

They grabbed Rudi in a corridor leading to the transit-tube terminal and bundled him outside into a waiting car. "Okay, okay, take it easy," the one in charge said in appalling Russian. "It's not you that we want. Where's the guy who put you up to this?"

Rudi looked at them fearfully. They were all lean, tough, and looked mean. He was rapidly coming to the conclusion that he'd had enough of this particular profession already.

One of them drew out a wad of FER notes and waved them provocatively in front of Rudi's face. "This could keep you comfortable for a long time. Come on, fella, you haven't done anything. You could be a thousand miles from here by midnight."

Rudi licked his lips uncertainly. "Or think of it this way," the leader suggested. "It's a bit like getting old: the alternative's a lot worse."

"Well," Rudi said, "if you put it like that . . ."

Meanwhile, Samurai had left to return to the Kestrel. They could spend their evening looking for him as Abraham Washington, while he got on with the job at hand.

Back at the hotel, he ordered a meal in his room and settled down to begin the tedious process of calling every hotel in the city in turn, asking to speak to a guest called Oleg Kubalov. Ever since Rostiescki gave him the name in Zittau, Samurai had been growing increasingly uneasy that even Pipeline, after their carelessness in using it on that occasion, wouldn't be so lax as to book Kubalov's room under that name also. But now that he had come this far, he had no choice but to press on.

He struck lucky after a little under an hour, with a place called the Kosmogord.

"Yes, sir, one moment," the voice on the line said when he inquired. "Putting you through now."

Samurai hung up. So Pipeline, apparently, could indeed be that amateurish after all.

"Ashling, I've got you!" he breathed.

While in another part of town, Colonel Hautz's men were setting up their stakeout of the Hotel Marko. All the angles were covered. Samurai would be back around midnight, the Russian had said.

It was going to be a long night.

forty-two

The Kosmogord was one of the city's more prominent hotels: an orientally inspired extravaganza of marbled halls and pointed arches, with an indoor arboretum and cascading rock pools giving its main lobby area something of the look of a Moorish palace garden.

Samurai arrived shortly after 9:30, disguised since Ashling knew him, and booked a single room, again as George Lincoln—although by now what name he chose didn't matter. Having deposited his briefcase, he went back to the elevators and visited every floor, noting down the room numbers indicated on the direction signs at each level. That gave him a list of all the rooms in the hotel. He then returned to his own room and began calling each of them in turn to pose the same question:

"Hello, is this Mr. Kubalov's room? . . . I'm sorry, I must have the wrong number."

But when he tried Room 1205, a woman's voice responded. "Yes. Who is this?"

Samurai penned a heavy circle around *1205* on the list he'd been working through. "Room service here, ma'am. Sorry to trouble you, but we've got some confusion over an order here. Was it 1205 that wanted a chicken salad for two and a carafe of wine?"

"No, not us."

"Oh, then it must be the other one. Sorry again for disturbing you."

"That's all right. These things happen."

"Thanks. Good night."

"Good night."

In room 1205, Kay replaced the phone and turned back toward Scipio and another Pipeline member called Julius, who were watching her expectantly. Julius had also been involved in the Ashling business and would be traveling to Luna with them tomorrow.

"He's here," Kay told them.

In the staff section at the rear of the second floor, the hotel security manager came back to his office, unlocked the door and went in, and never knew what hit him.

Samurai relieved him of his blue blazer, tie, badge and ID, and passkeys. He didn't like these kinds of impersonations, but there was no time left for fooling around. This would be his last chance to intercept Ashling before the launch tomorrow morning.

Ten minutes later, after using the emergency stairs to stay out of sight as much as possible, he came to the door of Room 1205. He checked the gun inside his jacket and the other items concealed about his person, looked each way to be sure he was alone, and rang the bell. There was no answer. He tapped on the door, waited, and then rang again. Nothing. After checking around him once more, he produced the security manager's passkeys, slid the gun from its holster beneath his arm, then entered swiftly and silently, closing the door and swiveling to cover the room from a crouch against the wall in one smooth movement.

It was deserted.

Samurai straightened up slowly, nonplussed. There were no people, but the signs of rapid departure were everywhere: ruffled beds, one with pillows stacked at the end; drawers half open; a folded newspaper on top of the vanity; used napkins in the trash bin. He went through to the bathroom. Sink and shower used recently, towels damp and crumpled. He came back out and rummaged through the trash bin. There was a receipted bill from the Harbor Light Bar in Hamburg, along with a couple of Ukrainian Airlines boarding passes from Odessa to Novosibirsk direct, dated December 3. He picked up the newspaper and saw that it was the *Berliner Zeitung* from the day previous to that. Some papers that had been inside the fold dropped out and fell to the floor. Samurai picked them up and examined them. Most were of no interest. One, however, had written on it among other things, *Dr. Andre Ulkanov, Neurophysiology Dept., Science Institute at Copernicus 3,* and a phone number with a lunar access code.

Still uncomprehending, Samurai returned to his own room and called the hotel on an outside line.

"Kosmogord, good evening."

"Hello, Room 1205, please. Mr. Kubalov."

There was a pause, then, "I'm sorry, sir. The person of that name has already checked out."

"What? How recently? I talked to him less than an hour ago."

"He left within the last half hour, sir."

"I see. . . . Thank you." Samurai hung up and stared at the phone.

So perhaps he hadn't been careful enough after all, he thought to himself as he put his own clothes on again. His call as room service must have tipped them off, and obviously they were taking no chances. He wouldn't locate Oleg Kubalov again tonight, anywhere in the city. There was nothing for it, then, but to return to the Kestrel and go on to his fallback plan of pursuing Ashling to Luna tomorrow morning.

On his way, he reflected on the incredible sequence of bad luck that had dogged him all the way from Pearse. It was uncanny. He had managed to miss Ashling by a hair's breadth every time; and in not a single instance had Samurai actually caught a glimpse of him.

If he hadn't seen him with his own eyes before whoever it was jumped him in the hotel in Atlanta, he could almost have believed that Ashling didn't exist at all.

forty-three

Passengers and well-wishers began arriving early the next morning, and by eight o'clock the Aerospaceflot departures hall was filled with people. For the most part they were younger, ambitious professionals, some traveling singly, others with partners, spouses, and families, bound offplanet because that was where the Offworld enterprises needed them and made it worth their while to go. There were scientists and engineers, drawn by what they had read and heard of breathtaking leaps in concept and theory that were already making Earth's contemporary technologies as obsolete as the stagecoach. There were teachers, eager to go where the creative potential of young minds was regarded as the most precious resource that the universe had to offer; entrepreneurs with an instinct for opportunity still to be uncovered; writers, artists, moviemakers, poets, searching for new elements and inspiration. And there were the restless, the curious, and the adventuresome, unable to resist the lure of challenge and an environment that would be unlike anything they had ever known.

Some sat quietly and stared, lost in thought as they prepared to leave for new worlds. Others milled around in constant agitation, checking and rechecking details needlessly, and talking incessantly in vain efforts to mask their nervousness and excitement.

Samurai arrived disguised, proceeded to the Aerospaceflot ticketing desk to confirm his reservation as Carl Zimmer and pay the outstanding balance. It was too easy: no documentation was required; nobody asked to see any ID.

"How can you people permit this?" he couldn't keep himself

from saying as he watched the clerk enter the transaction. "Do you really believe that resources out there are unlimited? You can't simply open up the Moon to the whole world."

The clerk smiled as if he had heard it many times before. "I'm no scientist, but they tell us they're on the verge of being able to turn moonrock into anything you want," he replied. "And nobody's shipping the whole world anywhere. We can only send as many as there are places on the ship."

"But you haven't told me where to stay. Nobody's asked me how long I'll be there. Isn't there any control? Doesn't anyone *plan* anything?"

"Of course they do. How many designers do you think it took to plan the construction of the ship? We plan the flight schedules, because that's what we do. The hotel and real estate people plan the accommodation, because that's what they do. It all works itself out in the end." The clerk slipped the ticket into a plastic holder and held it out. "Enjoy the flight."

Samurai took the holder and tried to summon a response from all the reasons why he knew it couldn't be so. But as he stood, trying to sort the words out in his head, he found that he could only stare in mute confusion. All of a sudden, something inside him didn't feel right.

The slogans marched through his head like obedient soldiers. But they rang hollow, playing themselves automatically as if from a tape. It was as if he had forgotten what the words meant. He searched in his mind for some significance behind the phrases, some bedrock of conviction that should exist underneath . . . but encountered only emptiness.

Forcing the thought, he repeated to himself that the day would come when all this would collapse under its own contradictions, and the Consolidation would stand strong. But again the fingers of his mind slipped around and away from the words in vain, unable to capture any substance. It was as if his mind were continuing to function as a collection of mechanical parts only, going through their prescribed motions but somehow incapable of attaining any depth of thought. For the first time, the unassailable, total self-confidence that he had never doubted for a moment was shaken. He seemed to be feeling pieces of his mind beginning to slip apart.

He took the ticket in its holder and moved away from the desk.

Several men were standing around in the vicinity, a couple of whom he recognized as the Americans who had followed Rudi from here the previous evening. They scrutinized all the passengers intently, including Samurai. But they had no idea what appearance he might have adopted. And as foreign agents operating under cover, they had no authority to interfere with passengers boarding a spacecraft in the Kazakh Free State. There was nothing they could do.

Expelling all other considerations from his mind and forcing himself to concentrate only on the mission, Samurai drifted away and around the hall to see if he could spot Ashling among the knots of people. But there was no sign of the scientist. It wasn't especially surprising. After the alarm last night, Ashling could be in disguise also, or was being kept out of sight until the last minute.

He realized that two children were looking up at him, a boy and a girl, both about ten. They looked like twins.

"Our daddy's a famous conductor," the boy informed him. "He's going to start an orchestra on the Moon. Are you coming to live on the Moon too?"

"We're going to have more brothers and sisters, and they'll be born on the Moon," the girl said.

Automatically the words formed in Samurai's mind: And in ten years' time, more hungry mouths will be coming back to Earth, begging to be fed. But another part of him didn't want to believe them. Something about these people was stirring a piece of him somewhere deep inside, but at the same time another piece rebelled and didn't want to be stirred.

"Where are you from?" the boy asked.

Samurai could only stare at them. He could remember fragments of pictures of what he knew was Minneapolis, others that were Denver, and then bits of yet other places again, all of them in conflict. He didn't know where he was from.

He turned and walked away. Concentrate on the mission. . . .

Boarding commenced at nine. Since the flight up to the orbiting lunar transporter would be short, the shuttle cabin contained mainly seating, as in a regular airliner. However, since the craft was in the shape of a short, fat cone, the seats, all elaborately sprung and pneumatically contoured, were in a number of boxlike container-cabins set on transverse decks, like the floors of a house—which suited the ship's vertical attitude when on the ground. Once in free-fall, of course, it wouldn't matter which way up they were.

"Thank you for choosing Aerospaceflot today, and welcome aboard our flight LTR-7 to orbit, connecting with LLL's onward service to Luna, Copernicus. For those of you who will be going offplanet for the first time, there are some procedures and safety features that you should be aware of. . . ."

There was no sign of Ashling in the seats on the deck where Samurai was. But that meant little, since there were two other decks above and more below. Samurai checked in his pocket that he still had the piece of paper that he'd found in the hotel room the previous night, giving Professor Ulkanov's whereabouts at Copernicus. So even if he failed to pick up Ashling on disembarkation, he still had Ashling's final destination.

Now that he was aboard the shuttle and settled, Samurai felt more himself again. Perhaps the confusion that he'd experienced outside had been just a passing effect, caused by the accumulated stress and conflict of the last few days. He thought back over all the obstacles that he'd overcome since leaving Pearse and felt a deep sense of satisfaction.

And now he was so close.

Talk around the cabin died away, and the air tensed with expectancy tinged with apprehension for the unknown as the moment for departure approached. But the actual lift-off, when it came, was smoother, though noisier, than the takeoff of an airliner, with no rumbling rush across concrete, sudden pull-up to unstick, or clunkings of landing gear being retracted to reduce drag.

Instead, rapid pulsations throbbed through the structure to mark ignition of the onboard start-up booster, growing quickly to a pounding roar to achieve positive thrust and set the craft into motion. Then the three ground lasers went up to full power to energize the main propellant, and within seconds the shuttle was accelerating fast, then streaking skyward, riding on a controlled, laser-sustained detonation wave, course-corrected by alteration of the beams following it from the ground. Onboard optics redirected the tracking beams to sustain drive for over a thousand miles downrange, by which time the shuttle was up to orbital speed and on a closing trajectory for its onboard auxiliary thrusters to complete rendezvous maneuvers with the transfer satellite where the LLL transporter was waiting.

The transporter was essentially a framework supporting two co-joining spheres that formed the manned section, along with a number of gas, water, and auxiliary propellant tanks, and a nuclear main-propulsion module. One of the spheres contained the crew's quarters, flight deck, and control room, while the other, which was larger, held the passenger lounge-cafeteria, galley and other services, and a playroom-nursery. There was no need for passengers to leave their seats and move through into the lunar transporter when the surface shuttle docked. The box-shaped containers holding the seating cabins slid out of the shuttle as sealed units, into slots in the transporter framework, where they mated with ports connecting to the main passenger module.

There were more announcements, reminding passengers of the effects of free-fall and instructing them to keep seat belts fastened and loose objects secured. During the next two hours, three more shuttles, one from the other end of Siberia, one from Japan, and one from Malaysia, arrived to exchange similar passenger and cargo containers for others inbound from Luna. When preparations were complete, everyone returned to their seats. Then the main drive fired to begin lifting the fully loaded transporter up through higher orbits and speed it onto the escape trajectory that would carry it from Earth.

For a long time the cabin's occupants, for the most part silent, stared from their seats in awed fascination as the full disk of Earth being captured by the rear-pointing imagers came into view on the display screen. The transfer satellite shrank and was lost against the surface detail, and then Earth itself could be seen diminishing gradually against the background starfield.

"I still can't get used to the idea that it's really out there," a woman's voice said from the row behind where Samurai was sitting. "I mean, it isn't just another movie that was sent back. It's right out there, on the other side of the wall."

"Makes this thing feel like an eggshell, doesn't it," a man replied.

After a while the atmosphere relaxed, and such being the adaptability of human nature, what had been new and wondrous only an hour before soon became the norm. Some of the passengers began moving about to stretch their cramped limbs and check out the menu and other facilities available in the communal services module. The nuclear main drive was still sustaining enough thrust to maintain a mild acceleration, so conditions were not entirely weightless. The ship would enter a fully free-fall phase later into the voyage, however.

Confusion and disorientation were beginning to come over Samurai again. Something catastrophic was happening to him, he could sense, but he didn't know what. Splinters of memories came together in his mind and tumbled apart again like the pieces of a kaleidoscope picture, forming patterns of chance associations that hung together for fleeting moments but made no sense. An apartment in Philadelphia; a girl with red hair in Chicago; a room in which soldiers lived; a corridor full of students in a school somewhere. . . . There were guns, all kinds of weapons; two punks lying crumpled on the ground in a dark, narrow street. . . . The red-haired girl again, this time lying naked on a towel by a lake surrounded by trees. A machine surrounding his head. . . . He saw a ship coming into dock in a port, he wasn't sure where. Some part of him thought it was in Germany. Had he ever been to Germany?

He didn't know. Who were these people who came and went through his awareness like fish glimpsed in a turbulent river? Which of it was real, which was fabrication? He couldn't tell.

Perspiration was damp on his forehead, slippery across his palms. A feeling close to panic gripped him. Suddenly the rows of people pressing in on him from every side in the confines of the cabin were asphyxiating. He undid his seat belt, mumbled his way past the people to the nearest aisle, and headed through the connecting port to the services module.

Two catering attendants were dispensing snacks, sandwiches, hot food, and beverages in closed cups with drinking tubes from a horsehoe counter projecting into an eating area of tables and booths. Samurai selected a plate of fish with potato salad and bread, and a hot tea, and took it over to an empty stool at a side bar where several other people were already sitting.

As he ate, he remembered a woman and a car. She was driving. They were on a road winding between snowy mountains. He didn't know where or when it had been . . . or even if it had ever happened.

But there was something about her that mattered. He tried to think what. She had been different, somehow, and cared about a stranger. Been something that he never could be. . . . And it mattered.

"Apparently we're doing almost fifty thousand kilometers an hour," a voice said nearby. "You'd never believe it." Samurai looked up. A gray-haired man with a short beard was looking at him genially. "Hello. My name is Piotr. It's going to be a long trip, so we might as well make the best of it. Why go out of one's way to be strangers?"

"Oh . . . yes," Samurai responded uncertainly, still half immersed in his reverie.

"I'm a petrologist," Piotr went on. "Rocks and soils, you know. Lots to do out there. They're going to be digging half of Luna up. Copernicus goes down hundreds of meters already." He waited expectantly for a moment, then prompted, "What do you do?"

Samurai looked at him blankly. "I kill people," he replied.

Back in his seat, Samurai stared unseeingly at the display on the forward wall of the cabin, which was now showing a movie. All around him were creators, builders, producers, discoverers: men and women who belonged to life, who were life; who extended life through the power to forge out of ideas and matter the tools that could transform deserts into gardens, and the lunar waste into cities. He had been programmed only to kill and destroy.

By now he had forgotten what his mission was, and why it mattered. He knew only that it was Ashling who had made him what he was. And that was why Samurai had to kill him.

That was all.

forty-four

Balanced on its descent jets like a metallic sculpture coming down out of the black lunar sky, the transporter sank between the opened outer doors of an immense subterranean docking bay. On every side stretched the clutter of domes, towers, and surface constructions forming the North Complex of the thirty-mile-wide interconnected sprawl of the Copernican base system. Beneath the arc lights inside the doors, tiers of access platforms and service gantries lined the sides of the docking bay, with freight hoists going down to deeper levels.

Shock absorbers disposed of the last remaining momentum, and the ship came to rest. The huge doors slid together overhead, and the dock began filling with air. Umbilicals and access ramps swung out to mate with the craft, and shortly afterward its passengers began walking through, moving warily and awkwardly to the unfamiliar sensation of possessing only a sixth normal bodyweight, into the reception area.

The hall was small compared to the arrivals lounge of a typical airport of any size, and the sudden flood of several hundred arrivals, augmented by others who had been waiting to meet them, quickly transformed it into a confusion of jostling and bustling, with relieved and excited talk breaking out on every side now that the voyage, with all its unknowns, was over. There was little evidence of officialdom or bureaucracy in action. A man and woman in pale blue police uniforms stood looking on from beside one of the exits, and a number of Lunar Link Lines agents in maroon suits and tunics were on hand to help people with directions. A sign above the main doors proclaimed WELCOME in a score of languages. Nearby was a clock showing local time, and above it a picture of earth and a footprint with the legend: One Small Step.

Samurai moved to the center of the hall and allowed himself to be carried along with the current of people that was beginning to flow through into a brightly lit concourse on the far side of the exit. Surrounding it were desks for information, transportation, and accommodation, and at the far end, several further exits with signs denoting ways to other parts of the spaceport and to local transitube terminals. Opening onto the concourse were several shops, a restaurant and bar, an employment, insurance, and real estate agency; a chapel; an entrance to a pool and gymnasium; and a massage and sauna parlor with scantily clad girls and several well-muscled studs in the foyer, with the invitation to "Rest, Relax, Enjoy. It's Out of That World!" flashing in colored lights above.

He searched with his eyes, one way, then the other. Everywhere the same milling tide of men, women, figures, faces, couples, groups, scurrying, standing, children looking lost, clutching hands. . . .

And then he saw them.

It was only a glimpse through the crowd: two men and a woman, one of the men in a long coat and with a hat pulled down low, just in the process of disappearing into an exit marked LOWER LEVEL & TRANSITUBE . In that brief moment and from that angle Samurai didn't see their faces; but their hurried pace and hunched postures, as if unconsciously trying to conceal themselves, signaled all that he needed to know. He began moving in that direction, slipping swiftly through the crowd.

Outside the concourse was a foyer with sales booths and escalators going up and down. Samurai joined the short tail of people moving onto the down-going one. Below, he could see the three figures just stepping off at the bottom and disappearing into one of several tunnels leading away in different directions. But he could do nothing to close the distance, for the moving stairway was filled with people.

He fretted impatiently while the escalator carried him down, then as soon as he was off at the bottom, dodged around the group immediately ahead and threaded his way through the people moving along the tunnel that the three from the shuttle had taken. It brought him to a crossway, with stairs going down on both sides, while a wide passageway continued ahead. He could see no sign of his quarry, but there were signs giving directions.

The note on the piece of paper that he'd picked up in the Kosmogord said, *Science Institute, Cop 3.* A sign by one of the stairways read: EASTBOUND, with a schematic map of the line. The loop at the far end was indicated as COMPLEX 3, FRANCINE, with stops at *Mineheads, Orchard, Astrakhan, Zagreb, University-Observatory, Central, Maindome, Shinjuku, Aquamarine, Eratosthenes Link, Valley, Gorky,* and *Junction.* People were emerging from the archway next to the sign, indicating that a train was already in. Samurai went through the archway and hastened on down.

He came out onto a platform with a transparent wall running along one side. A train consisting of three short cars was standing on the far side. But the platform was already clear of boarding passengers, and even as he watched, the gates through the wall closed and the train began moving noiselessly away.

Thwarted and exasperated, Samurai turned away. Already more people were coming out onto the platform. Between the seats set along the rear wall was a picture of a grinning Mickey Mouse face, with a monitor screen and audio grille. Above the screen an illuminated sign proclaimed INFORMATION. Samurai moved over in front of it.

"Hello," a squeaky voice greeted cheerfully from the grille. "How can I help you?"

"Copernicus Three, the Science Institute," Samurai answered. "Do I get there this way?"

"Sure. Get off at University-Observatory and just follow the signs."

"How long?"

"It takes about fifteen minutes."

"I mean how long before the next train?"

"With an Earthship just in, no time at all. In fact the next one's coming in right now."

In his office on Level 5B of Neurophysiology, Professor Andre Ulkanov stood watching one of several monitor screens set into a panel that took up part of one of the walls. The screen showed a side view of the head of Jason, one of Ulkanov's graduate students, who was posted on a gallery overlooking the entrance lobby above, in the upper levels of the largely subterranean institute. After a few seconds the head turned full-face. "I think this might be him, Professor." Ulkanov raised an eyebrow and caught the gaze of his assistant, Barbara, standing a short distance back.

"Now, we'll see," he murmured softly.

Another screen showed a view from a hand-held camera that Jason was operating, looking down over the floor of the lobby. A figure with fair hair, a mustache, wearing glasses, and carrying a black briefcase, had entered from the doors leading through from the Transitube and was looking around. Jason's voice reported, "He's going over to the information desk."

Ulkanov turned toward the three people, still in their traveling coats, who had arrived only minutes ago. "Is that him?" he asked them. "The man who showed up at the Kosmogord?"

Kay and Scipio came closer and studied the image for a moment. Julius, the other member of Pipeline who had come with them from Earth, sank into a chair and lit a cigarette. "Man, that was a long trip," he sighed.

Kay nodded to Ulkanov. "It's him."

"It's unbelievable," Scipio breathed. "He's here at the institute already? What kind of person is this?"

Ulkanov looked at another screen, this time showing two girls in white lab coats. "Okay?" he asked them. "Is everything ready there?"

One of them nodded nervously. "Yes."

"Be careful, now. Remember that he's dangerous."

"You don't have to remind us," the girl said in a shaky voice.

"Will this count toward grade points?" the other asked.

Ulkanov smiled thinly. "We'll see what we can do."

Jason said from the first screen, "The clerk at the information desk is sending him to the elevators. He's moving away . . . on his way over. Get ready. He's coming down."

Level 5B, Experimental Wing, Samurai repeated to himself as the elevator door closed. The first place that Ashling would have been taken to on arriving would almost certainly be Ulkanov's office. There was no call for stealth or elaborate planning now, Samurai decided. His world had reduced itself to the single, overriding obsession to kill Ashling. One fast, sudden stroke, and it would be over with. Then they could do whatever they liked.

The elevator descended a level and stopped. Two girls in white lab coats got in, carrying some items of technical equipment. Neither took any notice of him. The doors closed and the elevator resumed its descent. The girls talked in nervous, subdued voices, but Samurai didn't really notice as he softly fingered the lines of the automatic in his coat pocket.

Two levels farther down the elevator stopped again, and the girls got out. The doors closed. The elevator began moving once more. And only then did Samurai see the flask that the two girls had left in a corner on the floor . . . a split second before it burst, releasing a pungent vapor that filled the small volume of the elevator car in moments. Samurai tore his handkerchief from his pocket and clamped it over his nose and mouth, then punched the button to stop the car at the next level.

But it never reached the next level. It stopped halfway between, and the door remained firmly closed against Samurai's frantic attempt to force it. He braced his back and feet against the walls, intending to work his way up to see if there was a hatch in the roof that could be opened; but before even making the first move he could feel his strength failing. He slid down into a sitting posture, keeled slowly over sideways, and lost consciousness.

He awoke many hours later, in a treatment room near the machine facility in the institute's advanced research labs. Ulkanov was standing near the door, watching his patient's recovery and smiling.

For the person who was staring up from the cot was no longer the synthetic creation that had been named Samurai.

Nor the teacher, Richard Jarrow; nor Warrant Officer Demiro.

But the missing scientist himself: Conrad Ashling.

Ashling
Ashling
Ashling
Ashling
Ashling
Ashling
Ashling
Ashling

forty-five

After leaving the rear of the department store in the shopping mall, Josef and the other Pipeline agent, whom he introduced as Leon, drove Ashling on a zigzag route around Atlanta to be sure they were not being followed. When Josef was satisfied, they headed for the Hyatt, where Josef had already arranged a reservation. They brought Ashling in through a side door and took him straight up to 7319, which turned out to be a suite of two main rooms: a living room and a bedroom at the rear, each served by a separate bathroom. Two more Pipeline agents were there already when Ashling and his escorts arrived. With them was an Offworld scientist called Kay, a colleague of Ulkanov's, whom Ashling had talked to before from a public viewphone when the plans for his defection were being finalized.

"Good to see you again, Conrad," she said. "It won't be much longer now."

"Let's hope so," Ashling replied.

He sat down at the table, and Josef took the chair opposite. Kay perched on the side of an armchair nearby, while Leon and the other two men dispersed themselves around the suite.

"You'll be staying here tonight," Josef informed Ashling. "A courier will be arriving tomorrow, who will stay with you all the way through to the FER."

"What route will we be taking?" Ashling asked out of curiosity.

Josef showed his palms in a brief, apologetic gesture. "Just in case anything goes wrong . . . it would be better if you didn't know the details. That way there can be no risk of our methods being compromised."

Ashling nodded tightly. "Of course. I understand."

"But I can tell you that you will be launching from Semipalatinsk on December sixth," Josef said. "That gives us three weeks: time enough for you to take it slowly, and an ample allowance for contingency. We want to get you out of the Consolidation fast, before they have time to react. If there is time to spare, you can spend it relaxing after you get to the FER."

"Fine," Ashling agreed.

Josef looked at him. "How are you feeling?"

"Oh, I was a bit shaky earlier, but I think it's passing. Tired. I think I'll turn in early this evening."

"Kay has got some questions about Southside that she'd like to talk about while you're here," Josef said. "Are you up to it?"

"Oh, sure," Ashling said.

Kay reached for a folder of papers that she had with her and rose to pull a chair up to the table. "How about doing it over a meal?" she suggested.

"Maybe later," Ashling said. "I had lunch fairly late. And with all the excitement since, I don't have any appetite. Maybe something to drink, though."

Leon ordered tea, coffee, and soft drinks from room service, and for the next couple of hours Kay and Ashling talked about his work at Pearse and as much as he had discovered of Nordens's true motives. When they had finished, Josef announced that he and Kay needed to take care of a couple of other things.

"We'll be back sometime tomorrow," Josef said. "Leon will stay here, with at least one of the others at all times, so you'll be all right. And you know how to get in touch with me if there's a problem?"

"Yes, I've got the number," Ashling confirmed.

"Anything else you need for now?"

"No, I don't think so."

"We'll see you tomorrow, then."

Josef and Kay left. Leon and his companions talked with Ashling for a while, and then settled down to watch a movie in the living room. Ashling stayed through most of it, even though it didn't really interest him. Then he stood up, excused himself, and announced that he was going to get some rest.

In the bedroom, he sat down on a chair and sat thinking for a while about the journey that lay ahead of him over the next three weeks, culminating, if all went well, with his leaving Earth completely and going to Luna. It was a bit late in life for changes of environment as radical as that, he reflected. He hoped he was capable of surviving it. He patted his pockets to make sure he had his Panacyn pills with him, then remembered that he'd taken one on arriving and left them in the other bathroom. Not to worry. He didn't feel as if he needed one right now. Surprising.

Suddenly, without warning, the door flew open and Leon hurled himself through. He started to turn, but before he could close the door a chair hit it from the other side with enough force to make him stagger back. An instant later, a figure hurtled through the doorway in a crouching posture, its body canted away and leading leg doubled back in readiness, and sent Leon crashing back over the bed with a sidekick. Before Leon could move or recover, the assailant leveled a pistol and shot him through his shirt.

"Oh, my God!" Ashling whispered, rising to his feet, horrified.

The man laughed. "Don't worry. We don't want killings. Too many complications. It'll keep them out until I get back here to tidy things up."

Ashling stared, confused, as he recognized him as from the project. "But you're one of the volunteers. Demiro, isn't it? . . . I thought you'd been transferred away. What's going on? I don't understand."

Demiro turned with a wave and strode back through the living room. Ashling followed. Another of the Pipeline guards was unconscious on the floor. There was no sign of the third.

"Let's just say for now that there's more going on than you know about," Demiro said. "There isn't time now. Ask Nordens to tell you about it when we get back." Then Ashling felt a pain and clutched at his chest, falling against the side of the doorway.

"What is it?" Demiro demanded.

"Pill," Ashling croaked. "White jar . . . other bathroom."

Demiro sat him down, then went away and came back with the pills and a glass of water.

Ashling took one of the capsules and sat for a while, recovering. On the room's TV, a program was just beginning about tropical insects. Finally Demiro said, "Okay? Can you move now?" Ashling didn't respond, but continued panting, staring down at the floor.

"Come on," Demiro said, straightening up. "We have to get your briefcase. What else do you need?"

"Where are we going?"

"Back. Where do you think?"

They left the hotel through the side door that Josef had brought Ashling in through. Demiro had a car parked nearby. He handed Ashling the keys and, still keeping the pistol in his hand as a warning, gestured toward the driver's-side door. "Get in, and don't try anything clever. You're driving. . . . And things have changed since you last had anything to do with it. The name, to you, is Gordon. Maurice Gordon."

forty-six

They passed the Institute of Technology, and soon were on the familiar Northwest Expressway, I-75, heading back in the direction of the southern Appalachian fringe.

Almost thirty minutes went by before the paralysis that had seized Ashling's mind began to wear off. The suddenness and violence of the assault had left him stunned. Now, as fragments of his thinking processes started coming together again, the numbness that had protected him gave way to all-consuming despair.

After all the planning and preparations, the growing nervous tension that had been tormenting him for weeks, and actually to have pulled it off it seemed, without leaving a trace. . . . Now this. Even Pipeline, his last hope, which he had come to regard as so professional and capable, to whom he entrusted himself completely . . . before his eyes, in seconds, reduced to impotence and helplessness. What hope could he have now?

As he drove, staring rigidly ahead, tight-lipped and blank-faced, he could feel in his chest the imminence of another attack. He realized then that even if these last events hadn't happened, he'd been deluding himself anyway. He would never have survived the stresses of getting out of the Consolidation and going offplanet. And with these latest developments, he was beginning to wonder if he would even survive tonight. A part of him that he couldn't ignore was already seriously doubting it.

He needed medical help, and quickly; there was no alternative but to get back to Pearse. And what then? He would never be up to another escape bid. And after this, the only prospect that the future held was to be kept there under virtual house arrest. Living as a captive, forced to work for a regime that he now had no hesitation of condemning as decayed and corrupt. Working to contribute to what further misapplications of science? For what else did this transformation of Demiro into something ruthless and inhuman mean? Ashling had found out about the covert political objectives of the project, but here, it seemed, was something else, even more sinister and repugnant, and he had never suspected.

No.

Whatever the consequences, he would have no part of it, he resolved. At several points he toyed with the thought of simply steering the car off the road and ending it right there for both of them. But he didn't, because that would only have eliminated whatever opportunity might lie ahead for him to do something to stop all of it, entirely. Wasn't it he, more than anyone, who had made it possible in the first place, after all?

Beside him, Gordon remained alert, pistol in hand. After a while he began passing the time by taunting Ashling mercilessly.

"I ought to thank you, I know, but I'm afraid they didn't make me that way. I don't thank anyone because I don't need anyone. Know why? Because I'm more than any of you could become in a lifetime. It's called 'superiority.' Being ashamed to claim it is a weakness, and I don't suffer from it. I don't suffer from any of them."

Ashling stared at the road unrolling itself ahead, and said nothing.

"So you'll go back, and be nothing and timid, because that's what the rest of you are. That's what you're made for. I was made for something else: living. Living all of it, to the full. I like killing people, do you know that? Want to know why? Because killing them makes me more alive. That's something that you could never understand. You couldn't understand because you're not alive. Not fully. You never have been. That's why the weak think life is so precious: it's something that they desperately want, but can't have. It's natural to value what you can't have, isn't it? Come on, you tell me. You're the smart scientist. What's the matter? Does it offend your precious pride to even talk?"

They turned off the main highway onto the approach road to

Pearse. Gordon waved him onward when he began slowing at the main gate. "No, not that one. Farther around."

Ashling knew that there was a separate section known as the Permanent Quarters Annex, where some officers and high-clearance personnel resided. He himself was housed in a billet section inside the main establishment compound, and had never had reason to visit the Annex personally before.

It had its own gate and guardpost at the end of a road leading in from the perimeter road, but security was less stringent than at the regular entrances. From its position relative to the rest of the layout, Ashling estimated that it backed onto the experimental wing inside the Restricted Zone, which he knew from his work inside.

Past the guardpost, they drove across a dark yard with parked vehicles, and then around a projecting building to enter what seemed to be, as far as Ashling could make out in the shadows between the widely spaced lamps, one of several interconnecting enclosures of chalets and apartment units jumbled together among screening clumps of foliage and trees.

"That way," Gordon said, waving. "Park next to that truck."

What happened then was completely out of Ashling's conscious control. The pickup that Gordon had indicated was parked at the limit of the glow from one of the lamps, nose to the curb. In the back it was carrying several lengths of thick piping, four inches or so in diameter, lashed together and projecting back from the tail. As Ashling came toward it, he registered subconsciously that all was dark and still, with nobody around.

Perhaps it was an expression of a hopelessness that made him simply not care anymore. Maybe it was his accumulated emotions, now fermented into hatred. Instead of parking alongside the pickup, he accelerated at the last moment and ran the car straight at the projecting pipes to drive them through the windshield, right in front of Gordon's head.

Nine hundred ninety-nine men in a thousand would have died right then. Gordon's reflexes, however, were all but instantaneous, and he managed to duck—but not without cracking the side of his head on the dash panel, and in the process stunning himself for one vital fraction of a second. The pistol dropped from his fingers, and Ashling, still not really aware of what he was doing, grabbed it and shot Gordon in the neck, just below the ear. Without thinking or considering anything, he started the motor again, backed the car off the impaling pipes, and eased it up alongside the truck. Then he sat numbly in the darkness, waiting for retribution to come.

But none did. The court remained deserted; no light or sound came from the buildings around.

Ashling stared disbelievingly at Gordon's inert form, slumped back in the passenger seat, shards of windshield glass glinting in the light from the lamps outside. He felt himself turning cold and starting to shake uncontrollably. His chest pounded, with searing pains tearing through him at every beat. He waited, fully expecting a terminal attack right then, but gradually the feeling eased. He got out unsteadily.

There was a path, leading to several steps going up between shrubs and a grassy mound to a covered walkway. The walkway brought him to a door of what seemed to be one of the residential units. There was no sign of light from inside. Ashling explored around but could find no other door nearby. He decided that this had to be where Gordon had been bringing them. Presumably it was where he stayed. From its location, Ashling wouldn't have been surprised if it connected on the inside, somehow, through the Restricted Zone boundary and into the experimental wing. So that was how Gordon had intended to get him inside. Did that mean that whatever had happened to Demiro was too secret for its subjects to be allowed to go in and out through main-gate security.

Or too unofficial, perhaps?

But whatever the answer to that, it was the only available place to hide Gordon, and that was the uppermost concern in Ashling's mind right now.

He went back to the car and returned with the keys that Gordon had given him. After some trial and error, the door opened. Ashling stepped inside, closed the door behind him, drew the drapes across the single window facing out frontward, and turned on the lights.

It was stark, harsh, brutal in its assault on eye and sensibilities; a visual percussion of black and white, metal and glass, porcelain and leather; acute, angular forms, unrelieved by warmth, curve, or any concession to softness. Yes, Ashling decided, looking around stonily, there could be no mistaking it. If that was what they had turned Demiro into, this was where he would live.

He checked quickly around the remainder of the place: bedroom, kitchen and breakfast area, and bathroom, all echoing the same theme. It was deserted. He paused in the bathroom to gulp down a pill and stare at himself in the mirror, asking himself what he thought he was doing. Then he went back to the car and, with a lot of puffing and heaving, moved Gordon inside and dumped him in the recliner, after which he went back for their briefcases. Miraculously, nobody had been roused. He closed the door again, then slumped down on the couch and stared at Gordon's inert form while he considered what to do next.

Going back to the Hyatt was out of the question. For all he knew, the whole Pipeline operation could have been blown, and he might be walking straight back into a trap.

Besides, what would be the point? He was already a dead man. He could feel it, a dull, heavy lethargy taking hold deep inside, like cold creeping up into a house that has lost its heating. Why consider anything?

He stared again at the motionless figure in the recliner, Demiro, who now called himself Gordon. As far as Ashling was aware, the first phase of the project had been completed months ago and the volunteers sent back. So what was Demiro doing here still? . . . He remembered Demiro from their occasional contacts: easygoing, personable, unconvinced by most of the propaganda but too intelligent to make an issue of it, popular with everyone. The cold, precise, purpose-built combat machine that had appeared in the Hyatt and demolished three guards in virtually as many seconds was somebody else.

The phrase that had come to mind repeated itself again in Ashling's head: *purpose-built.*

Was *that* what Nordens had been doing? Suddenly, lots of things that had been happening during the previous few months came together and made sense. Long calculations and pattern-manipulation algorithms that Nordens had wanted, that went far beyond anything needed for the limited transfers called for by the initial specifications. New symbolic syntaxes for manipulating entire groups of system pathways. An entire macrofunction transform calculus.

They had created a synthetic pseudo-personality. Ashling swallowed dryly as all the sinister implications unfolded in his mind.

And then he sat up slowly in his chair as a new possibility

dawned on him. Suddenly his eyes, only a moment ago dulled by despair, were bright—bright from the thought of the sheer audacity of it. His chest was thumping rapidly again, but this time from excitement.

He had long ago cracked the access codes into Nordens's private sectors of the computer system. Therefore he could retrieve all those personality-synthesis and transfer routines that Nordens had been developing. And if so, maybe he could take it a step further.

Maybe he could transfer a complete set of patterns defining *himself* into Gordon!

He licked his lips as he thought about it. What was there to lose, after all? He was as good as dead if he did nothing. And even if that was not the case, he could never have survived the stresses of getting himself out to the Offworld independencies to place his work at the disposal of the free scientists out there, such as Ulkanov—which was his only real goal now.

No, *he* could never get there. He accepted that now. Or rather, *his* body couldn't. *But Gordon's could!*

He got up and explored the apartment again. At the back he found what he was looking for: an ordinary-looking door that, when opened, revealed a second, heavy-duty door leading in the direction of where he estimated the Restricted Zone perimeter and the experimental wing to be. It was locked of course, and one of Gordon's keys seemed to fit. But there was a second lock too, and the door remained unmovable. So close, yet thwarted. Ashling came back into the living room and looked around frantically. The desk! He went over to it and went through the drawers. In a box in one of them he found more keys. One of them was similar to the one that had fitted the door—a reasonable precaution: one key kept on Gordon's person, the other in a different place. Ashling hurried back and tried both keys simultaneously. The door opened.

There was a short, bare corridor leading to a second door. Beyond that, Ashling found himself in the familiar lab area. It was late Saturday night; nobody was about. He went back into the apartment and retrieved from his briefcase one of the sheets that he had taken with him, giving the access codes into Nordens's filing system. Then he went back through to the labs, activated a terminal in one of the computer rooms, and began picking his way in.

An hour and a half later, Ashling sat back tiredly, yet intrigued.

His human and ethical side apart, Nordens had greater scientific capabilities than Ashling had given him credit for. He had delved more deeply into the problems of total personality integration than Ashling had even contemplated, solved a lot of the problems, and in some cases hit upon methods that Ashling had to concede were highly innovative and effective. There was a lot that Ashling couldn't be sure of, and of course his biggest hazard was lack of time. . . . But it seemed, basically, that with a bit of hasty improvisation and more than his due share of luck, Nordens had furnished him the tools to do the job.

There was a further problem, but Ashling had been turning that over as he worked, and now thought he had a solution.

It was all very well to think of re-creating himself in Gordon's body, and using that to take him across to the FER and then offplanet. But Ashling could never hope to pass himself off as Gordon—what did he know about violence and aggression, and the rest of the world that Gordon had been engineered to function in? But suppose that he could deactivate his own, implanted Ashling personality temporarily, letting Gordon resume functioning as himself, and none the wiser. What better cover could he ask for than that?

If he could somehow contrive for Gordon to be sent off along that very route on an official mission, Gordon would travel with the aid of all the permits, foreign cooperation, and other resources that would be available to an agent of the state, but which Ashling as himself could never enjoy. The government would get him there more surely than Pipeline could ever hope to. Yes, he rather liked the thought of that, Ashling decided. He liked the thought of that a lot.

By the time he had his plans finalized, it was close to midnight. He moved Gordon through into the laboratory area and coupled him into the transfer machine. Then, working feverishly and praying that he hadn't made any major errors in his haste, he used one of the auxiliary scanners to read the layers of superposed connectivity functions that had been accumulating throughout life to form the essence of his being, and assembled them all into superconvoluted megaplex code, using the facilities that Nordens had developed. As far as he could tell, it was complete. The machine now contained a full representation of Ashling's persona, coupled with transform parameters that would activate an emulation of it in Gordon's particular neural configuration.

He then added two further functions.

First, he set up an inhibiting code that would deactivate the implanted Ashling personality during the first period of natural sleep to occur after completion of the implanting process. Thus, Gordon would recover consciousness tonight as Ashling, which would keep Ashling in control to get his transferred self—in Gordon's body—away, dispose of Ashling's own body, which didn't feel as if it had much longer to go, and set in motion the remainder of his plan. But after going to sleep tomorrow night, Gordon would awaken as Gordon once again, with no knowledge that he was carrying another personality suppressed below his level of awareness.

Second, for the plan to work, Gordon would need to awake unsuspicious that anything abnormal had taken place. That meant that he couldn't be allowed to remember anything about the most recent events of this evening: taking Ashling from the Hyatt, the drive back to Pearse, Ashling's shooting him in the car when they arrived. To achieve that, Ashling erased the most recent parts of Gordon's memory, back to the time when he was still in the room at the Hyatt, having dealt with the three Pipeline guards. There was no way to change that event, and eliminating the memory of it would serve no purpose. True, there would be a discontinuity in Gordon's recollections, but there was nothing to be done about that. Given the human capacity for inventiveness, Gordon would doubtless fabricate his own rationalization.

When they were leaving the hotel room, a program had just begun on the TV about tropical insects, Ashling recalled. He checked the time of that from the published schedule, and erased Gordon's memories back to then.

The next problem was to arrange for Gordon to be sent offplanet. A promising way of achieving that would be to make it appear that Ashling himself was heading that way, and hope they would send Gordon in pursuit. In fact, if a suitable trail of clues could be set up, it might be possible to lead Gordon all the way to Andre Ulkanov's laboratory at Copernicus, on Luna, which was where Ashling wanted to go. And Andre would be the ideal person to reactivate Ashling when Gordon obligingly got him there.

But that side of things could wait until Ashling knew whether the copying of himself into Gordon had been successful or not.

He made a final check over the machine settings and couplings to the probes around Gordon's head, and entered the code to commence the process. Then he sank down in a chair in the next room to wait. Now that the need for concentrated effort was over, he could feel himself fading rapidly. He grew weaker, his arms dropped over the sides of the chair, and he lost consciousness.

forty-seven

Ashling opened his eyes and found himself looking up at a ceiling past parts of machine and loops of cable. The only sound was the subdued humming of motors and cooling fans, punctuated by the intermittent beeps of check routines timing out. His head was restrained by pads, and he could feel probes positioned around his skull. He blinked, hardly daring to believe it. Was this real? Had the machine really done its task?

He moved his hands up to his head and, working by touch, carefully removed the probes and slackened off the restraining pads. Then he sat up cautiously. Yes, this was the machine chamber at Pearse. He felt strong, young, and vigorous—sensations that he hadn't known for years. On looking down, he saw that he was wearing Gordon's clothes. But to his surprise, there seemed nothing unusual about his arms and hands. Evidently there was an effect that he hadn't thought through sufficiently. But there could be no doubt that what now constituted him was functioning in a different body. His watch showed it to be a little after five, not yet dawn.

He braced himself, and then went through into the adjoining room. But curiously he experienced little of the emotions that he had expected. The figure slumped over in the chair was a stranger. Oh, yes, it possessed all the attributes that Ashling could recite in a purely intellectual fashion as having pertained to himself: white hair, hawkish nose and chin, tired features, but the details were all as he might have remembered of an acquaintance. He felt no sense of identity with the person he was looking at, no intuitive recognition of *self*. He turned and found a glazed panel on the front of one of the instrumentation racks, which in the prevailing light returned a reasonable reflection of himself. Young, olive-skinned face, wavy black hair, large, dark eyes, and full mouth. Again, he *knew* from his memories that he should be seeing the face of an old man, but the face peering back at him *looked* familiar. He shook his head, unable to explain it. Then he turned away and moved closer to the form that had been him, in the chair. It was dead and already cold. There could be no going back now.

In his intended defection, he had planned to take with him information on the most important aspects of his work. It was all in his briefcase, written onto a thin package containing an ultra-high-density holographic storage film that he had concealed behind the lining in the lid. The papers that the briefcase carried ostensibly were innocuous. To supplement the film, he now wrote the procedures he'd discovered in Nordens's files onto a second holofilm, and sealed it into a sandwich between two inch-square pieces of card. That would be his present to Ulkanov. Then he reset the equipment to its quiescent condition and cleared away all traces of his activity. That done, he lifted the Ashling body from the chair—a much easier task than before, now that he had Gordon's musculature to work with—and took it back through the connecting corridor into the apartment. He retrieved the holofilm of his own work, and put both of them in his pocket, to be prepared for Gordon to carry with him, later.

While tidying up the apartment, he thought over the next step: getting out. He didn't want to use Gordon's car if he could avoid it—the smashed windshield would be bound to attract attention. He wondered about the pickup truck. It was parked at the end of the path leading up to the apartment, and there seemed to be no other doors nearby. Maybe Gordon had been using it for some reason. If so, he should have the keys. Taking both sets with him, Ashling went back outside and tried them. Sure enough, he found a key that did the trick. He got out of the cab and checked the toolbox in the rear. It contained tools for just about every eventuality imaginable, including a shovel. The first streaks of daylight were showing. He would have to move fast.

He carried the body out, put it in the back, covering it with a tarp, and he went back inside for the two briefcases. On checking the clothes he was wearing he found a magnetic passcard to a room in

the Hyatt, along with a card reminding that the door number was
1406. His jacket pocket contained a wallet with ID and contents
carrying the name Maurice J. Gordon. So, everything seemed fine.
Gordon would wake up tomorrow back in his own room, but with
a gap in his memory from the time he'd been with Ashling in suite
7319. He could place his own interpretation on that.

Ashling took one final look around the apartment and closed the
door. He backed out and drove at a leisurely speed to the Annex
gate. The guards there evidently knew him and waved him through.
Minutes later he was back on the highway, heading south, with the
tip of the sun's disk just breaking over the hills to the east.

When he was about ten miles from Pearse, he turned off into a
narrow lane leading up off the main road and disappearing among
trees. He followed it and came to a deserted spot, hidden in a dell.
There, amid the undergrowth, he dug a grave and placed his former
body in it, along with his briefcase, which he would no longer need.
Before covering the body over, he removed the container of Panacyn
medication and a few other personal effects that might prove useful
for constructing the kind of trail of clues that he had in mind.

He completed the task and stared at the spot for a while with
mixed feelings. Then he replaced the shovel in the toolbox and drove
back down the trail. At the highway he stopped and looked around,
noting the landmarks to the place, wondering if he would ever
return here. There was no obvious reason why he should. He drove
back onto the highway and headed south once more, back toward
Atlanta.

He arrived at the Hyatt less than two hours later and went
straight up to room 1406. There was a leather traveling case of
Gordon's there, and some clothes in the closet. The first thing to take
care of was the three unconscious members of Pipeline who were
still in suite 7319. At least, he assumed they were still there—Josef
had said that he and Kay wouldn't be back until later today. He
called the number and let it ring for a while. Nobody answered. He
called the hotel switchboard on an outside line, but was told there
was nobody there. If anything irregular had been discovered concerning that room, he reasoned, the operator would surely have
shown more interest in him. Therefore it was as Gordon and he had
left it.

His first thought had been to call Josef on the emergency number, relate the whole story, and recruit their cooperation in getting him, as Gordon, across to the FER. But as he thought more, he decided that wasn't the way to go about it. When he awoke as Gordon tomorrow morning, he would know nothing about the events of today. Any contact or action by Pipeline that hinted of cooperation would be the surest giveaway that something was wrong. If he was going to believe himself, totally, to be Gordon, then so should everyone else who might get involved; then they would all play their roles faithfully.

Better, then, if only Ulkanov knew. With the advantage of unrestricted communications to the FER, Ulkanov would be in a far better position to coordinate everything, even from Copernicus. And Ashling already knew that Pipeline had its own ways of getting messages up to Luna.

He didn't want to talk to Josef, since that would have invited too many awkward questions. Besides, with Gordon's body his voice would have changed. He therefore composed a text message and sent it via the room terminal to Josef at Pipeline's number. It began:

Unforeseen developments have resulted in drastic change of situation. Regret am unable to proceed with plan. Imperative you clear your suite at Hyatt immediately. Also convey following to Ulkanov. Will explain all when opportunity permits. Grateful for your efforts. Ashling.

The message that he appended was encrypted in a code of scientific jargon that scientists inside the Consolidation had developed among themselves to flout official restrictions and censorship, and had been using to circulate information around their own professional network for some years. Basically it outlined Ashling's scheme for luring Gordon to Luna and indicated the kind of help that he needed, though leaving Ulkanov plenty of latitude in implementing the details. It also advised that the physical clues listed—Ashling's Panacyn container, a matchbook from the Hyatt, and a few other things that he thought Ulkanov might be able to use—would be forwarded to a scientist in Volgograd, whom Ashling and Ulkanov both knew. All further references to Ashling, the message stipulated, were to be coded as "Headman." Satisfyingly amusing, Ashling thought to himself.

He obtained some packaging and wrapping material from the bell captain, made a parcel of the Panacyn container and other items, and handed them over to the front desk to be mailed to the scientist in Volgograd. On the required customs form he described the contents as "personal mementos," which was accurate enough if it was checked, and sufficiently innocuous. Then he returned to his room to take care of the rest.

The next part was to launch Gordon on the course that would lead him to Ulkanov. However, to allow Ulkanov enough time to get the communication through Josef and lay his own plans in turn, Gordon shouldn't be dispatched too soon. Ashling should be made to "disappear" from Atlanta and the U.S. as soon as possible, however. That meant that Ashling should leave soon but travel slowly. The obvious way of achieving that would be to have him go by sea.

Ashling used the room terminal to access published tables of shipping routes and schedules, and after some studying found a connection from Jacksonville to Hamburg that suited his purpose. In case there were problems with the later clues that he hoped Ulkanov would arrange, it would be preferable if, right up front, this initial pointer also included a hint of Ashling's final destination. Accordingly, he took the hotel memo pad supplied for the use of guests and wrote on the top page: *Headman to ship out via J'ville, sometime Nov 19. Check ref "Cop 3."* Gordon would find that waiting for him when he awoke the following morning.

Now, Ashling was a scientist, not an intelligence agent. He didn't know if Gordon would communicate such information back openly to Nordens. Somehow he doubted it. So he called Nordens's number at Pearse and left a message on the machine there, saying only: "The bird has slipped its cage and is planning to migrate. Have details of route and destination. Will advise tomorrow." Gordon and Nordens could then figure out what it meant when they compared notes, and would deduce that Gordon had discovered Pipeline's plans somehow during the period in which he was blacked out following a presumed attack by somebody unknown, but nevertheless had enough presence of mind left to record the information.

Lastly, he bought a pack of razor blades and adhesive from the shop in the lobby, and back in his room carefully opened a seam in the lining of Gordon's briefcase, into which he inserted the two holofilms that he had brought from Pearse. He resealed the seam and satisfied himself that the join was practically invisible. That would be another item that Gordon wouldn't know he'd be carrying.

By the time he had completed his preparations, it was afternoon. He went out of the hotel to walk in the fresh air, then returned for an early dinner. Afterward, he went back to his room, feeling tired. He looked around the room, took a long look at himself in the mirror, then showered and retired to bed. If this fantastic scheme went as planned, a lot of things would have happened and he'd have traveled a long way from Atlanta by the time he was next aware of anything. The words echoed through his mind again as he lay back on the bed. *If it went as planned* . . . But nothing was certain. It had all been done under too much stress. There hadn't been enough time.

He closed his eyes, and slept . . .

. . . and woke up in a cot in a bright, clinical-looking room that could have been in a hospital. He lay for a while, letting his senses reintegrate themselves, and wondering. Could it really be possible?

Out of curiosity, he extricated an arm from the sheets and stretched it out. It felt extraordinarily light.

By the cot was a cart with a pitcher of water on top. He picked the pitcher up and weighed it experimentally in his hand. It too seemed very light. About a sixth of what it ought to have weighed, in fact. He still found it hard to believe, but already an expression of wonder was spreading across his face.

And then a figure who had been watching from the doorway came forward, smiling. He was big in stature, with gray hair, clear, striking features, and rebellious eyebrows. Ashling's face creased with exuberance as he recognized him. "I'm here?" Ashling murmured. "This . . . it's really Luna?"

"Correct," Professor Andre Ulkanov told him. "Yes, my old friend, you are on Luna. Welcome to Copernicus."

Slowly, the message sank in. In spite of it all, somehow he had succeeded. Ashling closed his eyes again, smiling. His mind let go, and he drifted away again, into sleep.

forty-eight

"That was how Conrad Ashling hid himself, and how he contrived to get himself here," Ulkanov concluded. "Small wonder, then, that this 'Samurai,' as Maurice Gordon was officially designated, could never catch him. Samurai *was* him!"

The professor was speaking mainly for the benefit of Jason, Gunther, and the two girls—all students of his—who had helped spring the trap when Samurai got to the institute. Kay and Scipio, who were sitting on one side of the center table in the small conference room adjoining Ulkanov's office, had given Ulkanov a full account of the events in Minneapolis and Chicago while they were waiting for Ashling to come round. Ashling, in his coded message to Ulkanov from Atlanta, had urged against divulging the secret about Gordon to them—in order that they would play their roles faithfully. Ulkanov, however, knew them better and had considered this overcautious. Needing all the help he could get, he had waited until they were in Europe and then filled them in on as much as they needed to know to take part in laying the trail that led Gordon to Semipalatinsk, and to act as bait for him to follow to the institute after he reached Copernicus.

Ashling, recovered enough by now to have joined them, smiled thinly over a mug of strong black coffee—not coylene. "But from the things I'm hearing now, it doesn't seem to have all gone as simply as I planned," he said. "I've been leading you people on quite a dance."

"You . . . could say that," Barbara, Ulkanov's assistant, agreed from one of the chairs opposite.

Ulkanov looked at Ashling. "Do you want me to go on with

what I think? After all, it was you who set the whole thing up, Conrad. It's your show."

"You'd better," Ashling replied. "Just at this moment, I think you know a lot more about it than I do."

"Very well." Ulkanov nodded and sat back for a moment to send a look around the room, taking in the whole company. "Conrad's intention, of course, was that after he sent the parcel from the Hyatt and got the message off to me through Josef, the Ashling personality would deactivate overnight, and he would wake up the next morning, thinking and functioning as Samurai, but with his memory erased from the time he was in Pipeline's room two nights before."

Ashling interjected, "I knew that Gordon would have a gap in his recollections of what had taken place. There was no way to get around that. But I figured he'd assume that he'd been jumped by somebody in Pipeline's room that he hadn't seen, or something like that." He tossed up a hand briefly. "However, he'd find the note about Headman, Jacksonville, and Copernicus, and when he combined that information with the message I'd left for Nordens, they'd conclude that during the blank period, Samurai had established that Ashling was heading for Europe by sea."

"Hoping they'd send Samurai after him," one of the two girls said.

"Right." Ashling nodded. "The sea crossing would take ten days, and by that time I hoped the parcel would have gotten to Volgograd, and Andre would be able to set up more clues to draw Gordon on from there." Ashling looked at Ulkanov wryly. "But I, ah, gather it wasn't quite that easy."

Ulkanov sighed. "There was a lot that you had never tried before. You were working under stress and in haste. . . . I don't think Nordens knew all the answers quite as well as you give him credit for, either." He glanced around the table again, and resumed, "After they tried to cover their tracks by faking the record of Demiro's death, Nordens and whoever else was in it with him were left with Demiro, overdosed with codes derived from Richard Jarrow."

"Overdosed? He thought he *was* Jarrow!" Scipio said.

"Jarrow was this Minneapolis schoolteacher that they got the source codes from to reprogram Demiro, right?" Ashling checked. Ulkanov nodded.

Kay frowned and extended a finger to halt things there for a moment. Ulkanov raised his eyebrows at her inquiringly.

"Yes, I reached the same conclusion when we were back in Chicago, but there's something that isn't clear to me," Kay said. "If that happened, it means that the Jarrow personality was reactivated sometime in that interval period at Pearse, between Jarrow's death and the creation of Samurai. And yet Jarrow had no recollection of such an event. He was quite adamant that his last memory before waking up in Atlanta was of his final visit to Valdheim." She looked unconsciously to Ashling for confirmation as she spoke, but Ashling could only shrug in a way that said that had been somebody else; it was all just as much a mystery to him too, now. Kay looked back at Ulkanov.

The professor showed his hands and sighed heavily. "Who can say? At this stage we have no idea what, exactly, took place during that period at Pearse. One possibility is that Jarrow's condition was too confused for him to have registered any coherent recollections. Alternatively, Nordens might have erased that reawakening in the mistaken belief that he was erasing the complete Jarrow personality that shouldn't have been there in the first place—as a prelude to the creation of Samurai." Ulkanov shook his head and spread his hands open again. "Whatever the true story, by the time he began building Samurai, Nordens would have believed that the scrambled Demiro-Jarrow personality had been obliterated. But that wasn't what happened. Instead of being substituted in place of the Demiro-Jarrow entity, the Samurai persona was *superposed on top of* it."

"You mean the time-out code that was supposed to deactivate Ashling went too deep," Barbara said.

"Exactly!" Ulkanov said, thumping the tabletop with a palm. "It not only deactivated Conrad, but Samurai as well, and then the Jarrow level that lay below that. So the person who woke up the next morning to find himself in an Atlanta hotel was Tony Demiro—completely bewildered, not knowing what he was doing there.

"What was he to do?" Ulkanov looked around, then answered his own question. "He called the person who was closest to him and the first who would naturally come to mind: the girl he intended to get married to one day, Rita Chilsen. That was on the Monday. Rita got there the same day." Ulkanov looked at Kay. This was the part that she and Scipio had supplied.

"They talked and puzzled over it, but of course they couldn't figure it out," Kay said. "Tony's last recollections were from when he was still with the program at Pearse. That had been something like five months before. He'd gotten fitter physically, and a lot tougher—that was from Samurai's training, but they weren't to know that. Everything was a complete mystery. But they were lovers, together again. She stayed that night."

"Demiro slept," Ulkanov said. "But the deactivation code set up by Conrad, which was triggered by a condition of natural sleep, remember, hadn't switched off as it was supposed to. During that night it suspended Demiro, and the self who woke up on Tuesday morning was the transferred personality of Richard Jarrow that had been in a dormant condition all the time. His last memory was from April third, which was the last time he visited Valdheim before dying unexpectedly from a stroke early in May."

Jason's face knotted into a frown as he thought this over for a second or two. Then he turned to his colleague, Gunther. "So why wouldn't the next period of sleep deactivate Jarrow and restore Samurai again?" he asked. Gunther could only shake his head helplessly.

"A good question," Barbara agreed. Everyone looked at Ashling.

Ashling eased himself back in his chair and returned a tired smile. "I don't know why not," he told them. "To be honest, I'm astounded that it worked the way it was supposed to at all. You have no idea of the pressure and the haste I had to work under when I set it up that last night at Pearse. It depended on a complex coding procedure that I had not devised and wasn't familiar with . . . added to a tangle of convolutions pertaining to different personalities that were already jumbled. Probably no one will ever be able to know exactly what took place."

"But whatever the reason, Jarrow he remained," Ulkanov went on, getting back to the point. He looked at Scipio. "And that was when we lost him, wasn't it?"

Scipio replied, "Josef had been away since the previous evening. He got a message from Ashling the next morning, telling him to clear out of the room in the Hyatt. But it didn't say where Ashling was. When Josef went there with a couple of the others, they found Leon and the other two out cold and Ashling gone."

"So they had no leads at all," Barbara said.

"None."

"So how did they pick it up again?"

"That was the amazing thing," Scipio said. "After what happened Saturday night, Josef just got everyone out and laid low all the next day. On Monday he went back with Leon to settle with the hotel. And lo and behold, Leon spotted the agent who had gone in after Ashling on Saturday!"

"He was still there, in the hotel?" Barbara said, sounding mystified for a moment. Then she looked at Ashling. "But wait a minute. That's right. You were Demiro by then, weren't you."

"But registered as Maurice Gordon," Kay said. Ashling just shook his head hopelessly and said nothing.

Scipio resumed, speaking to Ashling. "Josef notified me, and we kept an eye on you. But the next morning you suddenly vanished. We didn't know it at the time, but you'd gone back to Minneapolis, now as Jarrow. All we had left to go on was Rita. We followed her back to Chicago, and then discovered that Gordon was none other than her former fiancé, who was supposed to be dead! What did that mean? Nobody had a clue. So we did the only thing we could and kept a watch on her place in the hope that you'd show up there."

"And so did the feds," Kay interjected.

"Anyway," Scipio went on, "we traced you after you and Rita got away from them, and to cut a long story short, eventually you agreed to go back to Pearse, essentially to help us find out what the hell had been going on there."

Ashling looked uncertain. "I did? . . . You mean Jarrow did? I'm surprised that he would. I mean, from what I've been told, he sounded like a dedicated servant of the system. I'd have thought he'd be more against you than for you."

Scipio snorted. "Oh, he didn't mean it. It was just to get himself away. I'll bet that the first thing he did as soon as he was back inside Pearse was to spill all the beans. But we gambled that maybe what he found out there would change his mind. What else could we do?"

"And Rita was pushing him to go back too," Kay said. "For her he was Demiro literally back from the dead, but with delusions of being someone else. She hoped that something might happen there that would bring Demiro back again."

Ashling looked at them in turn, nodding intently as he strove to keep track of it all.

Ulkanov took over again at that point. "And that was when the most extraordinary part of all happened," he said. "You see, Conrad, by then your plan was totally screwed up. Samurai hadn't been reactivated. The information that was supposed to send him after Ashling had got lost. And the situation of Demiro thinking he was Jarrow had happened all over again, only now he was loose with the FSS chasing him." Ulkanov spread his hands and pulled a face.

"A mess," Ashling agreed. He looked around at the other faces and shrugged in a way that said well, he'd done his best.

Ulkanov went on, "But we can only assume that when you went back to Pearse, Nordens put everything back on track for us by reactivating Samurai. And once Samurai was functioning again, he picked up the trail as you'd intended in the first place. The irony was that it was *Nordens himself* who saved it."

Ashling shuffled in his chair and leaned forward to rest his elbows on the table. "Fine, okay. Now this is where it gets interesting. I don't remember anything after Sunday, which was the day I set everything up. I left a message for Nordens and wrote a note that Samurai was supposed to find the next morning. Between them they should have figured that I was sailing from Jacksonville to Hamburg on a German ship called the *Auriga*. It sounds as if that worked out in the end somehow, in spite of all the problems in Atlanta."

"So it would appear," Ulkanov agreed. "Exactly what happened at Pearse, we have no way of knowing. But I had gotten your coded message and so knew about the *Auriga*."

"What did you do?" Ashling asked. "How did you get me the rest of the way here?"

"Well, whatever did happen at Pearse, they rushed Samurai over to Hamburg in time to be there with the local police when the *Auriga* docked. Of course, no Ashling came off it. But it so happens that there's a certain brothel in Hamburg where one of the girls does a sideline as a police informer. Pipeline has known about it for a long time."

"Oh, God, I didn't go there, did I?" Ashling groaned.

"No, but a friend of ours called Nicolaus did. He'd had a lot to drink, talked too much, and mentioned that he was in town to meet an important scientist who was coming in secretly from the USA. He also let it slip that he was staying at a particular hotel-pub, not far away."

"Good enough," Ashling agreed. "What happened then?"

"That got back via the police, as it was supposed to. We even paid somebody who looked a bit like Ashling to put in a quick appearance there with Nicolaus. But when Samurai and the police arrived, it was too late, naturally. They should have found one of your medication containers there, though."

"So that parcel that I sent got through to Volgograd in time?"

"Yes. It made things a lot easier."

Ashling gave a satisfied nod. "Next?"

"Well, in case Samurai missed some of the other things we'd planned for later, I thought we should give an indication of your final destination right then. It turned out to be as well that I did."

"Good thinking," Ashling agreed. "How did you do it?"

"A telephone call from Volgograd, which we hoped would be picked up by the Consolidation spy satellites. It gave a rendezvous that you were supposed to make with a courier in Berlin the next day, and also your launch date from Semipalatinsk."

"And Samurai showed up in Berlin," Ashling guessed.

"Correct—which told us that the call had been intercepted. If it hadn't, we had alternative plans in hand."

"I assume that he missed me again in Berlin," Ashling said.

"Yes. However, a cooperative restaurant manager and a bribed taxi driver provided some snippets that got you to the border. You were to cross over into Bohemia at Zittau. There's a certain pair there—a border police captain and a Pole who gets people across for a fee—whom Pipeline have suspected for some time of working a double-dealing act. We set it up to look as if Ashling had gone across, and we assumed that the German authorities would let Samurai through officially. But that was when trouble hit."

"How?" Ashling asked.

"Somebody back in the States must have gotten wind of what was going on and alerted Berlin. German federal agents appeared in Zittau to take Samurai in." Ulkanov smiled impishly. "You were quite a star, Conrad. You demolished them with ease, from the account I heard. Then you went across after him on your own. You weren't in FER territory yet, and we were worried that the authorities would be looking for you. One of Pipeline's people in that area, an American woman called Roxy, spent half the night touring the hotels and guest houses on the other side of the border to find you. She drove you to Prague and got you on an unofficial flight into Transylvania, from where you'd be able to join the regular FER routes. That was when I was glad we'd fed you the final destination. We heard nothing more of you until you appeared in disguise in Semipalatinsk the night before Ashling was due to launch off. We'd been getting quite anxious."

"We were in Semipalatinsk by then, booked on the same flight, with another Pipeline guy," Kay said, indicating herself and Scipio. "We booked a room in one of the big hotels there under the name that Ashling was supposed to be using. Knowing Samurai's abilities by that time, we figured that if he'd made it to Semipalatinsk, he'd track us down. And sure enough you did. But Ashling had flown again. You found confirmation that he'd been there, though. And, purely coincidentally of course, the exact place that he was coming to, here at Copernicus."

"Okay, very good," Ashling conceded. "So here I am. And now that I am here, let me show you something else that Samurai didn't know he was bringing." He lifted Samurai's briefcase onto the table and opened it. "Does anyone have a razor blade or a sharp knife?" he asked, looking around.

Ulkanov felt through his pockets but shook his head.

"I'll get one," Gunther said. He rose and left the room.

Ashling started to say something more, then stopped, looking puzzled suddenly as a new thought struck him. "But if I was disguised, how did you know me when I got here?" he asked Ulkanov.

Ulkanov grinned. "Do you still have a piece of paper that you found in the Kosmogord hotel in Semipalatinsk?"

Ashling frowned and searched through his pockets. "This?" He produced a crumpled scrap and unfolded it. It read: *Dr. Andre Ulkanov, Neurophysiology Dept., Science Institute at Copernicus 3,* followed by a phone number with a lunar access code.

"Have you got the counter, Jason?" Ulkanov asked, looking toward the far end of the table. Jason produced a small silver box with an extending probe piece, and Kay passed it across. Ulkanov thumbed a switch on the side and directed the probe at the piece of paper in Ashling's hand. The box began emitting rapid beeps.

"Impregnated with a radioactive tracer," Ulkanov said, looking back at Ashling. "We picked you up the moment you walked in the door."

forty-nine

Professor Ulkanov sat at a console in one of the rooms across the corridor from the main laboratory area, contemplating the image on the large screen in front of him. It showed in symbolic form the dynamic relationships within an associative set of schematized neural constructs. Several auxiliary screens to one side presented command summaries and algorithmic syntaxes of the specially developed group-manipulation calculus that Ashling had brought from Earth, including the extensions that Nordens had added to it.

Even after more than a week of devoting himself to absorbing these new representations and techniques with a born-again fervor that had wrought havoc with his schedule of other commitments and appointments, reducing his secretary to the verge of distraction from having to dream up excuses for him, he was still only discovering the full power of this. Ashling had taken a big chance when he buried himself underneath Samurai's persona and trusted to Ulkanov to reactivate him after he got to Luna. For a start the equipment here, though adequate, still left a lot to be desired compared to what Ashling had enjoyed at Pearse—there were some immediate modifications that he could use, Ulkanov could see. But more to the point, some of the procedures that Ashling stipulated in his encrypted communication via Pipeline were completely different from anything that Ulkanov had employed before, and at the time had meant nothing. Fortunately, however, being always the meticulous professional, Ashling had given very precise instructions.

Ulkanov could *see*, captured within the equations, the changes

taking place when new sensory information, processed and corre-
lated in different parts of the brain, merged with and modified the
conceptual structures to which it related. By entering a line of
command code he could create the new associative net connecting all
the modifications effected by that same data input as a higher-level
mapping. One level higher still, and he could tag entire blocks of
experience as variables that could be combined into symbolic
functions and processed analytically. He could build a mind on the
computer screen.

"Global," he murmured aloud.

"Z mode?" the system vocalized from a grille below the auxiliary screens.

"Five five."

"Function required?"

"Correlation nexuses with sigma above point three for the last
five runs. Overlay at new level, sub VT."

"Section scan running. . . . Integrated and complete. . . . Cross-
links complete. Index mods complete. Functions available."

"Transform AG through BT to mode five. Combine, and reintegrate with all delta. Show result in green three as level-four
conformal."

"Processing."

"And put a message through to Gunther to send in some coffee."

"Done."

Ulkanov was impressed.

Yet at the same time, his face was troubled. He shifted his gaze
to another screen, showing the "hardware" activation dynamics as a
superposition of neural arbors, each depicted in its own color as a
network of branching pathways in a skein of multiply connected,
interwoven filaments. What, only two days ago, had been uniformly
dense, intricately extended networks were separating into island
groupings. Entire highways of associative cross-linkings, rich in
interconnections essential to preserving coherence and functional
integrity, were disappearing. The mind that he was looking into was
beginning to come apart.

There was a perfunctory knock on the door, and Kay came in,
looking her old self again. A week of rest after her spell on Earth and
the journey back, with four days at Tycho with her husband and
children, had made a big difference.

"Still at it, I see," Kay said. "Barbara did warn me. She thinks they're going to have to hire somebody else to run the department."

Ulkanov grunted. "You have to see more of this, Kay," he replied. "Then you'll understand. God only knows what we'd have been doing by now if Conrad had been here years ago."

Kay closed the door and came over to lean on the console while she contemplated the screen. "What is it that makes people like Nordens get twisted?" she sighed. "I've never understood this obsession with having to direct other people's lives."

Ulkanov leaned back in the chair, stretched, and yawned wearily. "I don't know, Kay. Some people are just like that, I suppose, and others are not. They'll never understand each other. . . . Anyway, did you have a good time back at Tycho? You look much the better for it."

"Wonderful."

"The family are all well, I trust?"

"Fine. Joao's going out for six months on a spaceborne experimental plant that Skypower's building. Max will be staying on at college, but the girls are coming here to Copernicus, so I'll be able to see more of them, which will be nice."

"Very good. . . . Skypower. That's the antimatter recombination thing they've been talking about, isn't it?"

"Right. They say that within twenty years they'll be sending primary power around the Solar System as gamma-ray beams."

"Hmmm." Ulkanov thought for a moment. "Which is the one who wants to follow you into AI? It was one of the girls, wasn't it?"

"Yes, Maria. The twelve-year-old."

"I suppose we'll be seeing quite a lot of her, then," Ulkanov said. "No doubt you'll be dreaming up all kinds of reasons for bringing her along here."

Kay smiled. "You do read minds. Would it be okay?"

"Oh, certainly. I'm surprised you ask. This place seems to be alive with children most of the time, anyway. Half of them belong to the students."

"I just don't like being presumptuous about things."

Ulkanov turned in his chair. "My mind-reading powers also tell me that you didn't come here to talk about things like that."

As if she had been waiting for a cue, Kay's expression at once became more serious. "No," she said. "I didn't. I wanted to talk about Ashling."

Ulkanov's face remained neutral. "What about him?"

Kay straightened up from the console and moved to the other side of the room, where she stood facing the other way for a few seconds. Clearly, whatever she had to say wasn't something that came easily. Ulkanov waited. Finally she turned.

"When I was down on Earth, the time that we were with Scipio and the others in the house near Chicago, when he was still Richard Jarrow . . . I got to talking quite a lot with Rita."

"Yes?"

This wasn't coming out the way Kay had intended. She tried changing to a different tack. "Look, Jarrow lived out his life and died naturally. The whole business about him reactivating again in Demiro was a freak accident. And Samurai was an artificial creation from the beginning. He was never what you'd call a . . . a real person."

"Go on."

Kay spread her hands for a moment, hesitating. "But that still leaves two others. There's Ashling; and there's Tony Demiro, who still exists and is alive inside somewhere, underneath all the mess that's been going on. And physically, the person walking around up here *is* Demiro. You see what I'm saying, Andre. . . . I guess I'm still seeing the look in Rita's eyes, hearing the way she talked. They had their lives, their hopes—hopes to come to Luna one day, and start their own family, without all the restrictions down there. Going home to Tycho brought it home to me. I looked at my kids, and I couldn't help thinking about those other kids who should have had the chance to exist, but didn't have. See what I mean? It just doesn't feel . . . right."

Ulkanov stared at her, but whatever he was thinking remained unfathomable. "What do you want me to do?"

Kay closed her eyes and sighed. She moved over to a stool by the hard-copy unit and propped herself against it. "I don't know, Andre. Maybe I just needed somebody to dump it on. . . ."

Ulkanov waited, guessing that she couldn't leave it at that.

And he was right. She bit her lip for a moment and went on, "Ashling's purpose when he copied himself into Samurai was to prevent his knowledge and his work from being lost—and he's accomplished that now. It wasn't to extend his life. His life was over. He died that night." Kay took a long breath, and then finally got it off her chest. "He didn't do it to buy himself a new lease on life at the expense of a young soldier who was just an innocent victim of the situation, and who had his own life ahead. That's what I'm trying to say. That's what isn't right."

There was a silence. At last, Ulkanov nodded. "I know what you are saying, of course. And I understand how you feel. But again, what would you have me—" A tone sounded from the viewphone on a shelf beside the console. "Excuse me." He touched the accept pad. It was Barbara. "Yes?"

Barbara was uncharacteristically brusque. "Professor, there's some kind of problem with Conrad. We're in the machine section. Do you think you could come here, please?"

"At once." Ulkanov cut the connection and tilted his head at Kay as he rose. There was a strange, distant look on his face. "You'd better come too," he told her.

Ashling was sitting on the edge of the vinyl-padded couch in the workroom next to the machine installation. Barbara was standing by him, looking concerned. The nurse from the department's medical dispensary, whom Barbara had also called as a precaution, hovered a short distance behind.

Ashling frowned at Ulkanov when he entered, as if he were having difficulty recognizing him. Suddenly his face broke into a smile of self-congratulations. "Ah yes, the professor. Hi."

Ulkanov nodded an acknowledgment. "What's happened?" he asked Barbara.

"He started acting strange while we were going over the machine. He didn't seem to know who he was for a while. It seems to have cleared a little now, though." She brushed a curl of hair from her eyes. "It had me really worried. Maybe it's delayed stress from everything that went on down there, or something. I hope I didn't interrupt anything important."

"No. You did absolutely the right thing." Ulkanov turned to the nurse. "How does he seem to you?"

"He's perspiring, and his pulse is fast. There's nothing obvious to worry about that I can see. But he should have a full check."

"Of course." Ulkanov looked at Ashling. "How do you feel now?"

"I feel . . . You're the professor, right?"

"Yes, I am the professor. I'm told that you weren't sure who you are? Do you know now?"

"I . . ."

"He's doing it again," Barbara muttered.

"Ashling, Conrad Ashling," Ashling pronounced. He thrust his chin out challengingly. "You thought I didn't know, didn't you?"

"Where are you from, Conrad?" Ulkanov asked.

"From? . . ." Ashling seemed about to answer, but then sat back and looked puzzled. "From different places. Different places, all at once. I don't understand it."

"Tell us about the places," Ulkanov said. Kay looked at him oddly. It was almost as if he had known what to expect.

Ashling's expression was distant. "One had lakes and a river. There was a city there, by the river. . . ." His face cleared, and he focused on Ulkanov suddenly, as if a different person were speaking. "I used to kill people. I liked killing people. They wouldn't let me be like them. . . . Next I'm going to kill Larry. He wouldn't believe who I was. And Shafer, Nimmo, that Lauer bitch, all of them. None of them believed me. . . . But not Vera." He looked confused again and peered around. "Why isn't Vera here?"

The nurse looked to Ulkanov with a worried expression. "He needs to rest," Ulkanov murmured gravely. "We'll take him to the dispensary. Do you have something you can give him?" The nurse nodded. Ulkanov put a hand on Ashling's shoulder. "Come on, old friend," he said gently. "There's a warm bed waiting for you downstairs. You've had a hard time. You need to sleep."

"You know," Kay said to Ulkanov as they left the dispensary and began walking back along the corridor toward the front elevators. "I could tell, watching you. It didn't come as a complete surprise to you, did it? You know what it is."

Ulkanov nodded heavily. "I was looking at it when you came into the computer room just before. What they were doing at Pearse was too rushed, maybe because of the political pressures. I don't know. . . . But the groundwork on basics wasn't covered thoroughly enough. The overlay group linkages have inherent instabilities in them. They're starting to break down. The same thing would have happened to Samurai. Maybe it did."

Kay stared at him as they came to the doors. The car was already there. "Break down? . . . What are you saying, exactly?"

Ulkanov replied without looking at her as they stepped inside. "I think your problem might be solving itself. Think of it as analagous to a tissue rejection with a transplant. In subtle ways that we don't yet comprehend, the mind, like the body, recognizes and protects its own. Maybe one day we'll know how to prevent it. But that time isn't yet."

The door closed. They were halfway down to the main laboratory level by the time Kay had fully digested the meaning of his words. "There's nothing that can be done?" The fervor that she had spoken with earlier was gone, and her voice was suddenly very quiet and sober.

Ulkanov shook his head.

"I'm sorry."

"Don't be. Probably it's better this way."

They came out into a foyer with offices behind glass partitions, and corridors leading off in several directions. Ulkanov seemed to have been weighing something in his mind. "Kay, would you do something for me?" he said.

"What?"

"Get on to the Pipeline people. I'd like them to contact Josef again, if they can."

She nodded. "Sure."

"Let me know what they say. I'll be in the computer room again."

"I'll call you there as soon as I've talked to them." Kay went away in the direction of her own office.

Ulkanov walked slowly back to the room that he had been in earlier and closed the door. He sat down and stared again at the images still showing on the screens. What he had seen before was even clearer now.

The story he had given Kay was true in a way, but oversimplified. Yes, the overlays were unstable, and the linkages were breaking down.

But there was a director function in there, linked to another self-activating time-out sequence, which showed all the marks of having been constructed artificially. What was instigating the break-down process wasn't something that had evolved naturally. Why should it be? Nature had never encountered anything like this, for which a natural defense would be required. It had been *put there* to do the job.

Ashling hadn't wanted to steal Demiro's body, just to borrow it for a while. But he'd known that once he experienced the change, he might feel tempted to change his mind.

And therefore he had arranged things this way.

Demiro
Demiro
Demiro
Demiro
Demiro
Demiro
Demiro
Demiro

fifty

"The whole business makes me sick," Rita declared. "You know, sometimes it's like I'm working for the Mafia or something. They say that the quotas we allocate are figured on the basis of best-interests need as figured by the Economic Coordination Bureau in Washington. But that's bullshit. The corporations get the quotas that they're prepared to pay for. Our people are raking it in all down the line. Everybody knows it. Nothing happens." She popped the cork from another bottle of wine and came back from the kitchen area to refill the glasses.

The door and frame that had been torn off the wall were fixed at last and the police had stopped bothering her with questions, but things were hardly back to anything that could be called normal. Having a fiancé rematerialize from the dead wasn't exactly something that happened every day, and now he'd disappeared the authorities were trying to make out it had never happened. All the people she talked to simply went back as far as the same records that said he was dead, and the line ended right there. Nobody knew, or wanted to know, of anything beyond that. She'd talked to a lawyer, but when it got as far as establishing that she had no money, he'd lost interest. Margaret, her roommate, and the other friends who knew about it were supportive and let her talk as much as she wanted to if it helped. But what could they do?

"I think the Mafia's better," Bruce said from the couch. "Like, on a scale of one to ten for ethics, the Mafia scores higher."

"I know. I've heard it," Sandy said, next to him.

"Tell me then," Margaret invited from the chair by the window.

Bruce nodded to Rita as she topped up his glass. "It's like this. If a guy gambles on horses, or does drugs, or wants to pay for his women, then he knows that a slice of the action goes to the firm, okay? But it's his *choice.* If he decides to have nothing to do with any of that, then they leave him alone. They don't send hit men with guns around to his place telling him he has to pay what they say he owes, and he doesn't get to say anything. . . . But that's not true with the IRS. So I say that on a scale of ethics, the Mafia scores higher."

"True," Margaret agreed, sipping her drink. "Did you hear they're talking about bringing in the same law here that they've got in California, to take it straight out of your bank? I mean, why don't we all just work for the Fed direct in the first place, and be done with it?"

Rita sat down to join them again. "I already do, remember?"

"I thought you were state," Sandy said.

"It's more or less the same thing these days."

"No, I meant make work for them obligatory," Margaret said. "You know, whether you want to or not, at whatever they say. It's getting that bad, isn't it?"

"That's what I meant," Rita told her. "They're saying I'm up for reassignment to Cleveland. What kind of present is that, less than two weeks before Christmas?"

"Do you have to take it?" Sandy asked.

"They've got you so tied up with benefits they can make you do anything they want," Rita replied. "Either cooperate, or don't eat."

"So, does that mean you'll be looking for someone else to share this place?" Bruce asked, looking at Margaret.

"I guess so. Know anybody?"

"Not off the top of my head, but I'll mention it around."

"Thanks. That'd help."

"We'll miss having you around, Rita," Sandy said.

"Yeah. Me too. You'll have to come and visit when I get settled in."

"We'll do that. Do you have a date yet?"

"Not yet. Probably it won't be until the new year now."

A wail went up on the far side of the bedroom door. Sandy glanced at the clock. "There's Wretch, right on time. Excuse me. I'd better go take care of it." She got up and went through.

There was a short silence. Margaret reached for the plate of cheese slices, crackers, and pickles, and passed it around.

"What's on TV?" Bruce asked.

"Garbage," Margaret said. "I don't know why we bother paying the license."

"Then get rid of it," Rita said simply.

"Although there was a movie the other day that wasn't bad," Margaret went on. "Did you see it? What was it called?" She looked at Rita. Rita shrugged. "From way back . . . one of those old romantic things. It was about a woman doctor and a police detective in Africa, when they had the trouble there. But they were on opposite sides, like in Romeo and Juliet."

Bruce shook his head. "Not my kind of stuff."

"Oh, I think it's nice to see people acting parts that actually project qualities you want to admire for a change," Margaret said. "You know, instead of all the—" The front-door buzzer interrupted her.

"I'll get it," Rita said, rising.

Margaret carried on talking behind her, to Bruce, "You know, nothing but morons who can't take charge of their lives, having to be straightened out by counselors and programs all the time. Never any real friends who know anything, or family like people used to have. No wonder everyone's turning into sheep."

Rita opened the door to find a bearded man in a tweed hat and a parka standing there. She frowned, knowing that she knew the face but failing to place it instantly, and then gasped in surprise.

"Hello again, Rita," Josef said quietly.

"You! . . . Is it about . . . ?" She left the question unfinished.

"Can we talk?" Josef said. "Privately?"

Rita looked back over her shoulder uncertainly. "Well, not here. We've got company."

"Outside then. It's something important. I won't keep you long."

Still in a daze, Rita nodded mechanically. "Who is it?" Margaret asked from inside.

"It's somebody for me. Look, could you guys excuse me for a minute? I'm just going out."

"Is everything okay, Rita?" Bruce asked, craning forward to try to see who it was.

"Oh, sure. We just need to talk."

"Bring a coat," Josef suggested. "It's bitter out there."

Rita took her tan raincoat from the hook behind the door and went down with him to the street. The night was starry and clear, with a moon casting pale light on the mounds of frozen snow cleared from the sidewalk, and the houses opposite. They began walking.

"Do you remember when Scipio and Kay were here?" Josef said, speaking in a low voice, his eyes constantly alert. "You used to talk about how you dreamed of going offplanet one day." He stopped for a moment and looked up, then glanced at her with a quick grin. "You wanted to go to Luna."

That was an opening Rita hadn't expected. She turned her head and looked at him bemusedly. "Yes, I did. What about it?"

"How soon could you be ready?" Josef answered. "A message came down through Pipeline yesterday. They want me to get you out."

fifty-one

Tony Demiro paced agitatedly about the floor in the room of the Atlanta Hyatt. Wasn't she ever going to get here? She'd called him from the airport over an hour ago now to say she had arrived. How long was it supposed to take? All day he had stared at the TV, wandered aimlessly around the hotel, sat in the coffee shop and bar. . . . Anything to kill time. This last hour was the longest of all.

His first shock had been waking up that morning with no idea of how he came to be there. And then it had turned out to be mid November! Over five months of his life had simply disappeared, and he'd found himself apparently living the life of a different person. And then, as if that wasn't enough, the reaction when he called Rita. He'd expected her to be astonished after what he presumed had been his disappearance during all that time; but the look of numbed bewilderment when she saw him was something he hadn't been prepared for. And then he'd discovered that he was supposed to be dead!

He looked at himself in the mirror and tried to guess how it would feel if he were insane. But it was no good; he had no way of telling. Perhaps if you could tell, that was how you knew that you weren't. He looked again in the closet at the clothes that weren't his and around the room at the things that weren't his. No shred of recollection or association came with any of them. Nothing made sense.

The call tone came from the room's viewphone. He crossed the floor in a couple of swift strides and answered it.

"Mr. Gordon?"

He almost said no, wrong room, then remembered that was the name in the ID he was carrying. "Yes."

"Front desk, Mr. Gordon. There's a person down here asking for you, a Ms. Rita Chilsen. She says you're expecting her."

"Great. Yes, that's fine."

"I'll send her on up."

Demiro cleared the call, straightened up, and felt butterflies in the stomach. Was it because of the weirdness of the situation? Sudden doubts at the imminence of seeing Rita again? Uncertainty about how they would react? All of them? He paced over to the table and chairs by the window and looked out at the evening creeping across the high-rises of the city, rubbing his palms together, forcing himself to stay calm. Then he went across to the door, opened it, and stood waiting.

She appeared coming along the corridor from the direction of the elevators less than a minute later, wearing a green coat with an orange dress and carrying a shoulder bag. Her pace quickened when she saw him, but as she got to the door she slowed hesitantly. For a moment they stood and stared, trying to read each other's faces: she as if needing to be sure that it was he; he not knowing quite what to expect.

"Tony!"

And then, they both responded simultaneously. She threw her arms around him and he pulled her to him, and they moved back into the room, holding, hugging, and locked in a kiss that continued long after he nudged the door closed. There was the mystery of what had happened to him, the riddle of his death, questions, queries, a thousand things that needed to be talked about. . . . But the taste of her mouth and the aroma of her body, the pressure of her breasts and thighs against him, were already reawakening more powerful impulses that swept such thoughts aside. As they remained locked together, he drew her coat off her shoulders and began unfastening the hooks at the back of her dress. Keeping her mouth pressed to his as he guided her to the bed, she drew him down on top of her as he struggled to remove their remaining clothes.

"Promise you won't go away again," she whispered.

"Never," he said.

They lay naked between the damp sheets. Rita lit a cigarette and offered him one. He shook his head. She put the pack and lighter back on the bedside unit, lay against him, and exhaled long and slowly. After a few seconds she turned and touched a finger lightly to the puncture and mild swelling below his ear.

"What happened here, to your neck?"

"I don't know. It was there when I woke up this morning, just like all the rest."

"Is it sore?"

"A little. It feels like one of those small boils you sometimes get."

"It needs a Band-Aid. Stop it rubbing on your collar."

"The shop in the lobby should have some."

"You've got a bruise on the side of your head too," Rita said. "No idea how that happened?"

He shook his head, then got up from the bed, pulled on his pants, and went over to the bureau-vanity running along one wall. She watched curiously as he came back with a black briefcase. "Look inside here," he said, showing her. "Guns. That's a 9mm H&K automatic: professional killer's weapon. The other one's a special-purpose, gas-powered lightweight that fires some kind of tiny dart, probably toxic—those, in the plastic case. And there's all these tools and gadgets. It's a complete break-in, larceny, and espionage kit. What am I doing with all this shit?"

Rita could only shake her head uncomprehendingly. "Oh, God, Tony, what have they done to you?"

He went over to the closet and pointed to the suits, shirts, ties, slacks, and a blue, hip-length topcoat hanging inside. "None of this is mine. It's not even anything I'd pick." While Rita examined the things in the briefcase, he went back to the bureau and picked up a wallet that was lying there with some keys, loose change, and the room's magnetic passcard.

"According to the ID in here, I'm somebody called Maurice Gordon from Philadelphia." He brought the wallet over and showed her. "But it's got my picture in it. The cards are signed in my handwriting, but they say Gordon. It's all crazy. . . . And now you're telling me the Army says I'm dead."

Rita opened another section of the wallet and whistled. "Wow, look here. This Maurice Gordon guy doesn't believe in being caught short."

"Yeah, I know. I counted it. It's nearly twenty-five hundred dollars."

"He seems to be some kind of businessman."

Demiro shook his head dubiously. "It doesn't fit with that other stuff. More likely some kind of a cover." He raised a hand and rubbed the marks below his ear and on the side of his head gingerly. "Anyway, what kind of business does this?"

Rita got up and slipped on a light maroon robe that was among Gordon's things. She took the briefcase back to the bureau and picked up the hotel memo pad that was lying there. "Did you write these phone numbers? . . . Oh, yes, one of them's mine." It was for the new flat that she'd moved into with Margaret in Chicago, when she left the place in Hodgkins.

"The others are nothing. I made a few calls earlier and ordered a pizza. Have you eaten?"

"A bite on the plane, but I could use something more." Rita flipped back the top sheet of the pad. "What this? It's your writing too." She read: *"Headman to ship out via J'ville, sometime Nov 19. Check ref 'Cop 3.'* What does it mean?"

"I don't know. I found it there this morning."

Rita put the pad down again and turned to move back over to him. "Oh, Tony, what are we going to do?" she sighed.

He put his arms around her and held her. "I don't know, hon. I don't know what any of it means. . . . But for right now, let's get you something to eat. I'll call room service."

A little under an hour later they were sitting at the table by the window, sharing a bowl of chili con carne with a side salad apiece and desert. Demiro had also ordered a bottle of Canadian Club to see them through the rest of the evening.

"So before this morning, the last thing you remember was when you were back at Pearse in June," Rita said.

"Right."

"What do you remember, exactly? I mean, the last thing that actually happened?"

"It's amazingly clear," Demiro told her. "As if it was yesterday, know what I mean? It doesn't feel like five months ago. They were doing those tests for transferring new things straight into someone's head. The guys liked it. We could do all kinds of things. Not just what was in the official program—you know, stuff that the Army was interested in—but other things on the side, to make it more interesting, I guess. One of the guys who was a klutz turned into a cardsharp. I was playing the guitar there. So it was all going okay. . . . Then, one day I went in for a regular session on the machine. They fixed the pads and things around my head the way they always did . . . and the next thing I knew I was here in this room, and it was this morning."

"And that's it?"

"Just like that. Zap. No feeling of time gone by at all. It was like a piece being cut out of a movie."

Rita tidied the dishes together on the tray and got up to go over to the bureau, where the bottle of whiskey and the ice bucket were. "So the last thing you knew was being in that machine," she said, pouring two drinks.

"Right."

"Do you want this over there?" She turned, holding the glasses.

"No, let's get more comfortable." Demiro got up, went over to the bed, and stretched out on it.

Rita joined him and handed him one of the glasses. She put her own down on the side unit, then reached for her cigarettes. The conclusion that the machine was the cause of it all didn't need to be spelled out. "So what does it mean?" she said, finally propping herself back against the pillows alongside him. "Was the whole thing some kind of trick to camouflage something else they were doing? Was it to recruit people for some different kind of work all along?" She bit her lip uneasily. It was obvious that she meant his false ID, the guns, the other equipment: the kind of work that it all implicitly added up to.

"Maybe," Demiro agreed. "It sounds crazy, doesn't it. But . . ." He shrugged hopelessly.

"Do you think that faking the record of you being dead was part of it?" she asked. "Something they planned from the start?"

"I don't know. It sounds too fantastic. . . . Maybe something went wrong somehow."

"But what do we do? You can't go back to Pearse, if that was the center of it. And if the Army records are wrong, then it sounds like they're part of it too. So you can't go to the top. What about your old unit at Kankakee? Surely they're not in on it as well. Couldn't you start with your old CO there?"

"And what would he do?" Demiro said. "They're nothing. It'd all get swept under the carpet somehow."

"So what do we do?" Rita asked him again.

He sipped his drink and put the glass down on the side, then turned to her and moved closer. "Why don't you put that cigarette out? I don't know about tomorrow, but I know what I want to do right now. There's one way in which I do feel as if it's been five months. . . ."

Afterward they lay with the lights out and the drapes open, in the cool light coming in from the city. "What I'd really like to do is get away from all of it, just us, like we used to talk about," Demiro said. "All the things we said: just work for us, have our own kids, without needing numbers or licenses." He turned his head to look at the outline of her face. "Has that changed in five months? You still feel the same?"

She nodded. "Where would you like to go, if we ever got out of this country?"

"Oh, I don't know. One of the FER territories, I guess. Or maybe in the South World someplace, if you really want to get away. They say it's hard work, but not so hectic."

Rita smiled at him and stroked his hair. "Not offplanet anymore? What happened to that idea of the Offworld independencies, maybe Luna? We used to talk about that too."

His eyes were closing. He answered distantly. "Oh, just a dream. . . . Nice thought, maybe. Who do we know . . . who'd get us out? . . . Just talk. Talk and a dream. . . ."

"Sometimes they happen, though," she murmured. "Who knows? Maybe, if we knew who to talk to." A new thought struck her. "It might even be easier if you don't officially exist. Perhaps the best thing would be not to go looking for explanations and stirring things up. Ride with it, instead. Just vanish. Let's find out first if there are ways of benefiting from the situation. Tony? . . ." His body had relaxed beside her. His breathing was deep and even. "Tony, are you awake?" There was no response. She smiled, kissed him lightly, and snuggled close to him, feeling his warmth. She didn't mind what they did, as long as it was together.

Her body felt clammy and sticky. First thing tomorrow, she'd go for a swim, she decided. Later they could start making plans.

*   *   *

When Demiro awoke, the surroundings had changed. Rita was there, sitting on a chair watching him, but they were in a smaller room with electronic apparatus and shelves of instruments. He was lying not in a queen-size hotel bed, but under a sheet and blanket in a single cot, with a light above. For a chilling moment he thought he was back in the machine area at Pearse. But no . . . it was a different place.

He moved to raise himself and found that his body felt strangely light. And then he realized that somebody else was there too, a man whom Demiro had never seen before. He was big in stature, with thick gray hair, vivid features, and huge eyebrows, and wearing a white, laboratory-style smock.

Demiro looked uncertainly at Rita. "Where is this place? Who the hell's he?"

Professor Ulkanov gave a satisfied nod. "He should be all right now," he said to Rita. "I'll leave you both together for a while. There is all the time in the world now." He went over to the door and left, closing it quietly behind him.

Demiro looked bemusedly at Rita again. "What's going on?"

"Tony, it *is* you! You're back!"

"Of course it's me. Who the hell did you expect?"

Rita's face was flooding with uncontainable tears of joy. "It's such a long story. . . ."